ANGEL'S INK

ALSO BY JOCELYNN DRAKE

THE DARK DAYS NOVELS

Nightwalker

Dayhunter

Dawnbreaker

Pray for Dawn

Wait for Dusk

Burn the Night

ANGEL'S INK

INK

The Asylum Tales

JOCELYNN DRAKE

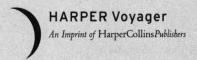

HARPER Voyager
An Imprint of HarperCollins*Publishers*

ANGEL's INK. Copyright © 2012 by Jocelynn Drake. All rights reserved. Printed in the United States of America. No part of this book may be used or reproduced in any manner whatsoever without written permission except in the case of brief quotations embodied in critical articles and reviews. For information address HarperCollins Publishers, 10 East 53rd Street, New York, NY 10022.

HarperCollins books may be purchased for educational, business, or sales promotional use. For information please write: Special Markets Department, HarperCollins Publishers, 10 East 53rd Street, New York, NY 10022.

FIRST EDITION

Designed by Paula Russell Szafranski

Library of Congress Cataloging-in-Publication Data has been applied for.

ISBN 978-0-06-211785-4

12 13 14 15 16 OV/RRD 10 9 8 7 6 5 4 3 2 1

To The Man Who Keeps Me

Acknowledgments

I'VE DELVED INTO a new series and with that comes a round of intense research and exciting discovery. First, I want to thank Tommy and Nate at Designs by Dana for not only my own lovely ink, but also for all the wonderful information you've supplied. Thanks for patiently answering all my annoying questions regarding the world of tattooing as well as telling some of the most insane stories of your own experiences. I love our two M's discussions and your ability to tell some of the most vulgar jokes I have ever heard.

Can you thank a place? I will at least try. I want to thank the Designs by Dana shop as it served as an inspiration for the tattoo parlor that is the center of this series. If you want to walk through my world, stop by MainStrasse in Covington, Kentucky. Too many times, it proved to be my home away from home.

As always, thanks to my amazing editor, Diana Gill, for being a guiding hand to my twisted imagination, and thanks to my tireless agent, Jennifer Schober, for being the perfect cheerleader, defender, and friend.

ANGEL'S INK

1

THE HAMMER OF a gun clicked as it was cocked.

That small, distinct sound sent a shiver through me despite the summer heat shimmering off the sidewalk. My heart skipped. I froze with my right foot on the bottom step leading up to the tattoo parlor—so close to sanctuary, and yet I didn't have a chance. The front door was locked. I was trapped, hanging helpless in that second waiting for the gunman behind me to finally speak or send a bullet screaming through the back of my head.

"You fucking lied to me, Gage!" snarled my assailant. The voice sounded familiar, but it wasn't until I slowly turned around that I realized why my life was hanging by a thread. I had tattooed the man just a couple of weeks ago and apparently he wasn't pleased with the result.

Russell Dalton was a large, beefy man full of muscles and a layer of fat around his waist from too many Big Macs and not enough core exercises. He was loud, obnoxious, and cheap. In my opinion, he had gotten what he paid for, but then it looked like he wanted to take his anger and frustration out on my hide, as he remained in the shadows of the alley beside the parlor.

"I never lied to you," I replied calmly, holding my hands open

1

and out to my sides to show that I didn't have any weapons. In this world, you couldn't be too careful. I resisted the urge to look up at the sky, knowing that it was not long after noon—hours away from when the hulking Bronx would be able to get to the tattoo parlor. Damn trolls and their weakness for sunlight. I was on my own for now, but then it was better that way. Just the two of us and no one watching.

"You promised me good luck," Russell accused. "Since I got this damn tattoo, I was fired from my job, my car was stolen, and my wife wants a divorce. That ain't good luck."

"You paid me fifty bucks for a shamrock tattoo the size of a quarter on the bottom of your foot." Balling my hands into fists, I let my foot fall from the step and turned around to fully face my attacker. "That was barely enough to cover the cost of the ink and my time and expertise, not to mention the leprechaun hair that I threw into the mix. Do you know how hard it is to get that shit?"

In all honesty, I had a contact at a popular beauty parlor across town and for a price she was kind enough to grab samples of hair for me. It wasn't that hard to get my hands on leprechaun hair. The only problem was that it so easily turned bad if you weren't careful. Obviously, my stockpile had taken an unexpected turn. I made a mental note that if I used it again I needed to cut the spell with water from a spring snowmelt or fuzz from a white rabbit to counter the negative energy from the leprechaun hair.

Unfortunately, this cheap-ass dirtbag hadn't paid enough for me to take those kinds of precautions. Hell, he shouldn't have gotten the leprechaun hair at that price, but I had been in a generous mood. Sometimes I can be a real dumbass when it comes to my clients, but then, my motto was you get what you pay for.

"You have to fix it!" Russell snarled, ignoring my question. "You have to make everything right again!"

"And let me guess, you want this work done for free?" I sneered.

"Damn right for free! You've ruined my life!"

I took a step forward, and to my surprise, Russell slid half a step backward into the alley. That worked for me. I didn't want this on the street should someone walk by. "If you want good luck, it comes with a price, and the kind of luck you're looking for is extremely expensive. You blew through my front door demanding lottery-winning luck while waving fifty bucks in my face. You got what you paid for. Buyer beware, buddy."

"You fucking asshole! You're not the only tattoo artist in Low Town! I don't need you!" he shouted, shaking the gun at me.

I took another step toward Russell, backing him farther into the alley. "Yeah, but I'm the best and that's why you came to me instead of some broken-down backroom operation with dirty needles and shady ingredients."

"You're obviously not any better!"

I had had enough of this shit. Keeping my eyes locked on his, I let the gym bag on my right shoulder slide off and hit the ground with a heavy thud. As I expected, he jerked the gun toward the bag. Taking advantage of his distraction, I edged forward and slammed both of my hands into the hand gripping the gun, knocking the weapon to the ground. Still holding his right hand, I twisted it at an awkward angle while dropping to my knee, putting Russell on his back in the dirty cobblestone alley. Before he could get his wits about him, I slammed my elbow into his face, feeling his nose fracture beneath my forearm while the back of his head hammered into the brick-covered ground.

"Asshole," I muttered. Standing, I dusted off my jeans and stepped back. "Don't show your face around here again or I'll tell the cops what kind of tattoo you really came in my shop for."

Sucking in a deep, cleansing breath, I summoned up a smattering of the energy that swirled around me, begging for my touch. I raised my left hand toward him and clenched my fist, as if I was grabbing his shirt, before throwing out my arm. Russell slid violent-ly down the alley until his head clanged into the side of a Dumpster.

My breath froze in my chest and I watched the sky for the tell-tale flash of lightning that would streak across seconds before the appearance of a guardian. I wasn't supposed to be using magic, no matter how minute. And the guardians were itching for an excuse to put my ass in a sling. I didn't need to push my luck, but Dal-ton had gotten under my skin. I was an excellent tattoo artist and I didn't need his kind of bad karma mucking up my business. After a couple of seconds and no lightning bolt, I relaxed. For now, I re-mained under the radar and intended to stay there.

A large hand appeared from out of nowhere and wrapped around my throat, picking me up and slamming me against the alley wall of the tattoo parlor. A sharp-featured face leaned so close that I could easily make out the silver eyes with a hint of green. Black hair flowed around his face, putting his features in dark shadow despite the bright sunlight.

"Gideon," I choked out as I held on to his hand, trying to loosen his grip before I suffocated. "It's been a long time."

"Not long enough," he said in a menacing voice as he raised his wand and dug it into my cheek.

My heart pounded in my chest far harder than when I was facing the barrel of Dalton's gun. I'd always known I could stop a bullet, but I wasn't prepared to stop any spell that this warlock was itching to throw in my direction. Apparently, someone *had* been watching. Fuck.

Gideon's sneer turned into an evil grin. "You've been warned more than once that you have been forbidden to perform any of the magical arts. As I recall, you were the one who turned your back on us, saying that you didn't need us or magic."

Gritting my teeth, I pressed my hands into the wall behind me and kicked Gideon in the chest with both feet, shoving him vio-lently away from me. I immediately erected a protective barrier as I slammed into the ground. A wicked flash of energy that shot from Gideon's wand was deflected by the shield, briefly lighting up the alley.

"Before I left, the council agreed that I could use magic in acts of self-defense," I shouted before Gideon could come up with another spell that would crash through my meager defensive shield. I had always been good at magic, but there was more to it than just being naturally attuned to the energies in the air. Being a powerful warlock took decades of study and I had stopped more than a few years ago. I didn't stand much of a chance in a magic fight against a warlock like Gideon.

He picked himself up off the ground and dusted off his black pants and shirt. Gideon even took the time to shake out his cloak before turning to me. In this day and age, the cloak looked a little ridiculous, but I was no fool. That thing was woven with enough protective spells that the warlock wouldn't be caught dead without it.

"I saw the fight," Gideon said calmly. "The man was already down."

"But not unconscious. I had to be sure that he wouldn't follow me into my shop where I would still be alone and defenseless."

"We all know you're never defenseless."

I shrugged, fighting back a smirk. "Relatively speaking."

"You used magic, when you were not permitted, in dealing with this human. You broke your agreement. You're coming with me."

"Not today." I shook my head as I dropped my protective shield and leaned against the wall so my shaking knees wouldn't have to fully support my weight. "Bring me before the council and they will see that it was self-defense. An unarmed man against one with a gun. The council would be forced to find in my favor. Think about it, Gideon. I know you and everyone else in the Ivory Towers is eager to see me dead, but do you really want to waste the council's time? They won't look kindly on it."

My only warning was a low, frustrated growl before he rushed across the alley and slammed my head against the wall. "I will let you go this time, renegade, but we are watching you. We will catch you eventually."

"Try all you like."

Gideon gave a little snort as he stepped away from me. "Why you've chosen to live among these useless flesh bags is beyond me."

"That's why," I said in clipped tones. I refused to view humans as little more than chattel.

Gideon frowned at me one last time before he disappeared completely, heading back to the Towers, I was sure. Each continent was dotted with gleaming towers made of white marble and granite that stretched above the clouds. These were the elusive Ivory Towers, their exact locations known only to the witches and warlocks who lived in them. And me. I knew where they were and had managed to escape with that knowledge, not that it was doing much good now.

Sliding down the grimy wall, I took a deep breath as I tried to slow my racing heart and my trembling hands. I had come too close this time. That self-defense argument was starting to run a little thin and I had a dark suspicion that Mr. Dalton might have been given a little shove in my direction in hopes of pushing my buttons into using magic. It had worked. I didn't like being threatened and I didn't like it when my abilities were questioned. Sometimes I had too much ego and not enough common sense.

If Gideon had had his way, I would have been whisked away to the council in the Ivory Towers, found guilty, and executed, all within an hour.

Pushing back to my feet, I paused for a second as I gazed down the alley and saw Dalton's chest rise once with a heavy breath. Then I picked up the gun in one hand and my gym bag in the other. This neighborhood was getting more dangerous by the day.

2

STEPPING INSIDE THE air-conditioned arctic of the tattoo parlor, I kicked the door shut while dropping my bag, along with the gun, on the floor. I twisted around and slid the dead bolt back into place and glanced around the parlor. The lobby had dark hardwood floors covered in ancient area rugs with worn floral patterns. An old ceramic fireplace stood against one wall, its mouth covered to hold in the heat during the winter and the cool during the blistering summer months. The wall was covered in plastic flip boards that held common tattoo designs we had done in the past to give potential clients some suggestions should they need them. But in most cases, clients didn't much bother with the flip boards, preferring to rely on the knowledge of the artist. A counter with a clear glass case stood before the doorway to the actual tattoo work space. It held a variety of old books and pictures depicting tattoos from the earliest of days, when only sailors were among the clientele. They had been handed down to me by the man I had apprenticed under when I decided to open my own shop.

A faint hint of antiseptic hung in the air from where Bronx had sterilized most of the surface areas in the back before closing up the night before. Underlying that was the smell of stale magic, which always made me smile a little. It was a distinct smell that only the experienced magic user could pick up, and I had more experience than I was willing to admit to anyone.

I leaned down and threw back the largest of the area rugs near the center of the room, revealing a pentagram deeply etched into the wood floor. Stepping into the center of the pentagram, I closed my eyes but still hesitated. I reminded myself that this type of magic fell under the self-defense clause. Besides, it was a rune spell and the guardians couldn't pick up on that kind of magic very well. Energy flowed around me, beating against my skin while trying to push its way into my brain. I started a low chant while keeping my arms lifted slightly at my sides. Magic energy coursed through me for a few seconds before shifting throughout the front room and flowing to the back room and down into the basement, completing my bidding.

After a second, I dropped my arms back to my sides and narrowed my eyes as I stared at the front door. A slight blue glow that only I could see clung to the opening. The spell was a small one, allowing me to see through anyone's glamour as they entered my tattoo parlor. You never knew who was going to walk through your door and I wasn't taking any chances. I had to recast the spell every day before opening the shop, but it was a small price to pay. Besides, security systems didn't come cheap, and getting one that included magical defenses was even more expensive since it involved finding a warlock or a witch willing to do a little menial labor. Not fucking likely.

The deglamour spell had proved itself time and time again, and very few could sense it when they walked through the door. Bronx had before I hired him—I remembered seeing him open the door and pause at the threshold. I had been sitting behind the counter at the time, and I remember seeing the troll narrow his eyes at me before he stepped boldly into the room. I doubted whether he could tell what the spell was exactly, but he knew it was there. I simply smiled and shrugged. The Asylum Tattoo Parlor wasn't in the greatest neighborhood, and I had every right to protect myself and any colleagues. Bronx never said a word about the spell and I think that was part of the reason I hired him. That, and he had some of the most impressive shading skills and creative line work I had ever seen. His potion-stirring skills hadn't been the strongest when he had been hired, but he proved to be a fast learner.

However, the greatest revelation had come from Trixie. She had given a little shudder when she stepped into the tattoo parlor, but by her expression, I could tell that she had simply waved it off as a cold chill. The spell had instantly stripped away the glamour spell she had been using, leaving it as little more than a hazy shadow over her tight, lithe form so that I could see she was truly an elf. I had never told her that I knew exactly what she was and had no intention of mentioning it. She was cloaking her true presence for a reason and I had no desire to go digging into something that wasn't any of my business.

Besides, Trixie was good for the parlor. Her long slender legs, revealed by a pair of short shorts during the summer, and her dainty tank tops filled out by perky breasts and topped off with a gorgeous face drew in more than a fair share of repeat male clients. Her sweet, outgoing personality and her skill with a needle made her an amazing package I preferred not to lose, so her secrets were her own.

Stepping out of the pentagram, I kicked the rug back and made sure that the corner lined up with the bit of masking tape on the floor I used as a guide to ensure that the rug hadn't been moved. No one needed to know about the pentagram. As far as anyone else was concerned, I was just a tattoo artist and didn't know shit about real magic.

I grabbed my gym bag and slung it over my shoulder. The front door was locked and the spell was back in place. It was time to get to work.

In the main room of the tattoo parlor, I flicked on the lights and let my eyes travel over the white counter space, the three large chairs, and the rainbow of ink bottles that lined one wall. Everything was neat and tidy, ready for another day. But then, Bronx was very organized and neat when he worked. He had no problem cleaning up the shop before he left at the end of the night. The only one who might have been more organized and clean conscious was a vampire, but I preferred not to have one on staff. I didn't need to worry about a staff member taking a nip at someone while in the middle of a job.

I crossed the room and headed down a narrow hallway to a windowless back room. This was where we completed some tattoos while offering clients privacy should the tattoo be in a place that was more than a little revealing. There were other, darker reasons for using the back room for tattooing, but then I always figured it was the decision of the tattoo artist to go down that path. I didn't ask too many questions, particularly since I used this room the most often of the three of us.

Shutting the door behind me, I went over to the floor-to-ceiling wood cabinet that covered one wall and pulled it open. Thousands of bottles, vials, plastic containers, and yellowing envelopes filled it. This was where we kept the main ingredients to stir into the potions needed for the majority of the tattoos people came to get. Sure, some customers just wanted a little ink. But most wanted something extra. They wanted the tattoo to do something for them, and whether it was a burst of good luck, a dollop of true love, or even a hex on an ex, we could get it done—for a price.

After scanning the vials for a second, I pulled down the one that held the leprechaun hair and glanced at the date on the side. It wasn't that old and shouldn't have gone bad on me already. It had to be the source of the hair that was less than . . . prime. In my limited experience, some leprechauns were just plain evil, running more toward their cousins the imp and the hinky-punk than their more compassionate faerie cousins. I had to be careful stirring with this ingredient or I was going to end up shot. Good luck spells were fairly common, though I generally relied on the leprechaun hair only for the cheap asses.

All the same, I pulled my cell phone out of my pocket and dialed Lana's number down at Curl Up & Dye. After a few minutes of mindless chatter and harmless flirting with the stylist, I got her to promise to bring me down a new tuft of leprechaun hair, from a different source this time, in the next couple of days. For now, I was stuck with what I had and we needed to be careful with it.

Slipping my cell phone back in my pocket, I walked over to the back of the room and pulled up the trapdoor in the floor with only a whisper of a creak. Most of the time, a chair was left on the trapdoor to make it look like it was unused, but I suspected that my coworkers were aware of my occasional disappearances down into the basement.

Despite the overwhelming darkness, I easily grabbed the pull chain on the single bare bulb in the basement and jerked it on before touching the dirt floor. Lined up along three of the walls were additional wood cabinets holding more volatile and rarer items. Some I had been lucky enough to inherit, while others were purchased on the black market. All of them were for my exclusive use, and they were what made me the most successful tattoo artist in town. When you wanted something done right and had the cash to pay for it, it was all about the ingredients in the ink rather than the design on the skin.

On the one bare stone wall was another pentagram spray-painted in black. This one held the power to attack any intruders. I glanced over the items one time and did a quick check on the spell to see that it was still intact and cast by me. No one had been down here without my knowledge. The same tension that coiled in my stomach every day I walked into the shop finally unwound and I breathed a sigh of relief. The basement held other spells, cloaking special items from view, protecting both them and me. There were things down here that people would kill for and ones that were an automatic death sentence for possessing without being a witch or a warlock.

Overhead, I heard the sound of the front door opening and slamming shut followed by the heavy pounding of heels across the hardwood floor. I knew that cadence. Trixie was in early.

Hurrying up the stairs, I shut the trapdoor behind me and dropped my bag on it to keep it partially hidden from view. It was time to get to work.

"Is there a reason a gun is lying on the floor?" Trixie asked casually as I met her in the main tattooing area.

Shit. I'd forgotten about the gun. It was now sitting quite obviously on the floor, beside the front door where I had left it. Not exactly the best thing to leave lying around a tattoo parlor where any of your more unstable customers could pick it up.

"Rough afternoon," I muttered, but the words didn't come out sounding as indifferent as I had hoped; then my eyes fell on Trixie's outfit for today. Instead of her usual shorts, she wore a pair of jeans with some strategically placed holes and tears. Her top was a black leather bustier that accented the swell of her breasts and left a broad swath of her flat stomach bare. Her long blond locks were pulled back in some twist thing that allowed some thick strands to frame her face. As she turned to drop her bag on the counter, I could easily make out the butterfly-wings tattoo between her shoulder blades. Somehow, they seemed to sparkle in the light as she moved.

Clenching my teeth, I ducked my head as I walked out into the lobby and picked up the gun. She was going to be the death of my sanity. I positively ached to touch her, to run my hands along skin I knew would be as smooth as satin, and bury my nose in her neck to drink in her sweet scent. I knew better than to mix business with pleasure. It NEVER worked out. Never.

To make matters worse, Trixie had gone out of her way to disguise the fact that she was an elf when it was well-known that some of the best artists in the industry were elves. They had the patience and the natural talent to not only learn to stir a good potion, but to also learn the art. Trixie was hiding, and that wasn't good under any circumstances. It had been on the tip of my tongue to ask her about it on more than one occasion, but I wasn't exactly sure how to start that conversation without giving away my own abilities and dark past. Among humans, the only ones who could identify a glamour spell were warlocks and witches. My hands were tied.

For now, I kept my mouth shut and my eyes open, content with her working five nights a week.

"What are you doing here so early?" I asked as I came back into the tattooing room with the gun. I opened one of the cabinets on the far side of the room with the toe of my worn black boot, removed the magazine from the bottom of the grip, and threw the gun and magazine in with the others that I had collected over the past few years. This was a somewhat dangerous business even under the best of circumstances. Luckily, having a troll on staff helped to keep the scuffles to a minimum.

"You said today was inventory day. I thought I would come in early and help," she said with a bright smile.

I made some nondescript noise in the back of my throat as I kicked the cabinet door shut, mentally plucking the wings off the butterflies that took flight in my stomach. After working with her for roughly two years, I would like to think that I could get through a workday without acting like a hormone-filled idiot.

My shift at the Asylum usually ran from the middle of the afternoon until midevening, while Trixie came in a few hours after me. Bronx didn't show up until a couple of hours after the sun set and stayed until a couple of hours before dawn. Oddly enough, these were typical hours for tattoo parlors. No one worked mornings. Who the hell wanted a tattoo first thing in the morning with their coffee?

"Are you ever going to do anything about those guns? Or are you just collecting them as mementoes of your past conquests?" Trixie continued.

One corner of my mouth lifted before I could stop it and I shook my head. "Would you rather I called the cops so I could hand them all over like a good boy?"

"And then try to survive the barrage of questions that would accompany that armory?" she scoffed. "I'd like to stay below the radar of *all* the local law enforcement."

"Agreed. I've got some contacts. I'll start asking around to see what I can get for them. We could use some new equipment," I said, letting my eyes skim over the work area while carefully avoiding Trixie. We could always use some fresh ingredients, and some of the tattooing equipment was starting to get worn in such a way that we were making personal modifications just so it kept working through a tattoo. I had made some nice cash from this business over the past few years, but it was obvious that it was time to start reinvesting.

Walking over to the counter opposite where Trixie was currently perched, I turned on the small television linked to the security camera that looked over the lobby of the parlor. It allowed us to see who came through the door when we were all busy with a chair. It wasn't completely foolproof—some creatures didn't show up on camera—but it caught most who wandered through our door.

"So are you going to tell me what happened?" Trixie prodded after a moment of silence had stretched between us.

I shrugged as I turned to face her. "Nothing important." I finally raised my eyes to look at her again, feeling as if I had better control over myself following the initial shock of her outfit.

"Nothing important, but it involved a gun," she said, crossing her arms over her bosom. "Come on, Gage. Spill it or I'll get Bronx to sit on you when he comes in and we'll crush it out of you."

"Russell Dalton caught me on my way into the parlor this afternoon. Seems he's a little pissed regarding the results of his tattoo."

"Dalton? I don't remember him."

"Came in a couple of weeks ago wanting a good luck charm. He had only fifty bucks on him."

"Oh, that idiot!" she gasped. She dropped her hands back to her lap and shook her head at me. "I still can't believe you took that one."

I sighed, once again forced to question either my sanity or my decision-making process when it came to clients. "I was feeling generous."

"So, I'm guessing the tattoo hasn't worked like he wanted."

"I put a shamrock on the heel of his left foot. Do you honestly think anything good could come of that?"

"Not really. But then, I wouldn't expect things to go all that bad for him either."

"Yeah, well, neither did I, but they did. Lost job, car stolen, and wife wants a divorce."

Trixie let out a low whistle as she leaned back against the set of cabinets above the counter that wrapped around the far wall. "That's odd."

"Not really. I put a leprechaun hair in the ink."

"It go bad?"

"That or it was bad to begin with," I said with another sigh. This wasn't how I expected my day to go. "I've already called for some fresh, but it'll be a few days. Just be careful and cut the mixture with something else to counteract it if you happen to use the hair between now and then. Pass the word along to Bronx if you see him before I do."

"Got it, boss," she said, hopping down from her perch on the countertop.

"Shall we get started?" I asked, trying to ignore the jiggle of her breasts as she landed lightly on her toes.

"Do you want front room or back room?" she inquired, looking over her shoulder at me as she walked toward the front glass counter and bent down so that I could catch the perfect roundness of her rear in the tight jeans. If I didn't know better, I'd say she was doing it on purpose. But she was just switching on the music like we did every day.

"Back room," I bit out, turning to look for the pair of clipboards that held the list of supplies we kept on hand. The front room held the random necessary items such as paper towels, latex gloves, petroleum jelly, needles, and ink. The processing of the items in the front room took less than thirty minutes and an order form was quickly filled out.

The back room possessed all the unique ingredients that we used in our potions. Each container needed to be checked, opened, and assessed as to whether the contents were still good or if we needed more. The back-room check could take up to three hours to process and the order form was even trickier because not everything could be purchased at the local ingredients shop. Some things had to be acquired through a series of back-alley transactions and black-market connections.

"If you need any help, just give a shout," she offered as I turned toward the back room again.

"I've got it."

"Gage . . ."

I stopped and turned half around to see where she was standing, one hand on the glass top of the counter in the lobby. "Thanks for not getting shot."

"No problem. I hear the job market is a killer right now." I winked at her, a wide, devilish grin crossing my mouth.

"Asshole," she mumbled under her breath as she turned back toward the stereo she was fiddling with. I didn't miss the smile that graced her lovely face. Before I could escape into the back room, Beethoven was blasted through the four speakers that were spread around the main tattoo room. I suppressed a laugh when I heard Trixie cursing Bronx's taste in music. By the time I had shut the door, she had hooked up her own MP3 player to the speakers and Dropkick Murphys was filling the air. Trixie had a thing for both punk bands and bagpipes.

3

ASIDE FROM NEARLY being shot in the alley, it was proving to be a slow night. Trixie and I finished the inventory in record time as the parlor remained dead for the first few hours of the night and I passed the next hour on the phone lining up sellers for the few hard-to-get items that I needed to put back in stock. Nothing that had to be acquired through the black market, but not all were through the most reputable channels. Just people who were willing to take some risks for the right price. One of the things I had learned quickly when I opened this shop was that in order to get the necessary and best resources it was all about the connections you made.

I had finished up my phone calls when Bronx lumbered through the front door and shrugged off the massive black leather trench coat he wore despite the heat. But then, even with the sun down, most trolls had a lingering fear of their skin being exposed to the sunlight. Hanging it on the coat stand near the front door, he grunted once at me in greeting before scowling up at the speakers still blaring the Dropkick Murphys throughout the parlor. I smiled as I leaned down behind the counter and picked up Trixie's MP3 player. I skimmed through her hundreds of artists and albums until I finally settled on a "Best of" Pink Floyd collection. It was a nice in-between band that both Trixie and Bronx could live with for the next couple of hours before the bickering began about music choice.

"Killjoy," Trixie grumbled behind me from where she was lying back in one of the chairs with her arm thrown over her eyes.

"It can't be that bad if it's on your MP3 player," I replied as I stepped back so that Bronx could enter the back room.

As I moved back to my position in front of the glass case, the front door flew open and four people rushed inside. By the horrified, panicked expressions twisting their faces, I knew they weren't in the market for new tattoos. In fact, a couple of them gazed around the lobby for a second, looking confused as to where exactly they were.

"What's up?" I asked, coming around the glass case to approach the front window where the four people were huddled together, staring down the street. I was trying for easygoing, but my question came out tight and tense. The door opened again and two women darted inside. Beyond the front window, I could see more people running up the street and slipping into any store that was open.

"One of them is down at Cock's Crow," one woman whispered. As she spoke, she backed away from the window so that she was nearing the shadows of the far corner of the lobby.

One of them.

At that utterance, it felt as if every muscle in my body tensed painfully. The world lived in daily terror of seeing one of them. Damn warlocks. Fucking witches. Because of them, fields had been dug up for enormous mass graves during the Great War. Because of them, both unicorns and dragons were now extinct, while others dangled on the cusp. Because of them, we all lived in fear.

"Gage?" Trixie's unsure voice snapped me from dark thoughts, jerking my head around to find her standing in the doorway between the lobby and the tattooing room. She had turned off the music, blanketing the shop in silence. Bronx stood behind her, a heavy hand on her slim shoulder.

"Bronx, take these people out the back door and direct them down the alley."

"The tunnels?" the troll asked, dropping his hand from Trixie.

"If they want, but I think this is just going to be an isolated incident," I said with a frown. I knew the warlocks and witches were aware of the tunnels, because I had learned about the tunnels from them. The only good thing was that they didn't know all the entrances or where all the tunnels led. They had been built under all the cities and into the countryside over the past couple of centuries as a means of escape.

I glanced back out the window, looking down the now empty street toward the Cock's Crow bar. Right now, nothing was happening on the street, but I could make out a form hovering near the entrance to the bar. It wasn't over yet. "Take Trixie with you to the tunnels."

"I'm staying," she declared, snapping my eyes back to her. I bit my tongue, fighting the urge to tell Bronx to flip her over his shoulder and carry her out of the shop. I wanted her safe and nowhere near another warlock or witch if I could help it. I knew why someone had appeared down at Cock's Crow and I didn't think anyone else would be affected, but I didn't want to take chances with her safety.

Turning back toward the people gathered in the lobby, I raised my voice. "Everyone follow Bronx! He'll show you how to get safely out of the neighborhood. Don't come back until you hear on the news that everything is clear." I looked out the window again, staring down the street as I listened to the thunder of feet across the hardwood floor toward the back room. Their whispers were rough and tinged with fear, which only made me angrier. These monsters didn't deserve to be feared. They were bullies, mocking everyone with their powers.

When the slam of the back door echoed through the silent shop, I pulled open the front door and stepped onto the first concrete step so that I could better see what was happening. I held open the door with my right hand while I leaned against the doorjamb. The night air was silent and thick, as if even Mother Nature was holding her breath, waiting for the evil to leave our midst. The only small relief I could find in this was that for once they weren't looking for me.

"Why do you think they're down at the Cock's Crow?" Trixie asked from over my shoulder. I hadn't heard her approach. I looked around to find her standing in the open doorway just behind me, staring down the street.

"They're looking for Dolan," I said, wishing she would at least go into the back room where no one could see her.

As if cued by some higher force, the warlock standing in the open doorway of the bar stepped aside in time for a large creature to come stumbling out into the middle of the street followed by a witch. Despite the dim light, I could see their arms extended toward the minotaur, keeping him under the point of their wands.

"Why?"

"He . . . He's been selling fix out of the bar."

"What?" she nearly shrieked.

Jerking around, I grabbed her arm and prepared to shove her back inside the parlor. "Keep your voice down. I really don't want them coming here."

Trixie winced, her eyes darting to the window to check that no one was approaching us. "Sorry." I released her with a grunt and turned back to where I had been just moments before, my gaze locked on the three figures in the middle of the street.

"How do you know?"

"I make it my business to know what kind of neighborhood I'm in. It makes it easier to protect yourself." Rather, it made it easier to judge whether a warlock or a witch might have a reason to stop in this part of town and happen across me. Per our agreement, only the council and my assigned guardian/parole officer, Gideon, were supposed to know my exact location. I knew Dolan's illegal activities might draw the attention of the Ivory Towers, but I had been secretly hoping they would go after the supplier rather than the dealer.

"Dolan was always so nice. Why would he sell fix?"

"The money's good."

"It's murder," she growled.

"On both ends."

Fix was a high-end drug, one of the few potent enough to affect the larger creatures such as trolls, ogres, and minotaurs. However, for humans, it was almost instantly lethal. Yet I had heard whispers that a few dealers had found a way to mix it with cocaine so that humans could use it. It wasn't because the owner of the Cock's Crow was dealing drugs in our neighborhood that Trixie was so upset. Hell, there wasn't a bar within a thirty-mile radius that didn't specialize in a little something.

No, Trixie was pissed over the source of fix. It was made exclusively from pixie livers. Thousands of pixies were trapped, ripped open, and harvested throughout the year simply for their organs. The pixie livers were dried and pounded into a fine powder, to be used later in a variety of ways.

Sadly, the warlock and the witch weren't at Cock's Crow because of the murder of countless pixies. They weren't even there because scores more creatures died every year from the use of fix. They were there because the drug dealers were cutting into their supply of the potent organs. There were more than a dozen potions that benefited from the use of pixie livers, not to mention a few charms and countercurses. The Ivory Towers didn't appreciate the competition.

A bloodcurdling scream ripped up the street as the minotaur buckled to his knees under a double blast of energy from the wands of the witch and the warlock. Dolan fell onto his back, writhing around on the asphalt in agony as the assault continued.

"He deserves what he gets," Trixie muttered. The hand she'd laid on my shoulder had clenched when his screaming started. I wasn't sure that I agreed with her. I thought that he deserved to be stopped, but the warlock and the witch had no business being the ones to mete out punishment. They were no better.

"You should go inside," I bit out through clenched teeth. I was tired of this. Everyone along the street was cowering inside in fear, terrified that if they were seen they could suffer a similar fate simply because they were in the wrong place at the wrong time. I was stepping down to the second step when Trixie's hand tightened on my shoulder and she started to pull me back toward the shop.

"No, Gage!" she said in a harsh whisper. "Get back inside. Please, they might see you."

I stopped on the second step, just above the sidewalk, still staring at the warlock and the witch laughing at the whimpering Dolan. There was a brief pause before Dolan's pain-filled scream rang out again and then abruptly stopped. I flinched at the silence, knowing he was dead.

Trixie increased pressure on my shoulder, turning me slightly back toward the entrance of the shop while placing her other hand against my cheek. "Please, Gage, come inside where it's safe. There's nothing you could have done. They would have killed you too. Please, come inside. Please."

It was the waver I heard in her final "please" that had me closing my eyes and releasing the breath I hadn't realized I'd been holding. I leaned my cheek into the palm of her hand for a couple of seconds, letting her soft touch push the last of the fiery anger out of my veins. She was right. There was nothing I could do, and if I had tried, I would be dead and she could very well be in danger as well.

"I'm coming in," I murmured, opening my eyes. Trixie dropped her hand from my cheek, but didn't release her hold on my shoulder until I stepped over the threshold of the shop. As I shut the front door behind me, I heard the back door open when Bronx returned. Pulling Trixie against my chest, I tightly hugged her. "They'll be leaving soon. We'll be safe." My lips brushed against her temple as I spoke. Her scent wrapped around me, helping to ease the last of the tension still humming in my frame. I didn't know whether I was trying to reassure her, or was simply clinging to something good and wonderful for a few moments in an effort to blot out the horror of our reality.

As I released her, Trixie looked up at me, a faint smile lifting her lips. "Thanks." I watched her walk back into the tattooing room where she patted Bronx's arm before disappearing from sight. Gazing back out the window, I found that the warlock and the witch had taken the time to set the bar on fire before disappearing. With any luck, everyone had escaped through the back exit before it was too late.

I moved back behind the glass counter and restarted the MP3 so that the first notes of "Comfortably Numb" drifted through the shop as the world started up again. We had two choices: ignore what had happened or die at the point of a wand. Those who still lived chose to ignore, but no one ever forgot.

Settling onto the stool, I watched as Bronx dropped onto his own stool at his workstation. The troll silently began organizing his area in the far corner, pulling together a collection of paper plates and ink caps and checking to make sure that he had an ample selection of tattooing needles still neatly packaged in their sterile casings. At the same time, Trixie pulled open one of the drawers and withdrew a large number of greasepaint sticks, tubes, and containers that she carried over to Bronx. Because of the thickness of his skin, Bronx could not be tattooed, which had always made him feel uncomfortable considering that he worked in a tattoo parlor. So at the start of his shift each night, if Trixie wasn't busy with a client, she would use greasepaint to cover him in a series of designs and images that could pass as tattoos. Despite their constant arguing over music, the two actually worked quite well together.

"What are you in the mood for tonight?" she inquired, lining up her colors along the nearby counter. Sometimes, it was just easier to pretend that certain things never happened.

Bronx pushed over a stool on wheels for her to sit on. "I want white ivy with green leaves all along my right arm."

Trixie arched one thin blond eyebrow at him in surprise and even I was taken aback. After more than two years of this process, Bronx had begun to run out of fresh ideas and simply let Trixie draw whatever she was in the mood to draw on him. He had even come to tolerate her preference for flowers and butterflies as long as she stopped drawing hearts and rainbows on him.

"Anything on the left arm?" she inquired.

"Nothing."

Leaning against the door frame, I crossed my arms over my chest and stared at the troll in the sleeveless shirt and spiked pale blond hair. I had known Bronx slightly longer than I had known Trixie. Trolls, from my experience, were naturally reticent creatures, preferring to keep to themselves. No one would ever accuse them of being chatty, but I had gotten pretty good at reading Bronx's moods. Something was bothering him and I wasn't sure that it was tonight's spectacle down the street.

"Is there a special reason for the ivy?" I asked.

"Got a feeling."

"Oooo . . . Do tell," Trixie purred as she settled on the stool next to Bronx.

The troll clenched his jaw as if he fought the words, but even the hardened creature wasn't immune to Trixie's charm. Hell, she could get a serial killer to confess his sins while sitting in the tattoo chair if she just batted her eyes and asked him in her sweet, come-hither voice. "Something dark is creeping toward us," he reluctantly said. "Like a vine that's going to wrap around us and choke . . . someone."

"Like tonight's . . ." she offered, letting her voice drift off.

"No, that wasn't it."

"Maybe the darkness has already passed," Trixie suggested. "I mean, Gage was shot at today and he survived."

"I wasn't shot at," I corrected quickly as Bronx turned his head to look at me. "Disgruntled customer, nothing more. Just avoid using the leprechaun hair for the next few days until I get some fresh."

"No, that wasn't it," Bronx replied, again turning his head to stare straight at the wall before him. I was afraid to ask more about the shadow that lingered in his golden eyes.

We all remained silent as Trixie patiently traced out a thick line curling down the length of his arm with a Q-tip and a container of white greasepaint. The elf had a knack for not only creating great beauty, but she also managed to work very fast. Within an hour, his right arm, from shoulder to wrist, was covered in a curling vine of ivy with thick green leaves highlighted in black to give them more depth. It was an exquisite work of art and it was a shame that he would wash it off before he left at the end of the night.

As Trixie cleaned up her greasepaint, the first of our customers for the night started to roll in, life once again trickling into our small part of the world. The first few were a handful of teenage humans looking to pop their tattoo cherries. They were giggling, indecisive, and squirmy in the chair when the needle was applied to their skin for any length of time. The two guys finally decided on some tribal bands around their flexed biceps, while the two females chose some tasteful and simple designs on their lower backs. All in all, as clichéd as they come, but for some, that was how the addiction started. Between the buzz of the needle and the sensual play of pleasure and pain, at least one of these kids would be back for something more intricate and interesting.

The hulking Bronx was more than a little intimidating under most circumstances so he was given the brash, cocky male, while I gave the most nervous female to Trixie. I took the remaining female first, knowing that if she was left to watch her friends, she would chicken out before she could get her tattoo. The second male wouldn't survive the ribbing of his friends if he chickened out, so I felt safe leaving him on his own for a while.

Humans came and went for the rest of the evening. Half scheduled appointments for later dates since one of us needed more time to draw a specific design, while others wandered in wanting something quick and simple. Sadly, less than half required us to go to the back room to mix up a little something extra for the ink. Tattooing in itself could be a lucrative business, but it was the potions added to the ink that made this venture truly worthwhile. For some reason, people were in no rush to get spells done tonight.

Until the drunken satyrs stumbled and fell through the front door. Asylum catered to all kinds of creatures, just so long as they could fit through the door and could be tattooed. Vampires were impossible to tattoo unless you used garlic in the mix, and then they tended to whine and scream through the entire process. Trolls, gargoyles, and ogres couldn't be tattooed at all due to the thickness of their skin. But everyone else, we would ink.

Swaying and boisterous, the satyrs on their little hoofed feet clomped through the parlor, bumping into each other. Normally, I wouldn't tattoo anyone that obviously intoxicated, but in general that was the only state in which you found satyrs. There was no helping it, and I wasn't about to pass up what was likely to be a very nice deal.

"What can I do for you gentlemen this evening?" I asked politely as I leaned over the glass counter to look down at them. At just over three feet tall from hoof to horn, they were easy to overlook, but that was generally something they used to their advantage.

"We want tattoos!" declared one as he threw his hairy fist into the air. The others joined in this cheer, their low voices rumbling around the room.

I suppressed an urge to roll my eyes and forced myself to keep a smile on my lips in the face of their obvious proclamation. "What kind of tattoos were you looking for?"

"Virility tattoos!" another shouted.

"Yeah, big dicks on our arms so that women will be attracted to us!" added the third satyr. I couldn't help it. My face fell into my hand and I shoved my fingers through my short brown hair.

"Gage!" Trixie hissed from somewhere in the tattooing room. I glanced over my shoulder, finding her standing in front of the security television, but she was glaring at me while shaking her head. I didn't know if she was more opposed to tattooing a penis on someone or the idea of being ogled by satyrs, which was inevitable if I let them into the back room. I decided to go with the penis reason and chose the route of tact and negotiation.

"You know, there are more subtle symbols of virility that can be tattooed on your arms. Items that could draw a woman close to you without being so obvious," I countered.

"Like what?"

"Like what . . ." I repeated. I glanced wildly over my shoulder, looking for a little help from my two companions in the back room.

Trixie gave a huff before she started ticking items off on her long fingers. "A stag with antlers, the full moon, the oak tree, holly, the bull or even the minotaur, and the eye of Horus."

The three satyrs looked from one to the other, quietly weighing each of the options that Trixie had listed for them, but I could tell by the tone of the conversation that not one of the choices had particularly won them over.

"You could also go with a mushroom or some particular flowers that have phallic undercurrents," Bronx added, to my delight.

The head of one of the satyrs popped up, excitement lighting his beady black eyes. "Don't some mushrooms have aphrodisiac qualities?"

"Possibly," I hedged. Hallucinogenic? Sure. Deadly? Of course. Aphrodisiac? I had no idea.

"That's what we want! Mushrooms on our upper arms."

"You got it," I said, somewhat relieved that the three of us weren't going to be drawing dicks on the arms of satyrs that evening. I had a feeling something like that would follow me into my nightmares later.

"Now, we don't just want tattoos," said what appeared to be the soberest of the trio. "We want more."

"An actual increase in virility," I supplied.

"More than that. We want to draw women to us."

"Allure."

"Exactly."

"Then that's going to cost a little extra." I mentally went through the potential list of ingredients that I might use, starting with the most expensive, before I quoted my first steep price. I fully expected the satyrs to hem and haw at the asking price, but they said nothing. All three reached into the little pouches hanging around their waists and slapped two gold coins apiece onto the counter. At today's going exchange rate for gold, and the quality of the product, I had no doubt that I had been overpaid by a lot.

"Now, gentlemen, you know I can't properly give you change for gold."

"Keep it," one said with a wave of his hand. "A tip. Can we get started?"

"Let's go," I said, motioning for them to step into the back room. As I suspected, their mouths immediately dropped open at the sight of Trixie. I quickly stepped in front of my coworker to stop the stampede as she backed into the far corner of the cabinets, effectively trapping herself.

"Trixie, could you go to the back room and draw up a design or two for these gentlemen while Bronx shaves down the area they want tattooed?" I asked quickly. She was already sidling out of the room before I finished the question. I threw a sympathetic look at Bronx, but the trio was less likely to cause problems with a troll wielding a razor. I followed Trixie into the back room where I started pulling down items for the potion.

"You're fucking insane!" she snarled in a low voice the second I shut the door. "Satyrs! Virility tattoos for a bunch of satyrs? Aren't they enough trouble on their own without your help?"

"They spend most of their time at strip joints and harassing prostitutes. I don't see them going after a bunch of soccer moms at the local bake sale." I pulled down another container. "I'm not making it that potent anyway."

"You do realize that certain fey creatures do react to natural aphrodisiacs," she snapped. "What if some poor unsuspecting wood nymph or sprite ran across these three? They could be helpless."

"Oh, please! Every wood and water nymph I've known has been more oversexed than these three and far more dangerous. Helpless, my ass." I threw some herbs into the mortar bowl and started to crush them into a fine powder with the ceramic pestle.

"Exactly how many nymphs have you known?" Trixie demanded in a surprisingly sharp voice that drew my eyes back around to her. She sat at a small drawing desk, glaring at me. "And how well did you know them?"

"Come on, Trixie. You know what I mean," I groaned as I focused on pounding the ingredients.

"No, I don't think I do."

"You're starting to sound like my mother," I warned. At least, it's what I imagined my mother would sound like. I honestly had no idea how she would sound in a conversation like this. I had been dragged from my home by a warlock at age seven and returned for only a few months when I was sixteen. Family was not something I had a lot of experience with.

A bright flush stained Trixie's cheeks and she turned away from me. Her sweet voice softened. "Please, Gage. This is dangerous."

"No, just a waste. You can't mask what a satyr is no matter the potion. You might be drawn in by the potion at first, but the innate curiosity has to be there in order for the person to succumb to anything. If the person isn't even a little attracted, nothing is going to happen. I'm just not that good. No one is."

"Promise?"

I turned from the counter to find her staring at me from where she sat at the drawing table. Half of a sketch of a tall, phallic-shaped mushroom sat on the drawing paper before her.

"I'll even cut it with nightshade juice so this will have practically no effect on the fey," I said with a sigh. I was a complete pushover when she looked at me with those wide eyes. It didn't help that I also knew she was fey and felt more than a little vulnerable around these tattoos I had promised.

"Thank you," she murmured before returning to her drawing.

"Just draw two designs and then hurry back. I want to get these three out of here so I can call it a night."

"Any way I can get out of this one?"

I snorted as I walked toward the door with my mixture and a tiny wooden spoon. "Not a chance. The pay is more than worth the twenty minutes it's going to take you to do this."

"Bastard," she muttered, but not with her earlier vehemence. I was at least partially forgiven.

While Bronx was shaving away the bristly hair from the area on the arms of the satyrs where the tattoos would go, I selected three small plastic caps and spooned in a bit of the potion that I had mixed up. I then squirted in black ink. The potion didn't need to go into all of the colors unless you were weaving a more complex spell and then it was different potions in different colors so that the spell created an interesting tapestry of power on the person's skin. In this case, the outline of the mushroom tattoos in black was the only part that actually needed the potion.

I was pulling out the needles and scooping out dollops of petroleum jelly to put on small Styrofoam plates, which would help to control the bleeding during the tattooing process, when Trixie reluctantly entered the room to show off her two designs. One mushroom was short and thick, while the other was tall and narrow. I kept my comments to myself as the satyrs argued over the merits of each design. In the end, all three decided on the long and narrow design, but with a variety of color combinations so that each one would be slightly different.

With our customers settled in their respective chairs, we three set to work quickly. The steady buzz of the tattooing machines filled the air, but was nearly drowned out by the constant chatter and bawdy comments made by the three satyrs. Despite Trixie's close attention to her one client, all three took turns trying to hit on her, even from across the room, mindless of what anyone was saying. And may the gods bless Trixie, she kept her comments to herself and silently worked on her customer. I knew that I would receive an earful later. But then she knew that this was part of the business. While Bronx and I would defend her against any type of physical threat in a heartbeat, she had seemingly grown accustomed to the occasional rude comment and had told us more than once not to bother calling a halt to it.

In less than half an hour, the three satyrs were tattooed and bandaged up with the appropriate care directions in hand. I only hoped that they paid some attention to the care of the tattoos, otherwise they would be back in for a repeat job and I was in no mood to put up with them again.

As soon as the door slammed shut behind them, I put one hand behind my neck and massaged the tense muscles there as I turned to face Trixie. I opened my mouth to apologize to her for what she'd had to endure for the past thirty minutes, but she held up one pale hand, halting the words in my throat.

"Did we make enough from them to make the night worthwhile?" she simply inquired.

"And then some."

"Then it was worth the hassle, though I am not looking forward to their eventual repeat visit for another tattoo. As long as they pay well and the work can be done quickly, I can tolerate it."

"Yeah, but you didn't have to shave the little buggers," Bronx groused as he stood and reached for a broom that was leaning in the far corner. Until now, I hadn't noticed the heavy sprinkling of short hairs that covered the floor around his chair. Satyrs were naturally hairy bastards, and the few I had tattooed had proved to be a waste of time since most didn't bother to keep the area of the tattoo shaved so people could see the art.

Glancing up at the clock, I silently cursed, dropping my hand back down to my side. It was already after one in the morning. I should have been out of the shop more than two hours earlier. Trixie would stay on for another hour or two before heading home, and then Bronx would close the shop around four. Business would remain relatively light, but there were enough nocturnal creatures in the world that it was worth Bronx's while to keep the late hours.

I was starting to head to the back room for my bag when a young woman with straight brown hair and wide brown eyes slowly pushed through the front door. She kept her jacket tightly wrapped around herself, as if for protection rather than warmth on this summer evening. Her eyes swept over the place once as she crossed the threshold before they finally settled on me. Her lips were pressed into a thin, frail smile, while lines of worry crisscrossed her brow. This was not the look of someone excited about getting a tattoo.

Glancing over my shoulder, I found Bronx watching the security television before he looked up at me and pointed to the vine on his arm. Yeah, that was the feeling I got too. Trouble. Something bad had just walked through my front door in the guise of a helpless young woman. I didn't exactly have the word SUCKER stamped across my forehead when it came to the damsel-in-distress types, but I also wasn't a cold-hearted bastard like so many in this world. I could at least hear her out. And then Bronx would gently show her the way back to the front door.

4

THE YOUNG WOMAN slowly crossed the room, as if still not sure that she wanted to be there. Her hesitance gave me ample time to check her out. There was no glamour clinging to her, no spells to set off any alarms in my head. Nothing out of the ordinary. Just a scared human. Common enough. Not everyone was a fan of needles.

So I formed my lips into an open, reassuring smile, hoping to put her somewhat at ease. It won me a weak smile in return as she reached the counter.

"Hi," she began with a little wave. "I was told to ask for Gage."

Something sank in the pit of my stomach when she said my name. It wasn't as if it was the first time someone had come in asking specifically for me. Hell, most of my business came via word of mouth and referrals from former clients. This little bit of trouble shrouded in fear had come looking specifically for me though. I would have felt safer if she had just opened her jacket and revealed a bomb strapped to her stomach. At least it would have been easier to smile through.

In my own defense, I am proud to report that I didn't flinch and my smile didn't waver when she made her request. "You've found him. What can I do for you?" I said, leaning forward on the glass case.

"I was told that you were one of the best tattoo artists in the area and that I should come to you. I was hoping to get some ink," she explained, focusing on the obvious because fear seemed to have her locked into place a few feet from me.

"Sure, what kind of tattoo were you looking for? Do you already have something in mind?" I silently prayed that she hadn't come to me looking for a bit of artistic direction as well. Guessing what kind of tattoo would fit a person's unique personality was like trying to guess what kind of person they would marry. It was intimate, and I wasn't currently privy to that kind of information. The young, bubbly, and brash teenagers were a little easier to guess, but I knew by looking at this young woman that she wanted something that would carry meaning for her for the rest of her life. It was going to be an emblem of who she was and/or what she believed.

"I know what I would like," she said, allowing me to suppress a sigh of relief. "I want wings."

"Sure, what sort of wings? I can show you Trixie's back," I offered, motioning toward the back room where the other artist was currently relaxing. "She's got a great set of butterfly wings between her shoulder blades."

The young woman looked away from me and frowned as she shoved her hand through her stringy brown hair. Her pale face was gaunt and her eyes were underlined with dark circles. Something was wrong here that I was missing. "Can we sit down?" she asked, looking over at the wooden bench, which ran the length of one wall of the parlor nearest the doorway to the back room.

"Of course." I motioned toward the wooden bench, waiting for her to precede me.

She sat down a couple of feet away from me, dangling her purse between her legs while twisting the strap around her clenched hands. She didn't look up at me and didn't speak for nearly a minute, as if she was carefully weighing her words.

"My name is Tera, and I've heard a lot of great things about your work," she finally said in a hushed voice, as if she was sharing some secret. "I've thought about it for a long time and I've decided that I want a pair of angel's wings drawn on my back."

"How big were you thinking?"

"My entire back."

"Your whole back?" I dumbly repeated. This was not what I was expecting.

"From the tops of my shoulders to my lower back," she confirmed.

"Have you gotten a tattoo before?"

"No."

"Are you sure you want something so big to start with? Most people start with something smaller before getting such a large tattoo."

"If it's the needle you're worried about, don't. Needles don't bother me." Her voice hardened for the first time, giving me a flash of some unseen inner strength. "The pain won't bother me either. I'll be fine."

"The other thing you have to consider is that tattoos are permanent, regardless of those stupid commercials and other so-called cures. You'll have to live with this very large tattoo for the rest of your life." In general, I wasn't in the business of trying to talk someone out of a tattoo, but I believed a person should make an informed decision before jumping into such a big commitment.

"I can't think of anything better," she whispered, hanging her head down so that her hair blocked her face. However, I didn't miss the quick motion of her hand sweeping up to her eye to catch what I was willing to guess was a tear.

Placing my elbows on my knees as I leaned forward, I cupped my right hand in my left, massaging out some of the tension that had settled there. I was beginning to guess where this was going and it was becoming increasingly harder for me to say no to this woman, which was going to be my downfall in the end.

Tera heaved a heavy sigh, as if she was finally prepared to bare her soul to me. "Look, Gage, I have to tell you the truth. I don't have a lot of money. I can scrape together about two hundred dollars. I have a feeling that that won't even begin to cover what I want, but this is my only chance. I'm dying. I've been diagnosed with terminal cancer and the doctors are saying that I've got anywhere from days to a few months. I haven't been the best person in the world. I'm not some mass murderer or rapist, but I haven't made the smartest of choices in life. I know I'm not going to get wings when I die, so I would like them now, even if it's only for a day or two. Will you help me?"

Sucking in a deep breath, I lowered my head into my hands, digging my fingers into my hair. What the hell was I supposed to say? Sure, she could be conning me, but I doubted it. There was something about her, some darkness seeming to hang about her that reeked of death. She might not have terminal cancer, but I was willing to bet that she was telling the truth when it came to the fact that she was dying.

I dropped my hands and sat up so that I could look over at her. "Tera, I can guess at some of the things you've heard about me, and I honestly can't help you with the cancer if that's what you're hoping."

To my surprise, she gave a little chuckle and sat back against the bench, looking relaxed for the first time since coming into the parlor. Of course, she had already shared her dark secret with me, so what was there to be nervous about now? "I know that. Trust me, if a tattoo artist had found a cure for cancer, do you think anyone would actually be dying of it right now? I know that you can't do anything about my situation. You can't even extend my life. I want to die knowing that despite what God thought of me, I still got my wings. I'll go to hell with my angel wings."

I turned my head and looked over at the brave woman who was begging for my help to jump out on one last adventure before her breath left her body for the final time. Her two hundred dollars wouldn't cover the time it would take to draw up the design and get half of it inked, but I would take the money because I didn't want to injure her pride any more than it already had been by having to admit the truth to me. I'd take the job because I knew about thumbing your nose at the authorities just a moment before you were sure that you would cease to exist.

"So when do you want to start?" I asked, forcing a smile onto my lips.

Her brown eyes finally lit up with some of the energy she had been missing when she first came into my shop. "You'll do it? Wonderful! I want to do this as soon as possible!"

"I need some time to get the design done. I'm assuming that due to the narrowness of your frame you want the wings to look like they're folded on your back."

"Yes, that would be perfect."

"And color?"

"Just black ink. I think I'm pale enough to make the feathers look snowy white."

Her enthusiasm was starting to become contagious. Most people who came in had been tattooed a time or two, resulting in a very blasé attitude about the whole process, or there was just the annoying, slightly intoxicated youth looking for that official badge of adulthood. But Tera was different. She might never have the chance to show the tattoo to the world, but she would know it was there; it was her way of trumping the great puppeteer in the sky. She had won my respect.

"All right," I said, pushing to my feet. I extended my hand to her and she eagerly took it in both of hers. "Come back by tomorrow around six o'clock and I'll have a design for you to look at. If you like it, we'll get started then."

"Awesome! Thank you so much!" she gushed for a second before sailing out the front door.

As I stepped into the back room again, I found two sets of eyes pinned on me in a mixture of worry and surprise. They both could easily have overhead all of the conversation despite the music that was still playing. The tattoo I had just promised to complete cost closer to a thousand dollars and I was doing it for a fraction of the price. I was happy to help people out when I could, and I cut friends a deal on occasion simply because I knew they would come back, but I wasn't in the business of charity, and it was extremely rare for me to be drawn in by some sob story.

"Boss, you know that I don't interfere in your business choices," Bronx started in his low and steady voice, bringing a frown to my lips. "But this doesn't seem like a good idea."

"What's the problem? She's dying. It's not as if I can do any more damage, right?" I snapped.

"Could the ink make her condition any worse?" Trixie demanded. "Or maybe the stress on the body during the tattooing process might aggravate her weakened condition."

"I don't see it being a problem. She knows what she's getting into, and hell only knows what she's already been through. Getting a tattoo couldn't possibly be worse than some of the tests and treatments she's already suffered."

"Who do you think recommended you to her?" Bronx inquired.

I just waved my hand aimlessly as I started to walk to the back room where the potion components were stored. "Heaven only knows. I've tattooed so many people over the years. It could be anyone."

"Maybe you should ask her when she comes back tomorrow."

I paused before disappearing down the narrow hallway and looked over at the troll's grim expression. "You know, you're starting to sound really paranoid about this one. You got something you want to tell me?"

"Wish I did," he muttered as he eased himself down into the tattooing chair he used.

Truth be told, I wished he had something more to tell me as well.

I thought I knew all there was to know about this particular client. Hell, I knew more about her than I knew about most of my clients. I tried to tell myself it was just the fact that she was dying that was bothering me, but there was something niggling in the back of my brain that wouldn't let the tension ease from my shoulders.

Before grabbing my bag, my eye caught on the enormous glass-fronted wood case that held hundreds of different potion components. With the right combination of herbs and rare ingredients, I could guarantee someone a varying degree of good luck, I could make them more attractive to a certain person, or I could even hex a person's ex for the right amount of money. Damn, for the right amount of money, I was positive that I could do far worse, but I tried to avoid getting myself into that kind of trouble, no matter how much green or gold was flashed in front of me. Karma could be a bitch.

Yet, as I stood there, it wasn't the first-floor cabinet I was picturing, but my wall of cabinets in the basement that was flashing across my brain. In seconds, I was running through the catalog of items, weighing the use, effectiveness, and strength of each one. What was I hoping to accomplish? I knew without a doubt that I couldn't cure her, but what if I could buy her a little more time? What if I could give her months versus days? Would they be days of agony or happiness because she had experienced more life than she had expected to?

It was only the pounding of Trixie's heels on the wood floor that made me realize I had been standing transfixed before the cabinet for several minutes, lost in thought. I quickly bent down and grabbed the strap of my bag before shouldering it. My mind was still rattling through ingredient after ingredient. It was a puzzle my brain couldn't let go of. There was something I could do. I was one of the best tattoo artists in the region, if not the country. I had a past that no other tattoo artist could claim. After all the centuries of torture, bloodshed, and death caused by the warlocks and the witches, there had to be something positive that one warlock-in-training could do to help someone without looking for something in return.

"You okay?" Trixie asked, poking her head in the door.

"Yeah, just thinking about the designs I've got to get done tomorrow. It's too late tonight to sit down at the desk. I'm dead on my feet."

Trixie arched one eyebrow at me for a second before shaking her head as she backed out of the room and headed into the tattoo parlor. I had to admit that I kind of felt the same way. What the hell was I doing? There were some things in this world that couldn't be changed, but I wasn't sure that I was ready to admit defeat on this one yet.

5

AFTER THE LATE hour I'd finished the previous night, it was a little difficult to pull my sorry ass back into the parlor before three o'clock the next day. It meant skipping the gym and packing a quick lunch/dinner, but at least I didn't have an unexpected run-in with any gun-wielding maniacs in the alley beside the tattoo parlor when I arrived in the afternoon.

I went through my usual routine of checking the spells and resetting everything before I trudged down into the basement and reset the spell there. Trixie wasn't expected for another five hours and Bronx wouldn't be here until another hour or so after that. The parlor was mine for a while, allowing me to work in peace.

In one far corner was a designer's desk with a bright overhead lamp. Sitting down in the ergonomically correct chair, I snatched several pieces of paper and started sketching the wings that I had seen dancing through my brain all night as I slept. This project consumed me like nothing else before. I had had clients come to me with some interesting concepts and art, but there was something different about this. I needed it to be perfect in every detail.

As I worked on the art there was something else eating at me that finally drove me down into the chilled basement of the tattoo parlor. Normally, I worked on all my designs in the windowless back room with the ingredients. But this one had taken on a secretive quality. I felt the need to be close to my personal ingredients, as if they were calling to me, wanting me to use them in the ink when I had already said that I wouldn't. This was just supposed to be a tattoo of angel wings and yet I felt as if I needed to do more, as if I had to do more. I didn't know if it was about trying to save one lost soul before it was taken too early. Maybe it was about trying to do something good with all my years of study when all the other warlocks and witches had only looked out for themselves.

After a couple of poor starts, I got down a design on paper that I managed to finish in just over an hour. I decided to go with an exceedingly simple design instead of something with heavy detail. I didn't want to distract from the sheer purity of the lines. The wings would break from her back and pour forth like a white cascade.

I took the design upstairs and checked the clock one last time. I still had a couple of hours until Tera was due to arrive, and to my surprise, I felt myself growing nervous. I had been tattooing long enough that I was never nervous before starting a piece of work. I had done more than a dozen tattoos in a single night and still gone on to have drinks with friends later. Tattooing was my life, and yet I was suddenly faced with what would probably be the last great act of this woman before she died; I was nervous about screwing it up for her.

Shaking my head at my strange feeling, I started to tidy up the windowless back room where I would be tattooing Tera. Considering that she would be forced to lie on her stomach with her back fully exposed, I thought she might appreciate a little extra privacy instead of being on display for any other customers who might come in. While I knew the tattoo would take close to two hours to complete, I figured that I would be able to finish it before Trixie came in the door and officially opened the shop.

As I prepped everything I needed, I took a long look at the plastic cap that would hold the black ink for her tattoo. It was a large, but simple, thin line tattoo. I wouldn't need more than a single cap of black ink. Mind swirling and conscience screaming, I tightly grasped the cap in the palm of my hand as I stomped down the stairs to the basement where my hidden ingredients beckoned me.

"Fine! I'm here!" I shouted to no one as I stood before the cabinets. I set the cap down on one of the counters of the largest cabinet before I started pulling open one glass door after another. It was only when I reached the one with the heavy padlock on the front that my mind grasped what I was searching for. My heart pounded and my mouth went as dry as the Sahara. I had never thought to use it. Part of me had convinced myself that it wasn't real, but then I had acquired it from my mentor and he wasn't one to lie about the veracity of a particular item. Every potion maker had to understand the potency and capabilities of every item he used. The only problem was that due to its extreme rareness no one knew how this item would react. But this once, I was willing to take a chance as the ingredients that I needed suddenly filled my brain.

Walking back over to the first cabinet, I reached inside and on the second shelf picked up a small vial. With a toothpick, I fished out a few particles of pollen from a white lily that had been sitting on a church altar during Easter mass. I wasn't the type to go haunting churches and cemeteries for the really interesting ingredients, but sometimes a person had to take some chances to get the good stuff. At least I had waited until everyone left mass and cleared out of the church before I made my own personal collection. The white lily has always been a symbol of rebirth and purity. There was a cleanness to it that appealed to my brain, as if I could use these particles of pollen to wash away Tera's sins.

Replacing the container in the cabinet, I closed the doors and carried the cap, with one finger over the opening and one below the bottom, to the cabinet with the padlock. Carefully setting the cap down, I fished my keys out of my pocket and, with the infrequently used lock making a slight screech, opened it. The wooden doors groaned as they were opened. Dragging over a stepladder, I climbed up to the last step so that I could reach the top shelf. I removed several items before I could reach a carefully sealed mason jar in the very back that seemed to glow with its own perfect light. The jar contained a single white feather that looked as if it was large enough to come from a giant eagle or condor. After coming down the steps, I walked over to my workbench and grabbed a pair of metal tweezers and a pair of wooden tongs. With shaking hands, I opened the jar and partially removed the feather by grasping it with the wooden tongs. I drew in a deep breath and held it as I used the tweezers to pull a single wispy frond from the feather and curl it in the bottom of the plastic ink cap. It was only after the feather had been replaced in the jar and the lid properly resealed that I started breathing again. I quickly put everything back where it belonged and locked the cabinet.

According to my mentor that feather had come from an actual angel. In fact, if he was to be believed, the feather had come from Gabriel himself. Other than my mentor, no one knew I possessed such a unique artifact, and I had always promised myself that I would never use it. It seemed to be too dangerous to ever use. And in truth, there had never been a call for anything so pure and perfect to be used in a tattoo, but at the moment it seemed to fit. I was drawing angel wings for a dying woman. What was more fitting than to have the ink first touched by the bit of a feather from a real angel? It had to do some good, right?

Placing my thumb back over the opening to the cap, I carried it up the stairs and kicked the trapdoor closed with a heavy bang. Setting the cap on the table, I grabbed a small piece of plastic wrap and placed it over the cap so that its contents would be protected until I could finally add the ink.

A knock on the front door suddenly woke me from the doze I had fallen into while stretched out in one of the tattoo chairs. I rubbed my eyes and stumbled out to the main waiting area. Tera was peeking through the front window around the stickers and signs, trying to see if anyone was actually inside. I waved at her as I crossed the distance to the front door and unlocked it for her.

"I saw the closed sign and thought maybe you had forgotten about our appointment," she said as she stepped inside.

"No, I just can't open the parlor until I'm done with your tattoo because I won't be able to work on you and man the front desk and phone at the same time. The shop probably won't officially open until Trixie gets here later tonight."

"I'm sorry. I didn't mean to be so much trouble."

I waved her off as I led her to the back tattoo room. "It's why I had you come in so early. The shop usually doesn't open until around seven during the summer. Most of my customers are the nocturnal sort."

"Isn't that a little dangerous?"

"Not really if you've got a troll on staff," I replied with a smirk. "Bronx tends to keep the peace with just a look."

"I can imagine," she murmured as she stepped into the windowless back room. There was a large, cushioned table in the center of the room surrounded by some small tables on wheels so I could easily move my supplies and tattooing machine around without forcing the subject to switch positions. There was one stainless steel sink against the far wall where we would sterilize some of our equipment that wasn't simply disposable. On the opposite wall was a floor-to-ceiling mirror that allowed the customer to easily see the new piece of work. I knew that it was intimidating being closed up in a windowless room with a total stranger and a pulsating needle while being half dressed, but it was part of my job to set her at ease.

Pulling around one of the stools on wheels, I patted it for her to sit down while I walked over to another table in the corner and grabbed my drawings. I held them up to her. Each was only one wing. I would make a mirror-image copy of the second wing so that it would be symmetrically perfect on her back.

"For the first one, I chose to go with long, slender feathers because your frame is so small and narrow," I explained. "I wanted to create the illusion of them flowing down your back. The second image is of somewhat shorter wings that stretch more across your shoulder blades."

A slow smile spread across Tera's face as she looked at the two designs. She lightly held the paper by her fingertips, as if she were afraid of harming the design. "I love the first one. It's perfect. Exactly what I had in mind."

"Excellent. I'm going to go and start getting these copied out to the right size so that the ink outline covers your back. That will give you a chance to get out of your shirt and bra. I just need exposure to your back, so feel free to hold your shirt to your front. Or not," I said, winking at her as I left the room in hopes that the teasing would take some of the tension away from the lines surrounding her mouth and eyes.

It took nearly half an hour to get the wings the right size and evenly spaced, let alone straight on her back. I had been forced to wash away the ink copy twice before I finally got it centered as perfectly as possible. Two-sided tattoos were a bitch to do, as they required that each side perfectly matched up with the other. However, they were usually some of the most elegant tattoos I have ever seen because of their symmetry on the body.

Through all my cursing and eyeballing of her back from one angle to another, Tera remained still and silent. The perfect little client, but then I suspected she wasn't going to give me any trouble considering that I was doing this tattoo for so little.

When I was finally satisfied, I told her to lie down on the table while I stepped into the other room and picked up a bottle of black ink. As soon as I returned, I found her lying on the table on her stomach with her shirt arranged in such a way that her breasts were covered as best as possible. Pulling on a pair of latex gloves, I glared at my hands as they trembled before I removed the plastic wrap from the little ink container. I hesitated for only a second, my mind questioning why I was so determined to do this, then I squirted the ink into the container, covering up the frond from the angel's feather and the pollen from the Easter lily. It was the right thing to do.

Settling on a low stool with wheels, I took a deep breath as I dipped the needle in the ink and positioned the foot pedal for the tattooing machine under my toe. "Okay, I'm just going to do a short line to make sure that you can tolerate this," I warned her before pressing on the pedal. The buzz of the tattooing machine filled the air and the tension oozed out of my body. I drew the first line and Tera didn't even flinch. She'd passed the test. I grabbed a glob of petroleum jelly and smoothed it over the area that I was going to be working on and then continued to follow the blue outline on her shoulder, working my way down her back.

As I tattooed her, we talked about nothing at all. We discussed the weather, places we had grown up, and bad relationships. We laughed and joked as I worked, allowing me to completely forget about the dangerous potion I was permanently embedding in her flesh. I reminded myself that I couldn't kill her, cancer was already doing that job, and quickly.

By the time I'd finished the first half of Tera's back, Trixie had stuck her head into the room, so we took a short break.

"How's it going?" my coworker asked with a cheerful smile.

"She's a trooper," I replied, setting the tattoo machine on the nearby table so I could pull on a fresh set of gloves.

"Putting up with your crude humor and lewd jokes, huh?"

"No, he's been a perfect gentleman," Tera said, defending me.

Trixie gave another snort of disbelief. "Give him time. He's only half done with your back."

"Thanks, Trix," I muttered, turning my attention to Tera, who was looking at me over her shoulder. "I'm going to go help Trixie open up the shop. That will give you a chance to change your position on the table so that you're facing in the opposite direction. It's easier for me to reach that part of your back without dragging all the equipment around."

Tera nodded and I followed Trixie out of the room, shutting the door behind me. We walked silently into the main room, where Trixie started to fiddle with her MP3 player, searching for tonight's music before she settled on some Three Days Grace.

"How long you been at it?"

I glanced up at the clock. "Nearly two hours. Took me thirty minutes to get the fucking outline on her back properly. The tattooing is going quickly. It's a simple design. I should be done with her in about another thirty to forty-five minutes. Can you handle things alone for that long?"

"Sure." Trixie paused for a moment, staring at me with a frown on her face. I knew I wasn't going to like what was on her mind. "I know it's way too late, but I still feel bad about this one."

"Why?"

"I have no idea. It's a feeling, and I've learned to trust my feelings. They've kept me alive this long."

"Yeah, well, I'm just tattooing angel wings on the back of a dying girl. I don't see the harm."

"Nothing in the ink?" Trixie inquired.

I frowned at her. "What could I possibly have put in the ink that would help her?" Evading her question wasn't much different from outright lying to her. Despite my intention of helping Tera, I didn't like myself much at that moment.

She sighed as she walked to the front door to flip the sign over to OPEN. "Nothing, I'm sure."

"I'm going to get back in there. Hold down the fort. I shouldn't be much longer."

"Be careful," Trixie whispered at my back as I headed down the hallway, my heavy footsteps echoing off the hardwood floor so that Tera had ample warning of my approach. When I opened the door, she was settled on the table with the shirt properly tucked around her.

"Ready for the second half?" I asked as I grabbed a pair of fresh gloves.

"Ready."

As I placed the first line on her lower back, she flinched. The tissue there was a little softer and the needle dug in more than when we had been doing her shoulders. I wanted to work my way up, getting the worst part of the tattoo done first. I continued working until she let out a little grunt, causing me to pause.

"It hurts more this time around, doesn't it?" I asked.

"Yeah."

"Sorry, but that's just how it works. When you do two halves of a tattoo, the second half always hurts more than the first half."

"You're kidding, right?"

"Does it feel like I'm kidding?" I resumed inking her back. I tried to quickly work my way up to where I knew she had been more comfortable during the first half.

"No, it doesn't."

"Sorry, I would have warned you, but you'd have spent the entire first half of the tattoo worrying about completing the second half. You'll get adjusted."

Tera gave a soft little laugh as she settled her chin on her folded hands in front of her. "Besides, it's not as if I can stop now. It would look ridiculous—a single angel's wing on my back."

"Actually, at this point, it's a wing and a half, so that would look even sillier. You have to grit your teeth and stick it out now."

I looked up when Tera sighed and found that her eyes were closed. "I've been through worse. This will pass too," she murmured.

I had nothing to say to that, so I went silently back to work, finishing the tattoo as cleanly and quickly as possible. It took me another thirty minutes to complete it and wipe it down, removing the excess ink, blood, and petroleum jelly. I gave her a chance to walk over to the large mirror and stare at the image. Her eyes were shining as she gazed over her shoulder at her back. It really was an impressive work of art. The wings actually looked as if they would rise off her back and carry her into the heavens. But that was an illusion created by the puffy skin that resulted from cutting into the flesh. It was just a tattoo, even if it was one of my better ones.

While she was still standing, I pulled off a large piece of plastic wrap and placed it against her back before taping it down with medical tape. "This is to protect that tattoo for the next several hours."

"I feel like a leftover," she joked, her mood instantly becoming lighter than air.

"Keep it covered until tomorrow. Don't sleep on your back, and wash it carefully with unscented soap for the next few weeks. Also, no matter how badly it itches, don't scratch it."

I closed my eyes as I helped her pull her button-up shirt on and then escorted her to the front room, where Trixie was already working on a client. She hadn't bothered to come back for any ingredients, so it seemed safe to assume that it was a regular old tattoo with nothing special added. I collected my fee and followed Tera to the door where she gripped me in a tight hug before she left the parlor.

I wanted to say something hopeful or happy or encouraging, but there were no words that I could push past my parted lips. She was one of the few clients who I knew without a doubt I would never see again.

THE SQUEAK OF the front door opening and closing accompanied by the door chime echoing above the sound of Marilyn Manson on the speakers caught my attention, but I couldn't hear any footsteps. The hairs on the back of my neck stood on end. I didn't let myself look up from the client I was working on until Bronx said my name. The troll was staring at the TV, which was showing the security-camera view of the lobby. No one was on the screen. Fucking vampires. I truly doubted that this was a pleasure visit. They rarely got tattoos and were never in a good mood when it came to dealing with anything remotely human. I guess it was simply a bad idea to get too friendly with something you viewed as food.

"Trixie, can you finish this tattoo for me?" I asked, dragging my gaze over to where she was sitting on the counter. "I need to take care of this." She nodded and hopped down from her spot. The man I was working on didn't seem to mind, as a smile crossed his lips when Trixie took the stool I had just vacated. I glanced over at Bronx, who was intently watching me. "Hang back for me."

I pulled off the soiled latex gloves as I started to walk toward the front of the parlor. Dropping the gloves into a trash can near the entrance to the lobby, I forced an easygoing smile on my face as I stepped up to the glass counter. A pair of men were strolling around the room in black trench coats. One had bright red hair that hung down his back in a thick braid, while the second had shoulder-length brown hair that curled at the ends—both shades looking darker against their ultrapale skin. Their thin lips were pulled down into frowns as they looked over the small shop. I couldn't make out their murmurs, but I had no doubt that they were critical and highly desultory. Asylum had never been designed for their type. There were a couple of high-end tattoo parlors around the city that a vampire might deign to visit, but I had my doubts as to whether they were actually turning a profit. This wasn't a business built for exclusivity.

"What can I do for you, gentlemen?" I asked, struggling to keep my smile in place.

The dark-haired vampire stepped forward and pulled what looked to be a leather wallet from the pocket of his coat. Flipping it open, he revealed a little gold badge that made my blood run cold. There was nothing I could do to keep the smile on my face. They were representatives from the Tattoo Artists & Potion Stirrers Society (TAPSS), and they could make my life hell. All tattoo artists had to pass a series of tests set forth by TAPSS that covered both tattooing skills as well as potion stirring before you were given a license to tattoo. In addition, a parlor had to maintain a separate license that promised to uphold a certain level of quality and cleanliness.

Unclenching my teeth, I forced out the question I had to ask, but I already knew the answer. "What have I done to warrant this unexpected visit?"

"I'm sure that you already know why we're here, Mr. Powell," purred the red-haired vampire, as if he was trying to use his voice to get inside my head. Neither of them was attempting to glamour me and a part of me prayed they wouldn't try to. The other part of me really wished they would.

"Look, Vlad, all my transactions and work have been on the up and up. You can look at my records if you want to," I offered, throwing up my hands. They both laughed at me as we all knew that records were frequently falsified to hide the true nature of a tattoo or the identity of a client. It was normal operating procedure in the business. Any tattooist worth his salt knew how to protect his clients.

"No one would trust your records."

I replied with a shrug of one shoulder, as if his opinion didn't matter to me. "No one has time to run background checks on every client. You have to trust them to tell the truth when they fill out their paperwork."

"Regardless, we've had an extremely dark complaint from one of your former clients."

"You'll have to be a little more specific. We do a lot of business every night."

"Russell Dalton," the vampire replied, and it was all I could do to not react to the name. I had a feeling this man was going to haunt me until he finally put a bullet in the back of my head, or worse. "I believe you personally gave him a tattoo of a four-leaf clover on the heel of his left foot with a potion earmarked for good luck. Recall him now?"

"Rings a bell," I sneered. "I believe he told me that he had a complaint about the tattoo while he was waving a gun in my face the other day. I would have offered then to make any reparations he might have requested, but I found myself reluctant to cave to the ravings of an idiot when he was pointing the muzzle of a handgun in my face."

"Gun or not, you should have fixed the tattoo," the dark-haired vampire chided.

"Of course, the tattoo and potion that you mixed were basic and there shouldn't have been a problem to begin with," the other vampire added as he seemed to glide silently across the floor until he was standing on the other side of the glass counter.

"I would drop this case, gentlemen," I warned them softly through clenched teeth. "Russell Dalton is a worthless piece of slime who crawled in here one night with fifty dollars to his name, wanting a tattoo that would give his wife an uncontrollable desire to give him a blow job every time he gave her a little pat on the back of the head. I talked him down to a good luck charm and sent him on his way, hoping he would never cross my doorstep again."

"His potential depravity and initial desires have no bearing on this case. You should have done the tattoo correctly after you agreed upon it," the vampire closest to me said.

"I did do it correctly, Dracula. It was simple. I used leprechaun hair, which is well within the bounds of use for a good luck charm. It was only after I spoke with Dalton yesterday that I discovered the hair had gone bad. I had had the supply for less than a week. By the standards set by TAPSS, that is still considered a viable resource."

"Then you should have fixed the problem when it was brought to your attention."

"Like I said, Lestat, I don't bow to the whims of idiots waving guns in my face," I replied in a low growl.

"Let me rephrase it for you," said the red-haired vampire, drawing my gaze back to his pale blue eyes. "You will fix—" He didn't even get the chance to finish the sentence as a burst of power threw him across the room so that he crashed against the wall between the front door and the picture window at the front of the parlor. It was all I could do to keep the smile off my face. The other vampire simply stood stunned, his head bouncing from me to where his companion lay crumpled on the ground several feet away.

The antiglamour spell had kicked in. Trixie didn't feel anything when she used her spell, because she used it on herself. The vamp, on the other hand, had tried to use a form of glamour compulsion on me, which was then thrown back in his face—hard.

"There's no spellcasting in my shop," I snapped in answer to the unspoken question of "How?" hanging in the air. "If you haven't figured it out yet, I don't like being forced into doing anything that I don't want to do."

The other vampire overcame his momentary shock and lunged at me with amazing speed. He grabbed me around the throat with one hand, nearly crushing my windpipe so that I couldn't draw a breath. His long white fangs were bared as he snarled at me. "As my companion was stating before he was rudely interrupted, you will clean up this mess you created."

"I'm not touching Dalton again."

The vampire squeezed harder and slammed me into the wall, causing white spots to dance before my eyes. As my vision cleared, I noticed that the second vampire had regained his feet and looked even more pissed than his companion. This was turning out to be a great night.

A part of me relaxed when I heard the heavy thud of Bronx's footsteps as he approached the front of the parlor. I expected him to execute some wonderful violence as he beat these two assholes to bloody pulps. If anything, I was looking forward to him freeing me from the vampire who was currently clamped on my throat, causing my lungs to burn from a lack of air.

To my surprise, the troll stopped at the glass counter and reached under it to some of the hidden shelves where we kept paperwork, ink pens, and our MP3 players. The troll pulled out a large mason jar of buttons of different sizes and colors, and unscrewed the top. I had no idea that the container had been under there, but then the troll was always full of interesting surprises.

The eyes of both vampires locked on the jar, and they seemed to grow even paler. I thought I even heard one of them whisper "No" before Bronx poured a large handful of buttons into his massive palm and tossed them in the middle of the floor. The vampire holding my throat released me so fast that I slid down the wall to the floor. Dark curses were muttered from each as they knelt on the ground, gathering up the buttons. With lightning-fast hands, they sorted the buttons, stacking them according to size, color, and design so that a rainbow of buttons covered the worn carpet on the floor.

Rubbing my throat, I patted Bronx on the shoulder as I stood. Instead of risking his neck and mine, the troll had decided to go the wiser route and take advantage of a known obsessive-compulsive trait in vampires. Seeds, buttons, and even flower petals: if they could be sorted and organized, the vampire was compelled to stop whatever he was doing and complete the task.

When the two were finished, they carefully eased away from the buttons so that they wouldn't be disturbed. They both looked frustrated and more than a little humiliated. They also looked eager to take that frustration out of my hide, but right now Bronx was still standing by the glass case with his hand on the top of the jar of buttons.

Reaching into my back pocket, I pulled out my wallet. I withdrew fifty dollars and threw it at the nearest vampire. "Here's Dalton's refund. Tell him to take his problem to another tattoo parlor and to never step into mine again. Case closed."

"This case may be closed, but it's not forgotten," said the dark-haired vampire as he scooped up the money and stuffed it into his pocket. "Dalton told us what really happened in the alley yesterday. You're going to attract their attention and bring them all down on our heads. We can't afford that. We will stop you before we come to that crossroads. TAPSS is watching you."

The two vampires glided out of the parlor while I fought the urge to throw a handful of fucking buttons at their backs. Bronx gave me a dark look but said nothing as he returned to the back room. I sighed as I grabbed the jar and walked into the middle of the room. I picked up the little piles of buttons and threw them back into the jar. At least I now knew it was there in case we had another vampire run-in. In most cases, such a tactic served as little more than a distraction. I was sure Bronx's presence in the main room had also helped to deter the two vampires from trying to attack me again. OCD or not, they would have gotten to me eventually.

I sat down on the bench and rubbed my neck. I listened to Trixie finish up with the client who had been present to hear the entire altercation in the front room (fabulous), giving him proper tattoo care instructions while collecting her fee. It was only after he left the shop, the door banging closed behind him, that I dragged my sorry ass into the back room, where I was sure there were a few questions waiting for me and only so much that I was permitted to say.

"What happened in the alley?" Trixie immediately demanded, sitting on the side of one of the tattoo chairs.

"Nothing important. He attacked. I fought back and I won. You should be happy about that," I teased, but I knew that it wasn't going to get me anywhere with her. I refused to look over at Bronx. His perceptive eyes unnerved me in too many ways. He simply knew things without being told. He watched while others talked, and he remembered things that were better left forgotten.

"Are we going to lose our license?" Bronx asked.

"They aren't going to touch your licenses. I was the tattooist. I'm the one they're pissed at. You're safe."

"What about the parlor's license?"

"I don't think they would go to that extent yet. They just wanted to scare me a little bit."

"I hope by the bruises on your neck, it worked," Trixie grumbled.

"Who are they so afraid of?" Bronx demanded, getting to the real heart of the matter.

"Don't worry about it," I said with a shake of my head, hating the words as they left my mouth. I hated evading their questions and I hated even more that I was forced to lie to them. Trixie and Bronx were the closest I had to family in this world. My own family had been lost to me in an attempt to protect them from the Ivory Towers. My coworkers deserved the truth, but I couldn't give it to them if I was going to keep them protected as much as I possibly could.

Trixie had her secrets. Let me have mine so I could sleep at night. "I swear to you, if shit comes down, I will handle it."

Bronx settled on one of the stools next to his tattoo chair, laying his beefy hands on his knees. "You know, it doesn't have to be that way."

I flashed him a smile that crumpled from my lips before it could fully form. "This time, it does."

I had done the impossible and walked away from something that no one was allowed to turn their back on. I knew that it was going to haunt me until someone finally killed me over it, but I refused to drag my friends into my mess if I could help it. And for the moment, I thought the best way to protect them was to keep them as ignorant as possible. The less people knew about me, the better. When there's a monster under your bed, sometimes it really is best not to look.

7

THE RE WAS AN unexpected gift waiting for me when I came into the shop the next afternoon. I paused as I reached to turn on the overhead bank of lights in the main tattoo room and saw Trixie's body outlined by the light seeping in through the shaded windows. She was stretched out in one of the tattoo chairs with one arm thrown over her eyes, her breathing even as she slept. In the stillness, her beauty seemed to have softened, as if I had just chanced upon Sleeping Beauty after scaling the castle walls to the tallest tower in the keep. Her long blond hair cascaded from the head of the chair in a golden waterfall, while her pale skin glowed in the dim afternoon light. Her beauty was nearly heart stopping.

When she was moving gracefully about the parlor, perpetually light on her toes, cracking jokes and intent on her work, it was easier to overlook or put aside her beauty and focus on the person. I could remember that she was just a friend and coworker. It was easier to put up that mental barrier against both the sexual attraction and the something more that ached in my chest when she smiled at me. But in the stillness of that vulnerable moment, it all came rushing back to me so that I could barely breathe.

There had been a few times during the past couple of years that

Trixie, Bronx, and I had all gone out for drinks at the local bars. I cherished those few memories as I watched her out in public, not as her employer, but as her friend. She was a beam of bright light slicing through the darkness. She laughed, overflowing with joy. And then there were times when she watched you with such intensity you could almost be convinced you were the only person left on the planet. I could feel the compassion that flowed from her heart and it caused an ache in my own chest. She made the world a wonderful place even in the grimmest moments.

But I couldn't have her.

Clenching my teeth, I flipped on the overhead light, jerking her instantly awake so that I could finally escape her hold. While she was looking at me with a slightly confused and dazed expression, I was able to focus on the bigger question at hand: why was she sleeping in the tattoo parlor when she kept a comfortable apartment just a few miles away? It was time to pack away my sexual urges and simple desires for something else, because it was obvious that Trixie needed a friend.

"In a little early, aren't you?" I asked with a smile as I tried to break the building tension.

A little smile tweaked the corners of her mouth, but never grew into anything more as she sat up fully and swung her legs around so that her feet touched the floor. She still looked exhausted, and she was having trouble meeting my direct gaze. I had a feeling that she hadn't been asleep for long when I'd found her. Usually, she worked later into the night than I did and then probably didn't settle into sleep until shortly before dawn each night. Of course, there was also the problem that had chased her out of her apartment in the first place.

"I thought you could use the help," she volunteered, but there was a slight waver to her voice.

"Yeah, tell me another one."

"I know this doesn't look good. I just needed a place to crash and I didn't have anywhere else to go . . ."

"That was safe," I finished.

Trixie stared down at her fingers, entwined in her lap. "Yes."

"What happened?"

She hesitated for a long time as she was probably debating telling me the truth or a somewhat believable lie. I frowned and shook my head at her. It was none of my business and I wasn't going to force her into telling me something she didn't want to talk about. I also didn't get a feeling of urgency, which meant that explanations could wait for another time.

Reaching into my pocket, I pulled out my keys, jingling them softly in my hand. "Let's go. I've got a place where you can catch a few more hours of sleep before you're needed here."

I walked through the main tattoo area to the back room, listening to her grab her bag from the counter before she followed me, her heels clomping across the old hardwood floor. I unlocked the back door and turned toward a set of old, rickety wooden stairs that led to the second-floor apartment.

"You rent the apartment as well?" Her voice drifted to me as I paused at the door to unlock it.

"I own the entire building," I admitted as I opened the door with a hard shove. I held it open, allowing her to follow me in. Glancing over my shoulder at her, I blinked twice at the sight of her. She was outside the parlor and her glamour had kicked back in. Gone was the luscious blonde with the high cheekbones and sparkling green eyes. She was now a brunette with deep chocolate brown eyes and a heart-shaped face. Trixie was still a beautiful woman in her cloak of glamour, but I had become accustomed to seeing through it to her true beauty. I pushed the disappointment away and focused on the tiny apartment.

The air in the room was heavy from the heat, and musty. It had been at least six months since I'd last crashed here and that was only because I had spent a late night out drinking at the bars within walking distance of the parlor. It had just been easier to sleep it off here instead of attempting to trek back to my apartment.

Closing the door behind her, I led her through the small apartment, past the couch with the stained cushions, sunk from too much wear, through to the tiny kitchen that barely allowed two people to stand in there at the same time. We turned down the hallway as I pointed out the bathroom and the one bedroom. A mattress and box spring lay on the floor, holding a couple of blankets and a pair of flat pillows. Thick curtains blocked out the light from the window, but a slight part between the two panels allowed a shaft of light to cut through the room. Dust particles danced in the light as it fell across the bed.

"Believe it or not, this place is actually pretty clean," I said, shoving one hand anxiously through my hair. "I come up here every few months and air the place out, clean the blankets and anything that's been used recently. I haven't actually lived up here for a couple of years, but it's always been a nice fallback place when I can't make it home."

"I didn't know," she murmured. "Have you ever . . . ?"

"I've never done any of my tattoo deals up here. This is just a place for me to crash," I quickly said. "Hell, it doesn't even have a TV."

"I really appreciate this, Gage. I just need a couple of days to get this worked out and then I'll be back at my own apartment, or at the very least a new one," she said. "I'll even pay you rent if you want."

I waved off the offer. "I don't ever use this except on the rare occasion. There's no reason for that nonsense. Just try to keep it somewhat clean and we're good."

"Not a problem."

"When are you going to tell me what the real problem is?"

"It's nothing. It's just best if I don't go back to my apartment for a little while," she replied, trying to make it sound as if it wasn't anything important.

"I can't help you if you don't talk to me."

"I can handle it. It's nothing."

"Well, it's going to be something when this problem appears on the doorstep of the parlor. I'm going to need to know then," I warned her as I started to leave the bedroom.

Trixie crossed her arms under her full breasts and leaned back on one foot as she eyed me. "Does that mean you'll finally get around to telling me why TAPSS is so worried about you catching the attention of someone dangerous? That's turned up on the parlor doorstep on more than one occasion."

"It's something I've got under control."

"And I don't?"

"A person has to wonder when you're sleeping at the parlor after-hours. I'm not the one on the run."

Trixie allowed her arms to drop limply to her sides as she took a couple of steps closer to me. In heels she was nearly taller than me. She dropped her head so that her lips almost brushed against my cheek when she spoke. "Well, then, I guess we both have our fair share of secrets that we're not willing to share."

"Someday I think both of us are going to come clean, but I guess today isn't going to be that day," I said, as my throat threatened to close up on me while the blood rushed from my head to my pants.

"Thank you for your help, Gage. You're one of the only friends in this world I've got who I can turn to," she whispered, her warm breath dancing past my ear.

"I find that hard to believe," I choked out. "You're a beautiful, energetic, sweet woman. How could you not have other friends who would have your back?"

"That's just it. I'm only a beautiful woman to them. They don't care about me. But you do, don't you? You care."

A soft sigh escaped me before I could catch it. I lifted my right hand and let my fingertips slip down her cheek, caressing from the line of her jaw to her stubborn chin. She looked different, but I knew I was standing before my Trixie. There was just something in her eyes, the tilt of her full mouth, that reminded me of the woman I had come to know over the past two years. No, I didn't know her secrets, but I felt like I knew her soul. She was kind and compassionate. She worried about others before herself. She drew a laugh out of Bronx and me when our moods were sour. She eased fears, wiped tears, and laughed freely.

I had loved Trixie for the better part of two years, perpetually watching her from afar because it was simply too dangerous to involve her in my life. The warlock guardians were watching me too closely, and bringing someone into my life only meant making them vulnerable to that kind of danger. I didn't want the threat of the Ivory Towers to ever touch her life because of me. We all lived under the shadow of the warlocks and the witches, but I knew that she would become a target if anyone knew of my feelings for her.

Even with that quite valid reason dancing through my head, I couldn't get myself to take a step back from her. I lowered my hand from her face, letting my fingers skim down her arm before returning to my side.

When I finally spoke, my voice was low and rough. "I have always cared for you. I want you to be happy and safe. I will do whatever I can to see to it that you are."

She leaned forward that extra little bit and brushed her parted lips against mine. My eyes fell shut as instincts immediately took over and I kissed her back with force. I felt as if I had waited a lifetime to touch her, kiss her, taste her. My body grew hard as I raised my hands, running them along her bare arms so that she gave a little shiver as we deepened the kiss, my tongue darting into her mouth to brush against her tongue. She tasted of fresh strawberries, sweet and ripe. My hands lifted and I cupped her face, holding her in place as the kiss became hotter. I wanted her. I wanted her more than anything else I had ever wanted in my life. I wanted to spend hours worshipping her body, exploring every inch and curve, making her moan beneath me.

But I wanted the real Trixie, not this magic-induced facsimile. I wanted to open my eyes and see her golden hair spread out on the pillow. I wanted to be lost in those green eyes I looked forward to seeing every evening. I wanted the real thing.

And in truth, she deserved the real Gage. Not this half-truth that I presented to the world. We both deserved better than what we were getting at that moment. With all the willpower I could summon, I placed my hands firmly on her shoulders, and pushed her away from me a step. Neither of us spoke. Only the sound of our heavy breathing broke the silence of the overly warm apartment.

"We can't do this, Trixie," I announced when my brain started working through the haze of sexual desire. "You've had a rough night and need some sleep. You're only going to regret this later."

"Gage . . ."

"I'm going to head back down to the shop. Just get some sleep and come down when you're rested. I'll be waiting," I said brusquely, forcing myself to meet her gaze. She didn't look heartbroken or wounded by my rejection. In fact, she looked as if she could easily see through my ruse as a smile played at the corners of her mouth. Not surprising when I had no doubt that she could feel the trembling in my hands and my erection when I had her pressed against me.

Eager to beat a hasty retreat while I still could, I slid around her and headed for the bedroom door. I was determined to do the right thing where she was concerned. She needed help, not being mauled by me.

"I wouldn't regret it," she murmured before I left the room. Her voice was so soft, I wasn't sure that I actually heard it, or just hoped that I heard those words.

No, I wouldn't regret it either, I thought. But for now, it wasn't right.

I shut the front door of the apartment a little harder than I had meant to and tromped down the wooden stairs as fast as I could. I needed to get back to the tattoo parlor where I was safe and the world made sense. I needed to get back to the place where there were invisible boundaries that protected both Trixie and me from having to make these kinds of decisions. I needed to get back to the one place where I felt there were no surprises waiting for me and I was the king of my domain. I needed my shop.

SO MUCH FOR no surprises.

I returned to the tattoo parlor and had started to set up the equipment for the day when I heard footsteps creaking across the wooden floor as if someone was pacing in the lobby area. I glanced over at the monitor set up for the security system that overlooked the lobby, but I saw no one. A cold chill ran through me as I knew that it couldn't be a vampire—the sun was too high in the sky— and I couldn't think of any other creature who had the ability to be invisible to a digital camera without the use of a series of spells. Walking over to the cabinet that held the guns I had confiscated over the past few years, I pulled out a large black handgun. I had no intention of actually firing it since I didn't bother to grab the magazine that had been removed. I hoped that waving it around would be enough to scare off the intruder.

Frowning, I stepped into the lobby to find a man standing in the middle of the room, looking down at the watch on his left wrist with a grim expression. He wore a pair of black slacks and a white button-down shirt with short sleeves. His dark hair was starting to recede, giving him a bald spot on the top of his head, and the clipboard he was holding rested on the slight paunch of his stomach. While I didn't have any clue as to who he was, I could easily see that he wasn't the threat I had feared. He looked like a census taker or some poor, middle-aged man stuck in a dead-end job selling kitchen knives door-to-door.

"Mr. Powell," he said in a low, even voice as he looked up at me. His eyes paused on the gun in my hand, causing him to arch one eyebrow as his frown grew a little deeper. "I hope you appreciate that I was willing to wait for you while you had your brief encounter with the elf on the second floor. I don't have time to waste like that. I'm on a very tight schedule."

I opened my mouth to ask how he had possibly known what I was doing with Trixie and how he could know that she was an elf, but no noise came out as he continued talking.

"You might as well put the gun away. It won't help you."

"Who are you? How the hell did you get into my shop?" I swept around the counter and walked over to the front door to find that it was still locked. I lowered the gun, guessing that he might have sneaked in through the back door while I was upstairs with Trixie, but he had to have been watching the parlor from the back alley to get his chance, and I couldn't recall seeing anyone in the alley as we ascended the stairs.

"I'm with the Grim Reapers' Union, local number 23466, and I can get into any place I want, Mr. Powell, locked door or not."

A snort of disbelief escaped me as some of the tension eased from my shoulders. "Grim reaper? You've got to be kidding me." I had to admit there were a lot of things in this world that were hard to believe and a lot of things I struggled to understand, but I didn't believe there was a single creature who controlled the life and death of every living thing. Let alone believe there was an actual union of reapers that saw to the demise of everyone on this planet.

"You're not supposed to know about us, Mr. Powell. We work much better when we remain in the shadows, handling the death of a person when it is their time with no one looking at us. It's just easier for everyone involved. Much less paperwork."

"I would imagine so," I said, still unable to lose the snideness in my voice. A grim reaper? He looked like an accountant or some corporate drudge trapped in middle management. "I thought the grim reaper was supposed to wear a black shroud and carry a scythe and maybe even an hourglass. You're really destroying all of my beliefs here."

"I would hate to do that," he said with an irritated sigh, seeming to finally get tired of my sarcasm.

In the blink of an eye, dark clouds spread across the sky, blotting out the sun so that the earth was blanketed in a false night. The man I had been mocking was gone and an eight-foot-tall black-shrouded creature leaned over me until I was pressed against the wall. In one skeletal hand was a reaper's scythe that seemed to gleam in some unholy light, while the rest of him was cloaked in thick shadow. On a silver chain around his waist was an hourglass with its sand constantly pouring toward oblivion. I tried to stare into the hood of the shroud to see the creature's face, but I could see nothing beyond a pair of unblinking red eyes that radiated power. A deep sense of hopelessness pervaded the room until I was nearly drowning in it.

"Has this convinced you of my identity, Gage Powell, or do you need to accompany me on my next visit to reap a soul from this existence?" the creature asked in a deep, resounding voice that echoed throughout my whole frame and rattled my eardrums. Without a doubt, I was dealing with a creature infinitely more powerful than I could ever be. He could squash me like a bug with a mere wave of his bony hand and there was nothing I could do to stop it. And yet I was still holding my gun on him, clasped tightly in both trembling hands. I knew that a shot wouldn't do a damn thing to stop him, but my brain wasn't working in any kind of logical fashion. I was looking into the face of death and I just wanted him to back off and get the hell out of my shop.

"I'm convinced," I replied, somehow managing not to stutter.

The shrouded creature, in the blink of an eye, turned back into the balding middle-aged man shaking his head at me. He sank onto the bench that lined the back wall, settling his clipboard on his right knee. Pulling a white handkerchief out of his pocket, he wiped some sweat from his brow.

At the same time, I slid down the wall as my shaking knees gave out on me. The heavy metal gun hit the ground with a solid thud, while I hung my head forward so that my chin rested against my chest. My breathing was heavy as well, while a fine trembling seemed to fill every fiber of my being.

"See? Isn't this form much easier to deal with when it comes to handling business?" the grim reaper commented.

"Yes, but it's just a little hard to believe at first blush," I said, laughing, one part relief and one part hysteria. "I thought the idea of the grim reaper was just an old myth. I would never have guessed there were unions that handled death."

"Someone has to manage the flow of souls from this world to the next. It's a very important job."

"Without a doubt, but how does one go about getting such a job? I have to admit that I've never seen a want ad for the position."

For the first time since he'd appeared, the grim reaper actually gave a small smile. "Another time, perhaps. It's something of a long story and I'm on a tight schedule as it is. In fact, I should have been out of here already, Mr. Powell."

"Gage, please. I think after that scare, you can use my first name."

"Thank you," he said formally, with a nod of his head as he grew serious again. "Gage, you've seriously fucked up."

"I was beginning to guess as much considering that you're here. I would think that if you were after my soul, you would have reaped it already and moved on. No time for chitchat."

"Exactly. This is about one of your recent clients."

"I hope this isn't more Russell Dalton shit. I really don't think I can tolerate another word about that man," I grumbled, resting my arms on my knees.

"Dalton. Dalton. Dalton," the grim reaper muttered to himself as he flipped through several sheets of paper on his clipboard before he found what he was looking for. "No, it's not his time just yet. Though it doesn't look as if you've been much help with his case."

"I'm not taking responsibility for his death whether it comes today or ten years from now. He dug his own grave."

"And you threw the dirt in after him."

"Whatever," I said with a wave of one hand. "He got what he deserved. If this isn't about Dalton, then which of my clients do you have a problem with?"

"It's a young woman by the name of Tera Cynthia McClausen."

It took me a moment to remember who he was talking about when I heard the entire name, but my stomach clenched when I suddenly focused on the first name. Tera. She had never given me her last name and I had never thought to ask. It would be on the paperwork she filled out, but I never looked that shit over.

My tattoo on Tera's back had brought the grim reaper to my door, and I had a very good guess as to why he was there. *The angel feather.* It had done something to mess up the flow of souls. Whatever it was, the grim reaper was calling me out and this was one of the last guys on this planet I wanted to go a few rounds with. There really was no winning.

For now, the best plan was to play ignorant for as long as possible. "What's the problem with Tera?"

"She was on my schedule to die and you've ripped her from my sheet!" he exclaimed, slapping his clipboard against his knee. "I can't have screwups on my watch. This isn't the kind of job where you can let souls slip through your fingers. When a person is slated to die, they have to die. Every soul must be accounted for." As he spoke, he punched the clipboard with one slightly pudgy finger for emphasis.

"What are you talking about? Did I extend her life or something? What's the big deal if she lives a few weeks or months longer? She seems like a good person, and the world wouldn't be a particularly bad place if a good person lived a little longer."

"It's not a matter of good and bad people, I'm afraid. I also haven't the time to go into a discussion of morals and the silly concept of right and wrong. It's a matter of when their time is due. Tera's time is up."

"Fine. She has to die," I said, throwing up my arms in frustration. She was a nice person, but I doubted that I would be able to sway the grim reaper on the matter of death. "How does that involve me? All I did was give her a tattoo before cancer finally took her life."

"You know what you did."

"'Fraid not. Please, enlighten me."

"You made her immortal! I can't reap her soul."

My mouth hung open for several seconds and I swear my heart actually stopped in my chest. *Immortal.* I was up a serious shit creek with this one. There weren't true immortals in this world. Vampires could be killed with a well-placed stake and the elves were simply a long-living race. Even the witches and the warlocks had found spells to extend their lives by a considerable amount, but everyone died. Tera was immortal? To hell with the cancer that I had been hoping to give her an edge on, I had fixed it so that even all-mighty death couldn't touch her. *Holy hell.*

I was screwed. On the one hand, I had death haunting my tattoo parlor, angrily tapping his clipboard of names for the chopping block. On the other hand, if the warlocks and the witches got wind of this massive screwup, they would squeeze me for information on how I did it and then kill me. Unfortunately, I didn't know which was worse.

Pushing to my feet, I kept one hand on the wall to steady myself, as my legs were reluctant to support me. "Okay. Okay. Let's just discuss this slowly."

"Discuss this slowly?" the reaper repeated incredulously. "There's nothing to discuss. She's immortal, Gage. In case you've forgotten the definition of that simple word, it means that She. Can't. Die. You're keeping me from doing my job!"

"I get it. She can't die. This news is all a little unexpected."

"Is it? You know what caused this."

The angel feather. Yeah, I knew what had caused this. "I didn't expect it to have this kind of effect on her. I've never used that ingredient before. Never thought to."

"So you took a chance with some powerful magic without actually considering the consequences of your actions? What were you thinking?"

I pounded my fist against the wall before taking a few steps toward the balding man, still seated on the gleaming wooden bench. "I thought I would try to help her. It's like I said, she's a nice person. This world could do with a few nice people after all the scumbags that I run into on a regular basis. Helping someone isn't a crime."

"But making them immortal is a crime against nature, and you're going to have to pay the price for it."

"What are you talking about?" I demanded warily, halting in my steps toward the increasingly frightening figure.

"In three days, I need a soul. On my checklist, it's Tera McClausen, but I'm more than willing to change that name to Gage Powell to suit my needs."

"You can't do that!"

"Really?"

"You can't kill me to fill in for someone else. That just can't be legal in your world."

"And who are you going to report me to? Until a few minutes ago you didn't even know I existed."

I shoved both hands into my hair and tightened my fingers, wanting to pull my hair out in frustration and sheer desperation. This couldn't be happening. The grim reaper was going to cut my life short because I fucked up by trying to do something nice for someone else. A low growl rumbled from my throat, my eyes scanning the tattoo parlor as if I was trying to find some way of escaping, but you couldn't outrun death. I could tattoo myself using the same angel feather, but I had no desire to be immortal. I just didn't want to die in three days. I was hoping to have a little more time. And even if I escaped, that didn't mean the grim reaper couldn't start going after other people in my life in an attempt to exact some revenge for screwing up his job.

"I wish it didn't have to be this way." The man sounded tired and genuinely sorry about the situation. His round shoulders slumped and he sagged a little on the bench where he sat. "After glancing over your paperwork, it looks like you've still got a lot that you need to accomplish in this world, but I will reap you if I have to."

Dragging in a slow, cleansing breath, I unclenched my fingers and dropped my hands back down to my sides. There had to be a way out of this. I had gotten myself into some nasty scrapes in the past and had managed to ease my way out of the messes with a limited number of bruises, scars, and broken bones. I could still fix this.

"You said that you don't need the soul for another three days," I started. There was only one way to fix this and I could feel my stomach starting to knot. A bad taste was forming in the back of my throat.

"Yes, three days from today," he confirmed.

"And you just need a soul."

"Preferably Tera's soul, but I will take yours in trade. Only yours."

"I'm not going to kill some random person off the street just so you can meet your quota," I snapped irritably. "What if I can make Tera mortal again?"

"Then you are in the clear."

"And there's no way to extend the time she has? Three days is so little time before she dies from cancer."

The grim reaper heaved a heavy sigh, as if he had heard this argument far too many times in his long career of collecting souls from the living. Lines dug deep furrows in his face, signs that this job was weighing heavily on his own soul, assuming that the grim reaper was still permitted to keep his soul. "I'll see what I can do, but at the very least I need her soul available to me three days from now. Extensions happen, but they are extremely rare. I'll put in the appropriate paperwork for you."

A light-headed giggle escaped me. My neck was no longer necessarily on the chopping block, though Tera's was back on it. But in trade, I might have actually managed to extend her life longer than she originally had in a legal, happy, grim-reaper manner. It was the best I could ask for.

"Okay, you work your magic with death paper pushers and I'll work on Tera. Hopefully, at the end of three days, everyone will be happy in some way," I said, trying hard not to look too closely at what was currently left of my sanity. I didn't think it was a good thing to spend the afternoon examining futures with the personification of death. It only led to panic and bargaining for things you didn't necessarily think you could accomplish.

Tucking his clipboard under his arm, he pushed slowly to his feet again; some arthritis in the knees was probably beginning to slow him down. "You have a deal. I will see you again in three days." And then he was simply gone.

I blinked a couple of times, wondering if I had hallucinated the whole thing. Did I really just have a conversation with the master of death in which I argued trading my soul for Tera's? A part of me felt dirty from the idea of conspiring with another person to end someone's life, but then again, no one was supposed to be immortal. I was just undoing a mistake I had made. If I was lucky, Tera was completely oblivious to my mistake and I would be able to fix this without her ever being the wiser.

The only major problem was that I didn't have even the beginnings of a clue as to how in the world I was going to make her mortal again. Causing immortality had been a complete accident on my part. But I knew that an accident wasn't going to save my ass. I needed help. Serious, experienced help and I needed it *now* . . . before the clock ran out on my brief reprieve.

Jogging through the parlor, I burst out the back door and pounded up the wooden stairs to the second floor where Trixie was supposed to be sleeping. I hated to disturb her, but I didn't have any choice. I had to find a way out of this mess. The elf could catch up on her sleep later. Throwing open the door, I saw Trixie peer out from the bedroom doorway and look down the hall at me.

"I need you to do me a favor."

"Sure," she replied, sounding a little taken aback by my sudden appearance.

"Can you open the parlor for me today? Feel free to grab a few hours of sleep and open it late. That's fine with me. I've got an errand to run that I have to do right now."

"Don't worry. I've got it. Is everything all right?"

"Not in the slightest," I muttered under my breath. "One other thing, can you look up the information sheet that Tera McClausen filled out yesterday when I gave her the tattoo? I need to call her."

"Anything else?"

"Yes—I'll lock the doors downstairs, but I want you to lock this door behind me. If someone is looking for you, or whatever tale you want to tell me, then you need to try to protect yourself by locking the goddamn door."

To my surprise, a bright smile graced her beautiful face. "Thanks, Gage. I've got it."

I hoped so. It was bad enough my ass was in the fire. I wasn't sure that I would be able to protect her at the same time if things suddenly turned ugly. But I could try.

"If you want, you can wait to open until either Bronx or I get to the shop," I offered as I turned to leave and pull the door shut behind me.

Trixie's wonderfully light laughter danced through the small apartment before finally sliding around me. "I'll be fine, Gage. Run your errand. I'm not completely helpless."

"I know," I mumbled, feeling more than a little silly for treating her like some witless damsel in distress. For her to have survived this long in this neighborhood, she had to have learned to take care of herself. "Just be careful."

Closing the door behind me, I descended the stairs, listening for the telltale click of the lock being shoved into place on the door before I finally entered the parlor again. I locked the back door and checked my pockets for my keys and wallet before exiting through the front door. I had only one chance of finding a way out of this. I just hoped that my old tattooing mentor Atticus Sparks was still in the area.

Or at the very least, still alive.

9

THE DRIVE ACROSS town took only a few moments, but the results were not as I had hoped. I turned into a parking lot that was situated just a few buildings from where his shop was located. With a quick glance around to take in the few people wandering the sidewalks, I jogged to the building and skidded to a sharp stop in front of dirt- and dust-covered windows. The sign over the shop was missing, and gazing inside through the dirt revealed an empty storefront that hadn't been used in what looked to be years.

I stumbled a couple of steps backward, clenching my fists at my sides in desperation as I looked up to the second floor. Sparks had always used the second-floor apartment as his residence. I knew it too well after spending the better part of four years sleeping on a narrow cot in a room the size of a closet while I was going through my apprenticeship. It had been anything but a comfortable period of time for me, and I certainly wasn't getting laid, but I *was* busy learning everything that Sparks could possibly teach me about the tattooing world.

"Sparks!" I bellowed up at the second floor, hoping against my better judgment that he might actually have stayed in the building but had moved his shop to another part of town. There was no answer, no movement in front of the windows, which looked just as dirty and empty as those on the first floor. Passersby gave me a wide berth as I cursed under my breath. Sparks had packed up shop and moved on to some other tantalizing spot. At least I hoped that was the case.

"Damn it, Sparks!" I growled, kicking the door to the shop. I could find the old man, assuming that he was still alive, but it would mean using magic, and I was in enough trouble already. The man had never been big on advertising and I didn't expect to find his name in the white or yellow pages. He lived by the creed that the best kind of advertising was word of mouth, mostly because it was free.

Now I was in more trouble than I had expected. Standing on the sidewalk, I was trying to think of some way of locating where Sparks might have disappeared to when the thick scent of magic started to waft around me. I spun around, my hands extended, barely resisting the urge to call up my own barrier to protect me from whatever was brewing. My skin prickled and a cold sweat beaded across my back and down my spine despite the growing heat of the afternoon sun. Someone was coming. Someone powerful.

The distinct smell of magic was that of a warlock or a witch, but it wasn't Gideon riding my ass again. No, the black-cloaked figure who suddenly appeared on the sidewalk a few feet from me was Simon Thorn. It didn't look as if he had aged since I had last seen him. Then again, the Ivory Towers occupants had long ago learned to stretch the years of their lifetimes. I hadn't seen him since I had given up my warlock studies years ago. I had barely survived the experience, but I did give as good as I got, making him wary of me.

Beneath the traditional black cloak, he wore a dark suit with a crisp white shirt. His hands were encased in black leather gloves as he tugged at the cuffs of this shirt. Instead of a tie, a large red jewel was tucked in the top button. It was a new addition to his traditional ensemble and I had to wonder if it added an extra layer of protection to his usual battery of magical defenses that I had once torn down. When I escaped Simon, I had been fresh from the schoolroom and spells flowed through my brain like a swollen river. But I was at a distinct disadvantage this time. I knew it was too much to ask that he wouldn't pick a fight. Hell, I had little doubt that Simon was ready to finally kill me after having failed the first time.

A woman's scream tore at the midday city sounds, followed by the hard clatter of feet on the sidewalk as people scattered, darting into buildings and ducking for cover at the sudden appearance of a warlock in their midst. Things had been quiet until recently. The scene at the Cock's Crow just the other day had shaken up our recent stretch of peace, and now Simon had descended from the Towers with the obvious intent of kicking my ass. Sometimes the people of this world couldn't catch a break.

"Back to the scene of the crime, I see." Simon's cold voice whipped around me like a bitter winter wind. He looked up at the building, his upper lip curling as he took in the abandoned business covered in a layer of dirt and dust. "I see that it has been a profitable choice for your former mentor. Of course, I've heard that you've done significantly better now that you've chosen to cut corners and work in the shadows."

I took a couple of steps back from him, keeping my hands open and extended from my body. Instead of being a nonthreatening stance, among warlocks it was an aggressive stance, as it was the easiest way to both catch and sling spells when needed. "Talking to Gideon?" I said with a smirk. "He's always been such a gossip."

Around us, the sidewalk remained frighteningly empty, leaving me half expecting to see a tumbleweed roll between us on a hot breeze. Even the cars rumbling down the street had gradually stopped and all signs of life seemed to have disappeared. To a warlock or a witch, there was no such thing as an innocent bystander—anything that breathed was just a potential target.

"I don't need reports from the guardians. You were never interested in the purity of the art. You were only interested in how magic could be used to benefit your ends."

I couldn't stop the derisive snort that escaped me. "You're just upset that you didn't have much to teach me. The art came naturally to me, allowing me to cut corners that you simply couldn't."

"You never appreciated what we were offering you," Simon snarled.

"And what exactly were you offering me?"

He waved his hands around our surroundings. "The chance to be a god among these creatures."

"You mean a monster. Not interested."

"And it's time that you paid the price for turning your back on us." As he spoke, he hurled a bluish-white ball of energy at me. I instantly threw up a protective barrier so that the energy washed harmlessly down the front of the barrier like water. Without giving Simon a second to come up with another spell, I collected my own fistful of energy and magically grabbed the front of his suit like I had grabbed Dalton's clothes just a few days ago. Surprise popped on Simon's face before I threw him through the front window of Sparks's old shop, sending glass splintering in all directions.

Smiling, I pulled all the shattered bits of glass back together with a wave of my hand, re-forming the window so that Simon was at least temporarily shut up in the old building. Dusting himself off, Simon stepped forward, holding out his hand before him as he approached the window. But to his surprise, he walked right into the window, bouncing off what was now plastic instead of glass. He had used the wrong spell to shatter what he assumed was glass and he had failed to break through.

I couldn't stop myself. It wasn't often that you saw a full-grown warlock smash his face against a plastic window and then bounce off in total shock. I bent over at the waist, laughing, my arms wrapped around my stomach. The surprised look disappeared from Simon's face, instantly replaced with fury. As he approached the window a second time, a hole appeared in the center and quickly grew bigger as he melted the plastic so that he could step through.

"It's all still a game for you," Simon said through clenched teeth.

Swallowing back the last of my chuckles, I shook my head once as I regarded the warlock. "If you can't laugh at life, then what's the point?"

From an inner pocket of his suit jacket, he withdrew a wooden wand. The sight of the device froze the blood in my veins. Simon was done playing nice, lobbing softballs in my direction. Now I knew that he meant to kill me. Spellcasters could perfectly direct their magic with their wands, making the magic spell stronger and more concentrated. It was also ten times harder to deflect and block.

"Simon, this is ridiculous. You've let me live in peace for years now. I haven't caused any problems, haven't been using any significant magic beyond a little self-defense," I argued as I took a step back from him. "What happened to the live and let live attitude of the past several years? I'm not causing you any problems."

"But that's just it. You are. Your very existence is a big problem for us."

"How? I haven't done anything!" I shouted. He couldn't possibly know about my mess regarding Tera, and even that fell under the realm of TAPSS and not the warlocks—not that some simple bureaucracy would stop them. In all honesty, I expected both sides to want a piece of my hide if either found out exactly what I had managed to do. Immortality tended to sound appealing when you were approaching the end of your life.

"You represent a blot on our perfect record. All of our students have either finished their studies and gone on to become skilled warlocks, or they have perished in the attempt. And yet here you stand, neither a warlock nor dead."

I was beginning to see Simon's dilemma. He was getting grief from the warlock community because my reputation was growing among my own group as a respected potion stirrer and tattoo artist. If I had rolled up into a little ball of failure and lived the rest of my short life in the gutter, then we wouldn't be having this argument. Failure on my part was just as good as my death. My success was making Simon look bad. He should have found a way to kill me much sooner.

"A blot? I've been called worse," I said.

Simon pointed his wand at me, an evil grin growing on his face. "Not ever again."

Clenching my teeth, I slammed the sides of my hands together with my palms flat out, facing him. I focused my energy on creating a single steel barrier in front of me. Even then, my feet still slid nearly a foot backward across the pavement under the force of the spell that hammered into my protective barrier. My strength wavered and my protective barrier cracked under the force of Simon's attack, but it held.

"You're only putting off the inevitable," Simon taunted.

"Death may be inevitable, but not today." I tried to sound confident, considering that I had already had a meeting with the grim reaper that day. Of course, that didn't mean Simon couldn't put me in a whole lot of pain, making it impossible for me to find a way to fix the Tera situation.

Whispering a couple of words under my breath, I twisted my own barrier so that it bounced Simon's spell back at him. Unfortunately, the old warlock was crafty, cutting off his own spell and dodging the remaining energy by falling against the brick side of Sparks's old shop.

My head throbbed and muscles twitched throughout my body from the excess energy running through me. It had been a long time since I had last dealt with this much magic. I was sorely out of practice and in deep trouble if I didn't do something about Simon soon.

The gun I had pulled on the grim reaper was starting to look really attractive, even if it would only serve as an irritant for Simon. Any kind of distraction would serve. Unfortunately, I had left the gun at the parlor.

Shaking out my hands as I dropped them back down to my sides, as if I was lowering them toward a pair of guns, I sidestepped away from Simon and moved out into the empty street so that we had room to wage the war that had been brewing for more years than I cared to count. I had been only seven years old when I had started to exhibit an inclination toward magic. Simon had swept into my family's normal suburban home, completely overwhelming my poor parents, demanding that I be taken by him to be trained properly to be a warlock. He was doing what was best for all parties. If I was left on my own, unchecked, I would only become a danger to myself and those around me, while at the same time, I would become frustrated by missing out on my own potential. He conned them with pretty promises of grandeur, while leaving out the cold, compassionless life that I would lead as a fledgling warlock. No loving parents. No companionship from older brother or younger sister.

But then, he had been shocked in the end. I'd been a true natural when it came to weaving spells—magic flowed easily through me, like air through my lungs, and I could wrap it around my hands and command it to do my bidding without their complicated words and hand gestures. It was a part of me, and it infuriated Simon in ways that pleased me. In truth, I left Simon not only because I found his pompous rhetoric insulting, but I was also bored. I was reaching the end of what he could teach me, but he was unwilling to admit it. I knew that if I hadn't left soon, he would have killed me for my trouble.

So now I stood in the middle of the street, an outcast of the Ivory Towers, and he could kill me quite legally, not raising a single eyebrow. But I preferred it that way—I didn't want to be a part of their cult. I didn't want to be a part of anything that looked down on this world and saw it as something to step on. Sure, life was dirty and crowded and more than a little messy, but it was worth the effort and just too amusing to miss out on.

"Come play with me, Simon," I mocked.

Reaching out with my right hand, I closed it as if I was wrapping my fingers around his throat. I dragged his slumped body away from where it was resting against the building until he was standing in the middle of the street with me. With a little push, I released him so that he was forced to backpedal a couple of steps to regain his balance before I took a daring chance and closed my eyes. Digging deeper into the magic that surrounded me, I felt a pulse of fresh life fill my limbs and circle my heart as the rest of the world dimmed around me. The energy sharpened in my mind into daggers and flew through the air with only the slightest nudge from me. I knew that I'd hit my mark when I heard a distinct "Ugh" not far from me. Not all of the daggers had hit where I'd wanted them to, but only one of them needed to pierce him.

I cracked my eyes open and a grin slipped across my face as his thin hand pressed against his right shoulder. Blood seeped through his slender fingers and his narrow face twisted with rage. There had been a hole in his defenses. I wouldn't be able to manipulate that same hole again nor any similar to it, but it was enough for me to have wounded him once like that. I wanted to see him bleed. I needed to prove to myself and any others who might be watching from some distant crack in a window blind that this bastard was still human despite his best efforts to distance himself from his birth race.

"Surprised?" I asked.

"Not as much as you will be," he snarled in response as he tucked his wand down his left sleeve. Odd—a wand always represented more powerful, more precise spells. What could he possibly prefer to wield with his hands over the use of a wand?

Releasing his shoulder, he raised both of his hands above his head before quickly lowering them. A burst of power shot out from him, but instead of hitting me, it surged toward the buildings running up and down the street on either side of us. Windows exploded, shooting glass inward toward the occupants watching the events unfolding in the middle of the street. Screams of pain and fear filled the air around us as innocent people were injured by the flying shards of glass.

"Stop it! They've got nothing to do with this!" I shouted, taking a few angry steps toward him with my hands in fists at my sides.

Simon's smile returned, carving across his face like a violent slash cut through flesh. His left arm lifted from his side and at the same time screaming penetrated the quiet along with a child's sobbing. I looked over to his left to see a woman hovering in the air in a broken-out window. Her legs frantically kicked at the air as she clawed at her throat. A child struggled in an older woman's arms nearby, reaching for the choking woman as she cried.

"Stop!" I shouted. I didn't think. I just acted, weaving a counter-curse to remove the spell that Simon was using to kill the woman. As the woman fell to the ground with a heavy thud, I saw Simon out of the corner of my eye turn around in a circle, his cloak cutting about him in a wide swath before he threw the ball of energy at me. I tried to shift my powers to summon up another barrier to deflect the energy, but I was too slow. Simon's attack pushed right through and punched me in the gut, doubling me over. My face slammed into the dirty concrete at Simon's feet a half second before the rest of my body followed. The warlock's cackle rose above the excruciating pain swimming through my frame before grinding into my bones. It felt as if Simon had released within my body large worms that burned and wriggled their way through my organs and were now eating into the marrow of my bones.

I screamed, forcing my body to straighten as I lifted my head to look at Simon, standing over me. The warlock rested his fists on his hips as he stared down at me, a smile breaking over his face again. It was only through the overwhelming need to rip that smile from his smug face that I found the energy to move again. My eyes rolled up into the back of my head as I turned all of the energy swirling around me into wards. Pain sizzled through my frame as I sent energy surging through my body, seeking out and destroying the worms. I felt hollowed out, my organs reduced to little more than Swiss cheese, but I was still breathing.

"Your concern for them has always made you such an easy target," Simon said. "They're stupid, worthless bags of flesh."

"It's where we all start. Where you started," I replied through clenched teeth as I tried to push past the pain.

"I rose above that dirty start. You were supposed to as well, but obviously you've got some unfortunate failings. The council should have killed you years ago so you wouldn't have a chance to spread your weakness to others. I will correct that oversight now."

Simon had taken me by surprise, which meant this bastard probably had a little more stored up his sleeve. He had let me walk away years ago because he hadn't been sure that he could beat me. But he had continued to study magic, while I'd allowed my skills to stagnate. Simon came to me now because he was sure that he could take me out.

The nice thing was, there was one approach I could rely on that would always take a warlock by surprise: the direct one. Heaving myself back to my feet with a giant shove, I ignored my shaky legs and closed the distance between us. As he raised his hand, shock crossing his face, I slammed my fist into his nose. His head snapped back, causing him to stumble a couple of steps away from me as he covered his face.

"I've had enough of your shit. I didn't come here to deal with you," I said as I delivered another punch to his face followed by one to his gut that had him sucking in a harsh breath. "I came here to take care of other matters. I don't care about you, the rest of your useless crowd, or what you want because I don't want any part of it."

"That's too bad," Simon said, leaning close while wiping his bleeding nose with the back of a shaking hand. "Because we need to be rid of you."

I should have taken a step away. I should have turned my back and run. I should have learned my lesson years ago and started walking with an actual weapon at all times, but I thought I was skilled enough to keep myself safe with only magic.

Simon lunged a half step forward and slammed his fist against my breastbone; the impact was followed by a quick surge of power from whatever spell he had been weaving while I attacked him physically. It felt as if his fist kept going through my body until long, gnarly fingers wrapped around my soul. I gasped, my whole body going as stiff as a board as my hands latched onto his narrow shoulders for support. I had never read of this spell before, but Simon had discovered a way to not only grab my soul, but I could feel the bastard starting to pull it from my body.

Energy swirled around Simon and cut through me, entering my chest. Forcing my mind to move past the pain, I focused on the patterns I could see within the power rolling off the warlock. I had studied a great number of spells with Simon in this way. Many warlocks used the excuse of casting spells on their apprentices as a way of teaching them. If we managed to survive the encounter, then we were deemed worthy of continuing to study. The spell that was digging into my soul was similar to others that Simon had thrown at me in my younger years. It was familiar enough that I was able to unravel its secrets.

Raising my head so that my narrowed eyes met Simon's triumphant look, I balled my right hand into a fist and slammed it into his chest in the same way he had with me. I shoved the energy through his body until the echo of my hand came across a wispy feeling deep within his body. It wasn't as neat and tidy as his spell. In fact, it was downright ugly and sloppy, but it would get the job done.

"No!" he screamed as I wrapped my fingers tightly around his soul, locking us together. He knew that if he pulled on my soul in hopes of killing me, I would do the same with him.

The dark chuckle that escaped from me seemed to dance around the empty street. "It seems that we've hit a stalemate."

"You're not walking away from here!"

"Try to kill me and you know that I'm going to happily take you with me," I warned. "Besides, right now, I've got death on my side." Well, inasmuch as the fact that the grim reaper required me to undo a mess I'd made. Regardless, it was enough to unnerve Simon so that he loosened his grip the slightest bit, allowing me, with a fresh surge of power, to tighten my grip not only on his soul, but on my own soul as well.

We were stuck. If I pulled away now, Simon would come at me with yet another and then another spell until he succeeded in killing me. He would keep coming, destroying everything in his path, everything in my life, until he finally wore me down. I knew Simon—he was ruthless when it came to getting what he wanted. Hatred bubbled within me as I glared at the warlock. I was ready for this to be over.

With a feral scream, I pulled my hand away from Simon's chest. My fingers ripped through his soul as I tried to pull it from his body. The spell I had tried to weave to match his was faulty and I couldn't keep his soul together. The warlock moved at the same time, tearing something inside me. Simon's scream matched my own as his fingers ripped through my soul, shredding it. There was no time to stop it or fight it. The energy surged out of us in a rush, like air surging forth to fill a vacuum. We were blown apart, thrown to opposite ends of the street. As the spell left my body, I could feel that a part of my soul was now missing. I had thought I had a strong enough hold on it that I could force him out, but I was wrong.

There was no time to think about it. I was weak, possibly dying from internal injuries. My insides were battered, bruised, and bleeding from the fight. I could barely raise my head from where

I was lying in the middle of the street. A cough scraped along my throat as I tried to suck in a breath. The street was splattered with my blood. I needed to escape if I was going to have any chance at living for another day. More important, I needed to escape with the little wisp of energy that was tightly clasped in my right hand.

Simon lay in the street several yards down from me, groaning in pain. He was injured, but still dangerous. It would have been nice if one of the bystanders had come forward and chopped his head off, but everyone knew from experience that a conscious warlock was a deadly warlock. They wouldn't take the chance.

With any luck, Simon would use what little strength he had left to take himself back to the Ivory Towers. He needed to heal. He wasn't dying. Not yet, and I was in no shape to finish the fucker off.

Taking advantage of his injuries, I closed my eyes and focused all of my energy on the back room of the tattoo parlor. I didn't like leaving the people here alone with Simon, but I was no good to them in my current state. In a flash, I was back at Asylum, lying in a huddled heap on the white wooden floor. My breathing labored, I lay limp, curled in a loose ball on the floor, staring at my clenched right hand. I couldn't see anything, but I could feel the energy writhing there. I had a piece of Simon's soul and I was going to find a way to put it to good use. Preferably before he found a use for the chunk of my soul in his possession.

10

"GAGE?" TRIXIE CALLED in a concerned voice from the main room of the tattoo parlor. There had been no masking the heavy thud created when my body hit the wooden floor of the shop or the grunt of pain that escaped me. Her heels clicked across the floor as she rose from a chair and approached the back room, which, luckily, still had its door shut. I didn't want her seeing me like this.

"I'll be out in a minute," I shouted back in a strained voice, struggling to sound as normal as possible despite the fact that I was curled up in the fetal position on the dusty floor, my body wracked with pain. Unfortunately, I hadn't been convincing enough because the door swung open as I was pushing into a sitting position.

"Oh shit! What happened?" Trixie rushed toward me, her hand outstretched to help me.

"Don't touch me. I'm fine." I didn't mean to snap at her, but I was holding on to the fragment of the powerful warlock's soul, I was missing a bit of my own, and I didn't trust Simon not to have potentially booby-trapped me as I made my escape. There was a chance that she could get hurt if she tried to help. My only option was to escape down to my private workshop in the basement and check over things.

"What happened?" she demanded a second time, still hovering close.

"Had a little run-in." I pushed to my feet, squelching the groan that was rising from my chest. It felt as if all of my organs were leaking blood and my head had a marching band stomping my brain. Death was starting to sound attractive. It had to be less painful. "I'll be fine. Could you go back out to the parlor and keep an eye on things for me for a little while longer? I need to get cleaned up and then I'll be out."

"Are you sure?"

"I'm sure." I wanted to smile to reassure her. I even tried, but my brain couldn't locate the muscles in my face that made me smile. It just kind of flipped me the bird and went back to screaming at the marching band.

By the look on her face, I knew that she didn't believe a single word I had uttered to her, but thankfully, she backed out of the room and closed the door behind her. With my fist still wrapped around Simon's soul, I kicked aside my bag and pulled open the trapdoor in the floor with my free hand. Stumbling down the warped stairs, I immediately headed to the closest workbench where I yanked open the glass cabinets. Bottles clashed as I scrabbled for an empty vial with a cork. When I finally hit upon an ampoule and stopper, I closed my eyes and focused all my energy on the bit of wispy soul that was writhing in my hand. I forced it to slither into the glass ampoule and quickly lodged the stopper in. A couple of whispered words placed a charm on the glass, holding the soul in place while cloaking it from any prying eyes. Turning back to the cabinet, I wrapped a length of worn leather around the top of the glass container before tying the ends together. It was only when the glass container was hanging around my neck, the cold glass pressed against my skin, that I sank to the dirt floor and breathed a shaky sigh of relief. This shred of Simon's soul would never leave my side, a bit of valuable leverage that could come in handy in an important moment. I'd find a good use for it. Simon certainly hadn't.

Breathing heavily, I leaned against the front of the wooden workbench, my hands flat in the dirt floor as the pain flooded my mind. When I returned to the parlor, my only focus had been on getting Simon's soul to a secure location before something happened that caused me to lose my newfound toy. Now, as I sat in the dirt in the nearly pitch-black room, all the pain came back with a new vengeance. The worms that had penetrated my body and bored holes through my bones represented a new spell. I hadn't been expecting that from the old warlock and hadn't been able to protect myself from it. I had a feeling it was only the beginning of what I faced when it came to Simon, particularly now that I had a bit of his soul.

Of course, he also had a bit of mine. Terrifying, but at least we were somewhat evenly screwed on that front. What had my attention was that he had chosen to attack me after several years of complete silence. He'd said he needed to be rid of me now, as if my presence in the warlock community had some kind of impact when I knew it had no bearing on anything whatsoever. I was a tattoo artist and a potion stirrer. We were beneath the notice of the warlocks and the witches who wove elaborate spells up in their Ivory Towers, changing the lives of helpless humans and other unknowing creatures lurking on the earth. I had suddenly become an important thorn in Simon's side and I needed to know why he was so desperate to have me plucked out before he found something interesting to do with the fragment of my soul he held.

Above me, Trixie's footsteps returned to the back room, but they remained in front of the cabinet containing potion ingredients. Based on the lack of other footsteps, I didn't think a customer had arrived in the shop, but it didn't matter. I couldn't remain seated in the dirt like a useless lump for much longer. I had to pull myself together and fucking locate Sparks. It was bad enough that Simon had picked this exact moment to reenter my busy life, but right now, I had to place my priorities on the grim reaper and his request for Tera's soul.

Which gave me pause. If he couldn't have Tera's, would he accept most but not all now that Simon possessed a fragment? A derisive snort escaped me before I could push it back. The grim reaper was going to take my soul regardless of its condition, and not even Simon and his pack of warlock flunkies would be able to stop him. In three days, if Tera wasn't mortal, my soul belonged to the reaper—not Simon. That at least seemed slightly comforting, but not much.

I was shaken from my grim thoughts by the sound of Trixie's footsteps descending the wooden stairs. "Gage?" she called into the darkness. I hadn't bothered to grab the pull-chain light when I came down the stairs, relying on the light from the opening in the ceiling and my own memory of the room.

Pushing off the workbench, I lurched violently to my feet and rushed across the room. "Stop! Don't come down any farther!" I ran until I hit the opposite wall with the flats of my palms, my body resisting every movement. The energy from the pentagram painted on the wall surged through my arms, jarring me even more awake. The spell that I had set down in the basement protected against the entrance of anyone other than me. The items in my private room were too dangerous.

"I made you something for the pain. It'll help you heal faster," she replied, not moving from the third stair from the top. Glancing up, I could see her cupping a white bowl in both hands.

My shoulders slumped under a combination of guilt and fatigue. She was trying to help, but she was going to get herself killed hanging around me. "Give me a second," I said in a low voice after a few moments. I closed my eyes and blocked out her presence while I focused on the aggressive energy that was hovering inches from her, waiting to strike. I had reached the pentagram just in time, putting the defense system in a state of hesitant and angry alert but not attack. Tracing my fingers blindly over the lines of the pentagram and other lines of protection drawn on the wall, the energy slowly dispersed until there was nothing left that would attack Trixie should she enter my domain.

Pushing off the wall, I stumbled a little into the center of the room until I reached the chain and gave it a hard yank. Harsh yellow light flooded the dark room, leaving me squinting as I tried to focus on the beautiful blond creature approaching me with a frown pulling down her full lips. It wasn't until she was standing in my private domain that I realized the antiglamour spell I had cast extended down here—to my pleasure. Had I really kissed those lips earlier today? Was there any chance of kissing them again?

"You're a mess," Trixie announced, still standing on the stairs.

No. No chance really. I plopped down in the middle of the room, grateful to be off my feet again and relaxing as I tried to will the pain in my bones to ease. "Thanks. You can come down now."

"What happened?"

"A visit from an old friend."

"Old friend?" she scoffed. She descended the stairs, her eyes sweeping over the room while her beautiful lips parted in surprise. I had no doubt both she and Bronx were aware that the room was down here, but I didn't think this was what she'd been expecting. I had enough supplies in these cabinets to keep three tattoo parlors in business and still maintain some illegal business on the side.

But it was more than the cabinets filled with ingredients that lined the walls. It was the symbols painted on the wall that protected both me and the room. It was the dirt floor instead of the typical concrete that had been dug out when I bought the place. There was no hiding that there was more to me than just a potion-stirring tattoo artist who liked to color outside the lines of the legal from time to time. But I didn't think she was going to be willing to utter the word.

"What did you make?" I asked when she stood silent and still as a statue at the bottom of the stairs, staring at anything but me.

"Painkiller," she choked out. "It will help ease your aches. I would have made something that helped you to heal, but I wasn't sure what was wrong."

I held out my left hand toward her, as it was the steadiest, forcing her to walk farther into the room. Her heels shifted in the dirt, but she stepped forward and handed me the white ceramic bowl. I paused, staring at the weak-looking tea that still had leaves floating in the steaming water. It smelled horrible, so I wasn't surprised when it tasted even worse. It was all I could do not to spit the first sip back into the bowl.

"What is it? It tastes like piss."

"Sorry. We're out of sugar. Drink as much as you can. It'll help."

"Thanks," I said, forcing down another mouthful. Small leaves wedged themselves between my teeth, leaving me to run my tongue over them as I wished I had something I could drink to get rid of the taste. Unfortunately, it was too early for a beer, and we kept the whiskey in a drawer upstairs. So far away.

Pushing back to my feet with a grunt, I walked over to another workbench. The mixture Trixie had made was already sweeping through my body, easing pain and removing the fuzz from my brain so I could concentrate. Once she left, I could cast a quick healing spell to mend the worst of my internal injuries. Setting the bowl on the workbench, I shuffled through some papers before coming up with an old, battered map of the city. It wasn't completely accurate any longer, but it showed a majority of the roads. Name changes didn't matter. I just needed a general vicinity in which to locate Sparks.

"Gage, what's going on?"

"I'm trying to find someone. He wasn't where I expected him to be, and now I've got to do a little digging. Has anyone come into the parlor yet? Had any problems since I left?"

"No, everything is fine, but you're changing the subject."

"I think it's better that I do."

"I don't think so. Gage, look around this place." I looked over my shoulder at Trixie as her voice gained in volume and found her motioning at the cabinets and the symbols painted on the far wall. A series of different types and styles of crystals hung on leather straps before me. "This room isn't about mixing potions and drawing tattoos for our clients. You don't use this room when someone walks in the door upstairs. What is this about?"

"Walk away now, Trix," I warned in a low voice.

"I can't! What are you doing down here?"

Slamming my fists against the wooden workbench hard enough so that jars clanked and rattled, I twisted around to glare at her. "What do you think this is about, Trixie?"

"You're not a potion stirrer."

"Of course I am. I'm a damn good one. Hell, I'm one of the best and you know it, but that's not the word that you're looking for, is it?"

"No! Potion stirrers don't use symbols like that!" she argued, pointing at the pentagram painted on the wall. "They don't use crystals or suddenly appear from out of nowhere looking like shit."

Shoving away from the workbench, I stalked over to where she was standing, in the middle of the room with her arms wrapped around her waist as if to protect herself. I stood so close that our noses nearly touched, my narrowed eyes meeting hers. " 'Warlock,' " I said in a low whisper. "I think that's the word you're struggling with."

"What?" she gasped.

I leaned in so that my lips brushed hers. "Warlock. I was trained to be a warlock."

"I—I don't understand. Warlocks are . . . I mean, I thought that once you started training to be a warlock—"

"You can't escape," I finished. "In general, that's the truth. They grabbed me when I was barely seven years old and I got sucked into the same system that has terrorized hundreds of children over the centuries as they were warped into learning how to use magic and look down on the rest of the world as if they were gods."

Trixie raised both of her hands to cup my face, sympathy filling her wide green eyes so that they nearly spilled over with tears. "But you did escape."

"I was better than they expected." I tried to be cavalier about the mess that had been my childhood. "I was better than they expected and that's what kept me alive. When I was about sixteen, I wanted out. I never bought into their type of mentality. They're not gods, reigning over us. They don't deserve to make life-and-death decisions for the creatures who inhabit this world. They don't deserve anything more than the right to study magic and bask in the beauty that is the power that surrounds us."

"How did you get out?"

"I told my mentor one day that I was walking away."

"I can't imagine that it went over well."

"He's still struggling with the idea." I chuckled harshly as I stepped out of her soft touch, giving us both a little more breathing room. The anger that had initially sprung to life when she'd pushed me to tell her what I was poured from my frame, leaving me feeling tired and a little light headed.

"What do you mean?"

"Simon, my warlock mentor, he's the one who attacked me today. I was forced to fight him when I was a teenager, and in the end he fled, giving me the chance to escape. When I got back to the real world, I hooked up with a man who taught me how to tattoo. I think he sensed my natural gift for magic because he taught me everything he knew around stirring and inking."

"But a warlock . . ." she whispered again. We all knew the warlocks and the witches as one thing—evil, domineering bastards who killed on a whim and destroyed lives simply because they could.

A warlock wasn't supposed to be standing in a dirt-floor basement with an elf, joking about how the world was fucked up.

"I was trained to use magic. I can't help that. It comes naturally to me. After I escaped from Simon, I was hauled up before the council. They decided that they would let me live if I agreed to not use magic in any capacity other than self-defense." Trixie arched one thin eyebrow at me as she let her eyes travel over the room once again. I smiled at her, barely resisting the urge to pull her into my arms. "Let's just say that I've learned to stretch the definition of what 'self-defense' means over the years. I've kept my head down, and the guardians generally leave me alone. I mix potions and tattoo people. That's enough for me."

"Is it?"

"Yes, of course." The answer came without a moment of hesitation, but there was something in Trixie's stare that had me wanting to swallow the words back again.

"I've always wondered, Gage. I've never seen anyone stir a potion like you. You come up with combinations that would never occur to me and that shouldn't happen. And then there's always been something more. Magic is a part of you, isn't it? You can feel it, hear it speaking to you—I don't think those warlocks can honestly feel that."

I smiled at her and let the comment slip by us both. Only the elves and other nature-based creatures could feel magic. They could hear it like a song that emanates from the earth and they used magic that danced along with the same song. Only an elf would understand my unique ability to use and feel magic—something that was incredibly strange and relatively unheard of among humans. Now wasn't the time to dig into that can of worms. It was enough that she knew I had been trained as a warlock and had more than a little magical ability.

That was why TAPSS was on my ass all the time, terrified that I was going to catch the attention of the Ivory Towers. They knew of my background and knew that if the warlocks decided to come down on the potion stirrers, they would use me as an excuse. But I wasn't about to let them take my shop from me. I believed in what I did. Everyone needed an edge these days, and that's what I offered. Hell, I was even giving the grim reaper problems now. The warlocks didn't know what kind of trouble they were in for.

"What I do, the tattoos and the potions, it's enough. I don't want to be a warlock. I don't want to rule the world," I said with a laugh. "I'm content ruling this shop with an iron fist."

"Yeah, you're a real dictator."

Smiling, I leaned forward and pressed a quick kiss to her cheek. "Thanks for understanding."

"Does Bronx know?"

I gave a little snort. "I've found it safer to live with the understanding that Bronx knows everything. I haven't said anything since hiring him, but then there have been a lot of times when I've not needed to tell Bronx things."

"You're probably right." She sighed as one corner of her mouth quirked into a smile. "I guess I should head back up to the shop and keep an eye on things."

"Thanks. I need to track someone down today."

Trixie laid a hand against my cheek, keeping my eyes locked on hers when I would have looked away. Concern was etched across her lovely face. "Does this have to do with the warlocks?"

"No, I got myself in another kind of mess and I need to see my tattooing mentor, if I can find the wily old bastard. That's where I was headed when I encountered Simon. I'm still trying to figure out what bug got up his ass."

"Do you need help with anything?"

"Keep an eye on the shop and forget everything I told you," I said.

"Told me what?" she asked with a coy smile.

"I'm serious, Trixie. It's safer for everyone if no one knows about my past. I don't want the warlocks to ever try to use you as leverage because you know something, anything, about my past. Just forget, please."

"You know I can't."

"Try."

She stared at me, the happiness seeping out of her face. "All right." Turning around, she headed back toward the stairs.

"One last thing, Trixie," I said, stopping her before she could reach the top stair. "Don't ever come down here without me being down here first. I've got too many protective spells in here. I don't want you to get killed. If I'm not here to unravel the spells, there would be nothing I could do to save you."

"I won't, I promise," she murmured and then finished climbing the stairs.

For several seconds I stared at the last spot where I'd seen her, a chill running through me as I thought about Trixie descending into my secret domain without me there to protect her. I didn't know her powers, didn't know her skill with magical spells, but the protective spells in the basement were vicious and ugly in order to protect myself and the rest of the world from what was down here. I didn't want to risk her. I couldn't risk her.

11

GRABBING THE WORN map from the workbench, I paused and looked over my selection of crystals before selecting a clear scrying one hanging on a leather thong. Taking one last sip of Trixie's tea, I took the two items into the middle of the room and collapsed on the dirt floor with a soft "Umph." My body ached, but the worst of the pain was easing, as if a warm wave was washing through me, pulling the pain out into the sea of my subconscious. I was grateful for the tea, despite its repulsive taste, since, not wanting to waste any time, I wouldn't have bothered to do anything about the pain. Now I could work with a clear head.

Crossing my legs, I spread the map out before me, positioning it so that true north matched with the north on the map. With my left hand, I reached down and grabbed a handful of dirt. I clenched it in my fingers, allowing the energy from the earth to caress my hand and filter through my skin to the rest of my body. In truth, it worked just as well as Trixie's tea to ease my pains and it shouldn't have.

Humans didn't have the same close connection to the earth as the elves, pixies, trolls, and other nature-linked creatures who filled this world. And yet I could still feel the energy, use it, and let it heal me. I never got a chance to find out why. When I was a child among the warlocks, I didn't see any other children so I couldn't ask anyone else my own age if what I was sensing was normal. And with the warlocks, you just didn't ask questions. You did as you were told and prayed that you lived to see the next day.

With a frustrated grunt, I pushed aside thoughts of Simon and my past. The combination of my run-in with the old warlock and my talk with Trixie had left me dwelling too much on things that I couldn't change. It didn't do anyone any good to think about the past, and in this case, it certainly wasn't helping me with my little problem of Tera and the grim reaper. Unclenching my fist, I carefully sprinkled the dirt across the map, linking the piece of paper to the earth. More specifically, I was linking the map of the area to this specific part of the city, narrowing my search for my old mentor Sparks.

Picking up the crystal from where I had set it beside my right hip, I cupped it in both hands and brought it to my lips where I released a warm, slow breath across it to awaken the magic captured within the fractals of the small piece of quartz. Gripping it in my left hand, I turned my right arm over and scratched a long line in my arm by using the tip of the crystal. I waited until a bead of blood welled up in one spot where I had broken the skin. Touching the tip of the quartz to the bead, the blood was sucked up into the crystal, yet its perfect clarity never wavered. I had made my offering for the spell and I could now begin my search. My only hope was that Sparks was still in the city. This wouldn't work with the same kind of accuracy using a map of the entire U.S. And it definitely wouldn't do anything if Simon or one of the guardians had taken the time to kill him.

I closed my eyes and rolled my shoulders once to ease some of the tension from my body as I centered my thoughts on my old tattooing mentor. Holding the leather thong with the tips of the fingers of my left hand, the crystal dangled free a few inches above the map. "Atticus Sparks," I murmured. "Find Atticus Sparks. Early sixties with gray hair and gray eyes. Potion stirrer. Smells of marigolds when working potions." The more details I could give the scrying crystal, the greater the likelihood that I would be able to locate him accurately.

When I opened my eyes, my heart sank when I found that the crystal hung completely still despite my descriptions. This was not good. Clenching my teeth and pushing back the building fear and frustration, I closed my eyes again as I pulled up distinct memories of Sparks while I was his apprentice. I remembered the way that he used to shuffle through the parlor in a pair of worn leather moccasins. I recalled that even when he wasn't tattooing, his left hand was kept in the formation of holding a tattooing machine. The scent of the incense he used to burn came back to me. He always had incense or candles burning to overcome the scent of the Chinese restaurant that was next door.

This time, I could feel the leather thong beginning to twist and move in my fingertips. I looked down to find that the crystal had begun swinging around in an ever growing circle so that it now encompassed the entire map. It was searching the entire city for him, sending out magical vibrations with markings that matched the descriptions I had given of him. I concentrated harder, watching the crystal finally start to slow in its revolutions around the map, its circles growing smaller. At the same time, I could feel a slight pressure on my hand, moving it toward the right so that when the crystal stopped it wouldn't be in the dead center of the map once again.

Nearly ten minutes ticked by before the crystal finally settled on the map on the opposite side of town. The color of the stone had changed from a perfect clear crystal to a murky pink. Slowly, I dragged the crystal across the map while leaning as close as possible so that I could make out the different streets—both business and residential. After a while, the color turned sharply from pink to bright blood red. I had found him. Sparks was living on the west side of town on Berkman Street in Over the Rhine.

I stared at the map, my stomach sinking. I complained about the part of town where Asylum was located. At night here, it was good if you kept one eye looking over your shoulder as you walked down the street, and it was even better if you weren't alone, but by day, the place was perfectly safe, if a little run-down.

Over the Rhine was different. There were few safe parts to the area and there was no good time of day. Sure, in the hope of attracting new businesses, the city was trying to clean it up with more cops and an infusion of money to help repair some of the crumbling buildings, but no one wanted to be in OTR, as the locals called it. You ended up in OTR because you either didn't have any money or you were hiding. I was afraid to ask which was the case for Sparks. I didn't have the time to get dragged down by some mess that he'd gotten himself into when I had death breathing down my neck. Normally, I'd jump at the chance to help my old mentor, but right now was not a good time.

Picking up the map, I let the dirt fall off the paper before folding it up again. As I rose to my feet, I shoved the crystal into my pocket and put the map back on the workbench. I knew where I was going. Pausing, I found my gaze snagging on a dusty wooden box with a brass lock. I hadn't touched that box since I had placed it down here after buying the building. My older brother, Robert, had given me the wooden box just before I left home for the second time. When the warlocks had taken me at the age of seven, I had not been permitted to take anything from my former life. When I returned at age sixteen, and then soon left in hopes of protecting my family, I had taken only a few things. Robert had been home from college and he'd given me the wooden box, filled with trinkets from our childhood. The few good memories that we had together.

With my hands flat on the top of the workbench, I stared at the box, my heart pounding in my chest. The original contents of the box had been moved to a cedar chest in my apartment, and I had put something entirely different in the box. I had hidden it from the council when I had been banished, claiming that it had been broken when I fought with Simon. This alone would earn my execution.

I reached into my pocket with my right hand and withdrew my keys. Selecting the smallest one on the ring, I inserted it into the tiny padlock hanging on the front of the box and turned it. The padlock came loose with a little click, falling away from where it had hung. I drew in a deep breath as I opened the long, narrow box and found a smooth stick from a Hawthorn tree nestled against a bed of black velvet. My wand. I hadn't touched it since leaving the Ivory Towers. I had returned to the world of my birth and packed it away in this wooden box so that I could never be accused of breaking our agreement. For defensive magic, I didn't need a wand. But with Simon once again hounding my steps, I was beyond just defensive magic.

I picked up the wand with my right hand, curling my fingers around the stick. An instant connection locked between the wood and my hand, sending a charge of energy through me to the tip of the wand and then back again. The world around me shifted, as if moving into focus. The glass jars filled with potion ingredients seemed brighter, the walls seemed thicker, while the dark brown of the earth beneath my feet seemed richer in color. The world around me was suddenly *more*.

The council would crush me without a moment's hesitation if I was caught holding my wand. It was supposed to have been destroyed. I had shown them a broken stick that I had imbued with just a taste of energy so they would believe it was my former wand. Simon had not been at the hearing to contradict my claim, as he had been recovering from our fight. Unfortunately, the alternative was facing Simon yet again without the wand. I wasn't sure that I would last much longer. He was proving trickier than I remembered.

Bending down, I jerked up my right jeans leg and stuffed the wand into my sock and shoe. It was far from comfortable, but it would be safe from harm and detection. At least, I hoped it would be. I was running out of other options.

I stood before the bench again and replaced the lock before shoving my keys back into my pocket. Everything was back to looking as it had. Grabbing the bowl Trixie had brought down, I paused before the pentagram and recast the protective spells that I maintained for my private domain in the basement. With everything reset as I had always kept it, I turned off the light and climbed the stairs.

As I reached the main floor, I was greeted with the comforting buzz caused by the tattoo machine as Trixie worked on a client. It was a relief that someone had come into the shop, as it gave her something to focus on other than what I was doing in the basement or, even worse, who I was. My mind settled back into this world, while thoughts of my former life drifted back to the deep shadows of my memory. The faint smell of antiseptic wrapped me in a feeling of security.

After closing the trapdoor and putting my bag back over it, I placed the bowl on the counter. I stopped in front of one of the mirrors that lined the walls and grimaced. My clothes were dirty but didn't appear to have any new holes in them. I looked ragged and my hair was sticking up in all directions, giving me a wild and hunted look, which fit my mood. I could use a drink, and a cigarette sounded good, even if I didn't smoke; anything to calm my frazzled nerves. A warlock was hunting me and possessed part of my soul, the guardians were hounding my every step, and now the grim reaper was tapping his watch as he impatiently waited for me to clean up the mess I had made. And then there was Trixie. Lost in my own problems, I had forgotten that I'd found her sleeping in the shop this afternoon because she was now on the run from someone. I couldn't let that go without helping her.

Shoving my hands through my hair, I tried to smooth it down slightly, give it some order. Once I talked to Sparks and got some answers that might help me climb out of this endless pit, I would see if I could pry some information out of Trixie. It might be a little easier now that she knew my big secret. Of course, that could always work against me and she could be gone when I returned to the shop later today. No one wanted to know a warlock, particularly one gone rogue.

After calling for a taxicab on my cell phone, I entered the main tattoo parlor and found Trixie working on a muscular man's bicep in what looked to be a tribal tattoo that would wrap around his upper arm. She looked up and shot me a crooked grin that I knew too well. We were both wondering when guys were finally going to get out of this phase that led them to believe tribals were cool. At first it was an interesting idea, particularly if the designs were well researched and possessed real symbols of protection that matched a person's heritage. However, in 90 percent of the tribal bands we tattooed this was not the case. It was a matter of one guy imitating another because it was cool, and if you didn't have some originality in the art on your body, what was the fucking point?

"How're things here?" I asked as I walked over to the cabinets directly behind her client. I was grateful she had him positioned so that he was facing toward the front of the shop and couldn't see what I was doing.

"No problems," Trixie replied in her usual easygoing tone of voice, as if nothing in the world could ruffle her beautiful feathers. "We've had a few calls, but I've told people that you're not inking today. Looks like you're going to be busy for the next week or so."

"That's cool. Everything should be back in hand tomorrow. I've got a taxi coming now. You got it here?" I bent down to one of the lower cabinets and quietly pulled out one of the handguns.

"Fine here." But this time there was a quaver in her voice. I knew without looking that she had seen the gun. To cut short the conversation, she immediately stepped on the foot pedal, starting up the tattooing machine again as she resumed her work on the client's arm.

"Great," I said as I headed toward the front of the shop. "Bronx will be here in a few hours, but I'm hoping to beat him into the shop so I can get some work done as well."

"Good luck."

If only it was that easy.

12

WALKING DOWN THE three cracked concrete steps to the side-walk, I squinted in the midday sun, gazing up the street and then down as I waited for the taxi to arrive. My heart jerked in my chest when a man in dark robes stepped away from the wall where he was leaning a few buildings down and started walking toward me. Gideon didn't look happy to see me, not that he ever did.

I quickly looked around, but no one else seemed to be reacting to the obvious presence of a warlock on the street. Perhaps I was the only one who could see him. He may have been trying not to cause a panic. Or maybe I wasn't supposed to see him either, but the pos-session of my wand at that moment may have been sharpening my vision, allowing me to see through his cloaking spell. Regardless, neither of us wanted to make a scene for the others to witness.

Backpedaling, I moved into the shadows of the alley that ran along the side of my building and leaned against the wall, waiting for Gideon to reach me. The warlock appeared around the edge of the building and was on me in a flash, his narrow face twisted in an-ger. He wrapped his fists in my T-shirt as he pinned me against the brick wall. I glanced out of the mouth of the alley to see if anyone was watching us. A car that had been passing down the street at that moment halted strangely. I looked around and found a bird hanging in the air as it attempted to fly over the alley, seemingly trapped in midflight. The world had completely stopped and had become blanketed in a suffocating silence. Gideon had stopped time. My breath escaped me in a harsh exhalation and my heart pounded in my chest. I couldn't do that, hadn't even the slightest clue as to how to do such a thing. It was as if we were trapped in a bubble outside of the world.

"It seems as if you can't keep yourself out of trouble this week," Gideon snarled, drawing my attention back to the enraged warlock, leaning close to me. "I had been hoping that my earlier visit might have had some kind of impact on you, but I can see that your arrogance made it impossible for you to heed my warning."

The gun I had shoved in my pants was digging painfully into my back and it felt as if my sock was growing warm where I had stuffed my wand. If I made a grab for either of them, I was toast before I could pull it completely free. "Arrogance, nothing!" I countered, fighting the urge to push him off me. Gideon was pissed at me enough. I didn't need to make it worse. In fact, I needed to find a way to calm him down so that he would at least try to listen to reason. "I was the one who was attacked. I was minding my own business."

Gideon arched his eyebrows, mocking me. "Why do I find that hard to believe?"

"I didn't start this!"

"And since you didn't start it, you felt that it was okay for you to use some very aggressive spells, spells that don't fall under the category of self-defense, which is the only thing you are currently permitted."

"Damn it, Gideon! Simon Thorn attacked me! He attacked in broad daylight without any kind of provocation!"

Gideon released me suddenly, looking genuinely surprised. Apparently, whatever he was using to keep an eye on me permitted him to see what kind of spells I was casting, but not who I was casting them on. I was a little worried that he knew all the spells I had been casting. I might be able to argue my way out of some of them, but not the one that permitted me to rip off a part of Simon's soul.

"Why was Master Thorn after you?" Gideon demanded in a deceptively soft voice.

Leaning my butt against the wall behind me, I bent over and dropped my face into my hands. I didn't have time for this crap. The aches in my body seemed to throb to life again and I felt tired down to my bones. "I don't know," I said in a rough voice. "I was honestly hoping that he had forgotten about me, but apparently not."

"Don't tell me you actually thought that?" Gideon scoffed. "You're a blot, a blemish. You should never have been allowed to live and your very existence is an embarrassment for Master Thorn. Of course he wants you dead."

"Well, that's not what we agreed to!" Jerking upright again, I pushed off the wall with one foot and walked over to the guardian until I was in his face. "The council agreed to a live-and-let-live attitude so long as I didn't use magic for anything other than self-defense. Simon's the one breaking the agreement by coming after me. Hell, he's not even supposed to know where I am. If anyone needs to be brought before the council, it's Simon."

"You know quite well that's not going to happen," Gideon replied in a low, warning tone. I got the message and backed a step away from him. There was no need to antagonize the warlock. At that moment, I desperately needed him on my side. If not, he was going to take me before the council. While Gideon had always been a harsh warden, he had also been fair. He could be reasoned with.

"Why now?" I paced down the alley, walking away from Gideon and the main street that ran by the front of the shop. I clenched and unclenched my fists at my sides in impotent frustration. "I haven't done anything to capture Simon's attention. I haven't stepped out of line. If Simon hadn't attacked me, you wouldn't be here now."

"Really?"

I swung around to look at him, a frown pulling at the corner of my mouth as my stomach twisted into a new knot. I didn't like that look on his face.

"As I recall," he continued with a slow drawl, "part of your agreement with the council was also anonymity. I believe you were forbidden to tell anyone of your past with the Ivory Towers."

Trixie.

"Hell! I appeared from out of nowhere looking like I'd had the shit kicked out of me. And then she goes down into the basement and sees—"

"Your collection," the warlock smugly provided. I had never had any doubt that he was aware of my basement hideaway. I just prayed that he wasn't entirely aware of its unique contents. There were things down there that shouldn't be in anyone's hands, and the council would definitely prefer that they weren't in my hands in particular.

"Yes," I said with a slight hiss. "I had to tell her something and I was tired of lying to her."

"Lying would have kept her safe."

I stalked angrily back toward the guardian, instantly throwing to the winds my earlier decision to try to win Gideon over with logic. "Are you threatening her?"

Gideon stopped me easily with an absent wave of his hand. An invisible force hit me in the chest, slamming me against the wall. I tried to push off, but I was pinned. "I wasn't threatening anyone, boy," he said a tad wearily. "I'm only stating the obvious. Anyone who knows about you is a potential liability. You risked her life when you told her about your past, and you know it. Your conscience should have overlooked the so-called discomfort of a lie in favor of sparing her life."

I stopped struggling and leaned back against the wall, letting his words soak in past the anger and fear. There were a few rare moments when I dealt with Gideon that I felt as if I was back in the Ivory Towers. But with him, it was never about learning how to use magic, it was learning how to manage life. While Gideon was persistently on my ass about using magic, he was at least careful to see that I didn't kill any innocent bystanders as I attempted to commit suicide by thumbing my nose at the council.

"She deserved to hear the truth," I said with a sigh.

"She needed to have her memory wiped."

"I respect her more than that!" I shouted, losing my grip on my temper. "You're not a god! You don't have the right to manipulate their lives with impunity."

Gideon surged toward me, pressing his forehead against mine so that I couldn't escape him. "You can try to wrap yourself in all these pretty ideas that you have, but they aren't going to protect you from reality. If you care about this woman, then you need to start taking some responsibility. Take a good look around yourself, Gage! You're not protecting her by telling her about our world."

The guardian jerked away from me, one hand propped on his hip while the other rubbed his forehead as if he had a headache. His eyes were clenched shut and I could see a muscle ticking in his jaw. I had succeeded, as usual, at pushing Gideon's buttons. But I didn't understand it. He seemed more peeved that I had told Trixie about my past than about my very public fight with Simon. The man made no sense, but then I also didn't know what was going on in the Ivory Towers. He could have received different orders from the council, or he could be getting some other kind of pressure regarding me. Politics were a bitch.

I forced myself to suck in a calming breath. I had Simon chomping at the bit to rip off my head, I didn't need Gideon hunting for me as well.

"Look, I'm sorry about Trixie. I was raised to believe that honesty is the best policy. I'm seeing now that it doesn't apply to . . . *our* world," I began, using his choice of words. I didn't see myself as part of the magic-wielding world any longer, but I guess I was if I was going to be policed by the guardians and carry a wand in my sock. Even if I never cast another spell for the rest of my life, I would still have to answer to the Ivory Towers, making me a part of that world despite my best attempts to escape. "Can you just tell me why Simon has a renewed interest in seeing me dead after so many years of ignoring my existence?"

Gideon dropped his raised hand back to his side and turned slightly to look at me. Some of the tension had eased from his jaw and he watched me speculatively, as if he were weighing my words against my sudden change in temperament. "I think you're the one who can best answer that question. Have you done anything recently that might catch his attention?"

I bit back my angry denial and waited until I knew I could speak calmly. Yelling at each other was getting us nowhere. And in truth, if Simon had somehow found out about my mess with Tera, then he would have a very good reason to be after my head. I just didn't think that he knew about Tera's newfound immortality. If he did, Simon would want the angel feather before he killed me. Right now, the bastard seemed focused purely on my gruesome and painful death.

"I've been a good little boy," I said sarcastically because I simply couldn't help myself. "I haven't done anything that would have caught his attention. I mix potions, tattoo, and sleep. Life is pretty dull. Nothing to interest an all-powerful warlock like Simon or even you."

A wicked smile slashed across his face. Gideon seemed to take great pleasure in stepping closer to me. "Then I guess I can't help you."

I snorted, trying once again to push away from the wall, but the warlock's spell continued to hold me in place. "Help me?" I laughed when I finally stopped struggling. "Since when have you done anything to help me?"

The grim smile disappeared from Gideon's face in a flash and I was left with a cold weight in the pit of my stomach as I stared, unblinking, at his dark expression. "You're alive, aren't you?"

And I had the sickening feeling that he alone was responsible for the fact that I still breathed. I didn't know why when he obviously hated me, but I had a dark suspicion that Gideon had more scruples and honor than most of the warlocks and witches I had met combined. For that, I was grateful, and I didn't want to be.

Gideon stepped back from me, brushing his hands together as if trying to wipe away all evidence of this distasteful conversation. "While I'm sure I'm wasting my breath, I'll tell you anyway in hopes that something will sink into that thick head of yours. If you want to live longer, keep your head down, out of trouble, and away from Master Thorn."

"I didn't do anything in the first place to attract his attention."

The guardian raised one eyebrow at me in disbelief, but he had to know better. In all the years he had known me, I had never gone out of my way to attract the attention of anyone in the magic world. I didn't want the attention. The few puny little spells that I bothered to weave were generally beneath his notice. What in the world could I have done that would attract Simon's sudden attention? Other than the Tera mishap, which I still adamantly believed he didn't know about.

"Can't you at least look into Simon? See what kind of bug suddenly crawled up his ass?" I asked. Gideon pinned me with a mirthful look and I dropped my head back against the wall, rolling my eyes skyward. "That's right. Silly me. I'm on my own in dealing with Simon unless it means using magic and then you're up *my* ass."

"I think that's a correct assessment of things," Gideon said, sounding as if he was trying to stifle a laugh. *Bastard.*

"Thanks for the help," I muttered as he started to walk toward the mouth of the alley and back onto the street.

Gideon paused, turning partially back toward me. "You want my help, then heed my advice and put that damn wand back where you had it hidden. Wave it once and I won't give you a chance to worry about Simon Thorn."

My heart felt as if it had stopped in my chest, only starting again when he rounded the corner of the building. The spell he had created to pin me to the wall disappeared and I collapsed to the ground, landing hard on my ass. I barely noticed, my eyes locked on the last place I had seen him. I was vaguely aware of the cars resuming their way down the street, the chirp of the birds, and the hot breeze that swept down the alley, carrying with it the rancid scent of rotting garbage.

Fuck. He knew.

The warlock had known that I was carrying my wand. Hell, he could have hauled me up before the council for just possessing it. I didn't have to wave it about to get my life revoked. And for some reason that I doubted I would ever understand, Gideon had just walked away from the perfect opportunity to get me permanently out of his hair. I would never understand that man, and I honestly didn't want to.

Leaning my head back against the wall, I closed my eyes and tried to will my heartbeat to slow to a normal pace. Simon Thorn wanted me dead. The grim reaper wanted me to clean up my mess or I was dead. But the one man assigned to kill me if I stepped out of line had walked away from the perfect opportunity to make me dead. I didn't know if he was hoping that Simon would take care of the job or if Gideon had other plans for me.

I reached down and patted the wand shoved in my sock, making sure that it was still secure. I was sorely tempted to grab the second chance that Gideon was giving me and put the wand back in the box in the basement. But I couldn't. Without it, I was dead if Simon attacked again. Of course, there was a chance I was dead if I continued to carry it. I was damned no matter what I did, so I might as well fight for my life.

13

THE TAXI LET me out at the end of Berkman Street in Over the Rhine, barely pausing long enough to allow me to pay the fare and give him a generous enough tip to make it worth his while for coming into this part of town. As the yellow car sped away, heading back into the secure bosom of downtown, I reached into my pocket and pulled out the leather thong with the scrying stone that held a drop of my blood. It was still bright red, and had begun once again to swing, as if a breeze had pushed it despite the relative quiet of the air.

I was more concerned with the dozen or so people watching my every move. Out of the corner of my eye, I could pick out groups gathered on street corners and on small concrete stoops that served as front porches for dilapidated houses. They whispered at the sight of me and wondered about the crystal I was holding out. Others didn't bother to speculate in so low a tone of voice. I had no doubt that some of the inhabitants of this part of town thought I was insane, convinced that this little bit of stone could protect me against any attack that might come my way, while others were smarter and warier. Only someone well-acquainted with magic would be brave enough to pop into this part of town waving around a bit of useless crystal. I might not look like a warlock, but then, as everyone knew, appearances were deceiving.

Keeping my gaze glued on the stone as I slowly walked down the street, I reminded myself that I had a handgun shoved down the waistband of my jeans and more than a few tricks up my sleeve. I already had Simon pissed at me, and Gideon wasn't in a much better mood, so what did it matter if I started throwing around some magic in hopes of preserving my life a little while longer? It also helped that the sun was still high in the sky. The vampires were still abed and the trolls were lurking in dark homes, waiting for the sun to finally set. While goblins could come and go during the day, they preferred to wait until at least dusk before showing their ugly mugs out of doors. There were a few other faerie folk that could be a nuisance, but I wasn't likely to find them here unless they were really down on their luck. OTR was way too far from anything that resembled forestland or even a small park, which would help to rejuvenate their meager powers.

In the end, it turned out to be a creature just as much of a pain in human form as it was under the caress of moonlight that finally stopped my progress down the street. I was passing by a sagging chain-link fence when a hand shot out to grab the crystal from where it dangled in front of me. Instinct took over. I jerked it away at the last second and took a quick sliding step back. At the same time, my free hand went to the gun at my back, but I didn't pull it free. I stopped in time to take in my surroundings, but the damage was done, as everyone gathered knew what I'd been reaching for.

Leaning on the fence was a large, bare-chested man with long brown hair and deep-set brown eyes. His thin lips curled into a smile, revealing a set of white teeth that possessed a pair of long canines, leaving me wishing I had paid more attention to the BEWARE OF DOG sign. The rest of his pack rolled off the nearby porch and fluidly moved across the small trash-strewn yard like a set of wolves loping across a verdant field toward an unknowing buck.

Werewolves. Of course, I'd run afoul of werewolves because I wasn't paying attention. I could have given them a wider berth as I trekked down the street toward Sparks's place, but no, I had to be completely lost in what I was doing. *Idiot.*

I eased my hand away from the gun at my back and allowed it to hang limply at my side while I tightened my grip on the crystal. I had lowered it so that it was hanging near my waist, glittering in the afternoon sunlight.

"Afternoon," I said, meeting the werewolf's narrowed gaze. "Is there some way I can help you?"

"Just wondering what you're doing in our part of town," he said in what seemed to be a friendly tone, but I wasn't convinced, as his companions joined him at the fence. One even went so far as to open the gate and stand there. "I can't say that I can recall your face."

"I'm not from this part of town. I'm Gage, owner of the tattoo parlor called the Asylum, on the other side of town. Maybe I've done some work for one of your friends?"

This gave the leader pause, as he actually looked around at his companions for confirmation of whether any of them had gotten ink in my shop before. Unfortunately, every last one of them shook their head no before the leader turned his attention back to me.

"Hmm. That's a shame." I slowly reached into my back pocket with my empty hand, sending them all back a step in surprise and wariness before I withdrew a business card. Experience had taught me that it was always good to have some cards on hand because you never knew when you would meet someone who needed a little help. "Stop in sometime. Let me handle some ink for you. I'm one of the best in the city, ask anyone. If I'm not there, my coworkers are just as talented." I handed the leader the card. He didn't bother to even look at it, but immediately ripped it into two pieces and dropped it on the ground. I just gave him a little, indifferent shrug. "Trixie will be disappointed."

"Trixie? Trixie Ravenwood? Dark hair and eyes? Tits?" demanded one of the other pack members as he held his hands out in front of his chest to simulate Trixie's ample endowments and appearance under the influence of the glamour.

"Yes, that would be her." It was a struggle to keep my voice light and indifferent when I wanted nothing more than to plow my fist into the man's face.

"Damn, she's fine!" he whistled, nudging one of his companions. "I've seen her and her work. She's good." He would have continued his praise, but one dark look from the alpha quickly shut his mouth.

"So, Gage," the alpha resumed, seeming to chew on my name before spitting it out. "What are you doing in this part of town? Scouting for new customers?"

"Actually, I'm looking for someone in particular. Maybe you've seen him around. He would be an old man, in his sixties, with gray hair and pale skin, going by the name of Sparks. He could be working as a tattoo artist."

"That's interesting," the alpha said with a nod, mocking me. "Unfortunately, information doesn't just rain from the sky in this part of town. You've got to pay for it."

"You've seen him?"

"Maybe."

"What do you want?"

"Oh, I think you know," he murmured.

My hand tightened on the leather thong that was attached to the quartz and I clenched my teeth. "It's useless to you, just a bit of stone. You can't even sell it for anything."

"It must be worth something if you're unwilling to let it go."

I had two reasons for being unwilling to release it. First, it was my only chance at reliably locating Sparks. And second, it held my blood. In the world of spells, potions, and warlocks, a person's blood was just a step down from having a piece of their soul. It was bad enough that Simon had ripped out a hunk of my soul already today, did I really need to give up a drop of my blood as well? I liked to think not.

"The crystal is not for sale. If you can't help me, then I'll be on my way. No harm, no foul," I said, my voice growing more clipped. I knew that I was letting my temper get the better of me, but it had been a rough day and I wasn't in the mood to be pushed and bullied by a pack of canine assholes.

"It's a little late for that. You've already trespassed into our domain and now you have to pay."

I smiled broadly at him as I shoved the crystal into my pocket. "No."

As I expected, he tightened his grip on the fence and launched his body over it with a ripple of muscle and more ease than I could have shown. I didn't move from where I was standing. Instead, I raised my right hand and palmed his face, stopping him dead in the air. Gazing deep into his brown eyes, I smiled as I quickly whispered a set of magic words. I swallowed a laugh at his look of shock and pain before I pushed him backward. When he landed in the yard, he had turned from a six-foot, muscular bully with a cocky attitude to a two-pound white Chihuahua.

The rest of the pack went into a frenzy of panic. Half of them immediately backed away from me, pulling toward the porch, while the other half must have stopped thinking because they moved toward me. The pack member in the lead immediately stopped as I pressed the muzzle of my gun to his forehead before he could react. I cocked the gun, capturing his full attention while the rest of the pack members came to a complete halt.

"I don't think you want to do that," I said calmly.

"What the fuck, man!"

"He's fine."

"Jack's not fucking fine!" he said with an almost desperate whine.

"Jack? That the name of your alpha? Jack?"

"Jack, yeah. You turned him into a fucking Chihuahua!"

"Yes I did, but if you'll recall, you really didn't leave me much choice. I could have killed him, but I didn't. I could still kill you, but I'm not going to because Jack will need a keeper for a few days." It was all I could do to keep from laughing. This was the most fun I'd had all this long day.

"But he's a fucking Chihuahua, man!" the werewolf continued to complain.

I shoved him a couple of steps from me with the gun and then put the weapon back in the waistband of my pants now that everyone's attention seemed to be on the shivering, yapping Jack just inside the fence.

"Jack is a dog, right?"

"Yeah, but—"

"And dogs are relatives to wolves, correct?" I slowly pointed out.

"Sure."

"So at the next full moon he'll be able to shape-shift back into human form as well as his natural wolf form."

"But that's two fucking weeks away."

"So in the meantime, I suggest keeping a close eye on him. Get him something to eat, and I'd keep the gate closed at all times. I'd hate for him to get hit by a car."

"Are you serious?"

"As a heart attack," I murmured as I bent down and picked up the two pieces of the business card that Jack had dropped on the ground. I handed it over to the pack member I had been talking to, who only stared at it in shock. "Stop by the shop when he's back to normal. We can get you guys covered with some decent ink for a change."

The werewolf looked at me in confusion, unable to understand my willingness to accept them as clients after they'd attempted to attack and I'd successfully changed their alpha into a shaking, whining ankle biter. "Really?"

"Yep," I said, and then stepped around the pack members standing stunned on the sidewalk and continued up the street. The run-in was to be expected and no one had gotten hurt, honestly. In truth, we'd all probably gotten a good laugh out of it (except maybe Jack, but then, he'd started the mess). When all was said and done, business was business. Werewolves were great clients. They healed fast; had a high tolerance for pain; and had nice, clear skin for tattooing. Furthermore, since they tended to be parts of clans and packs, there was a lot of tagging involved, which could get complicated and expensive—all good for the tattoo artist.

As I continued down the street, I didn't bother to pull my crystal from the pocket I had stuffed it into during the scuffle. A couple of houses down from where I had encountered the werewolves, I saw an old man standing on a stone porch stoop, wearing leather moccasins and with his arms folded over his chest. Sparks was waiting for me. He mouthed the word "Chihuahua" and shook his head with a grim smile. I shrugged my shoulders at him. He knew my secrets. He knew all my secrets because back then he was the only friend I had in the world.

The long years had changed things. I had opened my own shop, made lots of new friends, and kept my secrets tightly under wraps, with the exception of today. But then, I had always expected that one day I would end up on his doorstep and that it wouldn't be a pleasant visit. I had a feeling that he'd been expecting me as well. Atticus Sparks was not only a talented tattoo artist, but he was also a very wise man. He was the one who had advised me to maintain a distance from my family and to avoid getting involved with other people. It was always best if I didn't give the inhabitants of the Ivory Towers anything they could use to get at me. Letting me continue to walk the earth with their secrets was enough of a problem for them.

14

THE HOUSE MADE me hesitate. It was a ramshackle, shotgun style with its windows carefully covered to blot out all light as well as keep any nosy neighbors from peering inside. Claustrophobia set in as I stepped over the threshold into the living room. A sagging floral couch was against the far wall, while a small television with a wire clothes hanger sticking out of the top was against the opposite wall. The rest of the room was filled with stacks of old newspapers, boxes of stuff that had never been unpacked from his previous residence, and containers from old TV dinners. A blanket and a pillow were shoved to the far end of the couch, leading me to believe that he actually used it as a bed too.

Sparks had never been vastly successful with his tattooing business, but he'd made good money. The shop he'd owned had been big and he had maintained a nice-size apartment on the second floor. I couldn't understand how he had come to the point in his life where he was obviously scraping by. Even if he couldn't handle a tattoo machine any longer, that didn't mean his brain didn't hold a wealth of information that could be handed down to an apprentice for a nice price. Or at the very least, a price that would allow him to live in something better than squalor.

"So do you want me to start or do you want to go first?" Sparks inquired with a smug look on his face as he sat down on the couch. I stood in the middle of the room. There wasn't enough room on the couch and I didn't feel comfortable leaning against anything.

"Go for it," I said. I was sure that he had some scathing remark, but I could take it. At the moment, I had no tactful way of tackling what I was looking at or the man I had looked up to for so many years.

"Magic? In public?" Sparks began, raising one eyebrow at me. "That wasn't self-defense, Gage. I've seen self-defense, and that wasn't it. That was you having fun, and you're not supposed to have fun without risking the attention of the Tower twerps. You could have been killed in an instant for being so stupid, unless something has changed and you've moved back to the Towers."

"No, I'm still living down here among the dregs."

"Then what?"

I paused, trying to sum up the mess that had become my life during the past few days, but I couldn't come up with much that seemed helpful. So I decided to keep it simple. "Simon came looking for me today."

"Your old mentor?"

"I stopped by your shop looking for you and found him instead. He had one goal: to kill me. There was no discussion, no great reason or no law that I had broken this time. I'm beginning to think that my existence has gotten in his way up there in the Towers and he needs me gone fast."

"So what?" Sparks snapped. "Now you're playing fast and loose with the magic because you've got a bull's-eye on your forehead? Doesn't sound too smart to me. Sounds like you should be keeping your head down instead of sticking your neck out." His words sounded sickeningly close to what Gideon had told me just a short time ago. The sad part was that I wasn't sure I was going to listen to Sparks any more than I was going to listen to Gideon.

"They can find me anytime they want. I'm not changing my life or running because the warlocks have gotten their panties in a bunch."

"They're going to hurt those around you."

"They're going to try, but it's not going to happen while I'm around. I've lost enough because of the mistakes I made when I was a kid. I haven't seen my family in years. And the last time I did see them, everyone was terrified until I left. Why should I walk away from the rest of my life?"

"Because they are the warlocks."

"That shouldn't be an excuse."

"It is."

"Not for me. Not anymore. Not if they've decided that they're gunning for me for no reason at all."

Sparks heaved a heavy sigh as he shifted his weight on the sofa so that he was now leaning all the way back. "I wish it didn't have to be this way, boy."

"They chose this route. Not me."

Sparks snorted, relaxing. "Stubborn ass. I think this was a mutual decision. On a side note, the Chihuahua was a nice touch. I wasn't quite sure what you were going to do, but it was a nice surprise. I hadn't had a good laugh like that in a while. It'll take the wind out of the bastard's sails for a time."

I shrugged, a small smile slipping across my lips again. "Probably. I shouldn't have, but it's been a long day. I lost my temper."

"We all have bad days. You're just more dangerous than others when you let loose."

"I'm not that dangerous."

"Magic, a gun in your back pocket, and the last I heard you were studying a few styles of martial arts. Yeah, you're a real pussycat."

"Thanks. And what about you?"

"Oh, it's my turn now?" he asked innocently, snapping the brief good mood that I had managed to capture.

"What the fuck?" I demanded, motioning with both my hands to encompass the decrepit surroundings.

"That's it?"

"Seriously, Sparks! I went to the old shop and it looks like you haven't been there in years. What happened?"

"Business dried up."

"That's it? Business dried up? You weren't in a bad spot. If it was about business, you could always have come to me. I could have fit you into the rotation for a few days a week. You're a talented tattoo-ist and—"

"You smug son of a bitch!" Sparks snarled, pushing off the couch and closing the distance between us faster than I would have thought possible considering his advanced age. "You think I would ever come begging to *my apprentice* for a job? I'm the one who taught you everything you know. There's nothing on this earth that would make me come crawling—"

"Who said anything about crawling? I would have been honored to have you at the shop. You would have been a great asset. Like you said, you taught me everything I know about inking and stir-ring. You could have helped out the two people I did end up hiring. They're great, but they were a little rough around the edges starting out. It would have helped me immensely to have you."

"Would have? So, just like that you close the door on me? You would have taken me in years ago but not now?" he countered un-expectedly, leaving me flat-footed by the question.

"Now? I don't know, Sparks. When was the last time you held a tattoo machine?"

"It's like riding a bike."

"Yeah, but the skills get rusty from lack of use. Besides, you know the kind of trouble I'm in. That mess is going to rain down on my shop no matter how hard I try to protect my people. I'd rather you not be a part of that. The people I've got now . . . they have ways of protecting themselves."

I was babbling as my brain scrambled to decide whether I really wanted Atticus Sparks in my shop. Initially, my brain and heart had reacted to the rotting mess that was his life. He was a talented tattooist, but he was also a stubborn, crotchety old man who wouldn't listen to a thing I said because I'd been his apprentice. In many ways, having him in the shop would be hell on earth for me. But as I looked around at what I could see of his house, could I honestly turn my back on him?

"Easy, boy," Sparks said with a slight cough as he patted me on the shoulder. "I don't want a job in your shop. I appreciate it that you would think of me like that and that you're worried about your old mentor. That's enough."

"Yeah, but what happened?"

"Just got old," he muttered with a slight shrug of his slumped, rounded shoulders. "I couldn't keep up with the in-crowd. I wasn't getting any more apprentices to keep the shop interesting, so business died. I came here, and I've found ways to get by. I don't want you to worry about me. I'm managing just fine, regardless of what it looks like. Why don't you tell me why you really came looking for me?"

"I got myself into a mess and I need your help," I started as Sparks wandered back over to the couch.

He laughed as he sank into the flat cushions. "I can't do shit to help you with the Towers and you know it."

"Oh no, I've dug a hole deeper than just trouble with the warlocks right now. Hell, believe it or not, they're the least of my concerns. I've got the grim reaper breathing down my neck, trying to get hold of my soul if I don't get him what he wants."

"The grim reaper?" he repeated slowly, as if I had lost my mind.

"Don't fuck with me, Sparks! He's real. Or rather *they* are real. There's this whole union of them and the one I met is nice enough so long as I don't screw up his schedule, but I have."

"How could you screw up his schedule?"

I paused and took a deep breath. Raising both my hands over my head, I murmured a soft spell so that a shell fell over the small house, making it impossible for anyone to overhear our conversation either through natural means or through magic. I couldn't risk the warlocks finding out about this giant mistake. It was bad enough that they wanted me dead. I couldn't risk them wanting to take me alive. I dropped my hands back down to my sides and sighed once the spell was in place.

"I made a girl immortal," I said in a soft voice, hating to utter the words.

"What?" Sparks demanded, leaning forward as if he hadn't heard me correctly.

"Immortal. She can't die and the grim reaper wants her soul in three days or he's going to take mine in its place. I need some help."

"How the hell did you make her immortal? I didn't think such a thing was even possible. I mean, those fucking warlocks can't even claim to be immortal."

"A tattoo. She came in telling me she was dying and wanted angel wings tattooed on her back. I agreed. When I was preparing the ink, I put in pollen from an Easter Lily and a frond from the angel feather that you gave me years ago."

"Angel feather?"

"Yes, you gave me a sizable stockpile of contraband when I started my shop, remember?"

"Yeah, yeah."

"Well, it included an angel's feather. You even went so far as to speculate that the feather had belonged to Gabriel. I kept it under tight lock and key for years, never intending to use it, but this seemed like a good cause. I didn't know what it would do, but I thought it might wipe away her cancer. I never, ever thought for a second that it would make her immortal. Hell, if the thought had crossed my mind, I would never have allowed you to give me the damned feather."

"You used the angel feather," he breathed. He dropped his head into both of his hands as he placed both of his elbows on his knees. "I never thought you'd use it. I never thought you would come up with a good excuse to use it. I just wanted it to be in safe hands and I couldn't think of anyone safer than someone with a warlock's background."

"I screwed up."

"In a way. You saved a girl's life."

"I killed myself in the process and ruined hers over the long term. No matter how pretty it sounds, no one wants to be immortal. I have to undo what I've done."

Shaking his head, Sparks pushed to his feet and waved for me to follow him. "You know there's only one way out of this mess. You have to tattoo her again."

We passed through a kitchen that was a disaster area of dirty dishes, rotting food, and an overflowing trash can to a back room that had a large chair in the center; cabinets holding potion ingredients lined the walls.

"You're still tattooing," I murmured, my eyes taking in the room.

Sparks shrugged indifferently at me. "In a way."

"In a way? This is illegal, Sparks. If you get caught—"

"What? They gonna take my license away?"

"No, they're going to put you in jail. The bloodsuckers are going to come for you and they are going to put you away. You wouldn't survive, Sparks."

"You take your chances, Gage, and I'll take mine."

"Fine. You're right. This is none of my concern. Let's get back to the business at hand, making someone mortal again."

"What makes you think I would know how to do that?" Sparks demanded, throwing open the cabinets, one glass door after another, so we could look at the contents without any hindrances. "I didn't know you could make someone immortal, so how would I know how to kill them?"

"Killing someone is easy," I replied in a cold voice. I didn't know firsthand, as I had never killed anyone, but I had watched Simon succeed at the task often enough without even a flicker of guilt or remorse. "The hard part apparently is handing the soul over to the grim reaper after it's been protected."

Sparks heaved a sigh as he crossed his arms over his stomach and stared at the array of jars, wooden boxes, and yellowed envelopes filled with items. "Was there anything in the design that I should know about?"

"Nothing. Just wings."

"Easter lily pollen and . . . your unique item?"

"Yes."

"How old was the pollen?"

"Few months."

"Local?"

"The basilica downtown."

"Good choice," Atticus murmured softly, but I knew his mind was turning over the items that were before him. "The pollen was a nice touch, but it's unlikely that it did much except maybe bind the ink to the—"

"Yeah," I filled in. Neither of us wanted to mention aloud what I had used. "How about really potent venom? Even the Towers haven't come up with an antidote for basilisk venom. Kills every living thing it's injected into."

"That's rare stuff since basilisks are supposedly extinct."

"Not that rare," I muttered.

Sparks shoved a hand through his hair and shook his head. "Oh, yeah. Right." He finally remembered that he had given me a vial of it when I moved out on my own. "Regardless, it's not strong enough against immortality."

"How about red dragon blood? Or maybe a bit of horn from a black unicorn?"

"Come on! Why don't you just drop some strychnine in her

morning coffee and call it a day!" Sparks snapped as he turned back toward me. He reached up and clasped my face between both of his clammy palms. "This stuff will kill a mortal anything, but not an immortal."

I jerked away, pacing a little around the small room as my mind swirled in useless circles. "I don't know! If a heavenly agent can give a human soul immortality, what's the opposite? What can take it away?"

"A little piece of Hell, I guess," Sparks replied.

"Yeah, well, as far as I know no one has ever brought a piece of that back with them from the dead. Not even if they had to do time."

"What do you mean?"

Shaking my head, I reached into my pocket to pull out my cell phone and check the time. I didn't want to go into it and wasn't allowed to anyway. It was one of the few secrets I had learned from the Ivory Towers that I was willing to keep. There was one way to touch the afterlife and come back from it. It was easy to do, but impossible to control. All you had to do was kill someone with magic. Kill someone with magic and you were forced to give up one year of your life. Your body died and your soul traveled to the underworld, where it stayed for that year. Unfortunately, you never knew when you were going to die and those who came back were no longer in their right mind after the experience.

Other races knew about this little catch in the use of magic, but not many liked to talk about it. Among humans, it was largely seen as a myth. Warlocks and witches had found messy ways around it. Throw a body in front of a speeding car and the person is killed by the impact with the car, not magic. Push a body off a bridge and they drown in the river, not by magic. But pull all the blood out of a body through the pores with a spell and you're fucked.

"It's getting late. I've got to get going," I muttered as I walked toward the front of the house. "One of these days you'll have to tell me how you got your hands on the angel feather in the first place."

"Same way most people do. You know someone," Atticus Sparks said softly, his rumbly voice following me through the living room.

"Or you go get it yourself," I chuckled as I pulled open the door and left Sparks's small depressing house. Walking back down the street, I nodded to the werewolf pack on the porch as I passed while I pulled out my cell phone. I called for another taxi to take me back to my own shop on the other side of town.

Fear knifed through my stomach and sped up my heart so that it coursed through my veins. I had been sure that Sparks would know how I could get out of this mess. Atticus Sparks had always seemed to me to know exactly what items needed to be mixed together in order to accomplish whatever wish a client might have. Now I needed to accomplish the impossible for a second time, and I was beginning to realize that it would take a miracle.

Or a warlock.

15

PAPA ROACH SINGING about betraying the ones you love was the first sound to greet me when I pulled open the front door to my parlor later that afternoon. Rather than taking the taxi to the shop, I had the driver take me to where I'd left my car, near Sparks's old shop, which I then took to Asylum.

The heat of the day had left me feeling sweaty, sticky, and more than a little grimy. Given my fight with Simon, my scuffle in the alley with Gideon, and standing in Sparks's disgusting home, I felt as if I were wearing a coating of the filth of the world. I would rather have taken a shower before I picked up a needle, but I would have to do with sterilizing my arms and face with the soap we had on hand. When I crawled into my own apartment tonight, I would be able to turn on water hot enough to strip away the layers of dirt and lies. For now, I had to get to work.

When I entered the main tattooing room, Trixie was sitting in one of the tattooing chairs while she picked at a salad with a black plastic fork. She grimaced at the salad, looking less than enthusiastically at the wilted lettuce and collection of vegetables.

Leaning against the doorway, I shoved my hands into my pockets and smirked at her. "I always warned you that that vegetarian shit was going to kill you. Hamburger with everything on it is the way to go."

She gave a little jump at my voice. "Go to your grave," she snapped, and then turned grimly serious. "I didn't hear you enter or see you on the monitor. You powerful enough to get around the security system?"

My smirk disappeared at her question. "The music is loud and you're distracted. If you had been looking up, you would have seen me on the video monitor. Nothing has changed, Trixie."

"I know that nothing is supposed to have changed, Gage, but it feels like it has. The warlocks—"

"The warlocks are dangerous, and that's why I always thought it best to keep you and Bronx in the dark about my past. TAPSS knows a little, just enough to be wary of me, but at the same time keep a close eye on the shop. Beyond that, there's nothing that you or Bronx need to worry about. We're still friends, right?"

"Yeah," she said and nodded, dropping the salad on the counter-top with disgust. "One big fucked-up family."

"And that means that Bronx and I would do anything to help you," I said, circling back to her own problems, which had caused her to sleep in the tattoo parlor for part of the early afternoon hours.

"I know. You guys are great, but there's nothing for you to worry about. Everything is fine. I will be staying in the apartment upstairs for only a couple more days, I swear."

"Stay as long as you want. It's not a problem. My concern is what's chased you out of your own apartment. Tell me honestly, Trixie, was it a spider? I've got a troll on staff I can send over to squash it."

Peals of her laughter filled the parlor, signaling that we were do-ing okay. It was what I needed—the normalcy. I needed to know that everything was still solid between Trixie and me despite the fact that I was some freak of nature among the humans. I needed to know that she still felt comfortable enough around me to laugh.

"You're an asshole," she said around the last of her chuckles.

"It's the whole reason you love me," I murmured, leaning down to kiss the top of her head as I walked past to go into the back room.

"So you like to think."

I washed up, removing as much of the dirt and grime as I could. Standing in front of the mirror, I ran my fingers through my hair, sending it standing on end in all directions. It wasn't the normal style I went for, but at least it passed for a style, versus the disaster that it had been before. I looked a little bruised and tired, but it didn't appear as if I was fighting for my life. Sure, there were warlocks who wanted me dead and the grim reaper was counting down the hours until he could collect my soul, but I still had a job to do and time to think of a way out of this mess.

"You been busy?" I asked as I came back out to where Trixie was relaxing in the chair.

She gave an indelicate snort. "Molasses."

"It's not like you wanted it to be busy while you were by yourself."

"Appointments for future ink would have been nice," she complained. "As it was, I did one modest tattoo and two smaller tattoos while you were gone. I've got three more consultations on the books for later in the week. On the other hand, the phone didn't stop ringing for you. Your messages are over there." She absently waved her left hand toward a stack of little pink message notes piled neatly on the counter.

Leaning my hip against the counter, I picked up the messages and nearly choked, but managed to hold back the laughter. There were twelve messages and nine of them were left by females. For each of the females, Trixie had written in her swirling, delicate scrawl either "stripper" or "whore." Apparently, despite the knowledge of my warlock upbringing, my dear Trixie was feeling in a catty mood.

I softly drew in a steadying breath and only spoke when I was sure that I could comment without laughing. "You got most of these right, but I think you underestimated the stripper count."

"You would know, you're their favorite," she said in a supersaccharine voice that did earn a soft chuckle.

"It's nice to know that you think so highly of me," I said, stepping around her to walk toward the front of the parlor.

"Gage . . ."

"No, ink is ink. I'm not the type to judge. If some chick wants a butterfly just above her pussy because it might draw more clients, then what do I care?"

"Gage, I'm sorry. I didn't mean anything."

"I know," I murmured. Settling on a stool behind the glass case, I spread the messages out in front of me while I grabbed my planner from under the counter. It was only when I opened the calendar that I realized it was the eighth of the month. No wonder so many strippers had called me at once. They had a rush of cash from the excess business they enjoyed following the release of government money. They also tended to travel in packs when they got their tattoos done, and apparently a couple of groups were looking for some fresh ink. Once I got some of them scheduled, the rest would come in around the same day and time to get their ink done, assuming they all had an idea of what they wanted.

Since they worked nights, not one of them had been inked by Bronx. They had mixed feelings about Trixie. Some allowed her to handle the intimate tattoos, while others only allowed her to do the simple ones on the lower back or the shoulder. But it all started the same way, each of them requesting me and my list of skills. My potions were also cheaper than cosmetic surgery, though the effects weren't as long lasting. I handled as many as I could. After a while, they could no longer wait and had to get back to work, so they were forced to settle for Trixie's gentle hand.

After about an hour on the phone, I had everyone who'd called me scheduled for tattoos or consultations in the next week or two. I kept my schedule open for the next few days in case I once again needed to jump out of the shop and hunt down an ingredient or pin Tera down for a tattoo.

Tera.

What was I going to do about her? How was I going to tell her I had messed up on a colossal level that I couldn't even begin to explain? If she never discovered my mistake, never discovered I had made her immortal, then I had a shot at getting her tattooed a second time with the excuse of touching up the original. I wouldn't need to go over much of the old tattoo with the new ink to undo the spell. If she was completely ignorant, then I was in the clear. I could undo the damage I had done and she would never have to know. If I was lucky, only I would have to live with the knowledge that I had saved the life of a young girl from the ravages of cancer, ripping her from the cold grasp of death. I would be the only one who knew that I had personally delivered her back into the hands of the grim reaper as he waited impatiently on the sidelines.

"Trix, did you find that information sheet I asked you to dig up for me?" I called from where I was still seated at the glass case in the front room.

"Bottom shelf," she called back as she walked over to pick up a bottle of yellow ink from the cabinet. She was preparing to ink another one of her regulars, who had come in while I was on the phone. "It's right next to the MP3 player. That Tera chick, right?"

"Yeah, that's her," I murmured to myself as I doubled over on the stool to locate the sheet of paper. My hands were shaking and a knot had grown in my throat as I picked up the cordless phone to call her number. I just needed to dial the phone and kick off a simple, innocuous conversation, checking to make sure that she didn't have any trouble with her tattoo. I would then ask her to come back in to let me check it over in a day. With any luck, that would be enough time for me to find out what I needed to undo her immortality and also find the ingredients. It was simple.

There was no answer.

I dialed the number three times and each time I got her voice mail, but I didn't leave a message. My throat completely closed up in panic. She wasn't there. What if I didn't get hold of her in time? What if she had discovered my mistake and was gone for good? Then I was officially fucked and the reaper had my soul.

"You okay, boss?" Trixie inquired when the tattoo machine suddenly fell silent.

"Just peachy," I said through clenched teeth as I continued to stare straight ahead, toward the front door. I hadn't a clue as to what I was going to do. I had her phone number and address, but I was hoping to keep this civil. Drawing a deep breath, I closed my eyes as I slowly released it, suddenly wondering how far I would go to protect my own soul. Kidnapping? Murder? But then, wasn't it murder if I tattooed her a second time, stealing away her immortality so I could hand her over to the grim reaper? I didn't know.

With my nerves as settled as I could get them, I dialed her number for a fourth time and left an innocuous message on her voice mail telling her that I was just checking to make sure the tattoo had turned out okay. I also asked her to stop at the shop tomorrow evening. My fingers were tightly crossed.

As I ended the call and retuned the phone to its charging cradle, I smiled as I saw a large, hulking mass lumber up the stairs to the parlor. I had been so consumed with Trixie, Tera, and my own problems I hadn't even noticed that the sun had set at long last. Bronx had arrived at the shop, brightening my mood. If it was possible, there was an added level of security now hovering in the air with the presence of a large troll, relieving some of the latent tension in my shoulders.

"Bronx," I said with a weary grin as I leaned heavily on the glass case.

"Rough day?" he asked as he started to walk past me.

"Hardly," Trixie answered before I could. "He hasn't done shit all day." I shook my head as I bent over and picked up the MP3 player.

It was hers, but there were still some strange songs on there that she usually didn't play at the shop. I quickly shuffled through the music until I finally landed on the sound track for *Phantom of the Opera* and pushed play.

"Bastard," she snarled at me through narrowed eyes as I pushed away from the seat, leaving everyone stuck listening to the opening to the musical. I wandered into the back room to look through some of the ingredients and run through for the hundredth time what Sparks had told me. There had to be someone who knew what I needed to undo the mess I'd made with Tera's soul. Someone other than a warlock or a witch. Several minutes later, the music fell silent for an extended period of time before it changed over to Led Zeppelin. I always found it amusing when Bronx and Trixie had a moment of camaraderie and joined forces against me.

But our joking and laughter was interrupted when Trixie rushed into the back room minutes later, her face a stark white as she stripped off her ink-smeared latex gloves. "Help me!" she demanded in a harsh whisper as she paced right past me toward the back of the room so that she was hovering near the rear door that led to the alley. "They're here."

No hesitation. No questions. I rushed over to the trapdoor in the floor and kicked my bag off it before I lifted it up as silently as I could. Standing in the opening, I whispered a couple of words and waved my hand in the air, hoping that I'd wiped away most of the defensive measures wrapped around the basement.

"Go down the stairs and sit on them. Do not touch the floor. I will come get you when the coast is clear," I directed, moving aside enough for her to descend the wooden staircase. I would be leaving her alone in the darkness in a somewhat dangerous place, but it was better than leaving her out in the open up here. "And don't use any magic," I called softly after her as I closed the door.

Dusting off my hands, I briskly walked back out into the main tattooing room to find Bronx looking at me with one raised eyebrow, his mouth closed in a tight, firm line. "Could you see to that client, please? I can see that the outline is already finished."

"Hey, what about Trixie?" the man demanded at the same time the bell to the front door sounded, indicating that someone had entered. I spun around in a flash and grabbed the arms of the chair as I leaned in so close that my nose was an inch from his. I stared deep into his eyes, burrowing into his thoughts. "There is no Trixie," I commanded in a low, hard voice.

The man made no other sound as I turned back around and started toward the front of the shop followed by the sound of latex gloves being snapped on by Bronx. My only comfort was in the way he was sitting; he had a perfect view of the security monitor, allowing him to keep an eye on the progress of the conversation I was about to enter into. Considering that Trixie dove for cover before this person or persons even entered the shop didn't bode well.

Before slipping into the lobby, I waved my hand and several candles in jars popped into existence on the countertops, their wicks lit. I was hoping their perfume would mask Trixie's unique scent, still hovering in the air, but I wasn't going to get my hopes up. Sighing, I didn't bother to look around at Bronx. In less than two minutes, I had used magic twice in front of the troll. So much for keeping my secret tightly guarded. If the warlock guardians didn't come storming in to kill me any second now, I didn't know what it would finally take. All I knew was that I had to find a way to protect Trixie from whatever trouble she currently found herself in.

Pasting a smile on my lips, I stepped into the front room and was faced by three tall, lanky men with pale blond hair that reminded me of Trixie's. They had the same vibrant green eyes and pale skin stretched over high cheekbones. Not only were they elves, but they were obviously from the same clan as Trixie. My concerns were the swords strapped to their backs and the knives hanging from their belts. Citizens couldn't walk around heavily armed like that unless they were in some kind of official law enforcement capacity. This significantly complicated matters.

"Can I help you, gentlemen?"

"We're here looking for Rowena Lightheart," said the one standing closest to me.

"Sorry, I don't know anyone by that name." I was happy that I could answer honestly as I watched the other two elves poke around the lobby, looking closely at stuff and putting me on edge.

"We have been asking around the area and she is using glamour to disguise her identity. She would have brown hair and eyes. She is also going by a different name. We have reason to believe that she's working here. Do you have an employee by the name of Trixie?"

"Trixie?" I repeated skeptically. "No, I'm afraid I don't."

"More than a few of your customers would argue otherwise," he pressed through clenched teeth.

"Look, it's just me and my coworker, Bronx—a troll," I added with emphasis, hoping that the presence of a troll would keep them from pushing this into violence. "There are no Rowenas or Trixies tattooing here."

"Sir!" said one of the other elves, capturing our attention. We both looked down to where he had pulled up the rug, revealing the pentagram inscribed into the hardwood floor. "It looks like an anti-glamour spell."

"That's complex magic for a tattoo artist," the lead elf continued, taking a step closer to me.

"It was from the previous owner of the building. I don't know how it got there."

"Maybe, but considering the magic running through it, you obviously know how to use it."

I gave a little shrug, as if what he was saying wasn't of much importance to me. "A little self-defense isn't such a bad thing in this kind of neighborhood. A person has to know who they are dealing with."

The elf glared at me. "So you're that Gage. The rogue warlock they are desperate to kill." A weight sank in my stomach. Who were these guys and how the hell did they know about me? This wasn't good at all. "It should be no surprise that she would come here to hide. She would think you'd be the one person who could actually protect her."

"Look, asshole! I've got work to do and you're keeping me from it. There's no Trixie or Rowena here and, honestly, even if there was, I can't imagine handing some poor chick over to you three schmucks. So just get out of here before I call the cops for harassment."

He moved fast. Faster than the time it took me to gasp or blink. The elf closest to me grasped me tightly around the throat and lifted me off my feet before slamming me through the glass case. Pain exploded in my back as the glass shattered. He tightened his hand around my throat, nearly closing off my airway passage, before I could even think to grab his hand and tear it away.

As my thoughts finally caught up with the events happening around me, I heard the distinct *chunk* of a shotgun being cocked. I looked up to find Bronx standing next to the elf who was still leaning over me with his hand around my throat. The muzzle of the sawed-off shotgun was pressed into the elf's temple, giving him no room. I had little doubt that if the elf made a single move in the wrong direction, I was going to be splattered in his brains along with the fractured glass.

"Leave here," Bronx growled.

With amazing slowness, the elf released my throat and raised his empty hands as he stepped away from me. The trio edged backward out the door, looking as if they had all sucked on a lemon, before they left the building. It was only when they were no longer in sight that Bronx set the shotgun against the wall and offered me a hand as I climbed out of the shattered glass case. Shaking the broken glass out of my shirt and back, I turned around to find that all of the glass had been either shattered and knocked out of the case or was fractured in some way. The whole thing needed to be completely replaced and as soon as possible. Hell.

"You okay?" Bronx asked, which made me flinch. It wasn't a question that usually crossed his lips.

"I look that bad?" I asked in return as I glanced down at the scratches that lined both arms and then the fine tears in my jeans. Lines of blood crisscrossed every bit of exposed flesh that I could see. I'd had my ass kicked by Simon and an elf all in the same day. So much for being a powerful warlock. It was becoming questionable as to whether I could even take care of myself.

Bronx frowned at me as his eyes drifted down my arms. "You look like you lost a fight with a big cat."

"Thanks for stepping in."

"No problem."

"Can you take care of the client? I think it's time I had a few words with Miss Trixie."

"Sure, but take it easy on her. Those were Royal Guards of the Summer Court. You know that whatever she's mixed up in can't be good."

My heart seemed to stutter for a second at his words, but I nodded. "Leave this mess. I'll clean it up later."

Walking to the back room, I paused and grabbed a paper towel. After running it under water, I wiped some streaks of blood off my face, out of my hairline, and off my arms as the bleeding slowed. I didn't want Trixie to be worried when she caught sight of me. Unfortunately, there still wasn't much chance of stopping that. I was a mess. My clothes were torn and I was covered in cuts. And despite my fresh array of wounds and bruises, I doubted that I had convinced the three Royal Guards that Trixie didn't actually work here. I had a feeling that the tattoo parlor was going to stay under surveillance until they caught her. For now, she was trapped and I didn't know how to help her.

TEARS WERE GLISTENING on Trixie's face when I opened the trapdoor and started to descend the stairs. I pursed my lips together, trying to hold back a frown, but I don't think I really succeeded. I didn't know how to deal with the tears on her pale cheeks. I would have preferred it if she had been angry and ready to burst out of the basement, prepared to take on the bastards who had been hunting her. But all I saw was fear and shame in her wide eyes as I passed by her and down to the floor.

"Stay where you are," I murmured in a rough voice as I grabbed the pull chain for the overhead light. The basement flooded with dirty light, I walked over to the wall with the pentagram and placed my right hand against it. I closed my eyes a second and poured my energy into it, unraveling the last of the spells that protected my domain.

"Okay, it's safe to come down . . . Rowena," I said as I slowly opened my eyes to look up the stairs at her. She gave a little shiver at the name and remained sitting on the stairs. She leaned forward and wrapped her arms around her legs while placing her chin on her knees.

"How much did they tell you?" she whispered in a weak, thready voice.

"Nothing but a name. Rowena Lightheart. But I know they were members of the Royal Guard of the Summer Court. I also know that you're an elf. I've known since you first walked in the door of the shop the day I hired you."

"What?" she cried, her head popping up.

"There's an antiglamour spell in the lobby upstairs that covers most of the shop. Remember, I'm a rogue warlock."

Her head fell forward so that her forehead was against her knees and her shoulders were slumped. "Does Bronx know?" she asked in a dejected, muffled voice.

"Don't know. I'm the only one who can use the antiglamour spell, though he does know about its existence. Can't get much by the son of a bitch." When she didn't look relieved, I sighed. Walking over to the stairs, I stood next to the bottom step with my hands shoved in my pockets. "I prefer the real you, Rowena. Not this fake you present to the rest of the world. I love the way your blond hair curls at the ends, just past your shoulders, and the way your green eyes sparkle when you laugh. But then I guess I also liked being the only one who could see those things."

"The name's Trixie," she said. Her voice had grown a little harder as she finally raised her head. "I haven't gone by that other name in centuries."

She made it sound as if it had just been a few years to her, but that was the long-lived elves for you. Time meant different things to them when they had centuries lined up before them.

I paced over to one of the workbenches and leaned against it, wishing that I kept a chair in the basement. "Will you please tell me what's going on? You obviously don't have to, but I was just thrown through a glass case in your defense and I have a feeling that they're going to be back for more, so I would like to know why I am going to suffer physical harm for you."

"Went through the glass case? Is that what happened?" she gasped as her head popped up.

"Nothing major." I brushed aside her concern with a wave of my hand, causing a twinge of pain to shoot through my shoulder. I felt like crap as one beating seemed to bleed into the next, but she didn't need to know about that. "Bronx was right there with the shotgun, covering my back, so everything's good. Unfortunately, I doubt they left convinced that you don't work here. They're going to be watching the place."

"I'm sure they will." She loosened her arms and stretched out her legs so that her feet rested on one step lower. "They've spent a long time tracking me, but this is the longest I've gone since last seeing them."

"What did you do?"

"It's what I didn't do."

"And that was . . ."

"I didn't get married."

"And how long have they been hunting you for this?"

"For roughly three centuries."

"And the groom is still interested after three centuries? You'd think he would have moved on."

"The king can be a very stubborn man," she said with a shake of her head.

"The king? You mean, the king of the Summer Court?"

"Yes."

"But I thought he was already married. I can definitely recall his having a wife. Did she die?" A frown crossed my face as I wished I'd spent more time watching the entertainment news channels. The only thing more interesting to the races than the Hollywood celebrities was the royal families—both human and otherwise. And the elves had been blessed with three: Summer Court, Winter Court, and Svartálfar Court, though little was heard from the Svartálfar, or Dark Elf, Court.

"No, he's still married."

I rubbed my head against the headache beginning to form at

my temples, hoping it was the remnant of a concussion I'd suffered when my head crashed through the plate glass. "Trixie, you're going to have to start giving me more detailed answers here, because none of this is making sense to me. If the king already has a queen, how can he possibly marry you?"

"I would be taken as his second wife, more a type of concubine. The ceremony would make it impossible for me to ever leave him and marry someone else. It would also make any children he had with me legitimate heirs to the throne."

"Oh." Something clenched in my chest and weighed heavily on my heart as I listened to her talk about her situation. A deep sense of panic clawed at my chest, making it harder to breathe. It was becoming a struggle to stand still and not pace the small room.

"I grew up in the Summer Court and was taught to be an artisan. I spent centuries studying different art forms and techniques. During that time I caught the eye of the king, which would have made any family happy. Shortly before I left it was discovered that the king and queen could not produce children. To protect the throne, heirs were needed or the Summer Court could suddenly find itself under attack from either the Winter Court or the Svartálfar Court. Under our law it is only natural for the king and queen to take on concubines until children are born."

"What happened?" I prompted when she suddenly fell silent.

"I ran. When I heard the news that the search for concubines had begun, I left the court and never looked back. I didn't give him a chance to put the position before me because I would not have been permitted to say no. And if the Royal Guards are still looking for me it means that the queen has not succeeded in bearing a child yet."

"Shouldn't he have taken another concubine for the good of his people instead of chasing you?"

"Of course, but you know men," she said with disgust. Her eyes narrowed uncomfortably on me and I shifted from my left foot to my right. "They are only enticed by the chase. I'm more interesting to him now that I'm on the run."

I released a breath, rubbing both my hands over my face as the story swirled around in my brain. Centuries. This chase had been going on for centuries. Would the king still even really want Trixie if he was faced with her again after so long? I opened my eyes and looked at my companion with her wide green eyes and haunting face, and knew with no hesitation that the answer would be yes.

"I'm not sure what to do, Trix," I admitted sadly. "I've got some tricks that can keep them at bay for a few nights, but if they're confident you're here, they are going to keep coming until they flush you out. You can't stay captive in the tattoo parlor forever. That's not a life."

"Then I run again."

"That's not a life either!" I snapped, dropping both hands to my sides and forming them into fists. "You can't keep picking up your life, cutting off all ties of friendship and support, and running at the first sign of trouble. That's not living; that's surviving, and only barely. Trust me, I know firsthand what that's like."

"I've tried making a stand and fighting and I've just barely escaped. They'll kill me. The king would rather have me dead than allow someone else to have me."

"I'm sorry, but I don't know what to do for you."

"Would you marry me?" she asked softly.

I blinked twice, not sure that I had actually heard her correctly. I couldn't possibly have heard her correctly. "What?"

Trixie pushed to her feet, and with a snap of her fingers, the glamour that had cloaked her from the first moment I'd met her melted away. The vision of a woman with brown hair finally disappeared and I could clearly see the beautiful woman with the river of pale blond hair and sparkling green eyes. Her hips swayed hypnotically as she descended the last of the stairs. I knew that she hadn't captured me in any type of elfin glamour because I had protection against such things, but I felt as if I was wrapped in some spell she was weaving just for me.

She closed the distance between us until her breasts slightly brushed against the front of my shirt, while her body heat washed over me in warm, comforting waves. Lifting her left hand, her fingertips slid across my cheekbone and down my jaw, forcing my wandering eyes to meet her amused gaze.

"I said," she began in the same sweet whisper, "would you marry me?"

"I—I don't see what that would solve," I stammered, resisting the urge to step out of her reach. Of course, a part of me was itching to grab her with both hands and press her firmly against me so that every inch of her perfect body was molded to mine. My head stayed relatively clear only because I managed to keep my hands clenched at my sides.

"If I'm already married, then he can't have me. I would belong to you. He would have to drop his suit," she explained. Her hand slid around my jaw to my chin so that her thumb caressed my lower lip, parting it from the top lip.

She leaned in, gently kissing me, and by the gods, I didn't do a damn thing to stop her. Sucking my lower lip into her mouth for a second before releasing it, she moved on to the rest of my mouth. All thoughts of restraint snapped in a heartbeat as I plunged my tongue into her mouth, something I had dreamed of doing so many times. I reached up with my left hand and cupped the back of her head, holding her prisoner as I deepened the kiss until she moaned into my mouth. Trixie wrapped her arms around my neck, pressing her full length against me so that there was no hiding my erection, pressed firmly against her.

"Marry me, Gage," she murmured against my lips as she trailed her mouth against my cheek, seeking my neck.

Dropping my head back so that she had better access to my throat, I gave a low growl as I fought to think clearly with the right head. Marrying Trixie right now was not going to save her. I couldn't save her when my own life was hanging tenuously by a thin strand. Simon. Gideon. Death. They all swirled around me, waiting for their chance to chop off my head. Being with Trixie brought her within their sights as well. The king of the Summer Court wanted a lifetime of imprisonment, while the others could bring an end to her life. Loving something meant being willing to walk away from it. And I loved her.

"I can't," I said, grabbing her firmly by her upper arms. With every ounce of strength that I could muster, I pushed her a couple of steps away from me so that she could no longer reach me with her lips. "This isn't a good reason for getting married."

She arched one eyebrow at me. "Mutual attraction isn't a good reason?"

"That's the start of a reason, but I was referring to using it as a way of escaping your problems."

"It doesn't have to be the only reason we marry."

"Trixie . . ."

Trixie's full lips tilted into a teasing half smile that eased some of the tension from my frame. "I know, but a girl's got to try, and you're a catch."

"Thanks, but I'm more trouble than I'm worth, if you'll remember. Rogue warlock and all that." Because I simply couldn't resist the urge any longer, I pulled her back against me, wrapping my arms tightly around her. After everything that had happened, I needed her close, needed the feel of her pressed against me. Just for a couple of seconds and then I would find a way to keep moving. "I'll be lucky if I don't have the guardians breathing down my neck for the rest of my life. Right now, my life span is looking very limited, but I'm going to do what I can to help you until we can come up with a better solution than running, okay? Will you give me a little time?"

Trixie shook her head, stepping out of my grasp. "Gage, I don't want to risk your life or Bronx's any more than I already have. It would be best if I get moving now while they're trying to regroup."

"You're worth the risk, and I'm sure that Bronx would agree with me, so you stay. No more arguments. I'm just talking about a few more days. I need time to clear up some ugly matters and then I can turn my full attention to your problem, I promise."

Trixie stared at me in silence for several seconds, chewing on her lower lip as if she was wavering in indecision.

Reaching out, I grabbed her arm, rubbing my thumb over the soft flesh in a reassuring caress. "You've been running for so long, and this isn't such a bad life, right? Don't you owe it to yourself to take this chance at being happy in one place? At least for a little while longer?"

Trixie reached up and trailed her fingers across my forehead, easing some of the ache with her gentle touch. "You drive a hard bargain. I'll stay as long as I can, but if people start getting hurt, then I am out of here."

"I understand." I nodded, giving her arm a little squeeze. "Now, get back upstairs and get to work. This is still a business and we've got to make some kind of money today."

Trixie chuckled as she shook her head. At the same time, she waved her hand, putting her glamour spell back in place before she ascended the stairs. "You're such a slave driver."

"You better believe it. I've got to come up with the money to replace that damn glass case," I groused as the pains of being slammed through that piece of furniture suddenly came throbbing back. Trixie had managed to make me forget that my spine was killing me and that I was covered in a hundred little cuts along with having a nagging headache. Yeah, I was in great shape. I just hoped that Gideon didn't pick tonight to show up, because I really wasn't in any kind of shape to defend myself against an attack. Hell, without Bronx, the elves might actually have gotten the better of me. I wasn't accustomed to fighting something that moved so fast. My experience was with other witches and warlocks, who were quite dangerous but at least moved at somewhat human speeds. With all the problems I was having, I was beginning to wonder if it was time for me to crack a book and look over some of my old spell notes. Sheer bravado and reckless risk taking weren't going to carry me much further.

17

WITH A CHOKE and a stutter, life in the shop returned to normal. I trudged back up the stairs right behind Trixie and held her back from entering the main tattooing room until Bronx finished up the client she had been working on. Her sudden appearance would shatter the spell I had embedded in his brain, and I preferred that he go about his business believing that a woman named Trixie didn't work at Asylum. While we waited, I closed the door to the basement but didn't replace the wards out of fear that Trixie might need to use it as a sudden hiding place should the elves make a second appearance that night.

Once the man was bandaged up, the tattoo paid for, and he was out of the door, Trixie and I joined Bronx. The troll didn't say anything but gave her a little pat on the shoulder before slumping in his chair. He didn't need to ask any questions. He knew that the Royal Guard of the Summer Court was chasing Trixie for some reason. That was enough for him to defend his friend and coworker.

Trixie flashed him a weak smile as she stood in front of her workstation and started to pull out the greasepaint for Bronx's nightly pseudotattoo. "Thanks for covering that client for me."

"You owe me. He was a real squirmer. Couldn't keep his butt still in the chair," the troll complained.

Trixie and I gave a little laugh at the image of the small man squirming under the attentions of the large troll as he tried to work the tiny needle along the man's arm. "I can't imagine it had anything to do with the scary tattoo artist doing the work," I teased.

"Bronx! Did you growl at the client?" Trixie added.

"Not at first," he admitted, getting us all laughing.

Trixie came from behind her own tattooing chair and wrapped her arms around the troll's neck, pressing a kiss on his cheek. "You're just a big teddy bear in disguise and no one realizes it."

"Don't give my secret away," he said gruffly, but at the same time pointed to his other cheek for a kiss. Trixie laughingly obliged while giving him a hug.

Trixie wasn't far from the truth. Bronx was quiet and thoughtful. He was reflective and very purposeful in his decisions and his actions. It sometimes made him a slow tattoo artist because he was something of a perfectionist. Despite his frightening appearance, there was nothing brutal or scary about the troll. Unless someone attacked one of his friends, and then you could find yourself eating the muzzle of a sawed-off shotgun in a matter of seconds. I'd had to replace the front plate-glass window of the shop three times because of clients who'd become too aggressive with Trixie. I never said a word. Just picked up the phone and dialed the number to the glass shop. He had only done what I wished I could have.

Still chuckling at the silliness, I picked up the broom and dustpan while dragging one of the garbage cans behind me. I started with the task of cleaning up the broken glass. From the impact, the glass had scattered everywhere, forcing me to also drag out the vacuum cleaner to properly get it off the carpet as well. Clients came in as I cleaned, taking one look at me and another at the glass case, muttering comments under their breath before they were met by Trixie or Bronx.

As midnight approached, I neared the completion of my cleaning. I paused, locking the front door. I could hear the buzzing of two tattooing machines, as both Trixie and Bronx were in the middle of designs. I flipped back the edge of the carpet nearest the glass case and got down on hands and knees with the broom. I carefully cleaned the bits of glass out of the pentagram that had been inscribed in the wood floor. I didn't think the glass would interfere with the spell, but I didn't need to take chances right now when I had so many problems building. I certainly couldn't afford any surprises.

With the carpet back in place, I unlocked the front door. Putting the broom and dustpan back where they belonged, I carried the glass-filled trash can out to the Dumpster and replaced the garbage bag while Trixie and Bronx finished up their work. Other than the broken glass case in the front lobby, the place looked normal again. I picked up the phone, but caught myself. It was after midnight. I would have to wait until I opened the shop on Tuesday to call the glass company for a replacement. I was so used to working late hours that I half-expected the rest of the world to work the same hours. The nice part was that with so many nocturnal creatures in the world, there were a lot of businesses that did keep late hours. Unfortunately, Johnston & Johnston Glassworks was a human-run company as far as I was aware, which meant that they closed around six in the evening. To make matters worse, tomorrow was Sunday, and Asylum was closed on Sunday and Monday. While the case would have to wait, the timing was perfect for fixing Tera's tattoo, if I ever figured out how.

Shoving both my hands in my pockets, I watched as my companions cleaned up their stations after finishing with their respective clients. The tattoos must have been relatively simple, because each had taken just over an hour to complete, from setting the outline to bandaging the site. I could only guess that both clients had also come in with their own designs, since I didn't hear either go into the back room to complete a sketch or stir a potion. All in all, easy jobs.

Unfortunately, I was starting to drag. I was usually out of the shop by now, but I knew that Trixie worked until a few hours later. If I left the shop, it meant that Trixie would have to retreat to the apartment upstairs because I would have to set all the protective spells before I left. Considering that it had been a slow, rotten day, I was trying to last as long as possible to give her a chance to make a little cash, but I didn't know how much longer I was going to last without some coffee or an energy drink. I also had this lingering feeling that I was waiting for something, but I couldn't for the life of me remember what it was.

The bell attached to the front door rang as a new customer pushed it open. Lethargically, I leaned around the doorjamb on my shoulder to see how many people had wandered into the shop. If it was enough, I might squeeze in one more job myself and then call it a night. I might have been busy all day, but I hadn't done shit when it came to tattooing. Still, I was exhausted.

To my surprise, Tera bounced into the shop with a smile bright enough to light the night. It was then that it finally dawned on me why I had been waiting around in the shop so late. I had called her earlier in the day and been hoping that she might finally call me back.

"Gage!" she exclaimed as she rushed across the lobby of the tattoo parlor.

"Hey, Tera," I said, pushing away from the archway to enter the lobby. She paused at what was left of the glass case, her mouth falling open at the few large pieces of jagged glass that I couldn't pull free, leaving it looking like a hungry mouth standing ready to devour the foolish. "Don't worry about it," I said with an absent wave of my hand as I walked around it. "It was just an angry customer. I'm glad you stopped by."

My words seemed to finally rip her attention free from the broken case, placing her wide eyes back on me. She rushed toward me and wrapped her arms around my neck in a fierce hug, nearly strangling me.

"Oh my god, Gage!" she gasped, tightening her grip on me as if I meant to escape her. "I can't even begin to thank you."

"I'm not sure what you're talking about," I replied in a choked voice, resisting the urge to try to pry her arms from around my neck. Sure, I was lying through my teeth, but I had to play this one cool if I was going to have another shot at her back. I couldn't come right out and tell her she was immortal, that the grim reaper was demanding her soul, and that I just wasn't chivalrous enough to give him mine instead of hers.

She laughed, loosening her steely grip a little to hold me at arm's length. "You're kidding, right?"

"I just called you earlier today to make sure that you weren't having any problems with the tattoo. Most people who get their entire back covered have a little trouble getting it clean the first time—"

"No!" she cried. She fully released me and spun around in place hugging herself, this time to my relief. "The tattoo is wonderful! It's absolutely perfect!"

Guilt ate at me like acid through tender stomach tissue. I knew what she was going to say. I knew why she was so blissfully excited without having to ask her, but I had to. I had a role to play in this farce, maybe as a bit of penance for the mess I'd made.

"I'm so glad you like it," I said, hating myself a little more with each word uttered. "I just did what you requested."

"I know you did more! You had to have done more."

"I don't—"

"The cancer is gone!" she exclaimed. Her words seemed to be accompanied by an unearthly silence as one song on the MP3 player ended at the same time and the chatter in the next room went completely dead. It was as if those four words echoed through the void, shattering all my hopes of keeping secrets from my companions and the rest of the world.

"Really? That's wonderful!" I forced the words up my throat like fat chunks of sludge. I was happy for her, but it burned that I was going to be the one to steal all of that away.

"I went to the doctor this morning for a checkup and another round of tests. The doctor said that it's all gone. All of the cancer is gone. In fact, I'm completely healthy in every way." She closed the distance between us a second time and hugged me, a little more gently this time. "You've saved my life," she whispered in a tear-choked tone of voice.

Now I had to find a way to take it away from her again to save my own life. I thought I was going to be sick.

Carefully, I grabbed her upper arms and pushed her from me so that she could look me in the eye. "I didn't do anything, I swear. It's just a tattoo of angel wings on your back in black ink. I don't know what caused your cancer to disappear, but it wasn't me."

"But—" she stammered, her eyes wide.

"It wasn't me," I repeated firmly, but I softened my voice when I continued. "But that doesn't mean this isn't a wonderful thing that shouldn't be thoroughly celebrated!"

She jerkily nodded to me, her smile slipping back onto her lips, though confusion still lingered in her eyes. "Of course. I've been visiting with all my friends today and making plans again. After I was told about the cancer, I stopped making plans because I never knew how much time I had. But now that I have so much time, I can live again."

"Then let's make plans to have drinks Monday night," I suggested. It might be cutting it a little close, but this way I would have all day and night Sunday to try to track down a fix for her immortality and the shop would still be closed on Monday for me to do my work in secret.

"Monday night? Not tonight? It's not that late."

"I'm sorry, but I've been running since early this morning and it's been a rough day," I said with a heavy sigh. I grabbed one of her hands and gave it a squeeze. "I wouldn't be very good company, as I think I would fall asleep in my first drink. We can meet here at nine o'clock on Monday and make the rounds of the bars downtown. Remember, you've got time now."

"You're right," she said, her smile brightening. "I want to celebrate over several days and not try to cram it all into one night. It's just now that I have a second chance at life, I don't want to go to sleep. I want to keep moving and doing."

"I understand," I said, forcing a smile to my lips while I was choking on my words. "But try to get some sleep. I don't want you falling asleep on me when we're just getting started."

"I will, I promise." Tera laughed, giving me another quick hug. "I'll see you Monday at nine. Be ready to party."

"I will," I murmured as I watched her bounce out the door again, as bubbly as when she first came through it.

I stood there staring at the door for more than a minute, my hand pressed to my churning stomach as I tried not to vomit. I had screwed up in such a major way and now the only way to undo my mess was to kill her. Closing my eyes, I let myself dream that there was another option, but I knew there wasn't. If the grim reaper had someone scheduled to die, their soul was due for collection. It was not for me to step in and stop it. I was no god or great archangel or even demon that could put a halt to such things. I was a tattoo artist who stuck his nose into business that had nothing to do with him.

I fought the urge to pick something up and throw it through the front window. I needed to hear the sound of something breaking. I needed to feel as if I had something within my power, but right now I was under the control of the grim reaper if I wanted to live. And I did want to live. I wasn't ready to give up my life for someone else, no matter how I'd messed up.

Taking a deep breath, I reminded myself that I was not the one killing Tera. Cancer was. The grim reaper was calling in her debt to him; he wanted her soul. It had been scheduled long before I ever touched her. The only things I was killing were her hope, her dreams, her happiness while I pretended to be her friend so that she would allow me to stay close.

The sound of high heels on the wood floor shattered my down-spiraling train of thoughts. My head jerked around to find Trixie standing in the doorway, arms crossed over her stomach, a frown pulling at the corners of her mouth. She had turned off the MP3 player, and the silence nearly crushed me. I didn't need to look into the tattooing room to know that Bronx was also waiting for me to speak. They were both waiting for an answer to what they never should have heard.

"You cured her cancer?" Trixie demanded in a cold voice when I didn't speak.

Clenching my teeth, I turned and walked into the tattooing room where Bronx was waiting. He sat in his chair, his large hands resting on his knees and his face expressionless. Trixie returned to her station and leaned against the counter. Her expression was dark and disapproving as she waited for my response.

"Yes, I cured her cancer. Tera is perfectly healthy now," I said numbly, trying to push back the overwhelming feeling of guilt.

"Is this why TAPSS is now looking into the shop closely?" Bronx asked calmly. "Are they going to close the shop because of this?"

"No, this tattoo has nothing to do with TAPSS. We're not going to be closed," I said, shoving one hand through my hair. I was exhausted to the bone between the worry and the fights that had filled my day. And now I had to look my friends in the eye and find a suitable lie that they would believe because I certainly couldn't tell them I'd made the poor girl immortal. No one could know about her immortality. It was too dangerous. It was bad enough that I'd had to tell Sparks.

"Did you cure her with magic?" Trixie demanded. "Is that why the warlocks and TAPSS have been sniffing around here so much? Is Tera the reason you haven't been here today?"

I felt this conversation slipping out of my control, like water through my fingers. I needed to soothe their well-founded fear, but I didn't want to risk alienating them. They were not only my employees, but my friends as well. Two of the few friends I had, and I needed them. But I didn't want to lie to them any more than I already had.

"No, I didn't use any form of magic on Tera. It was a potion, just like every tattoo I have ever done," I said after releasing a slow, deep breath. So far, I was still telling the truth. "Unfortunately, there's been an unexpected side effect from the potion I stirred, and I need to find a way to undo it. That's why I haven't been here today. I sought the advice of my mentor."

"Why didn't you tell her about this side effect?" Trixie pressed. She still looked displeased with me and I couldn't blame her.

"I didn't want to ruin her happiness. She just got her life back. I'll talk to her when I see her on Monday." It was the truth with a few exclusions. I would talk to her about what I had done and its impact on her existence, but only after I had completed the touch-up of her tattoo.

Unfortunately, by Trixie's expression I had a feeling that she didn't completely believe me, but she kept her comments to herself, for which I was grateful.

"What ingredients did you use in Tera's tattoo potion?" Bronx inquired, drawing my gaze back to him.

I shook my head. "I'll never say. The items were from my personal stores, and they will be destroyed once this is over. The items were more dangerous than I had expected, and I won't allow them to fall into someone else's hands."

"And what about TAPSS? What drew them here?" Trixie pressed.

"Nothing to do with Tera," I snapped, but quickly stopped myself, clenching my fists at my sides. I was the one who'd made this mess. I had no reason to be angry with Trixie or Bronx for their concern for me or their livelihoods, and it was more than obvious that I was jeopardizing both.

When I was sure that I could speak again in a calm and even voice, I continued. "TAPSS was drawn here because of Russell Dalton's complaints about his faulty luck tattoo. I think they might also know that I used magic when I was attacked the other day in the alley. That is all."

"Why hasn't a warlock appeared tonight? You've been using magic for hours to protect Trixie," Bronx asked. When a stricken look crossed my face, he merely smiled at me. "I may be just a troll, but even I can smell magic in the air. You've been casting one spell after another tonight with no heed to the consequences for yourself."

I wanted to ask him how long he had suspected. Like him, I could smell magic too. Particularly on heavy users, as it tended to cling to them like a second skin. Was it like that with me? I didn't have the chance to ask.

"Gage?" Trixie whispered in a fractured voice. Her crossed arms slid apart and fell to her sides where they thumped against the counter. I didn't want her thinking about the warlocks and what hell might still come down on my head for what I'd been doing. She was worth the risk, worth risking my soul for. I wasn't going to let her fall back into the hands of the Summer Court if she didn't want to go.

"Don't worry about it," I said, peering deep into her wide green eyes.

"But if the warlocks come for you because of me . . ."

"They won't," I countered firmly as her voice drifted off. "If they haven't come by now, they aren't going to come. If the guardians are going to strike, they'll strike the second they sense anything going on that shouldn't be. I can tell you for a fact that they keep me under tight surveillance. Trust me, they know what I've been up to tonight."

"What if they're waiting for you to be alone?" Bronx said, drawing my attention back to his pool of calm. Despite the touchy topic we had been discussing for the past several minutes, his expression had never changed. Though I could now see some concern in his eyes that he hadn't been allowing to surface before.

"As much as I respect your strength, it's not enough to stop a guardian if they feel the need to strike," I said with a half smile. "They don't care if I'm alone or not. Hell, they prefer an audience. It helps to keep the rabble in line."

"Then why have we been left alone?" he asked.

"Someone is holding them back," I replied, letting my eyes fall shut. I slumped back opposite Trixie, against the counter that ran the length of the wall. I had little doubt that Simon was holding back the horde of guardians currently itching to take my head off. The struggle between Simon and me was personal, and he wanted to take care of it himself if he was going to regain any face among his peers. He needed to be the one to eliminate me or someone was going to take the opportunity to eliminate him in the name of pruning the weak growth.

"Do you know who?" Bronx asked.

"Yes."

"Do you know why?"

"Yes, he's hoping to kill me personally."

Trixie gasped, covering her mouth with both hands to stop whatever words had been about to rush forth.

"And I don't regret anything I've done tonight," I added, trying to alleviate any guilt she might be feeling. My problems with the warlocks had nothing to do with the elf, and in truth, I had a feeling that my ability to stay quiet and hidden wasn't going to last my entire life. I had used magic before I was collected by the warlocks and I knew that I would keep using magic until they finally killed me. It was too much a part of who I was, running in my veins with my blood.

"What's the next step, boss?" Bronx asked, bringing a smile to my lips. Only a true friend would continue to stand next to me when

I was talking about facing down the Ivory Towers. They ruled this world and crushed anyone who dared to speak out against them. Only a friend or a madman would continue to associate with me.

"Sleep." My eyes fell shut for a second as I sighed. "It's been a long day."

"Want me to close up?" Bronx offered.

"No, keep your normal hours. I don't expect you to have any trouble." I turned my attention to Trixie, who was watching me with fear filling her wonderful eyes. "Are you ready to call it a night? I have to set the protective spells for the upstairs apartment before I leave for my own apartment."

Trixie nodded once before walking to the back room and the door that led to the back stairs. As I walked past Bronx, I clapped the troll on the shoulder once and smiled. I couldn't have been luckier in the friends I had surrounding me. I just wondered whether they would remain so close if they found out what kind of mess I'd made for Tera. If I couldn't find a way to forgive myself, how could they?

18

TRIXIE WAS KIND enough to wait until I shut the apartment door behind us before she let loose with her real thoughts on the situation. Bronx didn't need to know that I was getting myself entangled in more than I already had on my plate.

"Are you fucking insane?" she shouted as I checked the one window in the living room.

I continued to move through the apartment, making sure that all the windows were still locked, as well as checking that no spells had been cast about the apartment that weren't my own. If the elves were smart enough to figure out where Trixie worked, then there was a good chance they also suspected where she might be hiding after she escaped from her own apartment.

"I've begun to wonder that myself," I said lightly as I moved into the bedroom. Sanity was beginning to appear highly overrated. I was managing quite well without it.

Trixie followed close on my heels, her footsteps heavy in her frustration. "This isn't a joke, Gage. You can't cast any of the protective spells you were planning. You're just throwing more fuel on the fire."

I couldn't stop the snort that escaped me. "It's a little too late to stop now. Simon is going to come after me sooner or later, regardless of whether I set these spells. I would like to get some sleep tonight rather than spend it staring at the ceiling and wondering if you've been found by those damn elves."

"I can take care of myself," Trixie said, blocking my exit from the bedroom by standing in the doorway, her hands braced against either side of the doorjamb.

"No offense, Trix, but so far your way of taking care of yourself is to run every time they get too close. And I'm not ready to let you run out of my life. I don't think Bronx is either."

"I've stood and fought them!" she cried, hitting my shoulder with the heel of her right hand.

"And then what?"

She fell silent, her eyes drifting away from my face to stare down at my chest as her initial bravado deflated before my eyes.

"You ran," I filled in when she refused to speak.

"You don't understand."

"I do. There are too many of them and they're too strong for just one person to fight. You did the smart thing. You ran, staying alive and free. If I'd been you, I would have done the same thing."

Trixie shook her head, refusing to look up at me. "No, you wouldn't have. You would have stood your ground and fought. Gage, you would have died fighting rather than spend a very long lifetime running and hiding."

"I honestly don't know if that's true. But if it is, then I'm glad you're smarter than me." I reached out and ran the fingertips of my right hand along her cheek, getting her to raise her teary eyes to my face. "Running brought you to Asylum and into my life. You've made both Bronx and me extremely happy over the past couple of years and I'm not ready for that to end. If it means that you need to make a stand with me at your side using magic to protect you, then that's what I'm going to do."

"And what if I'd rather protect you both by disappearing again?"

"I'd have to say that it's not an option. You're stuck here."

Trixie's left hand slid down from where she was holding the side of the doorjamb. She raised one hand and placed it on my chest, over my racing heart. "This warlock is hunting for your head because of me."

"Nah. Simon has had it out for me since I left his tutelage. We nearly killed each other when we parted ways, and he's looking for a chance to finish what was started."

"It's more than that. You've caught the attention of the Summer Court. While you're attempting to dodge and defeat this Simon, the Summer Court is going to be hunting for you as well because you're blocking their attempts to apprehend me. I couldn't live if you were killed."

Slipping my hand behind her head, I pulled her against my chest while I wrapped my other arm around her waist. Trixie wrapped her arms around my neck, laying her head on my shoulder. "I'm not going to be killed by Simon or the guards from the Summer Court. Trust me, right now I've got bigger problems than either of those two represent."

Trixie jerked backward so that she could look me in the face. "What are you talking about? Is there something going on with Tera's tattoo that you haven't told us about?"

"Yes, but I don't want you to worry about it. It will all be cleared up soon and then we can concentrate on getting the Summer Court permanently off your back."

"Gage . . ." she softly murmured as a tear slipped from her eye.

I leaned in and kissed her, silencing any more of her protests. I had heard enough and I wasn't going to change my mind. It had been an extremely long day and my defenses were crumbling. Logic said to release her, but I didn't give a fuck about what logic was demanding. Trixie and I might have no future together, but she didn't have a future with the king of the Summer Court either. I would content myself with stolen kisses and long looks from across the tattoo parlor. I just needed to touch her now, reassure myself that she was safely hidden while in my arms.

Tightening my hand on the back of her head as my fingers threaded through her soft hair, I deepened the kiss until I thought I could drown in the taste of her. A soft moan whispered from her throat as she pressed closer to me, putting her firm body against my entire length. Her legs straddled one of mine, tightening her grip while she moaned again, grinding her body against mine. I swept my tongue through her mouth as I wrapped my arms around her more firmly. One hand slid down and cupped her rear end, hitching her up slightly higher so that I could feel her pressed against my erection. Fire burned through my veins, turning all thought to ash. I wanted her, wanted her more than my next breath. Her breasts were smashed against my chest. I leaned back just enough to get one hand between us so that I could fill my hand with that soft mound. She squirmed against me, rubbing along my leg. Her tongue thrust into my mouth and I could taste a new urgency in her. Her taste, touch, and smell had become my whole world. She was everywhere, flooding my senses.

"The bed," she said against my mouth as she briefly broke off the kiss. "Move to the bed."

I had been trying to forget about the bed, just a few feet away, right behind me, so her mention of it only made me harder. My hands reflexively tightened their grip on her as I tilted my head back and closed my eyes. I tried to clear my thoughts against the kisses she was trailing down my exposed neck. I had to think clearly. I had to loosen my fingers from where they were digging into her flesh, but I couldn't move my hands. I had to think, to remember where I was and why I had come up to the apartment in the first place. I was there to protect her, not complicate her life and mine.

"We can't." Ripping those two words from me was like cutting off a limb. I'd rather remove my own right hand than release her, but I had to. Taking Trixie to bed wouldn't be some simple matter for me. It was more than just being attracted to her. Beautiful women had come and gone in my life, but Trixie was a hundred times more. I craved her laughter and her sweet voice. I needed her gentleness and her compassion and her fierce loyalty. I didn't know if this was just sex for her, but it never would be for me. Once we crossed this line, there was no going back and I didn't want to think about watching her walk away.

"Yes, we can."

"You've been through so much today. I won't take advantage of you."

I opened my eyes and looked down at her when her lips finally left my body. She was staring at me, her focus clear. "I'm a big girl, Gage. I know what I'm doing."

My eyes fell shut again because I had conned myself into believing that I could think clearly if I wasn't looking at her. It didn't work. Dragging in a deep breath only pulled her scent deeper into my lungs. When I opened my eyes, she had removed the glamour spell that constantly cloaked her so that I was looking into her wide green eyes, her face framed by her soft blond hair.

Trixie smiled at me. "Did you honestly think this wasn't going to happen eventually? We've been flirting with each other for nearly two years."

"I'm your boss."

Rubbing her hands up my back, Trixie leaned close, grazing her lips across my neck as she spoke. "I'll try not to hold it against you. Now move."

Laying both of my hands flat against her back, I held her tight for a second, not moving, savoring the feel of her. "Trixie . . . I can't do this if it's just . . . I need more than . . ." My rough voice drifted off as I struggled to find the right words. I knew the timing was bad. Her life was a mess and mine was a national disaster, but I couldn't stop myself from grasping this one perfect moment even if I was forcing her to slip through my fingers.

Trixie stopped kissing me to meet my gaze, tears glistening in her eyes, looking so much like ivy leaves after a summer rain. Taking my right hand, she placed it on her chest so that I could feel her frantically pounding heart under my fingertips. "I give you the beat of my heart, the breath in my lungs, and the joy in my soul. You are mine and I am yours."

Leaning back down, I kissed her gently, memorizing the feel of her mouth. As I slowly stepped backward, she slipped her soft hands under my T-shirt and pushed it up so that I was forced to release her and raise my arms over my head. She removed the shirt in one quick move and tossed it across the room before lowering her hands to my bare chest. Her fingers danced over the outline of muscles down to my ribs and across my stomach while I ravaged her mouth in another soul-searing kiss. It only lasted a couple of seconds before she broke it off and pushed me backward. I flopped onto the mattress and remained lying there as I watched her remove her shirt and lacy black bra. I stared at her exquisite pale skin and firm breasts with their perfect pink nipples, already starting to harden under my gaze.

With a smile, she bent over and peeled off her skintight jeans and slipped out of her shoes. She started to crawl onto the bed, but as she hovered over me, I grabbed her shoulders and pushed her onto her back. I swallowed her giggle as I kissed her again, covering her mouth with mine. Leaning on my side, my right hand danced over her skin, cupping her full breast while gently pinching the nipple between two fingers. She moaned and squirmed beside me, her hands dancing down my chest to the waistband of my jeans where I left her to struggle with the button and zipper as I moved my mouth to her breast.

"You have to stop, Gage," she said in a soft, breathless voice.

I chuckled as I lifted my head an inch from where I was lying against her chest. "I don't think I'm ever going to stop doing this." My hot breath skimmed across her wet skin.

"I can't get your pants off if you keep doing this," she complained. Her body jerked as I ran my tongue over her nipple again while my hand slid down to her hip. I was shifting to her other breast when she shoved me onto my back and sat up in bed. She attacked my pants with both hands, earning another laugh from me.

"All right, you win," I said, batting her hands away. I easily kicked off my shoes, as my feet were still hanging over the edge of the bed, and then slid both my jeans and boxers off in a single move, carefully tucking my wand in with the pile of clothes. I started to lie back down but Trixie caught me.

"Socks too!"

I glanced questioningly over my shoulder as I reached down to strip off my socks.

"I want you completely naked. I won't have sex with a man who is still wearing his socks."

With my socks joining the rest of my clothes on the floor, I lay on the bed again. Trixie leaned over me, her golden hair flowing around her face like sunlight. Fear had left her beautiful green eyes and she looked down at me with laughter in them. Placing my left hand behind her head, I pulled her down, kissing her slowly. I savored the feel of her lips and the sweet taste of her mouth. I didn't know what tomorrow was going to bring or if I would ever have another chance to kiss her, but I was going to enjoy every moment I could with her while I had her in my hands.

Trixie broke off and started to trail kisses down my chest and across my stomach. My eyes drifted shut and my hand fell from the back of her head as I soaked in her gentle touch. She paused, her hot breath dancing across the head of my cock. I sucked in a deep breath at the feel and opened my eyes in time to see her run her tongue across it. Sensations tightened in my body and I released the breath I had been holding with a hiss through my clenched teeth. Her mouth was so warm and wet, scattering all my thoughts to the wind. My hips reflexively lifted, pushing myself farther into her mouth. Her tongue swirled around the sensitive flesh, driving me insane.

Reaching out, my hands briefly squeezed her breasts before moving down her body. As I reached the soft mound of golden curls, my finger slid between the two folds of flesh. She moaned deeply, her fingers curling so that her nails scratched red lines along my skin. As I slid one finger into her slick interior, she moved her mouth off me and pressed her forehead into my stomach.

"Gage," she whispered, moving her body so that she could take me deeper. I simply smiled, closing my eyes as I relished the feel of her warmth and tightness. She let me stroke her for a minute, wringing a long moan from her, before she suddenly moved out of my reach. I opened my eyes to find her straddling me. I stared at her beautiful body in awe, loving the sight of her above me, loving the feel of her hand wrapped around my cock.

I don't know whether it was lucky or not, but suddenly my brain started to work as she placed the head just inside her. I roughly grabbed her hips, stopping her sweet descent. My arms trembled and every muscle in my body was clenched to keep from releasing her.

"Wait!" I cried sharply. "I don't have any kind of protection."

Trixie smiled broadly at me, arching one eyebrow. "I'm assuming that you're concerned about pregnancy."

"Yes," I hissed, my body still straining for some little bit of self-control. I was dying to just release her and allow her to drop over me, but I was afraid that once we started there would be no more thoughts about the consequences. "Considering all our concerns at the moment, I don't think we need to worry about a child too," I continued in a strained voice.

Her somewhat mocking smile softened and she leaned forward, pressing her lips sweetly against mine. "I promise to mix up something tomorrow morning that will protect me against tonight."

"Are you sure?"

"Positive. I do know a few potions beyond those used for tattoo-ing," she purred in my ear.

That was all I needed to hear. I hadn't realized that I was hold-ing up her entire weight, so when my hands relaxed, her body came crashing down on mine in a single, swift stroke. A groan was pulled out of us both as she was impaled on my hardened body. She was so tight I thought for a second that I would lose myself right there, but I regained my focus. She sat still, her head thrown back so that her long blond hair cascaded down her back in a waterfall of golden waves. Her white skin seemed to glow in the dim light of the room. Her lips were parted as if she were frozen, a soft moan escaping her throat.

"Ride me, Trixie," I commanded in a rough voice.

With her hands braced on my chest, she slowly rose up and slid back down, her body convulsively tightening about me so that I groaned again. By the second stroke, my hips raised of their own accord, meeting her so that I was buried that much deeper inside. I lifted my hands and cupped both of her breasts, rubbing my thumbs over her pert nipples. Her body jerked once at the new touch and I felt her muscles contract again, squeezing me tighter, so it was harder to slide inside her.

She rode me slowly and steadily, her breathing a soft pant while her eyes remained closed as she soaked in all the sensations. We could have gone on all night like this, but it wasn't what I wanted. I wanted to feel and hear her orgasm as it shattered her body.

"Faster," I said in a low, rough voice. As Trixie picked up her pace, I released one of her breasts and slid that hand down her body to where our bodies met. I pressed my thumb into her clit and steadily massaged her. Trixie jerked, losing her rhythm for a second as she leaned even closer, moving her hands from my chest to my shoulders. A shiver ran the length of her body while she tightened around me. She became even wetter, sliding over me so easily now.

"Gage," she gasped, staring down at me.

"Let go. I want to feel it," I said.

She squeezed her eyes closed while her breathing grew heavier. "Gage . . . I . . . I've never wanted anything so badly. Please . . ."

I lifted my hips, picking up the pace, pressing my body as deep into hers as I possibly could. Her body was unlike anything I'd ever felt before. So perfectly warm and wet and tight, as if she had been made just for me. A perfect fit. But it wasn't enough. I needed to feel her orgasm break across me. She was so close, I could feel it. Her body convulsively tightened and relaxed around mine while she softly cried my name over and over again, her breaths coming in sharp little gasps.

And then she shattered. She sat straight up, her back bowing as every muscle in her body tensed. She gripped me so tightly that it was as if I was pressing my body into a warm velvet fist. A scream erupted from her while I continued to move inside her, stretching out the orgasm as long as possible. It was only when she finally collapsed on top of me, her body still vibrating, that I stopped moving.

The feel of her orgasm had pushed me to my own breaking point, but I held on with clenched teeth. Her body continued to convulse around me even though neither of us was moving. Wrapping my arms around her body, I carefully rolled her onto her back with my body still buried deep inside hers. She blinked a couple of times, looking around herself and then up at me, a surprised expression crossing her face. With my hands braced on either side of her head, I slowly slid out of her and then pushed back inside with the same slowness. Trixie sucked in a deep breath, as if steadying herself.

"Ready for round two?" I said with a smile.

"Round two?" Her voice wrapped around me, warm and heavy, like honey.

I continued to move inside her, pulling out almost completely before plunging back in again until I felt her hips rise. "I want to feel it again."

"Another orgasm?" She sounded surprised. Her slumberous eyes widened as she gazed up at me.

"Yes."

She chuckled, slightly throwing off my rhythm as my own strained body was fighting my control. "Not this time. It's your turn."

"Are you sure?" I asked, stopping midstroke in confusion. "I want to make you happy."

"I'm quite happy, but I will be happier when I feel you. Please, Gage," she said softly, raising her hand up to trail along my cheek. "Give me that piece of you."

"Everything I can," I murmured.

I started moving inside her again without thinking about it. Leaning down on my forearms, I grabbed her mouth in a rough kiss. Behind me, I could feel her dig her heels into the bed so that she could lift her body to meet each of my strokes. I broke off the kiss suddenly as a deep groan escaped me. I was steadily losing my tight control as she clenched her body around my cock, holding me tighter. I squeezed my eyes shut, wrapping my mind around the last bits of control I had, determined to give her as much pleasure as I could, but she was determined to break me.

"You feel so good," she moaned in a heavy, breathless voice. "So hard. So deep. Please, Gage . . ." Her breathing sped up again and I could feel her body tightening around mine. She was close.

"After you," I gritted out.

"Stubborn man," she cried as I leaned back, balanced on my knees. I grabbed her ass with both of my hands, tilting her slightly upward so that I could bury myself even deeper while picking up my pace. Seconds later, a scream was ripped from her throat while her body convulsed around mine. The last of my control shattered as I pounded into her body. The orgasm I had been fighting since she first pressed her body against mine exploded over me. I came so hard that her name was torn from my chest in a rough cry. I moved inside her, losing myself to the perfect feeling that tightened every muscle until my body gave out and I collapsed on top of her.

It took me more than a minute to gather both my thoughts and strength again. I pulled my body free of hers and rolled onto my back, still breathing heavily. Beside me, Trixie rolled onto her side, pressing her body along the length of mine. I opened my eyes to find her looking down at me with an exquisite smile, while her hair was spread about us in perfect disarray.

"Please say that I don't have to move."

"No moving for a while," I said, still breathing heavily.

"Good, because I don't think I can."

I chuckled, causing her to lift her head to look me in the eye. "I take it you're pleased."

"Mildly so," she said with a shrug.

My head popped up. "Mildly so?" I rolled her onto her back while I hovered over her. "Really, Miss I Don't Want to Move?"

Trixie laughed as she leaned up and kissed me. "Well, that's what you get for asking stupid questions."

It was a stupid question. I had heard her scream my name and felt her orgasm twice. We worked well together, our bodies fitting together so perfectly. I rolled onto my back and heaved a deep sigh as I stared up at the ceiling. Fatigue gripped my body and I found myself fighting to keep my eyes open. I had been exhausted before I came up to the apartment with Trixie. Now it felt as if I had tapped the last reserve of energy I had. I still had to find some way to drag myself back to my own apartment. I was tempted to just pull the covers over both of us and go to sleep where I was, but I didn't want to complicate things more than they already were. I wanted to take this slowly.

Besides, I still had to find the answer to my problem with the grim reaper and Tera. I preferred not to have Trixie looking too closely into my activities since it was unlikely that they were going to be of the legal variety. She had enough to worry about with the Summer Court. I didn't want her dragged into my mess if I could protect her from it.

"You have to go, don't you?" she suddenly asked, her voice filling the long silence that had settled between us.

I smiled, looking over at her. "Have you become a mind reader now?"

"No, you just had that look."

"What look?"

"That worried look."

"I'll happily stay if you want me to stay," I offered before I could stop myself. I wasn't ready to leave her alone. It was more than just a concern for her safety and the threat of the Summer Court. I loved the feel of her naked body against mine. I loved listening to her soft breathing in the silence of the room. There was something deep inside me that needed to hold her as she slept, but I kept those thoughts to myself. "I thought it would be best if I left. I didn't want to complicate things more. I wanted to take things slowly. I wasn't expecting this tonight."

Moving to lie across my chest again, Trixie threaded her fingers through my hair in a gentle caress. "I understand," she whispered with a smile on her lips. "You can leave on one condition."

"What's that?"

"You promise that we can do this again sometime."

I laughed deeply, wringing a laugh out of her. But her laugh was cut short as my left hand settled between her legs and rubbed against her still sensitive clit. Her laugh quickly deepened into a moan as she pressed her forehead to my chest.

"Definitely. There are too many things that I still want to do to your body, and I will never get tired of hearing you moan my name," I whispered in her ear. I returned my hand to my side and she slowly lifted her head.

"You're going to be the death of me," she said.

"Hopefully not for a very long time," I replied as I leaned up and kissed her.

Trixie slowly rolled off me and I reluctantly sat up. With a sigh, I pulled on my clothes, which were scattered around the room. Trixie also got up and put on her thin strip of silk panties and a T-shirt. I couldn't remember ever seeing her look so beautifully disheveled. Her hair was spread about her shoulders and her face was wiped clean of previous worries. I prayed this relaxed and sated state would follow her into sleep. She deserved a good, deep sleep.

With her hand entwined in mine, she accompanied me to the front door and pressed a long, lingering kiss to my lips.

"Stay inside. I'm going to set the protection spells and then leave. I have some errands to run tomorrow, but I will come back to see you as soon as I can. I'll think of a way to sneak you into my apartment," I said.

"Are you sure about this?"

"Movies and junk food with you?" I cocked my head to the side as my mouth curved into a broad grin. "I can't think of any better way to spend a Sunday."

"I'm talking about the spells."

"Positive. I'm not leaving you unprotected. Even if I stayed the night, I would cast the spells. I need to know that you'll be safe."

"I will be."

I pressed one last kiss to her lips and then stepped outside, pulling the door closed behind me. The sound echoed through my chest, rattling me for the first time. I had to deal with this business of the grim reaper, no matter what it took. If I was dead, there would be no one to protect Trixie, and eventually the Summer Court was going to get her if I wasn't there to intercede. And I would do whatever it took to protect her, even if it meant taking on the Summer Court, the warlocks, and death.

19

EXHAUSTION GNAWED ON my bones and tore at my muscles as I finished casting the first protection spell on the door. The only person who could lay a hand on the doorknob was Trixie or me. Otherwise, anyone else would be thrown from the small balcony and knocked unconscious before landing below in a useless heap. As I reached the ground, I grabbed a piece of broken brick from the parking lot and scratched some symbols in the first few wooden steps leading up to the apartment. I layered on a second spell, protecting the staircase from any intruders.

Heaving a deep sigh, I turned my attention to the small open area behind the shop that led to a narrow alley running between the buildings on this block. The night was quiet. The only cars traveling on the street could be heard in the distance, while there was no sound of people walking on the sidewalks to the local bars. A stray breeze caused an old aluminum can to rattle down the alley before hitting a building. I stood in the silence, trying to convince myself that there was no reason for me to feel this growing unease.

My eyes were skimming over the region one last time when they finally tripped over a lean figure standing on the opposite side of the alley. I hadn't seen him there moments ago, but I knew he had only just appeared. There had been no surge of magical power on his arrival, but Simon knew how to appear and disappear without causing a ripple in the energy that filled the air.

Adrenaline surged through my exhausted frame, reviving me. He wouldn't be allowed to threaten my companions. I hadn't expected him to seek me out again so quickly. I thought he would take more time strategizing. But then, I wasn't fully aware of what was at stake for him. There was something going on in the background that I wasn't privy to, and he was determined to take my life.

"You're not welcome here," I called out while mentally reaching for the energy swirling around me. This contest was only going to be won by the strongest and the fastest. My wand was still tucked in my sock, but I couldn't bend over to get it without exposing myself to Simon's attack. I had managed to keep Trixie preoccupied enough that I didn't think she'd noticed it when I got undressed or put my clothes back on. She didn't need such an obvious reminder of my otherness.

"I can't recall any time when I was welcome in your life," Simon replied. The warlock stepped closer, crossing the alley to enter the back area of the shop. The concrete that separated us was cracked and weeds were growing up through the fissures. Bits of trash speckled the open area, seeming to stand out in the moonlight.

I was suddenly aware of the glass ampoule around my neck, as if part of his soul was calling out for the rest of him. The container was still, but I could feel an energy brushing against me as his soul swirled within its cage.

"I had no desire to see you again so soon, but it seems you have something that belongs to me. I want it back," he said, his voice growing cold.

"I could say the same. Are you willing to make a trade?"

"Unfortunately, I can't do such a thing. I have a need for your patch of soul, though I'm sure you can't afford to be without what little you still possess."

"Then I guess you'll just have to come take it from me," I said, beckoning him forward.

Simon raised both of his hands, throwing a blue ball of lightning at me. I lunged out of the way, my arms scraping along the rough concrete as I landed on my stomach. I rolled onto my back so that I could see my attacker as I launched a similar attack. My ball of energy just missed as he slipped out of its path, letting it pound harmlessly against the brick wall behind him. The thick darkness of the alley was shoved aside in a brilliant flash. Shadows lunged away from us before the darkness flooded back in again, like bloodthirsty spectators eager for the first splash of red. The explosion of light lasted long enough for me to pick out some dark bruises and long cuts along Simon's face. I knew that I had caused some of that damage, but I wasn't responsible for it all. He had someone else causing him problems too.

I rolled to my knees when he threw the next ball of energy at me. A wave of pain tingled up my arms as I caught it in both hands. I gritted my teeth as the force shoved me backward, several feet across the concrete, but didn't waver. With a grunt, I threw the energy back at him and quickly followed it with my own. Simon easily dodged the first, but the second sent him spinning to the ground. Pushing to my feet, I thrust one hand toward the sky, summoning a boiling cauldron of black clouds. Thunder rolled above us and lightning jumped through the sky. A part of me longed for a nice sharp blade, but I would make do with the power from the heavens.

"Do you think that you actually have the strength to beat me with lightning?" Simon scoffed as he clambered to his feet again. I replied with a bolt landing just in front of him. The warlock stumbled backward, raising one arm to shield his eyes against the bright light that filled the small alley.

"There's nothing you can do that I can't do better!" he shouted. I concentrated on controlling the storm that hung right above us.

I had already pumped so much energy into it that if I wasn't careful I could quickly lose control of it. We couldn't afford the kind of devastation that would ravage the area if the storm slipped from me.

As I focused on directing more lightning at Simon, it felt as if a large hand wrapped around my throat and squeezed tightly, threatening to close off my breathing. I couldn't stop myself from raising both hands and clawing at nothingness as I struggled to catch my breath. The hand tightened and proceeded to pull me, on my back, across the open space behind the tattoo parlor. I commanded the lightning to pound the ground where Simon stood, but I was blind to his exact location. If I was lucky I would take him down before I was strangled to death.

And then the invisible hand released me. Holding my throat, I rolled onto my stomach and looked up at where Simon had last been standing. The air rushed from my lungs. Trixie stood behind him with one arm thrown across his chest, her other hand holding a large knife tightly against his throat. I don't know how she'd managed to sneak past us both unnoticed, but I wasn't going to question this change in events.

Shoving to my feet, I gathered together the energy swirling about me and reached out for Simon's soul once again. This time I would simply pull it from his body and release it into the air. The soul would not be able to reenter the body and the warlock would be dead. Sure, I would lose a year of my own life for killing him with magic, but it was a price I was willing to pay for Trixie. Only those with a death wish attacked a warlock.

As I pressed the energy into his chest, I could see Simon's eyes widen in shock. The warlock disappeared, preferring a hasty retreat rather than continue this fight. Whispered words tripped off my lips as I scanned the area with both my eyes and my powers. My breath lay trapped in my lungs for several seconds as I waited for him to reappear, but there was no lingering essence of him in the air. Simon was gone, and considering that he had suffered such a quick beating, I was willing to bet that he wouldn't be returning soon. I had some time to plan.

I breathed again as Trixie approached me, lowering her knife. Barefoot, she carefully picked her way across the pavement littered with rocks, broken glass, and bits of trash. She wore only a T-shirt and a pair of white panties. Noise from the struggle must have drawn her from bed. A part of me was grateful that Bronx had not heard the noise as well. It was bad enough that I now had to protect Trixie from Simon, I didn't want to worry about him exacting his revenge on the troll as well.

With the release of tension from my shoulders, the storm broke overhead. I had been carefully controlling it, manipulating its power so that I could pull forth one long string of lightning after another. Now all that was left was a cold shower of stinging rain that felt like an overturned bucket on our heads.

"Are you okay?" Trixie asked as she joined me. She folded her arms tightly over her stomach as her glamour-colored brown hair was plastered to her head and shoulders. Her thin clothes clung to her tanned skin, creating a contrast of shadows and shining rivers of water.

"Fine," I said through clenched teeth as I jerked my eyes away from her. Roughly grasping her elbow I led her over to the stairs that led to the second-floor apartment. "What do you think you were doing?"

"Helping you. It looked like you were getting your ass kicked," she replied stiffly, pulling her arm out of my hand.

"I was, but you shouldn't have taken such a risk."

"You're worth the risk."

"No! No, I'm not. Not when it comes to the fucking warlocks. Isn't it enough that you've got the damned Summer Court looking for you? Simon isn't going to overlook your attack. He's going to come after you now."

A flash of lightning snapped across the night sky, followed by a deep rumble of thunder. The cold rain washed over me and I half-expected to see steam rising as my temper rose to near the boiling point. I finally pull Trixie into my life and she risks hers by attacking a warlock. Another bolt of lightning slashed the sky, creating a large bang as it slammed into a telephone pole. Sucking in a calming breath, I forced myself to relax. The storm was still connected to me and I didn't need it to get out of hand because I couldn't control my temper.

Trixie laid her hand against my cheek, drawing my gaze back to her face. "He's a warlock. He had to know that I'm an elf."

"So?"

"So, the warlocks have given the elves a wide berth since the end of the Great War. He may keep his attention on you."

"The warlocks have given *the courts* a wide berth, not individual elves," I corrected. "Besides, if he finds out you're the missing elf, he may exact his revenge by just handing you over to the king of the Summer Court. Sometimes the best revenge isn't death."

Trixie glared at me, dropping her hand back to her side. "I can watch out for myself."

I bit my tongue, suppressing my every instinct to protect her. I was being unfair, even though the chest-beating Neanderthal inside me demanded that I drag her back inside the apartment by her hair. "Yes, I know you can watch out for yourself, and I'm grateful that you came to my rescue when you did. Just promise me that you won't attack another warlock any time soon, please."

Trixie narrowed her eyes at me, but she seemed to be fighting a smile. "I won't if you can avoid trouble for a little while."

A smirk tweaked one corner of my mouth despite my over-whelming fatigue. "I'll try."

"Go home, Gage. Get some sleep. You look like you're about to fall over."

"Great idea," I muttered. Sleep seemed like a distant sweet dream that I could never touch, a mirage dancing like a cool oasis in the middle of an arid desert. The day had been longer than I wanted to contemplate and tomorrow was going to be even worse. I still had to find a way to kill some innocent girl who had done nothing to me beyond walk in my front door.

20

"JUST KNOCK HIM out and let's get going."

"I can't."

I lay still, listening to the harshly whispered conversation flowing above me. The fog of sleep was dissipating fast and I recalled falling asleep on the couch in my living room after locking the door. I had told myself that I was going to stretch out for only a couple of minutes and that I would then set my protection spells and go to bed. Apparently, I never made it off the couch.

And now I had at least two unwelcome guests in my apartment, though I was grateful that at least one assailant was reluctant to attack me, but I didn't think that was going to last for long if I didn't do something.

"What do you mean you can't?"

"I mean . . . it's just that it's Gage. I can't knock Gage out. He's a good guy," argued the second voice, which I was finally able to recognize. Freddie the Moose. He stopped in the shop from time to time, getting fresh ink and generally catching up on local gossip. Nice guy, but definitely not the brightest bulb in the pack. Unfortunately, I didn't recognize the second voice, which was more adamant about me remaining unconscious.

"The boss said to fetch him and to be careful. Careful means unconscious."

Freddie's extended silence made me nervous. His friend's argument was starting to sway him and I needed to act before someone decided to take a baseball bat to my melon.

"You know, guys, you could just say please and I might come along quietly," I said as my eyes snapped open. Both large men jumped back. Freddie was stunned for a second before a wide grin spread across his face, cutting into his heavy jowls. The other man was a little warier, drawing a gun from heaven only knows where and leveling it at my chest.

Yawning wide enough to crack my jaw, I sat up and stretched my arms over my head. My body ached from yesterday's scuffles, and I felt filthy, but I didn't think Tweedledee and Tweedledum were going to let me slip into the shower. In fact, I didn't see coffee in my immediate future, which was enough to sour my mood. There were too many things I needed to get done, and I didn't have time to waste on unplanned appointments with a boss who felt the need to send two goons after me rather than just call.

"Afternoon, Gage!" Freddie greeted me. "Sorry we woke you."

Well, that answered my question as to whether I'd gotten any sleep. I still felt like crap, but I had apparently been dead to the world until after noon. "No problem, Moose. What do ya need?" I dropped my arms and leaned against the back of the couch while propping both my feet up on the coffee table in front of me.

"The boss needs to see you," Freddie said in an excited whisper as he leaned close.

"Who's the boss?"

"Mr. Roundtree would like to see you," the second man said, stepping a little closer as he relaxed his stance with the gun. He didn't put it away, but he wasn't pointing it at my chest anymore. I took a good look at him. Where Freddie was a giant mound of muscle and fat, this man was tall, broad shouldered, and full of what

I was willing to guess was lean muscle. Match that with his gold eyes, shaggy hair, the five o'clock shadow on his tan face, and a hint of a woodsy, musky scent and I knew that I was looking at a shifter, probably a werewolf.

I didn't know this Mr. Roundtree, but I knew the local mob that ran most of the city was composed heavily of pack creatures such as werewolves. I really didn't hope this had anything to do with Jack and the infamous Chihuahua incident. The local shady groups were nice enough to steer clear of me, and I dreaded finding out what had finally caught their attention. There just wasn't time for this shit.

"Look, I appreciate Mr. Roundtree sending the welcoming committee to fetch me, but could you tell him that I need to take a rain check?" Pushing to my feet, I started to walk between the couch and coffee table toward the hall and my bedroom. Freddie just continued to smile at me, but his companion wasn't smiling as he raised his gun. I stopped and glared at the shifter. "I've got things I really need to get done today. Maybe we could have drinks later in the week."

"Freddie!" the man barked.

"I'm really sorry, Gage," Freddie murmured. I twisted around to see him raise his meaty fist and then bring it down. I would have liked to think of a spell that would freeze everything or at least halt the descent of Freddie's fist. Instead, my only thought was that my day was already screwed. And then the world went black.

Holy shit! I'm drowning!

My eyes snapped open and my entire body jerked, fighting what I thought were swamping waves of water closing over my head. I sucked in a breath that wasn't filled with water and my gaze jumped around to find that I was sitting in a dimly lit bar or restaurant instead of bobbing out in the middle of the ocean. My eyes landed on a large man holding an empty pitcher. Apparently my host needed me conscious and I was awakened with a splash of ice-cold water. It could have been worse. I shifted in my seat, and was attempting to raise my hand to wipe off the excess water when I realized my hands were tied behind me. It *was* worse.

"It's unfortunate that we had to meet like this," announced a voice in front of me, drawing my attention away from one predicament to the next. I squinted, but could not make out my captor as he sat back in a dark booth. The hands folded on the table were encased in black leather gloves, sending a chill through me that had nothing to do with the ice cube sliding down the back of my shirt. The gloves hid what was most likely a revealing trait of his race, but I could already guess what was sitting across from me.

"As a business owner in Low Town, I figured that it was only a matter of time before I was approached by either you or one of your . . . associates," I replied, fighting to keep my voice flat and even. I wasn't in any physical danger, but I had to be careful if I wanted to get out of here without revealing all of my secrets.

When the inhabitants of the world weren't cowering in fear of the Ivory Towers, they were usually being harassed by the local organized crime families, particularly business owners in less than great neighborhoods. Asylum had been open for more than four years and I hadn't been approached by them until now. I didn't question my luck, hoping it was simply a case of Sparks putting in a good word for me. There was always the possibility that they were afraid of me, but something had changed, and not for the better.

"I'll admit that I've kept my eye on you, Mr. Powell, since you opened your quaint tattoo parlor. It's my understanding that you've been quite profitable."

I shifted in my seat, trying to find a more comfortable position that wasn't painful for my shoulders. "Helps being good at what you do, Mr. . . ."

"Reave. You may call me Reave. And, yes, you are good, aren't you?" There was something in his tone that made my blood run cold. I sat still, waiting to hear where this was going. I thought it was going to be a quick and maybe slightly painful meeting in which I would be told I would now be paying protection money.

"But you're only twenty-five, twenty-six?"

"Thereabouts."

"Pretty young for someone with your kind of skill. One might think that you've had some other kind of training."

I knew where this was going now. He suspected I was a warlock, but his approach didn't make any sense. Why was I attacked if he suspected I was a warlock? I could slaughter them all in the blink of an eye and walk out of there without a scratch. This mob boss seemed to think he had some sort of ace up his sleeve.

"What's your point? I'm a good tattoo artist, and I know how to stir a potion. There are a few people with those skills."

"But you have more than just a few interesting skills with a needle and ink. Jackson Wagnalls would certainly argue such."

"Who? Jackson Wag—" The blood rushed from my face as the name finally clicked in my brain. A part of me wanted to laugh at the ridiculously appropriate last name for the werewolf I'd turned into a Chihuahua, but I couldn't drag a breath into my lungs. This man had called me in because he did know I was something a little more than I pretended to be. The Chihuahua incident had come back to haunt me, but not in the way I had been anticipating.

"Yes, that Jack," the shadow man said with a chuckle. "Remember him now, or do you pass your afternoons amusing yourself by turning people into small mammals?" At that moment, one of the pack members I had seen the previous day walked up to the table from behind me, carrying Jack in one hand. The little dog growled and barked at me, flashing his tiny teeth in his irritation.

Narrowing my gaze on the dog, I sneered, "There are worse things than a Chihuahua. Try a fish out of water?"

Jack instantly fell silent with a whimper as he proceeded to tremble in the arms of his keeper. I looked back toward the shadows in time to see Reave raise one hand toward the werewolf and Jack, waving them away. He then motioned to me, as if prompting me to try to deny what we all knew.

"If you're so desperate to go down this road, let's do it correctly," I snapped. With a couple of whispered words, the ropes binding my wrists behind my back uncoiled like a snake unwrapping itself from around its prey. The rope then slithered across the room behind me, causing several of the men acting as guards in this meeting to gasp and curse as they moved out of the way. As I raised my arms, all the lights in the room came on. A quick glance around showed that I was in Strausse Haus Restaurant and Bier Garden, which wasn't too far from Asylum. Frowning, I turned my full attention back to my host, who was glaring at me.

Svartálfar.

Dark elf.

I was fucked.

The dark elves, or rather the Svartálfar, were known for only two things: ruthless cunning and merciless cruelty. I shouldn't have been surprised to find a dark elf running things, except for the fact that they didn't play well with others. But if you wanted to dominate a city like Low Town, there was no better way than to run it through the mafia.

"Pretty gutsy taking on a warlock," I said in a low voice. "I'm assuming that you had something in particular you wanted before I disembowel you and your associates."

To my surprise, the dark elf didn't flinch at my threat, as I had hoped he would. I knew a spell that would pull their intestines out of their belly buttons, but I had never actually used it and really didn't want to.

"Nice threat, but we both know that you won't do it." The elf chuckled, motioning for me to sit again while he removed his leather gloves. The dark elf was dark skinned, unlike his Summer and Winter Court brethren. So dark, in fact, that his skin held a bluish tint. It was a dead giveaway for their kind and nicely matched his long black hair and silvery gray eyes. "In fact, we know that you're not quite a warlock."

I froze, every muscle in my body tense as I waited for him to continue to explain how he had reached this conclusion. The Svartálfar reached down to the seat beside him in the booth and picked up a large piece of paper that he placed on the table.

"From what we've learned over the centuries, it takes a couple of decades to train a warlock or a witch, some even longer before they are considered full-fledged members of the Ivory Towers. And you're twenty-five, twenty-six? Kind of young."

"I'm a fast learner," I bit out, but my voice had lost all of its strength. I didn't like where this was going.

"And we all know that warlocks and witches live in the Ivory Towers. Not in little apartments on the west side of town."

"The Towers have gotten crowded."

"And warlocks never fight amongst themselves in front of the rabble." The dark elf flipped over the piece of paper to reveal that it was actually a large glossy photograph of the fight that had occurred the previous day between Simon and me in the middle of the street. There was a blue ball of energy between us. I couldn't tell from the picture who was throwing it, but it didn't matter. Not only did this Svartálfar have evidence that I was a former warlock, but he also knew I was on the outs with the rest of the Ivory Towers. This wasn't going to be pretty.

"I was . . . disowned," I admitted hesitantly. This was not something I wanted to discuss, particularly with a Svartálfar and the rest of his crew.

"What a shame for you," he replied with a smile that made my blood run cold. "So, it would seem that the Ivory Towers aren't a fan of yours and have banished you from their ranks. Yet you still have your powers. Interesting."

"What do you want, Reave?" I snarled, taking a step closer to the table.

"A business proposition."

"I'm not interested."

"I think you will be when I lay out your choices."

I clenched my fists at my sides and glared at the Svartálfar. "Which aren't really choices at all." There was no time for this game he was playing, but I couldn't leave. Not when he knew far too much about me. For now, I was just waiting for an opening.

"Your first choice, and really your best option, is to come work for me. You will be permitted to maintain your tattoo parlor, from which you will start paying me a percentage of the evening's take. And then on the random occasion, you will take care of a little business for me."

"And if I refuse?"

"Then we come down to the other two options. One is that I will hold an auction, where I will sell your evil warlock ass to the highest bidder. There isn't a race around that doesn't remember the pain of the Great War, and I'm sure I will find someone who would be happy to pay a nice price for the chance to spend many years torturing you. Or maybe just burn you in effigy during halftime at the championship football game coming up later this summer.

"The second option is to simply hand you over to the Ivory Towers. There has to be someone who would like to get his hands on you."

A stone sank in the pit of my stomach as I listened to Reave detail my options. There was more than one warlock or witch who would like to end my existence and that list started with Simon Thorn. And Reave was right in that there were more than a few races that would like the opportunity to slaughter a warlock, regardless of whether I had anything to do with the Great War. In almost all cases, witches and warlocks were all the same. I was just one of those rare exceptions. Maybe the only exception.

"Look, Reave, I think you need to consider this a little better. Who says that I'm going to allow you to pursue any of those options? I am a warlock after all."

"A warlock who has had his wand taken away. In the four-plus years that you've had a shop, this is the only evidence we have of your using magic," Reave countered, waving the glossy picture in front of me. "In battle with another warlock. I'm beginning to think that you've been banned from spell casting. But then, if I'm wrong, strike me down now. Attack me with magic and I'll set you free, never to bother you again."

Attack was the sticking point at that moment. I couldn't attack. I was only permitted to defend, and even then I was on thin ice. If I attacked Reave or any of the brutes filling the closed bar, Gideon would have to have my head on a platter to serve up before the council. Staring at Reave, I mentally ran through the list of spells I could sling across the room with a quick word or two and maybe a flick of my wrist. Of course, I could think of nothing that wouldn't immediately kill, and there wasn't shit that Gideon wouldn't instantly detect. I was in serious trouble. I had to escape Reave and his cohorts the old-fashioned way or I was going to be lynched.

Reave leaned forward and smiled wide enough to show that some of his perfectly white teeth had been filed to sharp fangs. "So I thought." His gaze darted to someone behind my left shoulder a couple of seconds before large hands gripped my arms and shoulders. "I'll be generous and give you a little time to think about my offer. I'll expect your cooperation before dawn."

The hands holding me started to pull me backward through the bar, but we didn't get far before Reave's voice rang out again. "And don't forget: he may be a warlock, but he can't do anything to you."

A deep chuckle rose up beside me just before a fist smashed into my jaw, snapping my head around. Reave's muscle had finally figured out the full implications of my discussion with their boss. I was a warlock, one of the group that had killed and tortured millions over long centuries, but I couldn't retaliate with magic.

Of course, that didn't mean I was without options. Relying on the hands that were still holding me in place, I leaned all my weight on them as I pulled my legs up and kicked my assailant in the chest. The large beefy man flew backward, crashing into tables and chairs, sending furniture flying. Another man released me in surprise and I took advantage of it. Swinging my fist around, I connected with a nose. Bone crunched under my fist, followed by a gush of blood. I managed a couple more swings before I was brought down by more assailants than I could handle in the confined space.

Awash in a surge of pain, my last clear thought was on Freddie as he stood slightly off to the side, looking afraid and more than a little worried. I focused just a little power on him so that my thoughts penetrated his. As blackness crept around my eyes and ribs broke under a well-placed kick, I left him with the compulsion to find Bronx and tell him everything. With consciousness slipping through my fingers, I prayed that he did.

21

THE SCRAPE AND crunch of heavy footsteps along concrete woke me, but I was soon left wishing that I had remained unconscious. My head throbbed in time with my heartbeat, bones were broken, organs were bruised, and there was a nasty copperish taste in my mouth from all of my own blood I had swallowed while I was out. This was becoming too much of a recurring theme in my life and I could really do without it. Whoever said a warlock's life was glamorous, filled with naked moonlit orgies and pixie livers, was an idiot.

My entire body flinched at the sound of the metal bolt scraping as it was pulled across the door to the little room I was in. A groan escaped me as a fresh wave of pain rippled up my nerve endings; I had yet to even attempt to sit up. My room was pitch-black except for a little sliver of light seeping under the door. I didn't know what time it was, but I didn't think I had been knocked out for the entire day and through the night. I couldn't see Reave yet. I hadn't had a chance to figure a way out of this mess.

I cringed as the door swung open, hoping that I wasn't faced with another beating.

"Oh, man! Gage! They beat the crap out of you!" moaned Freddie. His knees creaked and popped as he squatted down in front of me just beyond the open doorway.

"Yeah, Freddie. It's been a real bang-up day," I muttered, closing my eyes with relief. He didn't act as if he was about to kick the shit out of me, so I figured I was in the clear for now. I lay still, trying to collect my thoughts. I knew a couple of healing spells that would at least mend the worst of my injuries and shouldn't draw too many questions from Gideon if he noticed. However, the sound of another set of feet on the concrete had my eyes snapping open again, sending a fresh stab of pain through my brain.

Turning my head slightly so I could look up, I found Bronx staring down at me with a frown cutting into his broad face. His pale blond hair seemed to glow in the overhead light, while his brow cast his eyes in shadow. Apparently, the compulsion I'd pushed into Freddie's mind had worked. Sort of. I had hoped that Bronx would help me get out of this mess, but I was also hoping that he wouldn't be so obvious in his approach. I had wanted him to sneak in and then sneak me out. It was probable that Bronx had caught the attention of Reave. Not a good thing.

"Bronx," I rasped, laying my head back against the cool concrete floor. "I wasn't expecting you."

"Uh-huh. Tell me another." Bronx's sarcasm rumbled over me and I smiled, ignoring the pain that lanced through my split bottom lip. There really wasn't any use in trying to hide anything from the troll.

"It's not as bad as it looks."

"It will be when Trixie gets a look at you."

I groaned, squeezing my eyes shut. I definitely had to use a healing spell now. If Trixie saw me looking like I had been dragged through the city behind a pickup truck and then trampled by elephants, she'd knock the shit out of me as soon as I was healed. And that's nothing compared to the earful I'd receive while I healed. Besides, she had enough to worry about and didn't need this as well.

"How'd you get in?" I asked, trying to summon the energy to move.

The shuffle of feet and a grunt from Freddie drew my attention away from my pain. The thug had stood and moved out of the room so Bronx could approach. "Back door." My friend reached down, placing his large hands under my arms, and lifted me to my feet. A pained hiss slipped through my clenched teeth, but otherwise I managed to keep from shouting. "Can you move?"

I nodded, feeling my brain slosh around in my skull. "In a minute."

Bronx turned his head and looked at Freddie. "Tell Reave that I'll bring him in a few minutes."

"You've met Reave?"

The troll positioned me so that his hands were on either side of my chest as he held me up in front of him. He heaved a heavy sigh as his eyes darted away from me before wandering back. "I've had dealings with Reave in the past."

"Worked for him?"

Bronx flinched at the question, but continued to meet my gaze. "For a while."

"Well, at least you got out. Changed occupations."

"And yet, here I stand."

It was my turn to flinch. Because of me, Bronx was back in his old boss's clutches, putting him in a very vulnerable and awkward position. I couldn't imagine that it had been that easy to leave the first time and I doubted that it would be all that easy to leave tonight. "I'm sorry, Bronx. I didn't know. If I had, I wouldn't have sent Freddie for you."

"Not your fault, and if you hadn't sent Freddie, I would have been pissed." Bronx lowered his head and narrowed his eyes on me, his face taking on a more menacing quality. "And you don't want to see me pissed."

I smiled again at his attempt to scare me. "Trixie's right about you. You are a big teddy bear."

Bronx snorted. "You say that again and I'll let you fall on your ass."

"Actually, you ought to let me go so I can take care of this mess."

Bronx stepped back and dropped his hands to his sides. I stumbled a step backward as my legs were forced to support my own weight. Pain curled through my body, eating away at conscious thought for a moment before I managed to rise above it and concentrate on my healing spell. Closing my eyes, I focused on the spell, sending a wave of energy through my body so that it washed up from my feet to the top of my head. When the last of the energy dissipated, I breathed a sigh of relief. I still ached and my head throbbed a bit, but the broken and fractured bones were mended. My organs were no longer bruised and I felt like I could stand without falling over.

"You look a little better," Bronx admitted, crossing his arms over his massive chest.

"Good. Now, let's go kick Reave's ass."

I tried to take a step forward, but Bronx laid a restraining hand on my shoulder. "Gage, you can't."

"What?"

"If you were going to kick ass, particularly with magic, you would have done it already. At least you should have done it already, scaring Reave off. But you didn't or couldn't, doesn't matter. Freddie told me what's going on." Bronx paused, his shoulders slumping. His hand on my shoulder tightened, as if sympathizing or reassuring me. "You need to accept his offer."

"Are you insane? I'm not working for that murdering, conniving asshole!" I shouted, pointing toward the open door behind him.

"I don't see that you've got much choice. Death or Reave's offer." I dropped my hand, but continued to glare over the shoulder of my friend. Work for the mob. What a horrible, gut-twisting thought! My business was honest, relatively so, and it was my own. There were no threats or shakedowns. I didn't escape the authority of the Ivory Towers to now find myself under the thumb of a Svartálfar.

"Are you still working for them? Were you sent to my shop to spy on me and get me to bend to Reave's demands?"

Bronx gave me a hard shove. My back slammed against the wall in the dark room and I slumped there for several seconds as his low growl sent a shiver of fear through my intestines. "I left Reave's association. It was ugly and hard, but I did it. I haven't been back in contact with him or his people in over five years. Not until now and only because you needed me."

My heart lurched in my chest as I looked at my friend. What had I done to Bronx by dragging him here? What was he risking? "Bronx, I'm sorry. I—I didn't mean it," I stammered, hating myself.

The troll's shoulders slumped a little bit, but his face was still an unreadable mask. "I know you didn't. No one wants to find themselves in this position, and you just have to make the best of it. Death isn't an option. Trixie would never forgive either of us if I let you make that choice. We'll find a way out of this."

Staring at Bronx standing in the light of the open doorway, his head slightly bowed and his shoulders slumped, I realized that he was right. It wasn't just my life that was on the line when it came to Reave. If Reave handed me over to the Ivory Towers or to a lynch mob, I was done and Trixie was still in trouble with the Summer Court. It also didn't solve Tera's immortality problem. Furthermore, Bronx would once again find himself in the clutches of the Svartálfar. Of course, if I killed Reave, we'd all be in the clear. Unfortunately, I'd need to use a spell or two to accomplish that and then Gideon would kill me. And I was back at square one.

Forcing one corner of my mouth up in a smile, I pushed off the wall and patted Bronx on the shoulder as the troll stepped out of the doorway and into the hallway. "We'll figure something out," I murmured, my eyes slipping over the pair of armed figures standing at the end of the hallway. One particularly ugly troll with an eye patch stared at Bronx, a smug grin on his fat lips.

"Always knew you'd be back," the troll said as he leaned against the wall, blocking our way.

"Just a little business, Covington." Bronx didn't even look at the other troll as he stood, waiting for him to move so that we could continue on our way to talk to Reave.

The one-eyed troll leaned close to Bronx, crowding him, but my companion didn't waver despite the obvious threat. I clenched my fists at my sides, fighting to keep my mouth shut. "You think it's goin' to be that easy? You'll just slide back into your old spot?"

"I don't want anything to do with Reave and his associates."

"Trust me, you'll be begging to be welcomed back before Reave's done with you and him. And then you'll have to follow what I say."

"Doubtful."

The troll snarled as he stepped back. His large fist swung at Bronx, aimed for his face. Bronx leaned back just in time to see the punch slide by him, while he placed a hand on my chest to hold me back so that I wouldn't be hit as well. I waited long enough for Bronx to drop his hand before I launched myself at the unknown troll. Threading my fingers together, I slammed my doubled fist into the troll's face, snapping his head back as blood exploded from his large nose. As he stumbled backward, I kicked him between the legs, bringing the troll to his knees with a high-pitched cry of pain. It was a low blow and one I didn't often use, but the troll was more than twice my weight and had three times my strength. He was going to rip my head off. Sometimes you have to even the playing field in order to survive. Besides, he was harassing Bronx, and my friend didn't deserve it.

To my surprise, Bronx stepped forward and wrapped one arm around my waist. Picking me up, the troll carried me at his side down the hallway, past the wheezing troll I had attacked and his shocked companion.

"You can't help it!" Bronx barked, raising his voice for the first time since I'd met him. "You have to get in trouble no matter where you go."

"I do not!"

"My experiences with you prove otherwise."

I struggled against his grip, but it didn't budge. Bronx was undoubtedly right, but he didn't need to carry me around like a disobedient child. "Put me down!"

"Can you restrain yourself until we get out of here?"

"Possibly." I wasn't going to make any promises that I couldn't keep and we still had to face Reave.

Bronx made a sound in the back of his throat that didn't sound encouraging, but he paused long enough to let me return to my own feet before he walked down a set of dark stairs to the main room of the Strausse Haus.

"Try. I don't have any plans to die here today."

With that, my temper instantly deflated. I decided it was time to shut my mouth and start thinking because it wasn't just my life and future that were on the line. My actions would also have an impact on what happened to Bronx from here on out and I needed to stop acting like an idiot.

Reave was standing at the bar, talking to the bartender, when we entered the room. He straightened and smiled at us before returning to the same booth he had been sitting in when I'd first met him. The lights in the bar were on, but shadows still crowded thickly in Reave's booth, making it a little difficult to read his expressions. Not that elves were known for being the most expressive, but it would have helped.

"Bronx, it's so wonderful to see you again! Come for a visit?" Reave asked in mocking tones that instantly had me wanting to throw him into the wall of alcohol bottles behind the bar. When the dark elf failed to get a rise out of the troll, he turned his attention to me. Leaning forward so that he could rest his forearms on the table, he moved into a shaft of light, revealing a particularly evil grin. "Gage, you're looking . . . healed. Ready to talk?"

"It doesn't seem like I've been left with much choice," I said, forcing a lightness in my voice that I didn't feel.

"It really doesn't have to be that way." Reave settled back into the booth again, letting the shadows wrap their arms around him. "This could be a quite enjoyable arrangement for all involved if you just relax and do as I request."

"What exactly will you be requesting of me?"

"Oh, nothing too taxing for a former Ivory Towers resident. I've got a few places of business that could use some protection spells. Maybe a cloaking spell or two. I'm sure you're talented enough to handle something like that."

I crossed my arms over my chest while shifting from my left to my right foot. "Fine." Right now, it didn't sound too bad. The places he would send me would naturally be places where he housed the bulk of his illegal activities, but no one would be hurt by those spells. Unfortunately, I was sure that Reave would up the ante as time went by, compromising my morals a step at a time until I was in way over my head. I had to get out as soon as possible.

"There will be a few other errands here and there. Not too much. I don't want to interfere with your tattoo parlor."

"I'm not going to hurt anyone for you, so just get that out of your head now."

"No need for that. I've got plenty of muscle in my employ already. You're a fine instrument to be used for delicate procedures. Creatures, like your friend Bronx, are blunt objects used for basic things such as enforcement."

I clenched my teeth so tightly my jaw began to throb. I wanted to hit him, throw him, hurt him in some way, either with my bare hands or with magic. It didn't matter. I hated that Bronx was forced to stand there with me and endure his derisive remarks. Bronx was a skilled artist and a compassionate friend. He deserved to be treated with respect.

A large hand landed on my shoulder and gently squeezed. I looked up to find Bronx watching me, a half smile tilting up one corner of his mouth. It was only then that I noticed a crackle in the air. The lights in the bar were flickering and the sound of static crinkled around us from the charge of magic in the air. In my anger, I had summoned up energy, but wasn't releasing it, so the charge was building around us. Cocking my head to the side, I cracked my neck and released a slow breath out of my mouth to unroll the tension from my body. At the same time, the energy in the air dispersed and everything was quiet once again.

"Interesting," Reave murmured. He folded his hands together while remaining back in the shadows. I had little doubt that he also could sense the energy I had pulled together. "Since it seems that Bronx has a positive influence on you, I will generously allow him to serve as your backup. Think of him as someone to watch your back when you go on an errand for me."

"What?" I shouted at the dark elf, the exclamation bursting from me in a thoughtless rush. "You can't do that! He doesn't work for you."

"Of course he does."

"I left," Bronx said.

"You tried to, but look, here you are."

Stepping forward, I slapped both hands down on the table and leaned toward Reave so that I could clearly see his face. "He didn't come back to you. He only came to get me. Let him out of this."

Reave smiled, his gray eyes seeming to peer into my soul. "He knew when he entered this building that he would have to return to my employment if he wanted to get you out. So he did, and I'm not letting him go. It's not so much that he's a fantastic errand boy. It's more that his presence will make it easier for you to obey me. Accept it, Gage."

I shoved off the table and paced away from Reave. A quick glance around the bar revealed more than two dozen creatures lingering, closely watching the conversation. Too many for both Bronx and me to take on physically. My only means of successful attack was through magic. Kill Reave with magic and Gideon kills me. Refuse

Reave's offer and the dark elf hands me over to the Ivory Towers and probably still kills Bronx. Agree to his offer . . . and we both live.

Glancing over my shoulder, I locked eyes with Bronx. There was no anger or blame in his gaze. He didn't blame me for dragging him into this no-win situation, but I blamed myself. And I would find a way to get him out of this mess. To do that, we both had to live.

"All right, Reave. You win," I conceded, turning back around to face the Svartálfar. "What do you want me to do?"

"Right now? Nothing." There was a grin in the dark elf's voice as he claimed his victory. "You've had a rough day and I would prefer to have you in top form when I send you to work. You'll be contacted in a few days."

With that, we were dismissed from Reave's presence, but I could feel the shackle on my ankle. The only plus was that it was likely that the grim reaper was going to claim my soul in two days, freeing me of Reave, but Bronx would still be trapped.

Freddie stepped forward and motioned for Bronx and me to move toward the front door of the bar. Bronx followed me as we silently filed from the building, just grateful to be away from Reave and his companions. It wasn't until we were standing on the sidewalk, under the moonlight, in the warm night air that I started to breathe again. Looking up at Bronx in the nearby lamplight, I frowned as the weight of what had happened crushed down on my chest.

"Don't say it," Bronx warned. "I would have come no matter what. Reave would have found a way to drag me back in sooner or later. I'm just glad that he's teamed us up. Someone needs to keep an eye on you."

"I'll get you out of this," I vowed, clenching my right hand in a fist at my side.

"I know you will." Bronx tilted his head down the street toward a row of parked cars. "Come on. I'll give you a ride home."

I paused, staring almost blindly down the street. The day had been a total bust. I had planned on contacting a few people, trying to dig up an answer to my problem with Tera and her immortality. Instead, I had spent it unconscious, lying in a pool of my own blood. What's more, I still needed to figure out what to do about Trixie's dilemma, and now I also had to find a way to get Bronx free of our current bind. I needed to think, and I didn't do my best thinking at home.

"I'm going to stop by the shop. I'll catch a cab later."

"You sure?"

I nodded, forcing a smile on my lips when I really didn't have anything to smile about.

Bronx started down the street, toward his car, but stopped when he was only a couple of feet away. "I talked to Trixie just before I got here."

"She okay?"

"Yeah, a little bored, but good."

"Did you . . . tell her . . . about this?"

Bronx snorted and a wide grin cut across his face. "I'm not crazy. I'll let you tell her."

Chuckling, I waved to Bronx before turning and heading in the opposite direction, toward the shop. The laughter quickly faded as I got closer to Asylum. On my giant list of things to do before my life and my friends' lives were destroyed, I needed to first tackle Tera, the grim reaper, and the sticky problem of curing immortality. I could think of only one group that might know the answer and only one person who by some extraordinarily slim chance might be willing to help me. But asking wasn't going to be easy.

22

LIGHT CUT THROUGH the front window, sliding along the jagged glass teeth that rose from the edge of the case at the back of the lobby. The parlor was blanketed in a sickening, heavy silence. There was no magic in the air, as the antiglamour spell that generally encased the shop expired after twenty-four hours. There was no reason for me to reset it. I was hoping not to stay too long, and I wasn't planning to welcome in any customers. Only one person was going to stop by the shop tonight.

I thought about zipping up to the second-floor apartment to see Trixie, but I was only procrastinating. Seeing her would be a vain wish that she might be able to talk me out of my present course, which appeared to be quite suicidal at the moment. There wasn't any other choice. If I wanted to help Trixie, if I wanted to help Bronx, I needed to help myself first and that meant contacting Gideon.

Standing in the center of the lobby, on the old rug that covered up yet another of my crimes, I closed my eyes and focused on the energy swirling about me like small breezes dancing from all corners of the earth. Some energy I could use easily. Some energy I couldn't touch. Some energy I refused to tap. Selecting from the bands of magic that hovered close, I placed a dampening shell over the shop so that no one could overhear my conversation. I paused, opening and closing my hands at my sides. Did I just send out a call for Gideon, summoning him to my side? Which I'm sure would just piss him off. Or did I cast a spell that I shouldn't be using, and wait for him to show up to reprimand me? Which would also have him on my doorstep pissed off.

I dropped my hands, slapping them against my legs as I tilted my head back to stare at the ceiling. This was yet another no-win situation. I was going to piss off the man I really needed help from no matter what I did. And a mad Gideon was unlikely to be a helpful Gideon.

A loud banging on the front door of the shop echoed through the empty building. I jumped, nearly tripping over my own feet in my haste to twist around and see who was there. Just as my heart was returning to its normal pace, it skipped again at the sight of Gideon glaring at me through the window in the door. A small part of me was relieved to see that I didn't have to summon him, but I was looking at a mad Gideon, which meant I'd already done something that pissed him off. Hell, this really was turning out to be a shitty day.

Swallowing against the knot of anxiety that was tightening in my throat, I walked over to the door and unlocked it. Gideon was silent as he entered the room, not bothering to look directly at me as he swept by. This was one of the rare moments when I was alone in a room with Gideon. The warlock usually captured me while I was outside as I moved to or from my car. I think he liked to have plenty of room to knock the crap out of me. Now, the tattoo parlor felt smaller with him present, almost suffocating.

I turned away from him and closed the door. The bolt had barely slid home when it felt as if a hand was snaking around my spine, jerking me off my feet as I was pulled backward across the room. My breath exploded from my lungs as I hit the glass case at the back of the lobby. Sitting on the floor, I looked up to find Gideon standing over me, his arms folded on his chest, looking less than pleased to be here.

My thoughts were a jumble as I struggled to think of what I had done that day to bring him to my doorstep. Other than getting beat up by a collection of trolls, ogres, and humans, it had been a quiet day. I had healed myself and cast a silence spell. Hardly stuff to catch his attention. Unless he was there because of the spells I'd been slinging around the previous night to protect Trixie. I inwardly cringed. That stuff would definitely catch his attention and put him in a foul mood.

"Gideon, what a surprise," I said around a groan as I tried to push to my feet. I might have healed from my earlier scuffle with Reave's goons, but my body was still sore and resisting even more punishment.

"I find that hard to believe."

"If this is about last night, I can explain—"

Gideon paced away from me, wandering over to the large picture window to look up and down the street. If I hadn't thought it to be completely impossible, I would have said he was nervous. "Save your stories."

Wincing at the pain that shot through my back as I got to my feet, I walked to the center of the room, cautiously approaching the warlock. "I had a good reason for what I did and no one was hurt. It was a type of self-defense."

Gideon turned to look at me, frowning. "Yes, but I'm sure that when the council handed down their decision, they made it clear that the self they were referring to was you, not an elf you happen to be infatuated with."

I stepped back, my mouth falling open. Not only did Gideon have me on that technicality, but he knew more about my life than I wanted to contemplate. The warlock was supposed to keep an eye on my magic use, not every moment of my life and who was in it.

"She needed my help," I said softly.

"So I saw." His frown faded as his eyes shifted over my shoulder. I twisted around to see that he was looking at the broken glass case. "I was surprised that you didn't do something more . . . decisive when you were put through that."

"Are you serious?" I said, snapping back around to stare at him. "You would have had my head if I'd attacked them with magic. Err . . . right?"

Gideon chuckled, a thin smile pulling at his mouth. "I guess we'll never know."

"You're an asshole, you know that?"

"It's one of the few joys I have in life."

I threw my hands up and walked over to the bench that lined the back wall. Flopping down on the hard surface, I extended my legs in front of me and crossed my ankles before crossing my arms over my chest. I should have been calm, reminding myself that he hadn't beaten me to a pulp yet, threatened me, or even whisked me off to the North American Ivory Tower as he should have. Instead I was focused on the fact that the warlock was a freaking Peeping Tom. He sat back and watched my life unfold like some damned soap opera.

"If you're so aware of what I've been up to, why didn't you do something about this afternoon when I was getting the shit knocked out of me?"

Gideon slid his hands into the pockets of his expensive trousers and relaxed his stance, seeming genuinely amused by my question. "You mean, help you? I'm your warden, not your baby-sitter, Gage. When you get into a fight, you have to take care of it yourself."

"And you and the Towers don't care that I was beaten because they know I'm a former warlock. They know because people witnessed my fight with Simon in the middle of the fucking day. If Simon hadn't attacked me, today's mess would never have happened."

"If you want to effectively hide your past, you have to do what all the other mortals do."

"And that is?"

"Don't fight back."

Slamming my feet on the floor, I stood and stomped over to the warlock. "Unless you're planning to haul me in front of the council, or just do their dirty work now, leave. Leave now because I can't take anymore. Nearly every witch and warlock I've met since I was seven has made my life a living hell. I don't want to be one of you. I never did, but now I'm stuck tiptoeing around the lot of you for the rest of my life. To add to that, I could be hunted down by the people I'm trying to live among because I was sucked in by your group. I'm sick of it. Sick!"

Gideon arched one eyebrow at me, but didn't look all that perturbed by my outburst. "Are you done?"

"Yes."

"Feel better?"

I released a pent-up breath and it felt like all the anger and frustration whooshed out of my body with the air, leaving me feeling light headed and a little dazed. "Yeah," I said with a giggle. "Now get out."

"As much as I would like to leave, I can't."

"Why?"

Gideon motioned to the lobby with both hands held out to his sides. "The silence spell. I can imagine only two reasons for your casting it. You're either meeting with someone and don't want me to hear, or you wanted to get my attention. As to the first, I will kindly offer a warning. You're about a hairsbreadth away from me killing you, and a meeting that you don't want me to hear will undoubtedly tip the scales toward death. As to the second, you must be in some serious trouble if you need to talk to me. I'm here. So get talking before the last of my good mood melts away."

I snorted. "This is a good mood?"

"Have I killed you yet?"

"No."

"Then I'm in a good mood."

It was a struggle not to roll my eyes, but I managed. Gideon in a good mood. Next thing he was going to tell me was that he was actually a really nice guy and would prefer not to live with the other monsters in the Ivory Towers. Fat chance.

Several seconds ticked by before I managed to get my mind back on track and focused on the most pertinent problem at hand. *Tera. Grim reaper. Immortality.* This wasn't going to be an easy discussion, and after it was all done, I had to find a way to keep the feather out of Gideon's hands as well as anyone else's living in the Ivory Towers.

Clenching and unclenching my hands in front of me, I walked to the door and checked the lock again, simply needing to be moving. A moving target was harder to hit, right? "It seems I've had a bit of a problem with a recent potion I stirred." It was as good a start as any, allowing me to slowly work up to the issue at hand. I wanted to make him swear to never tell a soul or try to get the angel feather, but there wasn't a chance of me getting a promise out of Gideon. I just had to plunge forward and try to repair the damage that had been done.

"You? A bad potion? But you're known to be such a stupendous tattoo artist."

I spun around on my heel and lurched at him. "Damn it! This is serious, Gideon," I snapped.

The warlock was considerate enough to finally wipe the smug look off his face and at least appear to be serious. "Fatal?"

"No, not fatal," I slowly said, looking away from him to stare at the intricate design of the rug under my feet.

"Bad ingredients?"

"No. As far as I can tell, the ingredients were perfect."

"Then what? What's the issue here? You have to tell me plainly. I'm not in the mood for twenty questions and I have a number of other things I'd rather be doing tonight."

"I made a girl immortal."

Gideon's mouth opened and closed three times without a sound being made. He looked like a fish out of water, gasping blindly for a breath. I had started to turn away from him, shoving one hand through my hair, when Gideon suddenly grasped my shoulders, turning me so that I had to face him.

"Are you sure?" he demanded with a frightening desperation.

"Yes."

"Are you? Did you try to kill her? She can't die?"

"Yes. I mean, no."

Gideon gave me a hard shake, his fingers biting into my arms. "Which is it?"

"Yes, I'm sure!"

"You tried to kill her?"

"No, but a visit from a very angry grim reaper is pretty damn convincing. She also confirmed that her cancer is gone."

Gideon released me as if his fingers had been scorched by my flesh. He took a couple of steps backward, the desperation and fear on his face replaced by cold nothingness. "Tell me everything."

I did. I started with the moment when Tera first walked into my shop, telling him everything that she told me that evening. I detailed to Gideon the thoughts that ran through my mind, the designs I came up with, and even the exact ingredients I used. He had to know it all if he was going to be able to help me. I kept talking, telling him about the visit from the grim reaper, my timetable, and Tera's visit when she confirmed that she was completely cured.

When I was finally done talking, I noticed that Gideon was now seated on the bench. Even in the dim light filling the room from the streetlamp, he looked paler. He stared blindly straight ahead, saying nothing.

An uneasy silence filled the shop. There were a thousand things I wanted to say. I was afraid that he would just shrug his shoulders and walk away. He didn't have to do anything. In two days, the grim reaper was going to kill me if I didn't fix this. Gideon's problems would be solved. But it was bigger than that. Someone couldn't be left walking the earth immortal. Tera would figure it out eventually and it would cause massive problems. I didn't say anything, waiting to see what decision Gideon reached before I panicked.

The warlock's voice was soft and haunted when he spoke. "You have to fix this."

I breathed a sigh of relief, biting back my initial sarcastic response. Being an asshole wasn't going to help Gideon think. "I agree."

"Have you told anyone what you've done? How you did it?" Gideon started speaking a little faster, as if his thoughts were starting to congeal once again.

"Just my old tattooing mentor, Atticus Sparks. He's the one who gave me . . . the—"

"I get it," he snapped, glaring at me. But his anger melted before my eyes and he shook his head. "It could have been worse." Gideon leaned forward, placing his elbows on his knees while dropping his head into his hands.

"Do you have any ideas about how to fix this?" I ventured cautiously. Somehow Gideon was managing not to explode at me and I didn't need to tip him in that direction. When he remained silent, I pressed on. "I've considered hundreds of ingredients, all kinds of poisons and lethal items, but nothing seems powerful enough. I don't have time for trial and error. I have to get it right the first time. Any thoughts?"

"One."

"What? I'll try anything at this point."

"There's only one place where someone knows as much about death as heaven and that's the underworld's upper minions." The warlock paused, lifting his head to look at me and frown. "Charon and the rivers that lead to final judgment. Those rivers separate the humans from the upper and lower worlds, marking the journey into the land of the dead. A drop from one or all of those rivers should succeed in separating the girl from her soul, freeing her to travel to Charon and the underworld."

"You think?"

"In every story I've ever read, even the gods up on high steer clear of Charon and his rivers. Charon knows death, and he rides the rivers that carry the souls to the end." For one rare moment, a look of sympathy crossed Gideon's face as he stared at me. His expression was sad and worn, showing the weight of his existence for the first time. And then just as quickly, it was gone. "In all honesty, I don't know. It was sheer luck that you made her immortal in the first place, so I think it's going to be sheer luck that gets you out of this mess. Try a little River Styx when you tattoo her again. You either kill her or you don't."

"That's true," I agreed grimly. His logic made sense. I had used something from a heavenly body to get me in this mess, now I needed something from the other end to get me out of it. "Any chance you've got some water from the River Styx?"

Gideon shook his head as he pushed to his feet. "I don't know of anyone who's ever had that on hand. Not exactly easy stuff to acquire."

"Are you sure? Simon keep a bottle around? Dab a little behind his ear each morning to lure the devil to his side?"

"Doubtful. If he did, I'm sure he would have slipped some into your morning oatmeal many years ago."

"Thanks," I grumbled.

"As much as I hate to think of it being out there, I would try the black market first. There are some very resourceful people there."

"Seems like it would be incredibly rare. What if I strike out?"

"Then contact me immediately. We'll think of something else."

"There won't be time," I said with a shake of my head.

"Gage," Gideon said in a warning tone.

"I'll go after it myself if I have to."

"You have to die to go after it."

"I'm going to die in two days anyway if I don't succeed." I leaned forward and patted Gideon on the shoulder a couple of times, causing his frown to deepen. "If this all works out, I'll catch up with you in a few days. We can grab lunch and talk about shit that doesn't involve me getting killed."

"We can find another way."

"I doubt there is one."

The warlock nodded, slipping his left hand into his pocket while he lifted his right hand to check the time on his watch. "If you don't succeed, I will grab the girl and hold her in the Towers. I'll find a way to take care of her. We can't risk someone else finding out."

"Thanks," I mumbled, my stomach twisting at the thought of Tera being locked away in one of the Ivory Towers for the rest of her very long existence while a warlock worked to kill her. I'm sure it wasn't what she had in mind when she finally got the cure for her cancer.

"Regardless, you destroy that feather before your time is up. It can't fall into anyone else's hands no matter what."

I stared at the ground, trying to organize my thoughts and push past the guilt. "I will."

"And, Gage, one last thing."

As my head popped up to look at Gideon, his fist slammed into my nose. I stumbled backward until I finally fell on my ass. Raising my hand to my sore nose, I felt blood trickling past my fingers. I gazed up at Gideon to find him standing over me with his hands in his pockets, looking very calm and collected.

"Never again talk to me like you did earlier or the grim reaper will be the least of your concerns." With a quick nod of his head, Gideon turned and walked out of the shop.

Flopping back on the floor, I closed my eyes and murmured a quick spell to stop the bleeding so that it wasn't pouring down the back of my throat. What a fucking bad day! I didn't get a lot accomplished other than ruining Bronx's and my lives, but at least I had a lead. And for some bizarre reason, Gideon hadn't tried to kill me for what I had done or tried to get the angel feather. Too strange. It didn't make sense, but not much was as I lay on the floor thinking about my life. For now, I would just add Gideon's odd behavior to the growing list of things to look into once I cleaned up my mess with the grim reaper.

It was too late to head to the black market. I didn't have enough cash on me, nothing for trade, and the timing was just off. The black market kept a rotating schedule to avoid the Ivory Towers hassle and the other riffraff, while making it easier on other creatures who were bound by certain hours of the day. I would have to pop by to-morrow and see if my luck held.

23

SQUINTING AGAINST THE bright midday glare of the sun, I sipped my black coffee from my environmentally correct paper cup as I walked toward Diamond Dolls down the nearly empty sidewalk. I was on the other side of Low Town from Asylum. While run-down and slightly sleazy, this neighborhood didn't appear to be too dangerous shortly before one in the afternoon on a Monday. Most people were either at work or still in bed from another late night—the same place I felt I should be. By the time I finished checking on the protection spells outside Trixie's apartment and got to my own apartment, it was after three in the morning when I fell into my own bed fully clothed.

Despite a restless night, I was up relatively early. The problem with Tera was beating on my brain and time was slipping away from me. It also didn't help that I wasn't fond of being away from Trixie. I hadn't seen her at all yesterday, as I had promised, and though Bronx reassured me that she understood, I felt like shit that I hadn't at least called her. In truth, I was scared. I had screwed up yesterday, gotten myself into an even bigger mess, and I just wanted to come back to her with something positive to report. And so far, I didn't have anything positive going on.

At the very least, I wanted to tell her how I was going to help with her situation, but I didn't have a clue. In a moment of delirious insomnia I'd contemplated whether Bronx and I could rotate shifts watching over her until we found a way to extricate her from the king's interest. In the end, I tossed the idea away, not because of Bronx, but because I knew Trixie would never agree to being guarded. I had to come up with another way of protecting her, and I knew the key would probably involve taking care of the king.

Beating back a sigh, I stopped before a large orange door with a heavy, worn brass handle. With three fingers wrapped around the second drink I was carrying, I extended my remaining two fingers to grip the handle so I could pull open the door. I slipped inside, careful not to spill either of the drinks. Pausing just over the threshold, I blinked against the thick, hazy darkness broken by pulsing colored lights and a brighter light that illuminated a stage at the opposite end of the large room. After being out in the bright sunlight, my eyes slowly adjusted to the darkness, and in truth, I really didn't want them to focus completely. Diamond Dolls was one of the dingiest strip joints in the area, where desperate exotic dancers went when they could no longer cut it at any of the other clubs. Open twenty-four hours a day, seven days a week, Diamond Dolls catered to all walks of life and even some that preferred to crawl. Filthy, rancid, with a smell that defied definition, I felt as if I needed a shot of penicillin just to walk into the joint.

Unfortunately, it was the easiest access to Chang's shop. And for the truly rare and impossible to get, you went to Chang. He knew how to get his hands on anything, and I didn't want to know how. The man was older than dirt, and if I let myself think about it, I knew that he wasn't a man at all. But then, I didn't allow my imagination to go there, not even on the brightest day of the year.

"No outside drinks!" barked a gruff but familiar voice from out of the darkness.

"Not even a mocha coconut coffee with nonfat milk, whipped

cream, and toasted coconut flakes?" I replied as I walked toward the origin of the voice. My straining eyes focused on a large bar with an assortment of stools lining its front. A mountain of a man with a graying skullet and a broken heart tattoo on his right bicep leaned against the bar, glaring at me. When I raised the large drink at Jerry, his scowl relented and a crooked grin broke across his ugly mug.

"You're an evil man, Gage," he said as he accepted the drink. "You didn't happen to bring a cherry tart or a blueberry scone?"

I shook my head, trying to fight back a grin. "Sorry. The bakery was mostly cleaned out by the time I got there."

"Thanks anyway," Jerry said, lifting his cup to me before taking a big drink.

I settled on the stool directly in front of him and glanced around the bar, taking in my surroundings. An old rock song pumped out some tired beats on the sound system while one dancer went through the motions of gyrating around a pole, a bored expression on her face. Her lack of enthusiasm didn't detract from the shouting coming from the table that held the same three satyrs who had stopped at my shop last week. I ducked down and directed my eyes around the rest of the bar, hoping that they wouldn't notice and remember me. At the opposite end of the club, a trio of strippers sat around a table playing cards.

"How's business been?" I asked as I turned back to look at Jerry.

"Ugh," he grumbled, leaning both his forearms on the bar. He turned the paper cup around with his fat fingertips, staring at the drink. Jerry Caskey was the owner of Diamond Dolls. I had gotten to know him over the past several years as I waited for my turn to see Chang. He always worked the morning and afternoon shifts at the club with the excuse that he was too old to stay up so late to watch over things.

"That bad?"

"Customers have been steady. It's the girls who've been giving me problems. I recently hired this succubus with a solid résumé and a smokin' hot body. Her first night on the stage we discover that she can't dance to save her worthless soul!"

"You didn't interview her first?"

"I did, but I didn't make her dance. Her résumé had the names of some of the finest clubs in the area where she'd worked as a server. And honestly, have you ever heard of a succubus with no rhythm? I mean, you've got to think that she can't be that great a lay, particularly for a succubus."

"You fire her?"

"No," he moaned. "Like I said, she's got a smokin' body. I've got her coming in during the afternoon to have the other girls teach her how to move, and she works as a server during the evenings. I keep telling myself that she'll be a good investment one day, assuming she can stop dropping beer bottles."

"Training usually comes with hiring anybody," I said with a shrug. "At least you don't have to deal with potential life-and-death situations if something goes wrong."

"You'd think that, wouldn't you?" Jerry continued, his face twisting in anger. "I had to let my one vamp go. Do you know what a great draw it is to have a vampire among your dancers? They're impossible to get and impossible to keep happy. But I had to let Tiffany go. I found out she was draining clients during lap dances."

"I can see how that could be a problem."

"And the icing on that is that two of my human dancers just told me they're pregnant. I've got about another month before they will both need to be replaced. I've yet to run across a clientele that finds naked pregnant humans highly attractive."

"Sorry to hear things have gone so sour for you, Jerry. I'm sure it'll turn around soon," I said before lifting my coffee to my lips. I downed the last of the bitter drink in one gulp before it could cool to undrinkable sludge. The caffeine jolt had perked up my brain enough that I felt I could handle Chang without him weaseling away what was left of my soul in exchange for a handful of so-called magic beans.

"Hey, you still got that hot number workin' for you? What was her name?" Jerry snapped his fingers a couple of times as he searched for a name. His mood seemed to lighten with each word as the idea formed in his brain. "Trixie! You think she'd be interested in a part-time gig here?"

"I doubt it. She seems pretty content working with ink, but I'll pass your offer along to her," I said diplomatically, though I had no such intention. Trixie would stake me to the wall with a set of tattooing needles if I dared to mutter such a suggestion in her general direction. While she had proved that she was definitely no prude, she was very selective about who saw her and who touched her.

"Do you mind?" I asked, lifting my empty cup toward Jerry.

Jerry grunted, "No problem," as he took my cup and threw it in a trash can behind the bar.

"I should get going. Is anyone with Chang?" I asked as I eased to my feet off the bar stool.

"No one came through this entrance."

"Thanks. It was great talking to you and I hope things turn around soon. You should stop by the shop some night. I'll give you a nice discount on some fresh ink."

"Got anything for good luck?"

I couldn't stop my muscles from jerking at the question, as if he had thrown something at me. He didn't mean to touch on such a sore subject, but I couldn't help but flinch at the question. A good luck tattoo seemed to have started my recent problems. "I haven't had much luck with that particular tattoo recently, but I'm sure Bronx could set you up with something," I said, forcing a smile on my lips.

Waving one last time at Jerry, I turned and started weaving my way across the floor dotted with tables and chairs toward the back wall. I gave the satyrs' table a wide berth, managing to get past them without notice as their full attention remained on the dancer on the stage. Entering a small alcove, I sighed with relief when the music was dulled from its bruising thump in my ears. Before me were three doors, the entrance to the men's and ladies' restrooms and then an unmarked third. Pushing open the unmarked door, I entered a small, brightly lit room that was painted entirely in white. The only occupants of the room were a pair of Doberman pinschers looking alert and hungry.

"Gage Powell to see Chang," I announced in a steady voice. My gaze never wavered from the two vicious-looking dogs.

One of the dogs chuffed once at me before they stood in unison and walked over to the elevator, which had also been painted white. I pushed the call button and inwardly cringed as the dogs sat on the ground on either side of me to wait for the car to reach our floor. I suffered through this anxiety every time I visited Chang. It wasn't that I didn't like dogs, it was more that I didn't like these particular dogs. There was a frightening intelligence behind their black eyes and I suspected a cold-hearted cruelty that matched the sharpness of their teeth. I wasn't sure if they were even real dogs. They could have been part of a magical security system that Chang used to keep potential clients in line. Or they could have been highly trained canines. Either way, I knew that their teeth were real and that was all that mattered.

A soft ding jolted me from my thoughts just before the doors slid open soundlessly. I stepped inside the elevator followed by both of the dogs. I settled against the wall while one sat on the floor next to me. The other dog stood up on its back paws and leaned its front paws against the wall. Using its nose, it pushed the button for the third floor, which was where I usually met Chang. I had yet to see what was on the fourth floor and I had a feeling that I never would. The little man had more secrets than a Japanese puzzle box, and I knew better than to go digging in another man's secrets. The answer wasn't worth my life.

When we had descended to the third floor of the basement, I followed one dog out of the elevator while the second dog walked behind me, nails clicking on the bare concrete floor. We weaved through one row after another of shelves and tables containing myriad items. If I paused for a second to look at an object, the dog behind me growled, which was quite successful in keeping me moving. I didn't dare take my hands out of my jeans pockets.

We finally turned a corner deep in the enormous room and I found Chang sitting on a banged-up metal chair. A small transistor radio rested on the folding table beside him, playing some fuzzy jazz. I couldn't begin to understand how he was getting a signal so deep underground, below all these layers of concrete, but I let the thought go as a smile split the old Chinese man's wrinkled face. He clapped his skeletal hands together and the dogs darted to him.

Rubbing both dogs on the head as they sat before him, he looked up at me. "Patty is such a sweetheart." His words were wrapped in a heavy accent that he had never lost despite all of his years in the U.S. I had heard him speak a couple of times in a dialect that was akin to Cantonese, but had an older feel to it, the same way in which modern English is different from old English.

"I thought Cake was the sweet one," I said, looking from the dogs to Chang.

Chang looked up at me and his smile grew a little wider. "Does it matter?"

"No, it doesn't," I said, matching his smile. In truth, the dogs looked absolutely identical in every way. It didn't matter which one Chang said was the sweet one because I couldn't tell Patty apart from Cake. Of course, any man who would name his brutal dogs after a children's rhyme had to have a sick, twisted streak to him. I knew better than to press my luck.

"You're a smart boy, Gage Powell," he said with a nod. Chang patted each dog on the side and they left, returning to where we had gotten off the elevator to wait for me to finish with their master. It always seemed strange that he didn't keep his dogs with him when he discussed transactions with his clients. He appeared to be a weak old man who could be broken in half with just a thought, but then anyone who could actually use the items Chang possessed also knew that the easiest-looking targets were always some of the most dangerous. From what I could tell, Chang wasn't a warlock, but that didn't mean he was powerless. I just wasn't stupid enough to try to test his abilities.

"How have you been, Chang?" I asked as the old man stubbed out the cigarette burning away to ash in the aluminum ashtray on the table. Grabbing his wooden cane, Chang pushed to his feet. His thin body was stiff, but he was steady as he started to walk beside me down the aisle.

"Good. Very good, thank you," he replied. "My babies and I continue to expand my collection of unique items. I'm actually thinking of adding a new floor. I am close to making a very large acquisition."

I smiled at my companion as he positively beamed with pride. "Can I ask what you've acquired?"

Chang paused and stared at me, weighing my trustworthiness, before his smile finally returned. "You've been good to me and I don't think you would have any interest in stealing this item from me," Chang said, mostly to himself. "I'm working on acquiring the Great Library of Alexandria."

This time I stopped walking and stared, dumbfounded, at the old man. "I thought it had been lost or destroyed or something."

"Popular myth has it that Julius Caesar burned it down by accident centuries ago," Chang said with a derisive snort and a wave of his hand. "That library was the most important thing in existence to the Alexandrians. They would not have allowed it to burn. The building is long gone, but its contents have been hidden and protected these many years. I am close to completing a deal that will put the ancient scrolls into my hands."

"You're right that there's nothing I would want from that collection, but I would love to just see it some time."

Chang smiled up at me as we started walking again. "We shall see. If you have something interesting to trade, I might consider giving you the honor of looking at the library collection."

"Thank you," I murmured, respectfully bowing my head to him.

"Now, you do not visit me often and only when your need is very great."

"You're expensive, Chang."

The little man giggled, tapping his cane on the ground once as we came to a halt in front of a large jar sitting on a shelf that nearly reached the ceiling. "But my items are extremely rare. They have to be expensive." He reached inside the jar that held a human head, its dreadlocks hanging over the top, and pulled out an egg. "You want pickled egg?" he offered, holding the foul-smelling thing up to me.

"No, thanks. I'm good." Taking a step away, I looked back down at the head and something about the way one of the dreadlocks moved made me jump. It wasn't a dreadlock, but a withered snake. "Holy shit, Chang! That's Medusa's head!"

"Yeah, it's great. You interested? It still works."

"Be careful with that thing," I said, taking another step away from it while shielding my eyes with a raised hand.

"No worries. The safety is on. Her eyes are closed." He laughed maniacally at his own joke before patting me on the arm. "Open the eyes and bang! Instant lawn ornament. You need something like that?"

"No, something a little rarer," I said, looking away as my stomach churned at the sight of Chang popping the egg into his mouth.

"Mmm . . . Gorgon pretty rare. Sounds interesting," he murmured around a mouthful of rancid egg. We continued walking down the aisle and turned up another. My eyes slid over piles of dusty books, ancient scrolls, colored jars, and ornate boxes that held more secrets. I stopped as I felt the floor shift below me and looked down at an intricately woven Persian rug. Chang growled beside me and pounded the carpet with the end of his cane a couple of times. "Be still, stupid rug." He then looked up at me with a somewhat hopeful expression. "You need flying carpet?"

It was then I noticed that the four corners of the rug were held down by massive piles of books. Apparently Chang had some problems keeping the rug in one place.

"No, I'm good."

"It's a fast way to travel," Chang pressed.

"But I doubt it's all that reliable. It seems to have a mind of its own."

"You're a strong enough warlock to keep it under control."

I frowned down at the old man. "You know I gave that up."

Chang snorted again and shook his head as he resumed walking. "You gave that up like I gave up breathing for Lent."

I walked by him in silence. He was right, but I wasn't going to admit it. I didn't question how Chang knew I had studied to be a warlock because it was Chang's business to know things that other people didn't know. It was how he stayed ahead of the competition and acquired the true gems of this world.

"Okay, so no Gorgon head and no flying carpet," Chang said, breaking the silence that had stretched between us. "What is it that you are looking for?"

I stopped walking and took a deep breath. I knew I could trust Chang not to breathe a word of this conversation to another soul, but I still didn't like to say the words aloud. "I need water from the River Styx."

For the first time since I had known him, Chang lost his temper. The little man stomped his feet and swung his cane around, showing more agility than I thought possible for someone his age.

"How you do that?" he shouted. "Out of the millions of items that I have collected over the centuries, how could you pick the one item I have never touched? Never seen with my own eyes!"

Hope deflated in my chest and I shoved one hand through my hair. Chang had everything, and I mean everything. Pots of leprechaun gold, Damocles's sword, original handwritten manuscripts by Shakespeare, folded-up rainbows trapped in delicate crystals; Chang had it all and had never failed me.

"Are you sure?" I asked in desperation, dropping my hand back to my side.

"Sure? Of course I'm sure. Do you think I don't know my own possessions?"

"I'm sorry, but I'm desperate."

"You have to be to ask for such a thing," Chang snapped back at me. "Why you need it?"

"I'm sure you can guess." Death was the only thing that such an item could create, but I wasn't about to voice those words.

"You're right. You sure you can use nothing else as a substitute?"

"Yeah."

"Sorry, but I can't help you."

I stood sideways in the aisle, gazing back the way we had come, but I didn't see the towering shelves that surrounded us. I was left with only one other option and it was not going to be pretty or even easy. "I understand. Thanks for your time."

Chang nodded and clapped his hands once. I looked up to see both the Doberman pinschers turn the corner and stare down the aisle at us. They were patiently waiting to escort me back to the elevator. I started down the aisle alone and then paused when a new thought hit me.

"If I did get my hands on some water from the Styx, what would it be worth to you?" I asked, looking over my shoulder at the old man.

Chang's grin was positively sinister as his watery eyes narrowed on me. "I have a few truly rare prizes that I would be willing to consider trading for such an item."

"And for water from all five underworld rivers?"

Chang's hands spasmed and tightly clenched the handle of his cane. His watery brown eyes turned to vertical yellow slits as he lost his hold on his human form for only a split second at the thought of such a prize. His smile widened, and I could have sworn that I saw a thin curl of smoke drift from the corner of his mouth.

"Bring me such a prize and I will give you the pick of anything from my collection. And if I don't have what you want then I will acquire it."

"I'll keep that in mind," I said, suppressing a grin as I resumed walking toward the dogs.

"You won't give it to anyone else, will you?"

I turned around and walked backward a couple of steps so I could look at him. "You're the only one I would trust with such things."

"Good. Good. I will contact you in a couple of days to see how you have done," Chang said.

I turned back around to face the dogs and waved at Chang one last time, smiling to myself. I really didn't want water from the underworld rivers in anyone's hands, but if it could get me something of extreme value that would help Trixie with the elves or myself with the warlocks, then I would make the trade. I just had to figure out what the item would be. Besides, something as rare as water from the underworld rivers would never leave Chang's possession, and I believed he was the only one who could keep such a dangerous item safe and protected from the world.

My only problem now was figuring out how to get safely to and from the underworld. Getting there wasn't much of a problem. Getting out with my soul intact was.

24

DRYWALL CHUNKS AND dust covered my living room floor and furniture. I stared up at the bare wooden beams exposed by the hole in my ceiling, wondering for the twentieth time in the past ten minutes if I had lost my mind. Actually, I knew that I had lost my mind. I was planning to kill myself in an attempt to save myself from an early death. My only hope was to escape this death so that I didn't have to face a death I couldn't get out of.

Dragging over a folding metal chair, I picked up the heavy orange extension cord I had purchased at the hardware store before arriving at my apartment. I looked down at the noose I had tied in the cord and felt like I was going to be sick. My stomach churned and bubbled with anxiety, making me grateful that I hadn't stopped for anything besides coffee that morning. The world was closing in, narrowing to a dark tunnel that left me with only this noose and the bare wooden beams in the ceiling of my apartment. I didn't have a choice.

Reaching up, I threaded the cord around the beam above my head, wrapping it around the wood several times before tying it off. I yanked on it twice, making sure that it would hold my weight. The stoppered glass jars in the pockets of the trench coat I was wearing clinked together like wind chimes in the summer breeze as I moved. Gazing across the room, I looked at the clock in the kitchen. It was a quarter till three. I was out of time. I had already called Trixie, asking her to come to my apartment at exactly three o'clock because I desperately needed her help. I didn't tell her what I was doing for fear that she would come early and stop me.

My hands were shaking and sweaty when I finally lifted the noose over my head and wrapped it around my neck. I closed my eyes as I tightened it and dropped my hands back down to my sides, brushing against the note taped to my chest that read REVIVE ME!!! It was a struggle to slow my breathing down to a steady, even rate while my heart was pounding in my chest so hard that I thought I would have a heart attack before I could hang myself. Balancing one foot on the back of the chair, I tilted the chair so that it stood on only two legs. I had to be careful that I dropped myself slowly. I was attempting to strangle to death rather than snap my neck. While the drop was technically too short for a broken neck, I wasn't willing to take any chances.

I looked back up at the clock one last time. From what twisted notes I could find on the Internet, it took approximately ten to twenty minutes for a person to strangle to death. I was praying that it would take closer to the low end of that time frame as it would give me just enough time to wander around the underworld before Trixie was scheduled to appear at my apartment to save me. If it took longer, Trixie would appear before I was dead and I didn't think she would let me give this another try, even if my life *was* on the line.

Muttering one last prayer in my head to whatever gods there might be, I tilted the chair over until it fell away from me. My hands immediately surged up to the noose that tightened around my throat as I dangled from the ceiling. I couldn't get my fingers under the cord, it had tightened so much around my neck, sinking into my flesh. Air ceased to pour down to my lungs and I could feel the pulse pounding in my neck as blood fought to reach my brain. Panic filled my frame and crowded around my thoughts, coating everything in thick layers of fear.

In that grim embrace I finally entertained the thought that Trixie wouldn't show up in time. I knew that I was taking a significant risk in asking for her help. It wasn't that Trixie wouldn't come to my aid or that she would be late—I knew I could depend on her. But the elves tracking her could spot her on her way to my apartment and grab her. Not only would I be dead, but no one would be able to help her escape from the guards of the Summer Court.

Trixie was the one person I trusted above all others to help me. Bronx couldn't leave his house during the daylight hours. Trixie had to come and she had to be on time.

Yet even as I convinced myself that there was no one else to help me, Robert's young, smiling face drifted across my mind. Growing up, my older brother had been my closest friend and worst enemy rolled into one. We fought as hard as we played together, and I always knew that he would protect me no matter what. I hadn't spoken to him in more than ten years and yet I knew that if I had called him, he would come. However, I didn't want my dead body to be the first thing he saw after a decade of silence. It was better for both him and my younger sister if neither was involved in my dangerous life.

I twisted and tried to shift while hanging from my noose, but there was no give. Darkness started to crowd my eyes and my lungs, feeling as if they were going to explode in my chest, burned for oxygen. I squinted at the clock to see how much time had passed in this agony, but my vision swam and doubled, making it impossible to focus on the distant clock. Time slowed to a crawl. I didn't want to die. A part of me desperately wanted Trixie to come to the apartment early and save me from myself, but then I was only left with facing my death at the hands of the grim reaper.

As darkness closed in around me, leaving me feeling cold and light headed, I realized that I hadn't left a note in case something went terribly wrong. What if I died and no one was there to bring me back in time? I hadn't left a note to explain to everyone that I wasn't really attempting suicide. I hadn't left a note to explain the mess I had gotten into and how I was trying to fix it. My family would be left to think that my life had gone horribly wrong and that I was depressed. Trixie would be devastated, as she would believe that I had wanted to kill myself after having had sex with her. I had to fix it. I couldn't take the chance of destroying those who mattered most to me.

I reached up with my right hand to grab the cord above my head. If I could just hold it and concentrate, I knew a spell that would allow me to burn through the cord. I would have to start the whole thing over again, but I couldn't take the chance of hurting my family like this. They had to know why if I truly did die. Unfortunately, as I attempted to look up, my vision completely blacked out. The side of my hand grazed the side of the cord as I missed. I tried a second time, but my hand went wide of the cord, missing it completely.

Darkness swirled around me in an ever deepening vortex, sucking me down until I felt nothing. Not the tightness in my chest or the throbbing pain in my head. There was only a floating miasma of confusion and cold. I tried to blink my eyes against the darkness, but it didn't give forth any shape or sense of depth for several seconds.

And then there was earth beneath my feet. I shook my head, surprised to find that I was no longer hanging from a noose. I knelt on the cold, hard ground, feeling the smooth stones beneath the palms of my hands. My eyes focused on some vague shapes. In the distance I could see a faint blue glow emanating from a dark tunnel, while the earth shifted and swayed, reminding me of water. I was in the underworld, leading to final judgment and the realm beyond.

I had to move fast. I didn't know how time flowed in the underworld. The minutes until Trixie arrived could pass in the blink of an eye or slink by at a snail's pace. I couldn't take any chances that she would revive me before I had accomplished what I needed to. Pushing to my feet, I carefully walked down the gentle rolling slope to the bank of what appeared to be an endlessly wide river. The water flowed, but there were no waves. It was a flat plain, as if it were made out of black glass, and yet I didn't want to touch it. Without question, I knew I was standing on the bank of the River Styx.

Looking down, relief filled me as I found that I was wearing exactly what I had died in. Taking a glass container out of my pocket, I pulled out the cork stopper and knelt at the bank. Carefully filling the container, I made sure not to touch the water with my fingers. When it was full, I stood and replaced the stopper before putting it back into my pocket.

I had what I had come for, but this was also an opportunity that I wasn't willing to pass up. The River Styx represented hate, but it also led to the afterlife. It was a link to death, and it would be the only thing that could overcome the power of the angel feather. Yet there were still four more rivers that ran through the underworld—Lethe, Acheron, Cocytus, and Phlegethon. They represented forgetfulness, pain, lamentation, and fire. The water from those rivers could be used to create some of the most powerful potions in existence. Bringing back water from all five rivers would mean holding a fortune in my hands. More so, water from all five rivers would mean getting my hands on the one item that could free Trixie from the Summer Court. If only I knew what it was. It didn't matter. When I finally discovered it, I knew it would be found among Chang's treasures.

A dim yellow glow pierced the darkness and was slowly approaching me from across the Styx. Taking a step backward from the bank, I watched as a rickety wooden boat appeared from out of the darkness with an old oil lamp hanging from a bow that sloped upward. It was only when the boat pushed up on the shore with a scrape that I could make out the slender figure of a man standing at the stern with a long wooden pole that he used to direct the boat. Shrouded in a ragged black cloak from head to toe, I could see his bony white hands as they tightly clasped the pole. I was faced with the fearsome ferryman Charon.

Extending his left hand to me, Charon spoke, sending a chill through my frame. "Obol."

Without thinking, I felt myself reaching down to my jeans pocket, where I had stuffed the gold coins I had received from the satyrs. As I pulled one out, I finally caught myself before I could lay it in the ferryman's hand. My thoughts swirled frantically in my head as I fought the compulsion to heed his bidding. I wasn't trying to cross over to the land of judgment. I just wanted to travel the rivers, I reminded myself.

"I have your obol," I replied. My voice was shaky and soft, as I didn't want to disturb the overwhelming silence of the underworld with my presence. "But I have an additional request of you."

Charon's skeletal fingers curled into his palm and he pulled back his hand. He seemed to hesitate before pulling back the deep hood of his cloak to reveal a wrinkled old face with a long reddish-brown beard. His blue-gray eyes, partially hidden beneath a pair of wild, bushy eyebrows that wiggled like poisonous caterpillars on his brow, locked on my face. While not quite the fearsome figure I had expected, he still reminded me of the slightly mad homeless man who sometimes slept in the alley beside the tattoo parlor.

"You think you can bargain with Charon?" he asked, his fuzzy brows meeting above his large nose.

"Yes." I forced a smile on my lips as I met his stare. I held up one gold coin so that it flashed in the dim light from his lantern, causing his eyes to widen. It was tradition that the obol he was offered was typically the least valued coin of the realm. The ferryman didn't often feel the weight and slickness of a gold coin. "I don't seek passage to judgment. I want water from all five of the rivers and then to be returned to this shore."

"No one travels all the rivers of the underworld."

"No one but you."

He frowned at me, but continued. "Passage to the land beyond and back requires two coins. Standard fee. Ask the gods."

I nodded and reached into my pocket, withdrawing a second coin to show him. "I have the fee for passage back and forth, but I need all five rivers."

"No."

I tightly clasped the gold coins in my fist as I stared critically at the ferryman. I had suspected that I might have some problems getting him to acquiesce to my demand, but I had been hoping to avoid the only route I had available to me. It was dirty and despicable, but at the same time, I knew that if our roles were reversed, my opponent would not hesitate to do the same.

"How long have you been the ferryman for the dead?" I asked.

"Since the start of time."

"I imagine that you are looking forward to your own time of rest and peace in the afterlife following a long existence of servitude."

The frown on Charon's face deepened as he weighed my words. "I will not rest until the living fill the halls of the dead. Only then will I put aside my pole and rest."

"Could you not rest if someone came along to take your place?"

"The person has to volunteer to take my spot. None has ever agreed to such a thing." Charon paused, stroking his beard as he gazed at me. "Will you take my place as ferryman if I take you to all the rivers?"

I waved one hand at him and smiled. "I'm not quite so desperate, but I do have something else to offer." Reaching inside my shirt, I pulled out the small glass container that hung around my neck. Inside the glass swirled the piece of Simon's soul that I had torn off. Lifting it over my head, I held it out to Charon by the leather thong. "You may not need a willing replacement if you hold a piece of their soul."

Charon stood mesmerized by the fragment of soul that twisted in the glass container dangling from my hand. Before him was the promise of relief from his long existence of service to the dead. Of course, if I managed to return to the world above without Simon's soul, it was unlikely that I would ever be able to barter for my own fragment of soul. On the other hand, it was highly unlikely that Simon would ever willingly agree to a trade in the first place. I was better off using his soul in trade with Charon than attempting to trade for my own.

"You will give me two coins and the soul fragment if I take you to each of the rivers?" Charon asked slowly.

"Take me to each river *and* bring me back to this exact spot," I replied, lowering my hand back to my side.

"Agreed," Charon said eagerly, extending his hand to me again.

"I will give you one coin now for the start of the trip, and I will give you the soul fragment and other coin when we are safely back here."

A low growl slipped from Charon for a second as he glared at me. His extended hand balled into a tight fist and trembled slightly, as he was anxious to have his hold on his replacement. While Charon had no power to end Simon's life early and drag him down to the ferry, he would at least have the promise of a replacement when Simon died on his own.

"Very well," he grumbled.

Suppressing a sigh of relief, I handed over one of the gold coins as I climbed into the boat and sat on the single plank that ran from one side of the wooden boat to the other. Behind me, I could hear Charon shuffling with his robes before he pushed off the bank with his pole.

With surprising speed, Charon directed us across the Styx, weaving around sandbars and fingers of land stretched out into the water before we reached a new tributary. Where the Styx was like polished black glass, the next river was crystal clear, making it easy to see the various bodies of the dead that had settled near the bottom of the river.

"This is Lethe," Charon announced as we settled in the middle of the mouth of the river. "Feel free to take a drink. It's quite cool and refreshing. I'm told that it's the best-tasting water in the above or below worlds."

"I'm sure it is," I muttered under my breath as I knelt on the bottom of the boat while pulling another glass jar out of my pocket. Once again, I was careful not to touch the water as I filled the container. Lethe would wipe the memory of any who drank from it, a situation I was sure that Charon would be happy to take advantage of.

After I had the water from Lethe, we quickly moved on. Cocytus, with its deep blue waters, looked to be more of a lagoon found off an island in the Caribbean. The river of lamentation shifted and lapped against distant shores, sounding like the weeping of angels. But then, Cocytus was said to be made of the tears of angels gathered from all their centuries of crying for man. I wasn't sure that I believed the old tale, but I didn't take any unnecessary chances for fear of being swept away by an overwhelming hopelessness that could deter me from my endeavor to save myself, Trixie, and Bronx.

Phlegethon nearly proved to be the end of me as I jerked back in the boat when we drew close to the river. The tiny wooden boat swayed at my movement, but it didn't burst into flames as I had initially feared. The river of fire was red and yellow, as if it were made of flowing magma, but still had the same consistency as water. Intense heat radiated off it, causing sweat to bead and slip down the sides of my face. For the first time since entering the underworld, I wasn't cold and the darkness had been beaten back by the light that shone from the river. I nearly dropped the glass jar into the river, cursing the stinging heat that bit at my fingertips. When it was full, I placed it on the floor of the boat and replaced the cork stopper, waiting to see if the liquid would eat through the glass, but it held. Even the glass remained cool to the touch despite the fact that it looked like I had placed liquid fire in a jar.

Our final stop didn't appear to be a river at all, but a swamp. Acheron was the river of pain, and it reminded me of something I had read in Dante's *Inferno*. The boat frequently scraped bottom as we entered the swamp, the river remaining shallow, broken up by spits of land. The shore had moved closer, revealing black trees with twisted bare limbs. I stared out across the land and watched shadows shifting in and out from behind trees as we passed by.

"Are . . . are those people out there?" I asked as we paused in the center of the swamp. I hesitated to lean over the side of the boat with the glass jar, but held it tightly in one hand as I scoured the shoreline.

"The dead," Charon confirmed.

Glancing over my shoulder, I found him leaning against his pole as he gazed out at the nearby shore. "What are the dead doing here? This is Acheron, right? I thought the dead were to wait on the shore where I met you."

"That is where the dead start. Those who do not have my obol are forced to swim to the banks of the Acheron and wait for the end of days. It is only when the world is rent open and the living are judged that these poor souls will be able to freely move on to the land beyond."

"And if they don't swim to Acheron?" I asked as I leaned over the edge of the boat with the glass jar in one hand.

"Then they never move on to the next world. Most resist at first, but after centuries of waiting they eventually forget why they were resisting and begin the swim."

Sitting back in the boat, I put a stopper in the full jar and placed it in the large pocket of my trench coat. It was a good warning for the future that I faced. I should always carry some change in my pockets in the event that something bad happened to me while I was out and about. Of course, considering that I usually slept in the nude, that didn't make me feel any better about the prospect of potentially dying in my sleep. Shorts with a single coin in my pocket were starting to sound like a good alternative to sleeping commando.

As Charon turned the boat back toward the way we had come, a pale light caught my eye as it poked out from behind a massive tree in the distance. It reminded me of the Saturday morning cartoon version of a ghost, glowing and undefined. I twisted around in my seat and leaned over to peer around Charon, but the eerie glow was gone. Something that wasn't a member of the dead was watching me. I had stayed too long and now I was starting to attract the kind of attention that I had been hoping to avoid.

We passed easily through the other four rivers and glided soundlessly onto the Styx again. I needed to get out of here, and fast. Unfortunately, I didn't know how much time had passed since I had died. Trixie had to revive me soon if I was going to escape this world unscathed.

As I reached the shore, I knew that I had run out of time. Someone was waiting for me.

25

I SAT IN the boat, reluctant to move as I saw in the distance the same ethereal glow I had noticed in the Acheron swamp. Someone or something had come for me.

Charon tapped on my shoulder with his bony finger, causing me to jerk around and look at him. He extended his hand toward me and I could see a faint smile through the shadows of his hood. "This is where you wanted to be, correct? This was the bargain?" Charon demanded when I still hadn't moved.

"Yeah, this is the place," I murmured, pushing to my feet. Reaching into my pocket, I pulled out another gold coin and laid it in his hand. While two fingers closed around the coin, two other fingers wagged at me, beckoning for the soul fragment I had promised. Frowning, I lifted the leather thong from around my neck and placed it in his hand as well.

I didn't feel good about this decision, and the argument that Simon would do the same to me if he was in my position wasn't sitting well either. A promise was a promise, though, and my friends' safety and happiness were worth my own damnation if it came to that. Hell, I figured I was already damned for the mess I had created with Tera; what was one more mark against me at this point?

Holding on to the bow of the boat, I carefully disembarked and stood on the edge of the bank, gazing up the hill at the faint glowing figure that seemed to be waiting for me. In my pockets were only a handful of gold coins and the water from the five rivers of the underworld. Not exactly great bargaining chips for whatever I still faced, and Charon told me as much when he wished me "Good luck" with a rusty chuckle as he pushed his boat away from the shore.

Glancing one last time at the sight of Charon's boat receding into the darkness, I mounted the slope toward the figure waiting for me. The glow had faded to nothing, but the creature still loomed. As I drew close, I could make out a woman, with long dark hair and gray skin molded to a slim body, waiting for me. Her stormy gray eyes burned through me, while a smile slashed across her face like an open wound. My skin crawled to look at her, and I could feel something skittering around her in the darkness. I couldn't see the creatures, but I had a vague sense of their shape and number in the back of my mind, as if they were either shrouded in magic or existed on some other plain of reality that I wasn't fully privy to here in the underworld. Energy shifted and flowed in the air, magic that I had never come into contact with and didn't want to know.

"I take it that you've been waiting for me," I said in a neutral voice as I held back, several feet from her. In my mind, I desperately prayed that Trixie would soon draw me away from this world. Watching this woman, I feared for what was left of my soul.

"I've been waiting a long time for you, Gage," she purred. She closed the distance between us by several feet. I watched her legs take the necessary steps forward, but she moved as if she slithered across the ground like a snake.

My gaze jumped from her legs to her face as the muscles in my chest clenched around my lungs and heart in fear. There was only one female who walked the underworld, neither living nor dead, but trapped, supposedly tied to the one who had tempted her. Lilith.

Backpedaling several feet to reestablish the distance between us, my mind scoured the hours of mythology I had ingested during my studies with the warlocks. Was this the Lilith of Greek mythology? The vampiric, child-killing Lamia with second sight? Or was this the Jewish first wife of Adam who was tempted and seduced by Samael, only to give birth to Cain? Or maybe she was the more obscure incarnation of Istar and Asherah, who were born of the same power that gave birth to God? So many conflicting texts, but the same word was repeated again: evil.

"I can't help you, Lilith," I said in a steady voice, though I didn't feel it. I wanted out of here now. I could think of a dozen other dark creatures I'd rather be faced with than this woman, goddess, demon, known for both seduction and murder.

"I know you can. Anyone who can get in and out of here can free me as well," she continued in a deep sultry voice that seemed to curl around my thoughts like a smoky drug. "I've grown tired of my cage and I long to be back among the humans. Help me, Gage, and I can help you in countless ways. Your enemies would cower at the mere mention of your name."

"No thank you," I breathed, forcing myself to remain in one spot as she once again inched closer to me. "I would prefer to take care of things on my own. But I appreciate your offer."

Her smile dimmed a couple of notches and lines of tension appeared around the corners of her eyes. "I didn't mean to suggest that you had a choice in the matter."

"I can't help you."

"You can give me permanent freedom. I want out."

"No."

A sharp jerk broke my gaze from Lilith. It felt as if a string had been tied to the inside of my belly button and had been pulled out my back. Pressing my hand to my stomach, I briefly wondered if Lilith had caused it, but pushed aside the thought when she grabbed my other arm at the wrist while her smile completely disappeared.

"I will be the one to free you from this cage!" she snarled.

Trixie was trying to revive me, but I doubted she would succeed if Lilith was holding on to me. And nothing in this existence would allow me to take Lilith's offer to send me back. Such a decision would put me in her debt and at her disposal in the world of the living. I jerked on my arm, trying to break her hold, but it didn't budge.

"I won't help you."

"Then you will not be free of this place."

Closing my eyes against her distracting naked body and the fear that was rising in my chest, I searched my memory for all that I had been forced to learn about her. There was a bit of folklore about the prophet Elijah getting Lilith to tell him her various names, thus freeing him of her. I wasn't sure if repeating them back would free me in mythical Rumpelstiltskin style, but it was the only thing I could think of in my desperation.

"Abeko, Abito, Amizo . . ."

"Do you think such old magic can stop me?" she demanded, her voice cutting like shards through my brain.

Ignoring her comment as her fingers tightened on my wrist, biting into the flesh, I pushed on. "Batna, Eilo, Ita, Izorpo . . ."

Her grip started to slip as the tugging on my stomach increased. It felt like it was working as she grew steadily angrier. I prayed she wouldn't destroy me since she saw me as a source of escape, but at the same time I wasn't sure that she would let me escape if she believed I wouldn't help her. My wrist slipped out of her grip, but she caught the tips of my fingers. My eyes flicked over and met her fiery stare, shaking me to my core. My breath exploded from my chest as fear clenched in my gut. I was little more than a soul here and she was digging in her claws.

"Escape me now, but you will not be free of me. I've seen your future. I can still reach you, steal away your most precious love. I will come for you if you don't help me."

"K-Kali . . . Kea . . . K-K-Kokos," I continued in a fear-choked voice. My fingers slipped from her grasp and darkness consumed me while I was followed by her earth-shattering scream.

Burning in my chest caused me to suck in air again, which only resulted in a harsh coughing fit. I rose for a second and then immediately fell back again, hitting the back of my head on something. My throat was raw, my chest burned, and my temples throbbed with pain, but I welcomed it all as I knew that I was alive once again. Something wet hit my cheeks and I opened my eyes to see a bleary image of Trixie leaning over me with tears streaking down her pale cheeks. Her gentle hands smoothed my hair as she choked on a stifled sob of relief.

"Just breathe," she said, her voice fractured and raw.

Catching one of her hands, I pulled it over to my lips and pressed a kiss to the heel of her palm as I closed my eyes again. "Thank you," I croaked out as relief flooded my body, bringing tears to my own eyes. Images of Lilith danced in the back of my brain—I knew that I wasn't entirely free of her, but for now, I could push those worries aside.

"Are you okay?" Trixie asked soothingly, sweeping away the last of my fears.

"I'm fine, I swear," I said with a relieved sigh.

Pain exploded against my cheek, snapping my head to the side as she smacked me with all her might. My ears were ringing when my eyes popped open to look at her face, twisted with anger and pain.

"What the hell were you thinking? What's wrong with you?" she demanded, shoving to her feet. I made a grab for her hand but missed, falling onto my stomach as she lurched out of my reach. "You know, I should just have let you hang if this is how you're going to act after we . . ." Her voice drifted off in a heavy, broken silence.

Desperate energy filled me with fresh strength. I pushed to my feet and caught her as she moved for the front door. I pulled her roughly against my chest, wrapping my arms around her so that she was trapped. She fought me for several seconds until a fresh wave of tears fell from her luminous eyes. My head swam and the room swayed, but I ignored it, focusing all my thought on just holding on to her.

"How could you?" she whispered.

Tightly clutching Trixie, I grabbed the back of her neck, threading my fingers through her silken hair. I had almost lost her, lost everything. I had to risk it all if I was going to not only save myself, but save her as well.

"I wasn't trying to kill myself," I murmured against her neck. She jerked in my arms to argue with me, but I held tight. "Think, Trixie! If I had been trying to kill myself, would I have called you over to my apartment at a very specific time? Would I have put a 'revive me' sign on my chest? Would I have risked your exposure to the guards of the Summer Court if it had not been for a very important reason?"

"No, but how could you do that? How do you think it made me feel to see your dead body hanging there when I walked in the door?"

"I never wanted that for you, but you are the only person in my life I trusted to come to my rescue. I'm sorry I put you through this. I'm so damned sorry and I will apologize for this every day for the rest of my life if it helps to erase the memory."

"I don't think I will ever forget it," she murmured, her lips brushing my shoulder.

"I'm sorry."

"Why? Why would you do such a thing?"

Brushing a kiss against her temple, I loosened my hold slightly and leaned back so that I could look her in the eye. One hand dipped into the pocket of my trench coat and my stomach twisted in fear until I reached a glass jar filled with clear liquid. They had come back with me.

"I needed to get this," I said, holding up the jar so she could see it.

"What is it?"

"Water from Lethe."

Trixie eased away from me a bit as she looked from the jar to my face, her brow furrowed in confusion. "Lethe? Why? What could you possibly need it for?"

"That I will not tell you," I said as I tucked the jar carefully into my pocket again. "I would rather you forget that I showed it to you at all. I just want you to know that I would not have taken this chance if I had not been completely desperate."

"That doesn't make me feel any better."

Closing my eyes, I lowered my head again, pressing my face against the side of hers. My heart lurched and skipped in my chest while I breathed in her intoxicating scent as it wrapped around us. I needed her like I needed air. I hated myself for hurting her, but it had been a necessary evil. I might have killed myself to save myself, but right now I lived to save her. "I know and I am sorry. Just remember that I promised I would help you get free of the Summer Court and I will keep that promise. I will not leave you if I can help it. Please say that you at least believe that."

"I do," she whispered.

"You saved more than my life today, Trixie. You saved what's left of my soul. I will never be able to thank you enough or apologize enough for the pain and fear I've caused you. I will do everything within my power to help you, whatever it takes."

I felt Trixie stiffen at my words and she lifted her head so that she was staring at my face. "Did you kill yourself for me?" Her voice was faint and sounded as if she was haunted by some horrible thought.

I shook my head while I buried deep my thoughts. "No, to save myself."

She stared at me for another second before lowering her eyes. "I don't understand, and I don't think I want to."

Raising my hand, I cupped her cheek while rubbing my thumb across her cheekbone. "Please don't leave me yet. I can feel your need to run. Give me a second chance. Stay."

Trixie looked away from me, staring over my shoulder at the wall, causing my heart to almost stop in my chest. It felt as if she was pulling away, throwing up a wall to protect herself, and I couldn't blame her. I had betrayed her in the worst way.

"I'll stay," she murmured in the softest voice.

"Thank you." I sighed, breathing again. "Will you go back to the apartment above the shop?"

She frowned, refusing to look at me. She may have promised to remain in the area, but I had a feeling she was thinking of a place to go that was out of my reach. Unfortunately, that would make her vulnerable to capture by the Summer Court.

"Trixie, hate me. Be mad at me for what I've done. It's no less than what I deserve, but don't put yourself in danger because of that hatred. The apartment is protected, hidden. I won't come by until you say I can. I'll send Bronx by to check on you and bring you some food. You need to stay safe."

"I'll go back to the apartment," she agreed after a painful silence.

"Can I take you back?"

"No," she said sharply, finally bringing her gaze back to mine.

I chewed on the inside of my mouth in thought. If I took her back to the apartment, I could be sure that she wasn't followed. I could protect her from potential attack. I didn't like her moving about the city alone. "Will you at least promise to keep something with you? It will tell me where you are and if you are in trouble. If something happens, I'll be able to find you."

"Magic?"

"Yes."

"It's dangerous. You're not supposed to use it."

"You're worth the risk."

"You'll follow me if I don't?"

"Yes," I admitted with a weak smile.

Frowning at me, Trixie nodded after a couple of seconds of tense silence. "I'll carry it."

"Thank you," I breathed as I hugged her quickly. Reluctantly releasing her, I stepped away and searched the living room for something small I could use as a locator beacon. My eyes snagged on a fork on my living room table. Snatching it up, I rubbed it clean with the hem of my T-shirt before casting a spell on it. It would only activate if she was suddenly frightened by something. It would then alert me to the trouble and tell me her location. It wasn't a perfect spell, but it was the only one I could think of on short notice.

Trixie slowly took it from me as I held out the fork toward her. She arched one eyebrow and her mouth smoothed from the frown that had been there. "A fork?" she asked, turning the silverware around with her fingertips before shoving it in the back pocket of her jeans.

"At least it's clean. Sort of. It's the best I could do on short notice."

She nodded and walked to the door without looking at me. As she opened it, I gently grabbed her arm, holding her in place. "I am so sorry for putting you through this. I understand if you can't forgive me, but I wish you would."

Trixie looked over her shoulder at me. Her red and puffy eyes would be forever burned in my brain, knowing I had been the cause of her pain. "I will try. It may take a while."

I wanted to pull her back into my arms and kiss her until I wiped the memory from her mind. I wanted to use magic to go in and erase the image of my dead body from her brain, but it wouldn't be fair to her. It would also be cheating. I had a price to pay for my choices. So I just released my hold on her arm and watched silently as she walked out of my apartment, praying that she wasn't also walking out of my life.

26

TURNING BACK TOWARD the living room, my eyes skimmed over the overturned folding chair that had been pushed farther away from where I had hung. A section of the orange extension cord still dangled from the ceiling and a small knife lay on the floor from where Trixie had cut me down. It was only then that I realized the noose was still hanging from my neck. With a grunt, I jerked it from around my neck and threw it on the ground.

I noticed drywall chunks crushed into the stained beige carpet as I crossed to the low wooden coffee table. Bending over, I carefully lifted the five glass jars from my pockets and placed them on the scarred tabletop. The various colored liquids sloshed in the jars, but all were unbroken and safely corked. Somehow they had managed to survive the trek between the underworld and here, as well as a slight struggle with Trixie, with no problems and I was grateful.

Shedding the trench coat, I tossed it onto the sofa and started to walk toward my bedroom where I had left my cell phone. I would call Bronx and check to make sure that he had not had problems with Reave or any of his minions. I'd also ask him to stop by and check on Trixie sometime during the early evening. He wouldn't have any trouble as long as he didn't attempt to open the door. I knew he wouldn't mind looking in on our mutual friend and co-worker.

I jerked to a stop halfway to the bedroom as an unexpected pain shot through me to my core. Trixie was in trouble. Pivoting around on my toes, I surged forward, running out the front door. I took the stairs two at a time, racing down the narrow hallway. The feeling burning in my bones strengthened while anxiety roiled in my gut, tensing my body until I thought my stomach would purge its contents. I should never have asked Trixie to come to my apartment, putting her back in danger as the elves continued to watch the area for her.

Busting out the front door of my apartment building, I ran around the side of the building and down the driveway to the small parking lot behind the old yellow brick building. Trixie was struggling with two elves while a third stood back with his hands on his hips as he watched his companions. One elf held Trixie from behind, his arms wrapped around her stomach while pinning her arms to her sides. Trixie leaned back into her captor and kicked out at the other elf who was trying to get her to be still. I didn't know if they could use magic to instantly transport her back to the home of the Summer Court, but I knew I had to act fast to get her out of their reach.

"I don't think the lady wants to go with you," I shouted as I closed the distance between us. A quick flash of relief jumped across Trixie's face as she spotted me before she turned her attention back to her attackers. My heart pounded in my chest as both fear and rage poured through me. I wasn't going to let her go and I wasn't about to let these assholes force Trixie into a marriage that she didn't want.

"Rowena does not belong here," replied the one elf overseeing the struggle. "She must be returned to the king. She has no choice in the matter."

"I think she does," I snapped. "She left her people so that she could have her freedom. The king of the Summer Court has no dominion over her. She's given up everything. Why are you doing this?"

"She's being selfish. Her people need her and she has turned her back on them. It's not as if she's going to be tortured. She'll become a member of the Summer Court. She'll be royalty. Her children will be revered among our people. What more could she possibly want?"

"I want the right to choose who will use my body and how it is used!" Trixie snarled, increasing her struggles so that she had one arm free. "I want to be more than a pretty object for the man who will possess me."

"You want too much," muttered the elf trying to hold her.

"Leave, human! You've interfered and hindered our efforts enough. We will take her back to the king. It's best if you walk away now."

"I can't. There are too many people here who need her." Frowning, I looked over at Trixie, who had stilled as she watched me. There was a sad expression on her face. I didn't want to bring this to violence, but they were leaving us with no other option. "I don't want to hurt you, but I won't let you take her."

"Please, Eldon, just walk away. I don't want you to get hurt," Trixie pleaded in a softer voice.

"Then you should have thought of that before you ran," snapped the elf who still hung on the fringe of the struggle. "You should have stayed and submitted to your duty."

"How could you want me to be a prisoner? I'm your sister!"

My heart stumbled in my chest as I looked from Trixie to the elf called Eldon. There was a similarity in their coloring and features, but then I had thought that was just a trait of all the elves of the Summer Court. I didn't think it was possible that Trixie was being tracked by a member of her own family, by her own brother.

For the first time, Eldon's hardened expression softened a bit and he looked more than a little weary. There was some small comfort in that he didn't enjoy his task, but it didn't erase the fact that he was handing his sister over to be raped by their king for the salvation of their monarchy. "He's my king. I obey his commands."

There was nothing more to be said. He had made up his mind and turned on his own flesh and blood. I lunged at Eldon, aiming to smash my fist into his face, but he was quick, sidestepping me while sinking his own fist in my stomach. Doubled over, I stumbled past him while gripping my stomach. Elves were known not only for their innate grace, but also their speed. I was outmatched in many ways as a human, but I had one advantage that I was trying to avoid using.

A pained cry rent the silence of the sleepy afternoon. I twisted around as I gained my balance to find Trixie pulling the fork I had given her out of her captor's hand as she spun away from him. The second elf made a grab for her, but she easily slipped free of him while dragging the tines of the fork along his cheek. My eyes jerked to Eldon, who was intently watching his sister, seeming undecided as to how he could jump in without getting hurt or hurting her.

Lowering my shoulder, I ran at Eldon, intending to plow into him, but he saw me and started to dip out of my path. As he moved, I grabbed his arm and pulled him to the ground. His narrow shoulders slammed against the broken concrete, but the pain didn't slow him as he rolled to his feet again, facing me.

Breathing shattered and heartbeat rapid, I swung my right fist at him. He dodged it, as I expected, allowing me to hammer my left into his jaw as he moved. Trixie's cry snatched my attention from Eldon. I looked over and found her watching the struggle with wide eyes. I couldn't tell if she was worried about me or her brother, or maybe both. Unfortunately, the distraction lasted long enough for Eldon to come back at me with his own punch, knocking me to the ground. Lying on my back for a second, I gazed up in time to see Eldon bringing his boot down toward my face. I grabbed the rubber sole and stopped it a mere inch from crushing my nose. With a grunt, I pushed him off and regained my feet as Eldon edged away from me.

"Why are you even concerning yourself with Rowena's welfare? This is none of your business," Eldon demanded.

"She's my friend and my family," I said, bracing my feet for another attack.

"Her people need her."

"I need her!" The words exploded from my lips.

I chanced a glance at Trixie out of the corner of my eye. She was once again being held by one of the elves, but she had stopped in her struggles as she watched me with her brother. Her glamour spell was gone, revealing long blond hair that danced in the growing breeze. Tears streaked down her cheeks, lighting her green eyes so that they resembled leaves shivering in a spring rain. I could understand why the king was so desperate to have her, because in that crystalline moment, she was perfect.

"Trust me, I need her more," I murmured, dragging my attention back to Eldon. "She is perfect in more ways than I can count, and if she wants to stay here, then I will do everything in my power to make it so."

"She can't stay," Eldon growled through clenched teeth.

"Then you won't live long enough to take her," I announced, straightening from my defensive position. Eldon took the bait and lunged toward me with hands extended. Calling up the energy that surrounded me, I reached out with my right hand and imagined clasping his neck. Eldon immediately jerked to a halt as the invisible hand closed around his throat. He clawed at the empty air as I lifted my hand, hoisting him off the ground a few inches so that his feet dangled helplessly in the air.

"Gage!" Trixie cried, but I didn't take my eyes off Eldon. I had no desire to kill Trixie's brother, but I would not let them take her. She had suffered through enough torment.

"Release Rowena or I'll kill him!" I shouted, tightening my hold on the elf's throat. Eldon kicked and clawed at the empty air around his throat as he attempted to draw in a deep breath. I turned my head to the two elves watching Eldon in shock while still holding on to Trixie. I shook my hand slightly, shaking Eldon in the air. "Do it! Release her!"

The elves released Trixie and started to step away from her while closely watching me. In frustration at their slowness, I reached out with my free left hand and used magic to push them to the other side of driveway. They stumbled and fell so that they skidded on their sides along the rough concrete. When I felt as if I could breathe again, I moved over to where Trixie was standing, while dropping Eldon on the ground with his companions.

Coughing and rubbing his throat, Eldon shoved to his feet again, his face red. "She is not free of us! I will return her to the Summer Court."

"I won't allow it. She stays!"

Trixie laid a gentle hand on my shoulder and stepped around me so that I could look into her sad eyes. "Gage, I think it's time to let it go."

"No, you can't do this." I shook my head, tearing my gaze from her attackers. "You can't give in."

"I've been running for so long. I've lived a nice life, but maybe it's time I gave up this fight. It's not worth it if it comes down to either you or my brother dying, and I know both of you are willing to fight to that point. And if not that, then you are risking death from the Towers. It has to stop."

My arm shot out, wrapping around her waist before pulling her close against me. I glared at her brother as confusion twisted his expression. My hand clenched on her side, melting into her softness, but it failed to ease my black mood. Despite holding her tightly, she was slipping away. I was losing her. My heart tripped and stumbled in my chest, threatening to splinter. I couldn't let her sacrifice her happiness just for my safety. She had a right to live her own life, regardless of my desires, or the desires of her brother and her king.

"How could you do this? She's your sister!" I shouted at Eldon, my head snapping around to glare at him again.

"This is what is best for her!" Eldon snarled. "Do you think you could provide for her better than the king of the Summer Court? A pathetic tattoo artist?"

"I think I've already proved that I'm more than a tattoo artist."

"Even worse, a warlock! You're a danger to her and everything around you. Kill me and you declare war on the elves of the Summer Court!"

"Her love for you has stopped me from killing you, but that doesn't mean I won't protect her with everything I have. She's not leaving with you."

Trixie laid her hand on the side of my face, forcing me to look at her. Her expression was heartbreakingly sad, washing away the heated anger that burned in my frame so that I was left with only a bitter taste in the back of my throat. "Please, Gage. Look at where we are. I didn't want this. I never wanted to drag you into this mess and endanger your life. I know that because of me you would never harm Eldon, but I can't say that he would spare your life for me if we continued to fight him. I can be happy living with the king if I know that you're still alive."

I leaned forward, pressing my forehead against hers as my eyes slid closed. "What if I can't? I can't be happy knowing that you gave up to protect me."

A soft sigh from Trixie caused me to open my eyes and find a fragile smile lifting the corners of her mouth. "I guess I'm in a no-win situation."

"No such thing when I'm involved."

"What should I do?"

"Forgive me."

"Done," she said, her smile growing.

"Love me."

I felt her entire body tense at my suggestion, but to my surprise, her smile never wavered. In fact, it only grew on her beautiful face as she stared at me. "You're getting greedy," she teased.

"A man's gotta try."

"I'll see what I can do."

It wasn't a yes, but it wasn't a no either and I could accept that. It also wasn't the best time to be discussing emotions. I liked to think that it at least gave her one more reason to stay in my arms. I closed the last inch between us, capturing her slightly parted lips in a rough kiss. Her hands came up and cupped my head, holding me in place as her tongue slipped into my mouth while my hand tightened on her side. If she continued to kiss me like this, I was willing to carry her back into my apartment where I would keep her locked away from everyone.

"Rowena!" shouted Eldon, sounding more than a little shocked. I didn't know whether it was the fact that she was kissing a human, a tattoo artist, or a warlock that he found so appalling. It could have been all three. The truth was that I wasn't making a very good impression on a member of her family, but I really didn't care.

It was only the sound of gravel being crunched beneath boots that finally pulled my lips from Trixie's. Keeping her locked to my side, I turned my attention back to Eldon and the others, narrowing my gaze on them. I had to fix this, and there was only one way to fix the issue of Trixie's freedom and the rift with her family if she was ever to be happy.

"I've been told that the only reason your king wants Rowena is because he has been unable to father a child with his wife," I said in a neutral tone.

Eldon's brow furrowed as he stared at me. "She's been chosen to be his consort. It's an honor."

I bit my tongue against his "honor" comment, as Trixie didn't seem to see it as much of one. "What if he could father a child with his wife?"

"That would be preferred, but the queen has been unable to have a child with either the king or her own consort," Eldon admitted, his expression softening as he looked over at his sister. "Rowena is our only hope. The royal line cannot be allowed to die out. We would be attacked by both the Winter Court and the Svartálfar."

I wanted to say that Trixie wasn't the only hope, but the king was being stubborn because she was probably the first one to run from him. It wasn't just her beauty that made Trixie so valuable. It was her strength, intelligence, and wonderful spirit that drew those around her.

"What if I could find a way for them to have a child?" I pushed, forcing him to circle back to the idea.

Eldon frowned and shifted from his left to his right foot. He seemed hesitant to answer me as he looked over his shoulder at his companions. I had a feeling that court gossip was not something discussed with outsiders. I was just hoping that Eldon would be willing to take a risk on me for the happiness of his sister.

"There would need to be a reconciliation," Eldon admitted after a few seconds of silence.

"Between whom?"

Eldon's eyes darted away from me as he proved reluctant to continue. Luckily, Trixie spoke up when the others refused to look at me. "Between the king and queen. When it was declared that they could not have children together, the king did not search out any remedies, as others in his position have in the past. He simply jumped at the chance to have a consort. While I doubt that she would admit it, I think she was hurt by his readiness to abandon her."

"That's gossip, Rowena!" Eldon snapped.

"How would you feel if you could not have children with Alaina and she immediately jumped into the arms of another?" Trixie shot back at him while wrapping her arms loosely around my shoulders.

I looked over at her to find her intently watching her brother. "Alaina?" I asked, capturing her attention again.

"His wife. They were matched just before I left."

"It's different between the king and queen. They have their duty," Eldon interjected quickly, moving the topic away from his own life.

"Duty or not, she's still a woman. She can feel spurned and un-loved by his lack of concern for her," Trixie argued.

"He's the king. He has to think of his duty to the royal line," El-don contended, but even he failed to meet Trixie's angry gaze when he spoke. It didn't seem as if he completely believed the argument he was making.

"Regardless, this has to end," I slipped in before Trixie could dispute his claim. "If you've spent all this time hunting for your sister, you can't have been spending too much time with your wife. Wouldn't you like this to end so you can go back to your life? Wouldn't it be best if your king and queen were united rather than separated by Rowena?"

"What are you proposing, warlock?" Eldon hedged.

"His name is Gage and you will use it," Trixie snapped heatedly.

I smiled at Eldon, who stiffly nodded at me, hating to recognize my existence beyond the nuisance I was proving to be. "Can you ar-range for the queen to meet with me?"

"You want a meeting with the queen?" Eldon's entire body be-came rigid with the idea. "What could you possibly have to offer?"

"Possibly an answer to this problem—isn't it worth the risk? Just a short delay?"

"We've delayed long enough," Eldon growled, glaring at Trixie.

"Wouldn't you rather see your sister happy?" I said, causing the frown on Eldon's face to fade.

Eldon stared at his sister, his face devoid of any expression. "Are you happy as you are?"

"When I'm not being chased? Yes, I'm very happy."

"I would rather see you home with your own people where you are needed, but if this is the life you want, then I will try to speak with the queen. I can't make any promises. She knows I'm one of the king's guards searching for you and things have been . . . tense since the king and queen have sought their own consorts."

"Thank you, Eldon," Trixie whispered.

"Don't thank me. Like I said, I would rather have you home. I have a daughter now and I would like her to know her only aunt."

"Congratulations," I said to Eldon, who glared at me.

"I will be in contact as soon as possible." He then turned up the driveway and walked away. Watching the elves disappear around the apartment building, I wrapped both my arms around Trixie's waist and breathed a heavy sigh of relief. I had bought us some time. I didn't know how much, but it would have to be enough for now.

Trixie lay her head on my shoulder. "I have a niece."

"And he should be home taking care of his daughter instead of chasing you," I groused, staring blindly at the back of the building. There were a handful of balconies with metal railings covered in peeling white paint. I was lucky in that no one had stepped out onto their private balcony to watch the little family drama unfold. Elves were an extremely private people and I was sure that Trixie had no desire to air her personal laundry before an audience.

"Don't, Gage," she said, raising her head when I looked over at her. "This has been hard on Eldon. He was a member of the guard before I left, and I knew that he would be the one forced to search for me since I am his sister and we have a connection. I can't hide from blood. At least, not for long."

"Being your blood, he should have supported you. He should have protected you and believed in what you wanted for your life instead of trying to force you to submit to the king."

"You shouldn't judge him so harshly. We're not like you," she said, frowning. "We're raised to believe that we should do what is best for our people and that making hard choices isn't about sacrifice but about honor. I am an outcast among my people because of what I did. No one looks up to me or supports me."

"Then why did you do it if it went against your upbringing?"

"I didn't believe in what the king was doing. He was very forward with me even before it was declared that the king and queen couldn't have children. And maybe Eldon is right. I am selfish. I wanted more for my life than what I could have as a consort."

I shook my head, smiling at her. "Selfish or not, I'm glad you left. I'm glad that you came into my world, and I'm going to work very hard to keep you here as long as it is what you want."

Trixie leaned in and pressed a quick kiss to my lips. "Thank you."

"I am assuming that we can count on Eldon's word and that you'll be safe for a little while."

"Yes, we should have a minimum of a few days, but I wouldn't be surprised if it took much longer. I think it would be safe for me to return to my apartment. I can even open the shop tonight and work for a while to make up for all the recent chaos."

"No, leave the shop closed," I said quickly, then adjusted my tone to a more neutral level. "Take the day off. You've been through a lot and could use the break."

"And you've got some other plans in the works that you don't want me around for," Trixie added in a grim voice.

"Yes, I do," I admitted. I had lied and hidden enough from her during our friendship. I was tired of it, but in this one instance, I would not allow her to become involved. She was threatened by the elves and in danger with the warlocks. I didn't need her more entangled in the mess I had made of my life. "It's just one last thing that I need to sort out and then I'll tell you everything."

"You better," Trixie said, tapping the tip of my nose with her index finger. "You've been hiding too much from me and I don't want any more secrets between us."

"Agreed. Now go home and get some rest. I'll catch up with you tomorrow."

Trixie smiled at me one last time, but I could see the worry in her eyes. I reminded myself that I could still fix everything. I just needed a little more time and luck. Once Tera and the grim reaper were taken care of, I could then turn my attention to Trixie's problem with the king of the Summer Court. Unfortunately, that still left me with no answers when it came to the warlocks, and I still had to pull Bronx from Reave's grasp. I hadn't a clue as to what I could do about either problem, but I knew a couple of places where I could dig for some answers.

Waving to Trixie as she pulled out of the small parking lot in her little green hybrid, I forced a smile onto my lips. For the first time, I wondered if it would have been better to let the elves take her back to the Summer Court. As consort of the king, the Ivory Towers wouldn't be able to touch her without causing a war, and for now it seemed as if everyone was trying to avoid a war. Staying here meant that I was the only one who could protect her from Simon's wrath. The arrangement was less than ideal. Right now, I had to figure out what was the bigger threat and take care of it before I ran out of time.

27

AS I WALKED up the wooden stairs to the creaky front porch, I pulled my cell phone out of my back pocket and glanced at the time. It was just after six. Plenty of time for a quick visit with Sofie and then back to the tattoo parlor by nine so I could meet with Tera. I had already left a message with Bronx updating him on Trixie's status regarding her kin. On the way to Sofie's, I stopped off at the parlor and divided up the river water I had picked up from the underworld. I saved five small vials of the various rivers and carefully marked them before hiding them in the back of my padlocked cabinet in the basement. The other five were safely packed away in a small case and would be delivered to Chang as soon as I figured out exactly what I needed from the wily old man.

The wooden porch groaned under my feet as I crossed to the front door and rang the bell. I glanced up and down the quiet suburban street. The neighborhood was empty, but then it was likely that most people were sitting down to dinner at that moment, relating their tales of the day. Sofie's small yard was full of blooming flowers and green bushes, leaving little room for grass, which was probably for the best as the old woman would have needed to hire someone to maintain a large yard if she wanted to keep up appearances.

At the sound of the door opening, I swung around to face a white-haired old woman in a cotton dressing gown. A slow meow drew my attention down to her slippered feet where a large house cat with a distinct blue-gray coat brushed against the woman's legs. Wide yellow eyes gazed up at me.

"Hello, Sofie," I said with a smile.

"Hello, Gage. It's been a while," the old woman replied as she took a step back and motioned for me to enter. I stepped inside and closed the door behind me before following her and her cat into the crowded living room. Large, bulky furniture filled the tiny room so that I had to sidle sideways in order to sit down on the couch. The old woman paused next to a big rocking chair with thick cushions. "Would you like some tea?"

I shook my head, relaxing against the back of the couch. "No thank you. I can't stay long. I was hoping for some information."

The old woman laughed, wagging one bony finger at me. "Oh, you naughty boy! You've come here trying to get me into trouble."

"You know I would never do that to you, Sofie. I'm in a bit of a bind and I could really use a little insight into what's going on."

The old woman nodded and settled into the rocking chair. The Russian blue jumped into her lap and curled up while the old woman gently stroked her soft fur. Frowning, I leaned over to my left and turned off the old black-and-white TV, silencing the evening news. I didn't need the distraction.

"What can I do for you?" the old woman inquired.

"First, it would be great if we could drop the act," I replied with a shake of my head. "You know I find the whole thing too confusing."

The cat lifted its head and fixed its intense yellow eyes on me before giving its tail a quick flick. The old woman's eyes drooped and finally closed before soft snoring slipped from her. The cat sat on its back paws, facing me.

"Most people prefer the pretense. They feel it is easier to talk to an old woman," the cat said.

"Yes, but I find it uncomfortable since I know the truth."

The cat swished its tail back and forth in a lazy motion. "To each his own. You've always been an odd one, Gage Powell."

"Thanks, Sofie," I said and smiled at her. Some things didn't change despite the passage of time or even the unfortunate morphing of a body. Sofie still had an incredibly thick Russian accent that made her somewhat difficult to understand at first. It also didn't help that she was trying to talk around a mouthful of sharp fangs.

I had seen Sofie only a couple times in human form, and then she had been a relatively sweet old witch with a plump body and curly gray hair. Unfortunately, she had run afoul of someone stronger and found herself cursed to live the rest of her days in the form of a cat. What little I could get out of Sofie about her situation revealed that she couldn't change back into human form until the person who had worked the curse died. I didn't know who had cursed her and I wasn't brave enough to bring up the topic. Despite being a cat, Sofie was still a formidable witch in her own right.

As I understood it, after being transformed into a cat, she quickly realized that in order to maintain a comfortable lifestyle she needed to acquire an owner. The old woman was allowed to live her normal life under most circumstances, but Sofie put her under tight mind control when someone from her past, such as myself, appeared. Sadly, I didn't even know the old woman's real name. I just called her Sofie for the sake of simplicity. It didn't matter since she wouldn't remember my visit once I left.

"Have you had any problems?" I asked.

"None. You're one of the few who still visits me. I'm sure that everyone else has forgotten about me by now."

"You're a hard one to forget."

Sofie let out a long soft purr of pleasure. "While I certainly appreciate it, I know you didn't come to visit me just to throw sweet compliments at my feet. What's troubling you?"

"Simon," I grumbled.

"That annoying old windbag is still giving you problems? I thought he had finally let you go," Sofie said, her tail stopped in its swishing about at the mention of my former mentor's name. There seemed to be too few witches and warlocks in existence who had a good memory of Simon. Even if he hadn't been a warlock, I had a feeling that man had been born to be an asshole.

"It had been a while since I'd last encountered him. I've got my own personal guardian keeping tabs on me and generally harassing me whenever he gets the chance."

"Who?"

"Gideon."

Sofie nodded once as she settled down to lie on her stomach on the old woman's lap. "He's a fair one as warlocks go. It could have been worse."

"Possibly, but I'm getting the feeling that Simon has told Gideon to step aside for a while so that he can personally take care of me."

"Why do you say that?"

"A few days ago I used a little magic in a fight and Gideon was all over me. Since then, I've used magic several times in some questionable circumstances and Gideon hasn't taken those excellent opportunities to haul me in front of the council and let me get fried. On the other hand, Simon seems to be popping up all the time now even though I haven't seen him in years."

"That is odd," Sofie admitted as she rested her chin on her front paws.

"What do you think?"

"It doesn't look good for Gideon. He has always taken his job very seriously, and he was never one to step aside for anyone, particularly Simon. Unless, of course, Simon has gained enough power to actually ascend to the council."

"Not good for me." I frowned as my gaze drifted around the room, taking in the floral wallpaper, pretty landscape pictures, and collection of delicate porcelain plates. I shivered, but I didn't think it had anything to do with the air-conditioning, cranked to the max. I would be the last person to say that Gideon was a good guy, but Sofie was right in saying that he was fair. I could at least reason with him, whereas none of the others seemed willing to listen.

With a sigh, I slumped on the couch and looked back at Sofie, who was still regarding me with her bright yellow eyes. "Have you heard any news from the Towers?"

Sofie blinked once and then turned her head away from me and closed her eyes. "Not anything that you'd want to hear."

"What?" I demanded, jerking upright again so that I was sitting on the edge of the sofa.

"Have you considered moving?"

"Where? Where on earth don't they have an influence? Where can I run, because that's what you're telling me to do? Run?"

Sofie opened her eyes and looked at me again. "Peter died about a month ago."

"Shit." I sank back into the couch and dropped my head into my right hand while resting my elbow on the cushioned arm of the couch. The council was comprised of thirteen witches and warlocks who tried to maintain some kind of peace between the inhabitants of the Ivory Towers and the rest of the world. It was never an easy peace. When I decided to part ways with Simon, barely surviving the resulting fight, my case went before the council. The vote had been seven to six to let me live. Peter had been the deciding vote in my favor. I didn't know who the others were who voted for me and I doubted I ever would. As I was leaving the Towers, Peter had pulled me aside and given me one last bit of advice. *Hide.*

"Who has taken his place on the council?" I asked.

"No one yet, as far as I have heard. These things can take a while. But my guess is that Simon is trying to clean up his past so he can be considered."

"And I'm an ugly blot on his past," I muttered under my breath. Glowering at the coffee table, a new heart-stopping thought occurred to me. I pushed up so that I was sitting on the edge of the couch. "Can they retry a case if they get a new council?"

"No, they can't. Once a decision has been handed down, they won't bring it back up for review. However, at the moment, I wouldn't risk getting pulled in front of the council. With Peter gone, it doesn't look like you would have enough votes."

"And if there's a tie vote?"

"You'll be imprisoned until the council seat is filled and the deciding vote is cast. That could be years, my dear. But I wouldn't worry about that. If rumors are to be believed, you wouldn't get a tie vote."

"Why do you say that?"

If I hadn't seen it, I wouldn't have believed it possible for a cat to sigh, but then Sofie wasn't a normal cat. She sat up again on her back paws. She was a slightly larger than usual cat, but not so that you'd think it was too out of the ordinary. She had a regal bearing, making it easy to see why cats had been worshipped in Egypt.

"You're not the only renegade warlock running around now," Sofie admitted.

"What?"

"They did everything they could to hush up what happened with you, and wipe away all memory of you, because they were afraid that if other apprentices heard what you did, they would rise up as well."

"I wasn't trying to lead some kind of revolution for better treatment, I just wanted out."

"Whether you were the inspiration or not, three apprentices have left their mentors during the past several months. Two warlocks and one witch-in-training."

"Fuck," I whispered, flopping back against the couch. "Have you heard whether they've been caught?"

To my surprise, Sofie jumped from the old woman's lap to mine. Standing on her back paws, she leaned her front paws against my chest, putting her face just a couple of inches from mine. "No, but I wouldn't tell you anything about them if I did know. You can't seek them out. You can't help them in any way. If you are seen with them, the council will instantly see it as you trying to lead a rebellion against the Ivory Towers. They won't hesitate to send everything they've got against you, and they won't stop until you're dead."

I picked up Sofie and held her out at arm's length so that my eyes weren't crossing as I tried to focus on her. "I have no intention of leading a rebellion. I just wanted to escape Simon and live my quiet life unnoticed."

"Good luck with that," she mumbled, her ears twitching slightly. I lowered her back down to my lap where she sat looking up at me.

"So Simon wants me dead in order to get a position on the council, and the others would prefer seeing me dead so I can't assist those who have escaped. It's sad they don't take this as a sign that maybe times have changed and that the apprentices need to be treated better."

Sofie made a little noise in the back of her throat that sounded like she was trying to cough up a fur ball. I was starting to reach to push her off my lap when I realized that she had actually given a little laugh at my comment. "They've been doing things this way for centuries. They're not going to change."

"No, I guess not." I lifted my arms and dropped them over the back of the couch as I lounged there, staring at the sleeping old woman. Sofie was one of the most compassionate witches I had ever met, but she still had the mentality of her peers. She hadn't thought twice about moving into the old woman's home and taking over her mind for her own ends. The old woman had become little more than a fleshy puppet to be used. Was that how all the witches and warlocks saw the creatures of the earth, particularly the humans?

A substantial change to the council also didn't offer any promise of a bright future for humanity. The Great War that had been waged with the Ivory Towers had decimated the human and fey populations nearly a century ago and had led to the extinction of at least two races. The resulting peace when a surrender was finally tendered had always been a shaky one. Many who inhabited the Ivory Towers had argued that the warlocks and witches had not acquired enough concessions or enough power. I was sure that Simon was one of these. If he rose to the council, a new war seemed to hover just over the horizon.

But I couldn't worry about any of that. I had enough with my own problems. "So what am I supposed to do?" I asked.

"I think you know what you need to do," Sofie said.

"Run and hide again?"

"No."

"Kill Simon," I replied in a soft voice, to which Sofie simply nodded. Yeah, I thought so. Simon's death would not only buy me some time, but everyone else as well. "Murder isn't high on my to-do list and I'm not even sure I'm strong enough to accomplish such a thing."

"Well—" Sofie started and then suddenly stopped, her body going stiff while her ears perked up and forward as if she was listening for something. I turned my head as well, straining to hear a sign of someone coming up on the front porch, but everything was silent.

"Were you followed?" Sofie demanded, turning her face back toward me.

"I don't think so. Why?"

"Someone is here."

"Who?"

"Don't know," Sofie replied as she jumped from my lap and back over to the old woman's. She pressed her front paws against the woman's chest and meowed once. The old woman's eyes opened and closed a few times before she looked over at me. "We need to leave now," she announced.

I pushed out of the chair at the same time that the old woman rose. Laying my hands on her frail shoulders, I stopped her as she tried to shuffle toward the front door. The cat threaded through her legs, meowing desperately.

"She can't go, Sofie," I said, looking down at the cat.

"Why not?" the old woman asked, jerking my eyes back up to her face. I hated it when Sofie talked through the old woman. I wasn't sure who to look at when I replied.

"She's old, Sofie. She won't survive running from anyone who might have come looking for you or me. She has to stay behind. They are not looking for the old woman and won't harm her."

The old woman stared at me, frowning for several seconds before she finally stepped back, out of my grasp. She sat down in her rocking chair and promptly fell asleep again. She was out of Sofie's grasp.

Bending down, I scooped up Sofie while briskly walking toward the door. Propping the cat on my left hip while holding her by her stomach with my left hand, I slowly pulled open the front door and peered out. The neighborhood was empty. A bird chirped from the white picket fence by the sidewalk, which was a slight reassurance. When a witch or a warlock was about, wildlife was quick to flee.

"Wait!" Sofie commanded as I took a step into the doorway. I paused, still peeking out the slender opening. On my left, I could feel a stirring of energy as Sofie started casting a spell, for which I was grateful. She hadn't been banned from using magic, unlike me. In fact, she was still technically a member of the Ivory Towers community if she wanted to return. I wasn't sure if she'd left because she was stuck as a cat in a largely humanoid world, or if she was afraid that she'd be easier to kill in cat form. Either way, she'd left it all for a seminormal life as a house pet.

Just past the door, a Russian blue cat shimmered into existence. It bent its head and briefly licked the fur on its chest before darting off the porch and through the flowers in the front yard. A second later it vaulted over the small white picket fence and ran across the street where it disappeared behind a yellow house.

"Okay, go now," Sofie said.

I didn't question it or hesitate. Quietly shutting the door behind me, I slipped off the porch and jogged to my car parked a couple of houses down the street. Jerking open the driver's-side door, I tossed Sofie inside and slid behind the wheel. I was vaguely aware of the cat jumping from the front to the backseat where she leaned up against the window and meowed forlornly.

"Mae!" Sofie plaintively cried as I revved the engine and pulled away from the curb. I didn't look back as I drove out of the subdivision and headed for the nearest highway on-ramp.

"She'll be fine," I said, trying to reassure her. Unfortunately, I had more than I could deal with on my plate already. I didn't want to add concern over an old woman looking for her lost cat. "I can find a way to get her a new cat."

"Thank you," Sofie whispered.

As we slipped into evening traffic and headed back to my tattoo parlor, I turned my thoughts back to more pressing issues. "What was it back there?"

"Not sure," Sofie said as she jumped back into the front seat and curled up. "But there were two of them."

"How did you know they would go after you?" I asked, thinking of the decoy she had sent running off the front porch and across the street.

"I didn't. I sent a similar image of you running out the back of the house and over the fence for them to chase as well. They took the bait and I'm not going to question it."

"I'm sorry about this. I didn't mean to drag you into my problems. I know you had a comfortable life."

Sofie stretched out her paws, extending her long sharp claws, while yawning. "It was a life. It's better this way. I had grown fond of Mae and I didn't want her hurt should someone decide to finish me off."

"Where will you go now?"

Sofie gave a soft chuckle as she curled up again. "I'm your pet now, Gage."

"What?" I cried, jerking the wheel at her announcement. I quickly righted my bulky SUV again in the center lane before I plowed us into a semi. "I don't think so."

"They wouldn't have come looking for me if I hadn't helped you. You cost me a home, so I think it's only fair that you provide me with a new one."

"I'm not very good with pets. I could never keep my goldfish alive," I hedged. I really didn't need a cranky old witch trapped in a cat's body prowling around my apartment. I still had to deal with the grim reaper and Simon. My life expectancy wasn't looking that great, and I didn't want to worry about keeping a cat alive.

"I'm sure you'll do fine," she purred.

I frowned as I switched lanes, passing a slower car as it signaled to leave the interstate. This had not been a part of my plans for the day. "I also don't do mind control. I'm not going to be your puppet."

"I have no plans to do such a thing to you."

"Or my friends?"

"Or your friends," Sofie repeated, sounding a little put out.

"Fine," I huffed. "You can stay at the tattoo parlor for a while until we can figure out something else. I've got a lot of balls in the air right now and I don't want to worry about your safety or happiness."

"I'm stuck in the body of a cat, Gage. How much trouble could I be?" she demanded, sounding more than a little irritated with me.

"You're a witch. That in itself is trouble enough."

Sofie softly purred from the passenger seat as she stretched out on her back and closed her eyes with a look of contentment. She seemed to have gotten over her separation anxiety regarding her former owner relatively quickly. "I'll behave. Now roll down the window. I want to feel the wind through my fur."

I pushed the button on my armrest, lowering the passenger-side window while trying to keep my attention on the busy road before me. For the first time I wondered if I had been duped. I had never sensed a presence at Sofie's house, but then I trusted her more honed skills and years of experience. Could she have grown tired of her old life and wanted something more entertaining? Or was she now trying to keep an eye on me for her own purposes?

A sigh slipped from my parted lips as I slumped behind the wheel, squinting against the setting sun. It didn't matter for the time being. I was now the proud owner of a beautiful cat that could tell me exactly what it was thinking. Things were not looking up.

28

DRIVING TOWARD THE parlor, I found myself wishing I had dropped Sofie at Trixie's place for a while until I could figure something out. I really was no good when it came to animals and I didn't want Sofie at my apartment. I stopped at a red light and frowned. But if someone was still looking for Sofie, dropping the cat at Trixie's would only put the elf back in danger. The light changed and I pressed the gas pedal, jumping across the intersection. The parlor would have to do for now. I stopped briefly at a pet store to pick up some odds and ends before parking behind the shop.

I trudged down the wooden stairs to the apartment on the second floor. Balancing everything in my left hand and on my hip, I unlocked the door. Sofie shot inside ahead of me, sniffing around the living room as I followed. I quickly set up food and water bowls in the kitchen, and was secretly grateful when she told me that she used the toilet rather than a litter box. My stomach had turned at the thought of cleaning up the droppings of a witch in cat's garb.

Pulling my cell phone out of my back pocket I glanced at the time before shoving it back in place. It was just after eight o'clock. I had some time to set things up in the tattoo parlor before Tera was to meet me. Turning back toward the door, Sofie jumped up on the sofa and stood on the arm nearest the front door, watching me with expectant eyes.

"Are you leaving already?" Sofie asked.

"I've got another appointment tonight that I can't miss. I want you to stay here until tomorrow and then we'll try to figure out something more permanent."

"This isn't your apartment?"

My eyes darted away from her face, and it was only when her front paw brushed against my arm that the words jerked out. "No. I own the building and sometimes stay here, but this isn't my apartment."

Sofie's eyes narrowed to thin yellow slits. "Are you thinking that you can just dump me? I warn you—"

"Geez, no! I'm trying to find a good place for you to live. My apartment isn't it."

"Well, don't think you can just forget about me. I'm not going to let you. Besides, it seems like you could use a little help with your life considering all the messes you've gotten yourself into. I have some experience in dispensing good advice and direction to the young."

It was a fight not to roll my eyes at that announcement. Sofie had decided to become my own Jiminy Cricket with fur. A little magic advice would be appreciated if I was to go up against Simon, but I had a feeling that Sofie had no intention of limiting herself merely to the teaching of spells. No, this nosy cat was going to meddle in my personal life because, while in the Ivory Towers, she had been the only one to have any kind of motherly attitude toward the apprentices. Meddling was who Sofie was.

"My life is not a mess," I grumbled, pushing away the nagging thought that the claim was a blatant lie.

"Honestly, Gage, you've got Simon chasing you and you're on the least-favorite list of the members of the council. Heaven only knows what other scrapes you've gotten into. And you've got no girlfriend.

You're a handsome, talented young man. You should have a girl-friend."

"How do you know I don't have a girlfriend?" I demanded, feeling more than a little silly glaring at a cat. The fact was that I might have a girlfriend. Trixie and I hadn't had that exact discussion yet and it wasn't one that I was particularly looking forward to considering that I had hung myself and threatened her brother on the same day, but I was hoping that our arrangement was more than a "friends with benefits" kind of thing.

"Because you said you had an appointment tonight. Not a date," Sofie pointed out, batting one paw at me for emphasis.

I ran a hand roughly over my face. I was wasting time that I needed to get things settled before Tera arrived. Focusing on Sofie, who was once again waiting for me to respond to her accusation, I frowned. This could be the last time I'd see Sofie if things didn't go well tonight.

"Look, I've got to take care of something important this evening," I started, my voice thick and heavy. "If . . . if things don't go well, I'm going to leave a note in the parlor explaining everything. I will ask my friend Trixie to take care of you. She's a very sweet, wonderful person and I know she'll watch over you. I would just like you to promise not to use mind control on her. She doesn't deserve that kind of treatment."

Standing on her back paws, Sofie rested her front paws against my chest so that her face was closer to mine. "What's going on?"

"It would take too long to explain and I don't have the time. Just promise me no mind control."

Sofie dropped back down to the arm of the couch, sitting on her haunches as she stared up at me. "I promise." I didn't think a cat could look worried, so it might have been something in her voice telling me she was. I forced a smile on my lips as I reached up and scratched the top of her head. I suddenly jerked to a stop when I realized that I was treating the witch like a cat, but to my surprise she leaned into my hand, closing her eyes as she purred deeply. Apparently she wasn't opposed to a little physical attention, just like a regular cat. This was going to get more than confusing.

Slipping out of the apartment, I stomped down the wooden stairs and then went around to the front door of the parlor and inside. I locked the door and didn't bother to turn on the lights in the front of the shop. I didn't want to draw the attention of anyone who might be walking by. We all had a number of friends who frequented the bars in the area and I didn't want to take the chance that someone might stop by for a visit. Weaving in the dark through the chairs in the back, I headed to the room in the very rear of the building, where I shut the door and flipped on the light. I retreated to my storeroom in the basement and retrieved the vial of Styx river water and carefully carried it back up to the main floor.

Setting the vial on the middle shelf of the large cabinet that dominated the far wall, I quickly turned and searched out a plastic pipette and a plastic cap for the ink. I soundlessly gathered the last of the equipment I needed, pulling it all together on the shelf with the water. When I got Tera situated on the table, I didn't want to worry about running around to get my supplies. I wanted everything on hand so that I could get the job done quickly.

As I placed the sealed packet of needles next to the paper plate, petroleum jelly, and stack of paper napkins, I looked down at my hands and found them shaking. My heart was pounding in my chest and my breath was coming in short rapid bursts, as if I had been running. Wiping away the sweat that had started to bead on my forehead, I walked over and sat down on a stool while flexing my hands. I needed to calm down. I wouldn't be able to work if my hands were shaking.

I didn't want to do this. It wasn't right for Tera to be given immortality because of a careless mistake on my part, because no one should be immortal in this world. Yet I didn't want her to go rushing to her death either. There had to be some kind of middle ground.

She was young and sweet, and should be allowed to live out her life to a more natural end in her seventies or eighties.

Leaning forward, I dropped my face into my hands. People died every day—young and old. It wasn't my job to decide who got to live and who had to die. I was more than happy to leave that to my visitor the grim reaper. I didn't envy him that job. Did he even have a life? When he wasn't running around reaping souls, did he have time off to play golf or date?

I rubbed my face to clear my thoughts of the strange bent they had taken and rose to my feet. There were things I still needed to get done. Glancing up at the clock as I entered the main room, I had about thirty minutes before Tera was to arrive. I flipped on the light and grabbed a couple of sheets of blank paper from the printer before sitting on one of the stools. Laying the paper on a thick book on my lap of tattooing designs and techniques, I started a letter to Trixie and Bronx.

It was with a weary sigh that I explained everything. I briefly admitted my warlock background, warned of the danger of the basement, detailed the mess I had made with Tera and the promise I had made to Chang. I didn't want them going into the basement should I be killed, but I asked that they allow Chang to try. I trusted the old man to not only get past my defenses, but to also pay my friends a fair price for the items that he would find. I was on the third piece of paper when I finally got around to asking Trixie to take care of Sofie and explaining what little I knew of the witch's problems. I told them where to find my will, which left them the tattoo parlor if I had been killed or was missing for more than eighteen months. I concluded with telling Trixie to demand that Chang find her a proper fertility relic that would help with her problem in exchange for the items in the basement. Unfortunately, I had no fix for Bronx's current situation and I only hoped that Reave would release him if I was no longer around to torment.

Looking over the letter, I felt a swell of disgust rising in my stomach. My life had been quickly detailed over three pages in brutal, unflinching honesty. It was a mess. There was no mention of the family I hadn't seen in a decade, no tender words for Trixie, or even an apology for hurting her and Bronx. There was nothing telling my two best friends in the world how much they had meant to me and my sanity over the years. There just wasn't time.

A knock on the front door jerked my head up. Walking over to the doorway leading into the lobby, I motioned toward Tera, who was peering through the glass, that I would be there in just a minute. Turning back toward the tattooing room, I folded the thick letter twice and wrote on the outside "Read If I Don't Appear by 9 P.M." That would give me twenty-four hours to clean up the mess I had created of my life and Tera's. If I succeeded, I would be able to get back to the shop and destroy the letter before anyone saw it. Laying the letter on the chair that Trixie used for tattooing, I looked over the room as I reached for the light switch. There had been so much laughter here. Before I had decided to dabble in the realm of life and death.

Forcing a smile on my face, I turned off the light and moved toward the front door where Tera was waiting. I had the acting job of a lifetime before me. I had to pretend to be excited and happy while planning to steal a young girl's life away. I was a monster.

29

TERA'S SOFT MOAN brought my gaze up to where she lay on her stomach, tied down to the table. Everything was going according to plan, except for me. Actually, it had started out better than I'd planned. Tera realized as we walked down to a bar close to the shop that she had forgotten her ID, so we quickly popped by her apartment. While there I convinced her to have a celebratory drink with me to christen our night. She missed me dropping the strong sedative I had crushed up into her beer bottle. The sleeping pill mixed with the alcohol took quick effect once we had returned to my car. By the time we had gotten back to the shop, she was out. Parking behind the parlor, I entered through the back door. Quickly removing her shirt, I laid her gently on the padded surface and taped her hands together under the table.

I had gotten the red ink and Styx water mixed, as well as the needles placed in the tattooing machine, before reality started to set in again.

Now I sat on the floor against the cabinet in the dark, listening to Tera's slow breathing and my own erratic heart rate. I didn't need to retattoo her entire back. I planned on adding a few red highlights to her existing tattoo by using the red ink mixed with the underworld river water. But now that I was faced with her limp body, I couldn't do it.

My own will to live easily conjured up the argument that I was returning things to their natural order. Humans weren't meant to be immortal. It was as simple as that. I was correcting a mistake I'd made and I couldn't take the chance of Tera fighting me on this matter, so I had to tattoo her while she was unconscious.

But that argument tasted like ash on my tongue when I thought about the fact that she was facing an almost immediate death should I succeed at my task. Was my problem that I was still determined to cheat death? Was I really so cocky that I thought I could save her when the grim reaper had already laid claim to her soul? I wanted it to be, because she seemed like a nice person and I didn't want a nice person to die when there was so much evil in the world. I wasn't sure. Maybe I didn't want the guilt of being linked to her eventual death in any way because the guilt would be suffocating.

Tera groaned as the sound of tape stretching and scraping the underside of the table ripped through the silence. My muscles tensed as my eyes lifted to her face, waiting for her to fully awaken. She gave a soft grunt in the back of her throat as her struggles with the tape on her wrists became more pronounced. I hadn't wanted to do this while she was awake. Not only would she then know that I was robbing her of her life, but the still-healing skin on her back would be extremely tender and sore as I laid the tattooing needle down for a second trip. She didn't deserve the extra helping of pain to go along with the death that loomed.

As she woke, I knew that my conscience would only allow me to proceed if she realized what the situation was. I'd been afraid that if I'd told her sooner, she would have run. Even now, knowing that I was going to tell her the truth, I was unwilling to release her. I couldn't take the chance. My life was on the line too.

"What's going on?" Tera demanded in a rough, groggy voice. She lifted her head, her eyes blinking against the thick, inky darkness that filled the room. I doubted that she could see anything. I had been sitting in the dark for nearly an hour and could make out only shapes in the blackness. I could hear her struggling to free her hands again as her breathing started to become heavier. "Help! Help! Please, someone—"

"It's okay, Tera," I interrupted in a low voice. "I'm not going to hurt you." It had been on the tip of my tongue to say that she was safe, but I swallowed those bitter words. She wasn't safe. Not from me. Not from death.

Staring at her in the darkness, my will hardened. As distasteful as I found it, I knew that I was going to do this. It had come down to either me or her. If that was all that was at stake, I think I would have at least considered trading places with her. But it wasn't. If I died, Trixie would be left to fend for herself. Bronx would be stuck with Reave because of me. And if the world found out there was an immortal walking the earth, there would be a war, resulting in the death of many, many more. Sure, I had made certain there were contingencies in place that could head off those problems for the most part, but so much could be solved it I simply let Tera die.

Her head whipped around to look in the direction from where my voice had originated. "Gage?"

"Yes." It looked as if a lock of hair had fallen in front of her eyes and I resisted the urge to move over and brush it out of her face.

"Wh-where am I? Why am I tied down to this table? What's going on?" Her tone grew angrier as she spoke now that she realized that she was alone with me. She had trusted me, was starting to count me as a friend, and I was going to betray that.

"You're at the tattoo parlor," I replied and then paused, my mind struggling for a way to launch into this ugly topic. "There's something that we need to talk about."

"Okay, fine, but why am I tied to this table and why are we in the dark?"

"Because I can't take the chance of you running."

"Running? What's going on?"

I drew in a deep breath and slowly released it. Pulling my legs up toward my chest, I rested my elbows on my bent knees and dropped my head into my hands. "Do you remember when you came in and said that I had done something to your tattoo?"

"Yes, but you said you didn't," she replied softly.

"I lied. I did." I paused and licked my lips as I searched for a good explanation. "After you left following our initial talk, I started thinking about what you had told me. I wondered if I could come up with some way to heal you. I didn't want to tell you because I wasn't sure that I could actually succeed and I didn't want you to get your hopes up for nothing."

"But you did succeed," Tera argued. "I'm cured. The doctors said all the cancer is gone."

"No, I didn't!" I countered more sharply than I had meant to. I was angry at myself, not her, and I didn't need to take it out on Tera.

"What do you mean?"

"I didn't cure your cancer. I made you immortal."

I waited, letting the information sink in. The only response I received was the sound of duct tape stretching and scraping.

"I don't understand. If I'm immortal, why can't I break out of this tape?"

A fraction of a smile tweaked one corner of my mouth. "I said I made you immortal, not superhuman."

Tera stopped struggling with the tape and looked back over at where I sat on the floor against the cabinet of potion ingredients. "Immortal? So I can't die?"

"No, you can't die."

The soft "Oh" that followed my confirmation was somewhat reassuring, as she apparently didn't seem overjoyed by the prospect of being immortal. While most people were afraid of death and sought to avoid it at all costs, few truly considered the overwhelming idea of forever while you watched everyone around you die. I was in no hurry to go rushing off to my own death, particularly considering that I still had so much that needed to be done, but I had no desire to live beyond the normal human life span.

"But there's a problem."

"Besides being immortal?" she snapped.

"No, it's about being immortal. The grim reaper had already scheduled your death and he can no longer reap your soul because of what I've done. He's informed me that if I don't return your mortality so that he can do his job, then he will take my soul in your place."

"Wait! He can do that? He can kill you instead of me?"

Threading the fingers of my left hand through my hair, I glanced up at her. "I don't know if it's particularly legal, but the grim reaper isn't the type of guy I want to get into an argument with about his job."

"Did he tell you when I was scheduled to die?" she asked in a small voice that shot straight through my chest.

I closed my eyes and for a brief moment I considered lying, but quickly pushed the temptation aside. Lying was what had gotten me into this mess. "He didn't give any exact figures, but I got the impression that it was soon."

"Well, that would be in keeping with what the doctors were saying," she mumbled, talking mostly to herself. Pressing her forehead against the padded table under her, Tera heaved a heavy sigh. "I'm assuming that you've got me taped down to this table because you've got a plan for undoing this."

"I was going to retattoo you with a different potion."

"Will it kill me?"

"Honestly, I don't know," I admitted in a rough voice. "I am hoping that it simply counters the ingredients of the first tattoo, returning your mortality. With both the first tattoo and the one I want to do tonight, I am working with materials I don't know the effects of."

Her head popped up so that she could glare at me. "How can you use materials when you don't know how they're going to work?"

"Because the items are extremely rare and no one has ever used them," I admitted. I gave a little snort. "I even had to die to get one of them," I added under my breath.

"What do you mean you had to die?" she asked, her tone losing some of its earlier venom.

"It's nothing." I shook my head, not wanting any sympathy. She was the victim here.

"No, you said you died, but how? Are you dead . . . now?"

"No," I replied, unable to stop the smile at her tense question. I wasn't a zombie, ghoul, or member of the undead. "A friend revived me before it was too late. There was one ingredient I had to travel to the underworld to get."

"Wasn't that dangerous?"

"Yes, but then so is leaving you an immortal."

"I understand." She sighed.

I dropped my hands and stared at her in surprise. I hadn't actually expected her to understand. And for a moment, I wasn't sure if that made my job easier or harder. "You do?"

"Please," she scoffed. "I'm in no rush to die, but then I've been living with the idea of dying young for a long time. Even if I hadn't had this stupid disease, I wouldn't want to live forever."

"You're very wise," I said, which earned me a derisive snort.

"Nah, just not crazy. Should we get started? I'm beginning to get a little cold."

Pushing to my feet, I shuffled over to the wall and flicked on the bright overhead light, leaving us both squinting and blinking for several seconds. I settled on the stool beside the table and moved the foot pedal underneath the toe of my sneaker as I pulled on latex gloves and took up the tattooing machine in my right hand. After spreading down some petroleum jelly over the area near her shoulder blades that I planned to start with, I gently set the side of my hand against her back and paused when a thought suddenly occurred to me.

"When we first met, you mentioned that someone had recommended me to you. Do you remember who?" I asked, holding my hand still on her back with the needle hovering an inch above her flesh.

This time, Tera paused for a long moment. I had started to lean down so that I could look at her face when she finally spoke.

"His name's Atticus Sparks."

I drew my hand away from her as my heart skipped once in my chest. Why had my former mentor sent her in my direction? I didn't like this.

"He doesn't have the best or cleanest setup," she continued, unaware of my growing unease. "But a friend said that he works for cheap. I told Atticus Sparks about my situation and he sent me to you, saying that you could help."

"He said I could help? What did he mean by help?"

"I'm not exactly sure and he refused to explain. I kind of thought you might be able to do something about the cancer, but I wasn't about to get my hopes up. The doctors proved to be useless and I knew that it was just as useless to go begging a witch or a warlock for an easy fix. I had never heard of a tattoo artist curing a disease with some ink, but then this Sparks guy seemed pretty confident about your work. I guess he was right about you."

Yeah, Sparks did prove to be right and it was more than a little disturbing. Why had Sparks sent her to me? I trusted Sparks. He knew my secrets, and had never done anything to make me doubt him. But as I sat on the stool with Tera taped down to the table before me, I had a sick feeling that I had been set up.

Closing my eyes for a second, I pressed my foot down on the pedal a couple of times, listening to the distinct sound of the buzz of the machine surge through the room like a bolt of wild electricity searching for an outlet. The sound eased some of the tension from my shoulders, placing me back into a comfort zone in which I could work. It wasn't quite eleven. I had plenty of time to tattoo Tera and then head over to Sparks's for a quick, informative visit.

A feeling of control crept into my frame and I opened my eyes. I was back in the driver's seat of my life and I was ready to move forward. Lowering my right hand onto her back again, I pressed down the foot pedal and drew my first line along the black line I had drawn only a few days earlier. Beneath my hand, I could feel Tera flinch and her muscles jump as I tore at her skin. She didn't make a sound, but I knew it hurt. There was nothing I could do to ease the pain short of knocking her out again.

"I'm sorry," I murmured as I continued down her back. "I'll try to work quickly. I don't need to go over the entire tattoo again. I'm just adding some highlights."

"It's okay," she said in a fractured voice that cut through me.

I worked without speaking. The only sounds in the room were the buzz of the tattooing machine and the occasional creak from my stool as I shifted my position. It was one of the fastest tattoos I had ever done. I completed one side of her back and then pulled all my equipment around to the other side so that I could reach the far side of the table. A part of my mind kept anticipating her request that I remove the tape around her wrists, but she never did. For that I was grateful since I wasn't sure that I would be willing to remove it. Everything she said indicated she wanted me to tattoo her, but I didn't want her to risk trying to run. I would have to stop her with magic, and I knew there would be no gentle way to do that.

Less than an hour ticked by before I finally pulled my hand away and sat back on the stool to look over my canvas. I carefully inspected the lines and looked at the tattoo from several different angles, taking in the effect the red ink was having against the black lines of the wings. The whole tone of the tattoo had changed with the addition of the red lines and I frowned. For its simplicity, the tattoo was still beautiful, but it now had a demonic feel. I had moved Tera from Archangel to Fallen Angel. Keeping my thoughts to myself, I put the tattooing machine on the table beside me and carefully wiped off her back, removing the excess ink, jelly, and blood.

"I'm done. Would you like to see it?" I asked, inwardly dreading her answer. She had just suffered in silence for nearly an hour so that I could put her back in the clutches of the grim reaper. I doubted that she really cared what the tattoo looked like.

"Of course!" she replied with a little laugh that surprised me.

Grabbing a pair of scissors from where I had left them by the sink on the opposite wall, I knelt under the table and carefully cut her hands free. I turned and replaced the scissors as she sat up on the table with a loud groan. I could imagine that her arms and shoulders were sore from where they had been trapped under the table for an extended period. As I turned back, she was holding her unclasped bra to her chest as she moved to the floor-to-ceiling mirror that covered a section of the wall nearest her. Holding up a hand mirror in front of her, she looked into its reflection so that she could see her back in the large mirror. To my shock, a slow smile formed on her lips before she looked over at me.

"I liked the original tattoo, but I have to admit that this one looks good as well and it seems more . . . fitting. You do some fantastic work."

I lowered the hand mirror and returned it to where it had been on the sketch table, dropping my eyes from her face. "Thanks. How do you feel?"

"Sore," she said with a little groan.

"Sorry. It should pass in a couple of days," I said absently, then inwardly winced as I wondered if she even had a couple of days. I turned back to my table of supplies and began the process of bandaging her and cleaning up my workspace. Tera silently watched me work while sitting on the stool that I had used while tattooing her.

When everything was finally put away and there was nothing left that I could busy myself with, I turned to face her. She flashed me a weak little smile. In her hands, she tightly clutched her bra. She hadn't wanted to put it back on, as the straps would dig into her tattooed back and shoulders. Instead, I had politely averted my eyes as I helped her with her button-up blouse.

"What should I do now?" she asked in a soft voice.

"Live. Live as fully as you can."

She smiled at me and I tried to smile back. "You feel guilty, don't you?" Tera cocked her head slightly to the side as her gaze slid over my face. "I'm still alive. So I'm going to die young. That was going to happen before I met you. Nothing you did tonight changed that inevitable outcome. I got exactly what I came in here for: a kick-ass tattoo. Thank you."

"I got your hopes up for nothing," I murmured, shaking my head.

She gave a little snort, bringing my eyes back up to hers. "Hope isn't a bad thing."

"I'll try to remember that." I didn't quite feel better about anything that had happened, but it was nice to know she didn't think I was an insensitive, evil asshole. She was actually a lot more understanding about it all than I would have expected from anyone. I leaned in and carefully wrapped one arm around her neck, hugging her. To my surprise, Tera wrapped both her arms around my waist and hugged me tightly.

"I really appreciate you trying to help. It means a lot, especially since I'm a total stranger," she whispered.

"I just wish it had worked out better."

She pulled away and smiled. "Doesn't matter. You get points for effort."

"If you want to wait outside, I'll go around back and get my car so I can drive you home."

Tera shook her head, her smile not wavering. "Don't worry about it. There's a taxi stand that starts about this time each night to handle the people coming out of the bars. I'll grab a cab."

"You sure? It's not a problem."

"Yeah, I kinda want to be alone right now. Besides, I've always wanted to take a taxi. Can't imagine that I'm going to get many more chances," she said, but her positive mood never wavered despite talking about her own coming demise.

I let the offer drop and walked her to the front door. Our footsteps were nearly silent until we reached the creaky wooden floor in the lobby. I couldn't blame her, as I was probably the last person she wanted to spend more time with. Unlatching the dead bolt, I pulled open the old wood-and-glass door so that she could exit. She hopped down the three cracked concrete steps and paused to look back at me over her shoulder. Tera gave me a little wave, a smile still lifting the corners of her mouth.

I smiled back. Staring at her, I knew that I wouldn't see her alive again. A small part of me wished that I hadn't succeeded, while another part secretly wished I had.

In the end, so much was centered on the life and death of a single girl. She wasn't a world leader, an influential activist, or a powerful magic weaver. If I had never gotten involved, she would have died without a problem and the world would never have missed a beat. But in my stupidity, I tore the tender fabric of the world, shifted the balance so that everything ran screaming toward chaos.

I fixed my mistake and centered the scales once again, but the damage had been done. There were now three people who knew immortality was possible and how to achieve it. It was knowledge that should have stayed tucked away, hidden from the world. While I didn't think we three would ever reveal what we knew, it was like opening Pandora's damn box. Once the knowledge was out there, it was only a matter of time before someone else discovered it.

The world seemed a slightly darker place now, as if there was a new edge that hadn't been there before. The slant of light that shot through the city dimmed and the shadows deepened. Children clung a little tighter to their mothers and lovers huddled together a little closer against the bite of some unknown threat that had come one step closer.

I left the Ivory Towers wanting to take control of my life, but I never thought that maybe if I had stayed in the Towers, the world would have been better protected from me.

30

CLOSING THE DOOR and setting the dead bolt back in place, I reached for the light switch next to the door frame as I turned into the lobby. My heart lurched when my eyes fell on the grim reaper standing a few feet away, wrapped in the shadows. *No.* I jerked my gaze across the room to the old clock hanging on the wall to find that it was roughly seven minutes after midnight, marking the third day. My deadline. The evening had slipped away from me. I had stalled, cleaning up the back room with Tera watching me as I tried to find something helpful or even consoling to say.

"No!" I shouted, pointing one finger at him. "You can't! Not yet!"

I didn't give him a chance to respond, I was already spinning back toward the door. My fingers fumbled with the dead bolt, but it was too late. The sound of screeching tires on asphalt screamed through the night, followed by the horrible thud of something heavy hitting a metal surface. My stomach clenched and I gritted my teeth against the bile that rose in the back of my throat. Muscles tensed and refused to move as my fingers gripped the cold metal lock in one hand. *No, not like this.*

Only a couple of seconds passed, but it felt like an eternity before I managed to unlock the door and surge out of the tattoo parlor. I paused on the sidewalk, eyes darting up and down the street until they focused on a late-model Chevy sitting at the intersection just a few buildings up from my shop. The driver had jumped out of the car and approached a dark lump lying in the middle of the street.

With jerky, stumbling steps, I ran toward the car and the body in the middle of the street. Sliding to a stop, I knelt next to Tera's limp body. Blood was spreading across her forehead and down the side of her face. Her breathing was light and feathery as she gasped a couple of times before she stopped breathing completely.

"No! Tera!" I shouted, grasping her shoulders.

"You know she must go. Let her," urged a gentle voice. My head popped up and I looked over my shoulder to find the grim reaper standing a short distance away, his clipboard resting on his hip. Behind him, people were running up the street from the nearby bars, attracted by the noise. But I was the only one who could see him.

Glaring at the warden of death, I raised my voice. "Call 911!" He was right. Tera was gone and wouldn't be retrieved from the gates of the underworld because of anything I had managed to do. Her time had been preordained before she walked into my parlor a few days ago. All the same, I had to go through the motions as if I didn't already know the outcome.

"You bastard! She was coming from your shop! You killed her!" proclaimed an angry voice that grated against my ears.

Lifting my narrowed gaze from Tera's inert body, I found Russell Dalton kneeling near her feet. It had been his car. He had been driving when he struck Tera, killing her. Obviously, the bad luck tattooed into his skin was still having a strong effect on his miserable life.

My hand shot out toward him and clenched into a fist several inches from his face while power surged through my shaking frame. Russell slammed backward into the door of the car as he scratched at his throat. He made a gasping, choking noise while his feet scraped on the ground as he attempted to get some kind of leverage to push away from me, but I held him tight. My eyes never left his struggling form.

"Is he on your list too?" I whispered through clenched teeth. It didn't matter if the people who were starting to gather around us could hear me. I knew that the reaper could and he was the one I was talking to.

"I can't tell you that," the grim reaper replied in an even tone. There was nothing in his voice to indicate whether he cared if this worm lived or died.

I stared at Russell as his face became a splotchy red and white in the darkness. Tears ran from his eyes as he watched me. I tightened my hold on his neck. With just a little twist of my wrist, I could snap his neck and end it quickly. Or I could continue to hold him like this, crushing his windpipe so that he slowly suffocated to death. The people around me wouldn't do anything to stop me. I was using magic, and humans had learned years ago to not involve themselves in a matter where a human was using magic. It meant only one thing to them: warlock. And it was the job of the warlock to keep the scum in line.

Russell needed to die. He was walking scum. Days ago, he had tried to convince me to work a potion that would have had a negative effect on his wife. He'd threatened me and tried to kill me. He was a bully, walking over those who surrounded him. He had killed Tera. Dalton needed to be wiped clean from the earth.

The small thump on the car hood drew my attention. I looked up to see Sofie sitting on the edge of the car, just above Russell's head. I didn't ask how she had gotten out of the apartment or even how she knew what was going on. She was a witch. Sofie just sat there, staring at me with her wide yellow eyes.

"She's gone," I choked out as if it was an excuse.

Sofie stared at me, waiting. I looked back down at Russell, still hating him with every fiber of my being, but some of the fire had died. If I killed him this way, with magic, I would lose one year of my own life. I would die at some point and would remain dead for one full year, hurting my friends and family and leaving everyone vulnerable.

And deep down, I knew that Russell was not really responsible for Tera's death. He may have hit her with his car, but she was dead before she stepped out of the shop. If he hadn't hit her, then she would have died in a car crash on her way to her apartment, or choked to death alone while eating a midnight snack. She would have died in her sleep from a heart attack or cancer. The list was endless. Death had finally caught up with her.

Drawing in a steadying breath, I slowly opened my hand and dropped it back down to my side. At the same time, Russell slumped against the car, sucking in large gulps of air while gingerly rubbing his throat. His eyes were wary as they watched me, as if he was waiting for me to strike again.

Barely resisting the urge to growl at him, I turned my gaze down to Tera. I shoved my hand in my pocket and pulled out some change, which I put into the right-front pocket of her jeans. I hoped she got it in time to give it to the ferryman. Rising to my feet, I turned and walked through the crowd, which soundlessly parted as I neared.

"Make sure she gets that," I murmured to the grim reaper as I passed.

"I will," he replied, but I was the only one who heard him.

In the distance, I could hear the approach of sirens from the ambulance that was racing toward this spot. With my head down, I trudged back to the shop to wait. Sofie padded along beside me, occasionally brushing against the pants leg of my jeans. I held the front door open for her before following her into the shop. Closing the door, I sat in the darkness of the lobby and waited.

As I had expected, the ambulance was accompanied by a set of police squad cars. The sea of people once again parted to let the ambulance through, while the police rushed forward to keep the crowd back and to take statements. Fifteen minutes after their arrival, a pair of cops came up the stairs of the parlor and rapped on the door. Pushing off the bench I had been sitting on, I crossed the room and motioned for them to enter.

Behind me, I heard Sofie give a soft meow as she settled on the bench to watch. I suppressed a small smile at her support.

They questioned me for the better part of an hour about what had happened. While it seemed that the observers refused to mention anything about me strangling Russell with magic, the scumbag had been happy to spin a few tales. He was also eager to blame the accident on the bad luck that I had cursed him with. I brushed away the strangling incident as fantasy and the cops quickly dropped it. They were not eager to pursue anything that might paint me as a warlock, resulting in them being in my bad graces. However, as a tattoo artist, I couldn't escape the bad luck accusations or the questions raised about Tera exiting my shop.

Luckily, I was able to present the truth for the most part. I had already dealt with Dalton's issue with TAPSS, which they would have on record, clearing me. After I had returned the money for his tattoo, it was then his responsibility to take care of his problem, absolving me of any blame.

As for Tera, I told a partial truth, for which I was able to present records with Tera's signature. It showed that I had given her a tattoo with nothing in the ink, so I was not under investigation for a dangerous potion. And while I didn't have any paperwork for tonight's touch-up, it wasn't out of the ordinary. Most tattoo shops offered free touch-ups and didn't submit any paperwork for it. Sure, it was a way around the system, but so far no one had done anything about it.

I knew it didn't look good for me. I had links to both people involved in the accident and there were some questions about me using magic. There was nothing I could do about it, but at the same time, I wasn't concerned because there was also nothing they could stick me with. In the end, they would do an autopsy, and find nothing, as potions rarely left any residue in the tissues or blood. Even if they were brave enough to try to call in a witch or a warlock to inspect the body, I wasn't overly concerned. They were the most likely to find something, but I doubted they would be able to identify either substance considering that no one had encountered the ingredients I had used. Most likely, the inspecting witch or warlock would come to me directly rather than admit finding anything to the cops.

The attending officers left, looking more or less satisfied by my answers. I knew they were stuck in a difficult position. I looked more than a little suspicious, but everyone knew their history well. Any human exhibiting magical abilities was to be avoided at all costs. The human race had barely survived the Great War, and they did not want to be responsible for starting another. I was just lucky they didn't know about my real past, where I was a renegade within the magic users society.

It didn't matter. I doubted I would hear from the cops again. They would turn my name over to TAPSS, who would take a particular glee in questioning me. I just hoped that someone from the council didn't catch wind of what had happened. TAPSS I could deal with. I didn't want to deal with Gideon, or any other guardian for that matter.

"Gage?"

I turned and looked down at Sofie, who was still sitting on the bench staring up at me.

"What's going on? I'm sure there's more to it than what you told those police officers."

There was a lot more going on than I was telling, but I didn't want Sofie involved. It wasn't safe. "Thanks for coming out. I really appreciate your help," I said stiffly. If she hadn't appeared outside when she had, breaking my destructive train of thought, I probably would have killed Russell Dalton, the consequences be damned.

Deep down, I knew that he wasn't to blame for the mess I was in right now. He was simply in the wrong place at the wrong time. I had to look no further than the mirror to see the instigator in this mess. Well, myself and Sparks. For some reason, he had directed Tera to me, somehow suspecting that I couldn't pass up the chance to help someone while thumbing my nose at the higher powers.

"What's going on?" Sofie repeated, her voice becoming more urgent.

I walked over to the large picture window at the front of the parlor and stared out with my arms folded over my chest while I tightly gripped both elbows. Most of the crowd had dispersed by now and the paramedics were loading Tera's covered body into the ambulance. One cop was pulling Dalton's car over to the side of the road, while another was escorting the man to one of the squad cars. In about another hour, the area would be empty, leaving no trace of the tragedy that had occurred.

"Death," I replied softly.

"Surely you don't have anything to do with this."

"No, not this one."

"But some other one?"

"I suspect so," I murmured absently. Releasing my arms, I let my hands drop limply back to my sides. I stepped over to the door and quickly turned the dead bolt. "I've already written a letter explaining everything. Trixie will watch over you if something happens. Just stay here and keep your head down."

"Where are you going?" she demanded as I wove around the remains of the glass case and moved into the tattooing room. The soft thump on the hardwood floor indicated that she had jumped down from the bench and was following fast on my heels.

"I have to take care of something."

"I'm coming with you," Sofie announced, bringing a frown to my lips. I couldn't lock her up in the apartment because it was obvious that she knew how to escape easily. There was no doubt in my mind that the little witch could follow me if she truly wanted to.

For a moment, I wished she would come with me. She may have been stuck in the body of a cat, but she still had some powers and abilities at her beck and call. It would have been nice to have someone there who could effectively watch my back, unlike my companions with little to no magical ability. While some of the best friends a person could ask for, Trixie and Bronx would prove to be more of a distraction than a help should they try to accompany me. They wouldn't be able to protect themselves if this led back to the source I was fearing.

But in the end, I knew I had to take care of this alone.

"Please, Sofie, stay here. I want to handle this alone," I murmured as I paused in the narrow hallway leading to the back room.

Sofie stood beside me on her hind paws while her front paws pressed against my leg as she stared up at me. "But you don't have to be alone."

"Stay here and watch over my friends. I don't think this will boomerang back at them, but I don't want to think about them being left defenseless. Just do this for me, please."

Sofie dropped back down to her haunches and looked into the tattooing room with the three large chairs bolted to the floor. I was offering her a different life, one that could prove to be more interesting than the hidden one she had been living for the past several years.

"I'll stay."

I nodded and proceeded into the back room. Shutting the door behind me, I unlocked the back door. The night air was heavy and thick as I stepped out into the wall of summer heat. I pulled the keys out of my pocket and paused long enough to lock the door again. My hand lingered on the old brass doorknob as I wondered if this was going to be the last time I saw my shop. A part of me cried out to just drop the matter. I had a good life. I loved my work and my friends. I didn't need to pursue this.

I couldn't let it go. The thought would nag at me day and night until I finally sought him out for the truth. I had to know why Sparks had put Tera in my path with the expectation that I could "help her." There would be no peace until I knew what he was up to. I had to see Sparks, and just hoped that the trail didn't lead directly to Simon.

31

I CROSSED FROM the back door to my car waiting in the light thrown down from a nearby security lamp. Shadows stood silent and watchful along the backs of the buildings and down the alleys. The air was still and hung like a weight, infused with the summer heat so that it was like pressing through a hot wool blanket. There was no one about, but the hair on the back of my neck remained on end as I waited once again to be jumped by Simon.

Fumbling with my keys, I unlocked the driver's-side door and slid into my SUV. As I slammed the door and shoved the key into the ignition, there was a sudden shift in the car under the weight of a second passenger. I looked up to find Gideon sitting next to me in the passenger seat, white light from the streetlamp gilding his features and reflected in his narrowed eyes. I jumped back in my seat at his sudden closeness. There was no room to fight in the car. Hell, I didn't feel like there was enough room in the large vehicle to breathe.

Twisting back to my door, I grabbed for the door handle. At the same time, the distinct *chunk* of the locks engaging around me echoed through the car. I tried the lock switch, but it didn't work. It was only when I was scraping at the door frame, trying to manually pull out the little lock, that I heard Gideon sigh wearily. Some part of my brain realized that I wasn't getting out of the car because he had locked the doors and didn't want me out. But the self-preservation side was still demanding that I get the fuck out of there at any cost.

"I'm not here to kill you, Powell," Gideon grumbled.

Turning in my seat to look at him, I found myself pulling away so that my back was pressed against the door. My heavy breathing was loud in the silence of the SUV, making it impossible to mask the terror gripping me. I had been expecting Simon. I had been searching the area for Simon's presence. I hadn't even given a thought to the possibility that Gideon would come for me.

"If I wanted you dead, you would have been before you could get into the car," the guardian continued when I had yet to comment. "You left yourself completely defenseless. One would think you'd have learned something about that during the past several years."

"I wasn't expecting you," I admitted as I watched him.

Gideon arched one eyebrow at me, looking more than a little skeptical. "Really? The attack on the human just a couple of hours ago?"

"Well, there is that," I said with a shrug.

"And the candles spell, the memory charm, the protective curses, the storm," he countered, ticking each item off on his fingers as he walked backward through all the spells I had cast during the past couple of days. Apparently, Gideon wasn't ready to let me off the hook for all those spells despite our recent meeting. Gideon then gave a little snort as he closed his hand and smirked at me. "Oh, and then there was the Chihuahua."

"A lot of those spells were defensive," I argued.

"You're getting a little broad in your definition of defensive spells." Gideon paused and stared out the windshield. "Though I probably would have given you the Chihuahua spell."

Staring at the guardian in shock, I noted for the first time that when he was smiling, Gideon didn't appear to be much older than me. While I knew that he could be using a spell to slow down his aging, making him significantly older than me, I doubted it. Most of the witches and warlocks waited until they were closer to their late forties or early fifties before invoking that spell, as a few wrinkles and gray hairs gave them an air of distinction and wisdom, whether they deserved it or not. Gideon may have been one of the few to move straight from apprenticeship to a position serving the council as a guardian, making him relatively young.

"I would have expected you to collect me much sooner than this for those infractions. Getting slow in your old age," I mocked, as the tension eating at my brain started to make me reckless.

Gideon's smile slipped away, replaced by a frown as he glared over at me. "I didn't step in because you've had your hands full with other issues as well as Simon. Why dirty my hands when I could wait for him to finish you off?"

Throwing my open hands out to the side as far as I could in the car, I smiled broadly at Gideon. "Well, I'm still here."

"And Simon isn't done trying."

My hands fell back down to my sides and I tore my gaze from him so that I was staring out of the car at the building next to my own. I had little doubt that my old mentor was still aiming to remove my head. A number of things would fall into place for Simon and the others in the Towers if I was simply gone.

"What are you doing here if you haven't come to kill me or take me to the council?" My head was starting to ache with all the problems that seemed to be mounting the longer I continued to breathe. Ivory Towers bastards. Summer Court. TAPSS. Reave. I really knew how to step in it.

"The girl?" Gideon asked tersely.

"Gone."

"Good."

It didn't feel "good." It felt like a whole lot of shit, but that's how it worked sometimes. "Like I said, what are you doing here?"

"I came to warn you, for what little it's worth," Gideon admitted, causing my head to snap back toward him.

"Warn me?"

"I'm sure you realized after speaking with Sofie that taking you to the council will do little good other than to leave you imprisoned for an extended period of time, at best. I thought letting you run around for a while longer might do a little good, but I'm beginning to have my doubts."

I rubbed my eyes, pinching the bridge of my nose as I was hammered by the assault of discordant comments. He knew I was with Sofie. He was looking the other way as I broke my agreement. And he was hoping that I accomplished a "little good." Following that announcement I didn't even know where to start.

I tried to start with the easiest comment and work from there. "You knew I was with Sofie? Were you the one at her house?" I asked, looking up at him through my fingers.

"Yes, you weren't safe there. She's always under surveillance, though I'm usually the one watching over her. But I'm not the only one and I couldn't risk you being discovered just yet."

There it was again. Gideon was helping me?

"You chased us from the house. Does she know it was you?"

"I'm not sure," Gideon said with a little shrug. He absently tapped the tip of his wand on the dashboard in thought. "She's always been a tricky one."

"So you know what she told me . . ."

His scoff cut off any further comments as my voice trailed off. "Of course. Who do you think told her? I knew she was one of the few vital people you kept in contact with and I conveyed to her the information that I thought might be of most use to you. It's not as if the exiled witch gets that many visitors. I doubt she realizes that she was being used in such a way by her own warden."

I threw up my hands in frustration and expelled my next breath in a huff. "What do you want, Gideon? You've obviously been planning something."

"I'm trying to keep you alive!" Gideon twisted in his seat to look at me, pushing me back into my own seat. "Though you haven't been doing much recently to help me in that respect."

"Oh, please!" I snorted. "You've been hounding my ass for years, snarling at me every chance you get."

"But have I dragged you before the council?" Gideon said, aiming his wand at me, but there was no gathering of energy to indicate that he was weaving a spell. He was only trying to get his point across. Of course, that logic did reach my heart, which was trying to claw its way up my throat. "I could have pulled you in front of the council for any use of magic until I finally wore them down, but I didn't. I left you with warnings. Roughed you up a bit. If you were scared of me and the council, then I thought you might be more selective in your use of magic. If anyone else caught just one of your blatant infractions against your agreement, we both would have been in trouble. I've cloaked what I could, but you've been reckless. You need to finish this business with Simon quickly."

Gideon sat back in his own seat, giving me some breathing room again. Shifting in my seat so that I sat forward, facing the steering wheel, I slumped down, knocking my right knee against the keys dangling from the ignition. They danced briefly, glinting in the fragment of light slashing through the car. My mind was struggling to keep up with all the information that Gideon was unloading on me. My entire perception of the world was changing before my eyes and I was having troubling keeping up.

Sucking in a deep breath, I dropped my hands from the steering wheel. "Okay, so you've been watching over Sofie and supplying her with information in the expectation that she would pass it along to me. You've also been protecting me from myself so that I wouldn't come up before the council, who would no doubt vote to lop my head off so they could finally be rid of me."

"Essentially."

"But why? That's what I don't understand. Why are you helping me?"

This time, Gideon seemed to hesitate, heaving a sigh as he stared to his right out the door window. I watched him in silence, waiting for his response. This was the most time I had ever spent with him that didn't involve me bargaining for my life while he strangled me.

"We're trying to push through some change in the mentality in the Towers," he replied softly.

"What kind of change?" I wasn't sure I liked where this was leading.

Gideon must have heard something in my voice because he looked over at me and smirked. "It didn't start with you, if that's what you're thinking, but you've become the most visible voice toward our cause whether you meant to be or not. We want a different life from what we originally walked into when we started our apprenticeships. The idea that warlocks and witches are empowered so that they can rule with an iron fist over humans and other races is outdated and cruel. We still support the idea of dedicating ourselves to the art, but we also want more. We want lives and families."

Reaching into the inside pocket of his black sport coat, Gideon pulled out a photograph and held it up to me. I slowly took it and held it so that it caught the light slicing through the car. It was a picture of a woman kneeling before a large house beside a young girl with black braided pigtails. Both appeared to be laughing on that sunny summer day.

"That's my wife, Ellen," he said, pointing to the pretty blond woman. "And that's my six-year-old daughter, Bridgette."

"Human?" I asked as I handed the photo back.

Gideon stared at the picture, rubbing his thumb across the faces of his wife and child. "Yes," he murmured, and then cleared his throat as he carefully put the picture back into his interior pocket. "Well, Ellen is human. Bridgette still has time to surprise me with powers, but so far she is just a human little girl."

Resting my left elbow on the car door, I leaned my head into my hand, my eyes wide with shock. This hard-ass guardian for the council and protector of its beliefs was a doting husband and father, breaking some of the Towers's most basic rules. Warlocks and witches were not to associate with humans and certainly not permitted relationships with them.

"If you're caught," I breathed, but I couldn't finish the thought out loud.

"Then we will be killed," Gideon said in a cold voice that drew my gaze back over to him. "My innocent daughter will be killed. My wife, who has done nothing more horrible than love me, will be slaughtered."

I squeezed my eyes shut, trying to block out the images of Gideon's happy family as I struggled to get my heart to stop racing. I felt myself getting sucked down this swirling vortex that was spiraling closer and closer to the utter destruction of everything—both human and Ivory Towers—and resulting in chaos. When I was sixteen, I had run from the Ivory Towers, just grateful that I still breathed. I had turned my back on everything and had started a new life. But now I was getting sucked back in.

"Does she know?" I asked in a choked voice.

"Who?"

"Your wife."

"What I am? Yes, she knows."

"Does she understand the danger she's in?" I pressed, anger growing inside me. Had Gideon not considered any of this when he decided to become involved with a human? Should anyone else discover the information he had shared with me, her life and her child's would instantly be forfeit.

"She knows and she loves me anyway. I'm very lucky," Gideon

admitted, though I was more willing to argue that he wasn't very lucky at all to be putting loved ones in the way of a speeding train.

I shifted in my seat again, feeling restless with pent-up energy and anxiety. Pacing the alley seemed like an appealing alternative to sitting in this cramped car with Gideon. The summer heat was turning the vehicle into a sweatbox. Unfortunately, I felt that getting out of the car wasn't an option—Gideon had probably set a silencing spell over the vehicle so that our conversation couldn't be overheard.

"So what do you want from me?" I said, unable to keep the anxiety I was feeling from spilling into my words. "I didn't leave Simon so that I could lead some kind of half-assed revolution. I don't want anything to do with the rogues who left their mentors. I don't want anything to do with what you're talking about. Don't misunderstand me. I support the ideas that you're discussing, but I just don't want anything to do with you people. I've worked really hard to set up this life for myself, and right now it's all on the verge of falling to pieces. Leading some crazy revolution against the Towers isn't going to help me fix the mess I've made of my life."

Gideon chuckled. "We don't want you to lead us." Surprisingly, his assurance irritated me more. His smile waned slightly as I glared at him. "We're not trying to strike out against the Towers and start a war. We are just trying to protect ourselves so that we can live in secret with some security. Change will only come slowly. Not in a great explosion or a war."

"Then what do you want from me? Why are you protecting me?"

"The only thing we want from you is that you live."

"Live?" I repeated dumbly as my sluggish brain fought to keep up with Gideon's brand of insanity.

"Just stay alive," Gideon said, whispering it like a prayer. "As long as you're alive, you give so many hope that we can escape the rigid ideas that still cage those of us in the Towers. You give hope that speaking out against the council and cruel mentors can be done successfully. You show that compassion is not a sign of weakness. You living your life outside the Towers will lead more to our cause."

"So instead of being the leader of your cause, I've become its symbol?"

"Yes."

"I don't feel good about this."

"I didn't want to tell you, but you and Simon keep hammering at each other. Eventually, it won't end in a stalemate. I thought you needed to know what's riding on this fight."

"Oh, yeah! Putting more weight on my shoulders ahead of the biggest fight of my life is always a good idea," I snapped. "It's not enough that I worry about the safety of my friends simply because they know me, but let's also throw on the success of an entire group looking for its freedom."

"We never meant for it to work out this way."

A sound of disgust jumped from the back of my throat as I shook my head. I had enough problems to worry about. I didn't need to worry about Gideon and his family, even though they were now stuck in the back of my mind like a maggot burrowing through rotten meat. If I died, would their movement die with me? Would Gideon attempt to go into hiding in an effort to save his family? Or worse . . . would he cut off all ties from them so they wouldn't be in danger?

"Unfortunately," the warlock continued when I didn't say anything, "we need you to kill Simon just as badly as we need you alive. He is one of the most violently outspoken against the murmurs of our cause. He is also the one running in the lead to take the open seat on the council. He'll shift the vote on the council and could potentially lead his own movement to seek out those who are thinking like us. Families would be wiped out in a single cleansing and I would be forced to either leave the Towers or lead the cleansing."

"So you're asking me to kill Simon and live through the process?"

"He knows he can't claim the council seat if you're still alive."

"Then help me kill him if you're so desperate to keep me alive!"

"I can't." Closing his eyes, Gideon leaned his head back against the headrest and his shoulders slumped. "I'm taking a big risk talking to you. As far as most know, my job is to find a way to bring you before the council so that they can finally vote for your death. Talking to you runs counter to those orders."

"Fine," I growled, gripping the steering wheel tightly. I pulled myself forward so that I touched my forehead against the sticky plastic. "I'm alone in this. Kill Simon. Stay alive."

"That's it."

"Thanks," I grumbled as I flopped back down in my seat.

Gideon scratched his chin in thought, his grim expression starting to lighten. He opened his eyes and looked at me. "But I can give you a small tip. You've got some newly acquired goods in your basement. Go to your black market connection."

"Chang?"

"Yes, trade him for a magic deflection amulet. Merlin grade. It might not block everything, but it would give you a serious edge over Simon."

I nodded, lost in thought. Most didn't believe that a warlock by the name of Merlin ever really existed, but his name was used to mark the highest power within the magic world. Merlin-grade items were extremely rare and valuable since they were nearly impossible to create and just as hard to destroy. It would give me an edge over Simon, but I was afraid that Chang would use it as an opportunity to get his hands on all the river waters. I still needed the waters to trade for something to get Trixie out of her bind.

"I'll see what I can do."

"And keep your goddamn wand with you!"

"Thanks."

"When you're done with Simon, make sure that all of that stuff is destroyed," Gideon admonished, making me feel somewhat relieved that he didn't want to get his hands on it. If I hadn't been so desperate, I would never have brought all of the various waters back, but I knew I needed something really enticing to tempt Chang.

"Not a problem," I agreed.

"Stay alive," Gideon ordered one last time.

"You too," I said with a snort, but when I looked over he had already disappeared.

Stay alive. He almost made it sound easy.

32

TUCKED UNDER MY T-shirt and out of sight, the silver amulet was cold against my chest. As soon as Gideon disappeared, I'd darted back inside the tattoo parlor and grabbed my wand and the corked bottle of water from Phlegethon, the river of fire, that I had put aside for the old black market collector. The water from Phlegethon wasn't the most appealing or dangerous of the set of five, but I'd suspected it would be enough to pique Chang's interest. With four more waters still in my possession, the temptation that he might be able to possess them all eventually made him willing to deal with me that night. I warned him that if something went wrong, he would be dealing with my friends for the other four underworld waters.

Chang had not been happy to part with his magic deflection amulet, throwing curses at me as he pounded his cane on the floor, but in the end, he acquiesced to my request and I was on my way to Sparks's run-down little house at last.

I parked my car down from the house where I had encountered the werewolves on my last visit to OTR. Closing the car door, I looked over at the ramshackle house and found that no one was outside. It was dark except for a flickering blue light that seeped between some curtains on the second floor. Either someone was still awake, or they had fallen asleep with the TV on. The yapping alpha-now-turned-Chihuahua was nowhere to be seen, but then I guessed that he was currently keeping a low profile until the spell wore off.

My footsteps slowed as I approached Sparks's house. The old man was sitting on the crumbling concrete steps leading up to the front door. A streetlamp outside his house lanced through the area, casting him in bright, unflattering light against the shadows that clung to the nearby homes and sickly trees. The old tattoo artist sucked on a cigarette, a thin wisp of gray smoke curling up from his right hand. Flicking off some excess ash with his thumb, Sparks stared straight ahead as he released another puff of smoke. He had yet to look at me, but he knew I was there. He was expecting me despite the fact that it was now close to four in the morning and I had given no indication that I would be returning to visit him so quickly.

Walking down the middle of the empty street, I closely watched my former tattooing mentor take one last drag from the cigarette before he flicked it across the sidewalk to where it rolled into a pile of dried leaves and gray cigarette butts.

"Late night," he said in a rough voice that rumbled to where I had paused in the street, across from him.

"Yeah." I resisted the urge to shove my hands in the pockets of my jeans as I stood there. I needed my hands out and ready at my sides should Simon decide to attack suddenly. But there was nothing in the stillness, not the wind or even a car easing down the narrow, pothole-laden street. Sparks didn't say anything as he leaned forward, resting his forearms on his knees as he stared down at the cracked sidewalk in front of him. He had yet to look up at me, and I was wondering if the old bastard could look me in the eyes.

"I've been thinking," I announced, my voice cutting across the distance so sharply that Sparks flinched. "You didn't seem all that surprised to see me the other day. I was wondering why. We haven't spoken in a few years."

Sparks gave only the barest of shrugs of his slumped, rounded shoulders. "I always knew that I'd see you around eventually."

"Why did you send her my way?" I asked, grinding the words between my teeth before I could shoot them at him. I started walking again, closing the distance between us so that I was standing in front of the curb.

"I thought you could help her," Sparks admitted. He lowered his head, and rubbed his hands over his face and through his thinning hair.

"Help?" I snapped, but quickly got my voice back under control. "She was dying of cancer. What did you think I could do?"

"Help."

"She's dead."

Sparks shook his head, his tired eyes remaining on the sidewalk. His face was thin, as the skin seemed to hang off his cheekbones, deepening the wrinkles that lined his frowning mouth. He looked as if he had aged several years since I'd last seen him.

"What were you expecting me to do? I'm a tattoo artist, not some goddamn miracle worker," I pressed when the silence stretched between us.

Atticus Sparks looked up, glaring at me through narrowed eyes. With a struggle, he pushed off the concrete steps and took a couple of steps closer. "I was expecting you to heal her, you cocky bastard!" he snarled. "Even when you were just learning how to mix potions and ink, you still walked around this place like you owned it. Okay, so you were a fast learner, but you weren't the best there ever was and you still ain't!"

"I never claimed—" I started in a slightly dazed voice, but Sparks was quick to cut me off.

"No? You weren't strutting around with your nose in the air? You weren't trying after the first year to correct *me* when I was stirring potions?"

"Hey, I wasn't as green as some of your other apprentices!" I snarled back at him. "I learned a few things while I was up in the Ivory Towers and I didn't see any harm in trying to apply some of that knowledge."

"You should have stayed in that damned Tower!" Sparks shouted, jabbing his finger at the sky. His voice lowered to a sneer, as he inched closer to me. "You don't belong here. You're not one of us anymore, probably haven't been for years. They brainwashed you, or maybe you were just born this way, I don't know. What I do know is that because you think you're better than the rest of us, you're as bad as those arrogant bastards trying to crush us into the dirt."

I jerked back a step into the street, feeling as if I had been smacked by my father. When I left the Ivory Towers as a young teenager and was wandering around, feeling useless and lost, Sparks had been the one to swoop in and save me. While gruff and harsh, he had still been like a father to me. He hadn't let on once during all the years I had known him that he felt like this about me.

"How long have you felt like this?" I asked in a subdued voice.

"Since the day I first met you," Sparks growled.

"Then why do anything? I was homeless, helpless, lost when you found me. I probably would have died out on the street if you hadn't done something. Why bother if this is how you felt?"

"Because for some insane reason I thought I might be able to change you. That was a waste of my time," Sparks grumbled and then turned back to the steps where he sat down on the top one with a soft grunt. He waved me off. "Much like what you're doing now. Get out of here. I don't have any more time to waste on you."

I paced a few feet away from where I had been standing, clenching my fists at my sides. None of this was making any sense. "If you hate me so much, why send Tera to me? Was it just to see me fail? You wanted me to watch her die, knowing that I couldn't do anything to help her? It looks like you could have used the money and yet you turned her away."

"It doesn't matter anymore. Just get out of here!" Sparks barked.

"Oh, I think it's a bit late for that," purred a deep voice from the shadows beyond the edge of Sparks's house. I jerked my head in the direction of the comment as Sparks lurched to his feet. The old man took a couple of steps backward, edging in my direction. The frown on his lips deepened, pulling at the lines so that they dug heavy furrows in his face. Keeping my attention on the edge of the house, I tensed when Simon strolled into view and leaned against the side of the house.

The warlock wore a dark suit with a crisp white shirt and dark tie with thin red stripes. His fingers were loosely threaded together and held just at waist level, his wand nowhere in sight. He was far from harmless, but at least he didn't appear to be actively targeting me with a spell. Hatred glittered in his eyes as he watched me with a mocking smile. In all those years, I never saw anything other than hatred and contempt in the man's eyes. He laughed at another's misfortune. He took joy in pain. Simon could not be permitted to ascend to the council.

"Don't look so sad, Gage," he cooed as he pushed off from the corner of the house and walked toward me with slow, deliberate steps. As he moved closer, I backpedaled into the street, keeping distance between us. "You had to know that the old man was lying with every disgusting word that slipped from his alcohol-laced lips."

I slid my gaze over to Sparks to find him also shrinking from Simon as he approached. His eyes didn't waver from the warlock, while his expression remained unreadable. Had Sparks been lying to me? His words had been shocking and didn't exactly feel right, but he had delivered them with such force and venom that I hadn't questioned it. They had played on my own fears. I had wondered time and time again when dealing with Tera if I had been too cocky when she had come to me.

Simon's dark laughter sent a shiver up my neck, drawing my full attention back to him. "You did believe him!" he exclaimed. "Amazing. I really did think you were smarter than that. Well, maybe you can be quite intelligent, but you really do lack any kind of common sense when it comes to other people. You should have taken the hint that he was nearly screaming at you."

"Hint?"

"Leave," Sparks grumbled under his breath.

"Yes, he was trying quite earnestly to get you to leave and you just weren't smart enough to take the hint," Simon mocked. He dropped his hands down to his sides and I jerked back an extra step as he paused. His smile widened at my edginess. "We both knew it would only be a matter of time before you connected the dots back to Atticus, and you would come running here for some answers. He was just hoping that you'd leave before I showed up."

My gaze jumped from my first mentor to my last mentor, my heart thudding in my chest. I had been right. As far as I knew, Sparks and Simon had not known each other. There was no reason for their paths to cross but for me.

"You set me up," I said softly, looking over at Sparks. The old man shrank back from me, his shoulders rising as if he expected me to throw a spell at him, or just punch him in the face. His eyes fearfully darted to me for only a second before fixing on Simon again. He was struggling to decide which of us was the bigger threat at the moment. Simon was winning that contest, but I doubted that it was by a large margin. Sparks knew my temper.

"Of course he did," Simon proclaimed.

Sparks jumped in before the warlock could continue, trying to soothe the wounds that he had inflected only minutes earlier. "I didn't have any choice. He came here, threatening to kill me if I didn't help him. He knew I was the only one close to you that he could manipulate."

"So you agreed to help him," I said, clenching my fists at my sides. "You jeopardized my life, my work, my friends—"

"Have pity, Gage," Simon interjected as my voice gained in volume. "He really did have no choice. I did threaten to kill him."

Somehow I managed to be angrier at Sparks than at Simon. The warlock was just being true to his nature and hadn't surprised me in the least. Sparks, however, had betrayed me, even if it was to save his own neck. I had believed that the old man would have my back, but then I had never really expected Simon to return to my life like this. Some part of me must have thought that I would be left in the hands of the guardians and the council, while Simon returned to his old life, pushing me out of his mind.

But Simon couldn't be free of me. I was a blot on his otherwise clean record. A grim smile curled the corners of my lips as I stared at the warlock. I was as much a thorn in his side as he was in mine. And the only way either of us was going to be free was to kill the other. I wasn't a coldhearted, bloodthirsty killer by any means, but I knew that if any of us were to have a shot at living, Simon had to die and there was no one else who could do it. Of course, as I thought about all the abuse I had suffered at the hands of this man as well as the dark future that lay ahead for the human race should he succeed, I found that I was more than willing to take on the task.

Taking a step back, I opened my hands at my sides and attempted to secretly draw some energy together for a spell, but Simon instantly sensed the shifting in the air and tensed. His left foot slid back a little to brace himself for whatever I was preparing, while his own hands shot in front of his body, fingers slightly curled as he wove together, like a spider's web, strands of energy. I gritted my teeth and threw my hands out, but not at Simon. The energy exploded from my fingertips and slammed into Sparks. The old man was lifted from his feet and thrown against the side of his house, where he slid, unconscious, to the ground. He had been knocked out before he hit the peeling wood siding, so he didn't feel the impact. I just hoped that I hadn't broken anything with the spell.

I shook off the concern and concentrated on Simon. Broken

bones would mend. Bruises would heal. I had needed to get Sparks out of the line of fire so Simon couldn't use him as a shield or distraction when I attacked.

"How sweet," Simon said. "The human betrays you and you gently move him out of the way so that he can't get caught up in the fight. Very noble of you." A sneer wiped the last remnant of amusement from his features.

"Maybe I'm just looking forward to dealing with him at my leisure once I've brushed you aside," I mocked, earning me a fresh scowl. It had always been easy to get under Simon's skin. But then, as far as I knew the man hated everyone, making it easy to piss him off.

The warlock's temper snapped. With a wave of his arm and a quick flick of his right wrist, he threw a ball of energy at me that was meant to sizzle through flesh and break bone. Raising both arms with wrists crossed in front of me, I conjured up a defensive spell in time to block his attack, leaving the energy to dissipate harmlessly over the softly humming blue shield. The amulet lying against my chest warmed at the presence of magic, as if suddenly waking from a deep slumber. I wasn't sure what it could and couldn't do, so I was more than willing to rely on my own abilities for now. I just hoped that the amulet managed to kick in a little juice should Simon succeed in getting through the defensive spells I did know.

"One last thing," I called as Simon sidestepped out into the street with me. "I would like that portion of my soul you stole before I kill you."

Simon chuckled, creating an uneasy twisting in my stomach. "It would seem that I no longer have it in my possession. I sold it to someone I thought could find some use for it, since I truly doubt you were using it."

The warlock's grin dimmed slightly when I failed to react with anger. Instead, I nodded at him and gave a little bow. "I guess we do have something in common after all."

"I doubt that."

"I no longer have that bit of soul I stole from you either. I traded it to someone I thought could put it to good use. He seemed to be quite pleased with the exchange."

"You bastard!" Simon roared at me as he charged. He reached into the left sleeve of his jacket and pulled out a gnarled wooden wand made from an ash tree. Giving it a quick twirl over his head, he pointed the wand at me with a snarl on his face. A bolt of electric green energy shot from its tip and hammered into the blue shield that I was still holding in place. The shield cracked under the intensity of the blast and the energy shot through, aiming for my heart.

A second golden shield burst into life before Simon's green bolt could strike me, knocking the energy back toward its creator. Simon shouted as he dodged the energy blast, flattening himself against the pitted asphalt street. The magic deflection amulet worked, to my great relief. I didn't wait for the bastard to rise to his feet. Skidding over to the gutter, I snatched up a jagged piece of glass glittering in the dirty lamplight before launching myself at Simon. The old man started to roll away from me as I landed beside him. The glass dug deep into his upper arm, wringing a scream of pain out of him.

The deep cut didn't deter him as he reached up and grabbed the collar of my T-shirt. Confusion ensued. I had summoned up some energy at the same time as Simon. Between the two conflicting spells and the power from the magic deflection amulet, there was an explosion centered between us, throwing both Simon and me in opposite directions. As we were pushed apart by the force of the blast, I heard my T-shirt rip, followed by a pull against the back of my neck. A glint of silver caught my eye as it hurtled through the air away from me. Simon had grabbed the chain the amulet hung from and had pulled it from around my neck. Yet the force of the blast sent it spiraling out of his grasp and flying through the air away from both of us.

I slammed into the ground with a painful crunch as at least two ribs fractured under the impact. Rolling several feet until I hit the front bumper of a stationary car, I winced as pain spiderwebbed throughout my body. I had lost the magic deflection amulet, but at least Simon didn't have it either.

With a grunt of pain, I rolled over to my hands and knees, trying to pick myself up again. My head was pounding and my ears were ringing from the blast. Lifting my head, I found Simon still on the ground, but moving slowly. A gentle hand slipped under my chin and tilted my head up so that I looked into a pair of deep black eyes. Dark hair framed her face, while pale grayish-white skin shone like a dirty pearl in the nearby light. I blinked a couple of times, my mind struggling to take in the figure kneeling before me.

"Wake up, Gage," purred a soft voice. "You still have to kill him."
Lilith.

My body jerked painfully away from her touch as I finally recognized the woman. Falling backward onto my butt, I looked up at her and found that she wasn't really there. At least, not fully there. She was transparent enough that I could see the beat-up red car and dilapidated house on the other side of the street through her. It was possible that she hadn't fully escaped the underworld, but I wasn't reassured by the fact that I could see her here at all. There were no positive stories associated with the myth that was Lilith. A destroyer. A seducer. A mother of demons.

"What are you doing here?" I demanded. Using my heels, I pushed away from her, trying to put a little distance between us so she couldn't easily touch me again. I hadn't exactly felt skin when she placed her fingers under my chin. There had been a cold sensation, as if I had been touched by death.

"I came to claim my freedom from you. I can help you destroy this creature before he can harm you again," Lilith offered, taking another step closer to me.

"Go back to the underworld and wait for the end of days. I'm not helping you," I growled as I shoved back to my feet. I turned my back on her as I walked toward Simon, who was now on his knees, rubbing his temple with the heel of his left hand. Blood trickled from a cut on his scalp, running across his forehead.

Lilith flowed in front of me again as if she were little more than a leaf dancing on a breeze. There was no anger in her face, but I could feel the pull of her black eyes, attempting to drag my gaze back to hers so that she could find some way to control me for her own purposes. A cold chill swept through me, but I kept my eyes focused on Simon as he rose to his feet and stared down the street at me. To my surprise, confusion skittered across his features as he looked not at me, but at Lilith. I had thought I was the only one who could see her. This was not good. While I didn't want to help Lilith, I also didn't want her turning her attention to Simon. I wasn't too sure that he wouldn't accept her help, no matter how dangerous it was.

With a frown, I whipped my right hand out and shot another bolt of energy toward Simon. He easily blocked the energy with a shield, as I had been expecting. The energy was enough, though, to knock him back over so that he was seated on the ground again, breaking his stare at Lilith and distracting him.

"Get out of here, Lilith," I growled at her while keeping my gaze locked on Simon.

"Lilith?" Simon demanded as his gaze snapped to the glowing vision of a naked woman. I inwardly groaned, smacking myself on the forehead. I really could be an idiot sometimes. If Simon hadn't known who she was before, he did now and he was certainly interested. I didn't need my two enemies joining forces to get at me.

Growling in frustration, I grabbed my wand from my pocket and pointed it at Simon. With a burst of energy exploding from the tip, I started to throw him across the street, aiming to toss him against the side of a nearby brick house. His feet slid across the street less than a yard before he stopped moving, and the spell completely dissipated with a wave of Lilith's hand. Panic clenched in my stomach. She brushed off the power as if it had been nothing more than an annoying mosquito buzzing around her head. Obviously, I wasn't going to be able to use magic to get rid of Simon.

"Quiet, Gage. We're talking," she murmured, keeping her gaze locked on Simon, who was staring at her, completely enraptured. She took a step closer to the warlock and smiled. "It seems Gage has been giving you some problems. Would you like my assistance in dealing with him?"

"Yes," Simon whispered. His hands were trembling in his excitement as he edged a little closer to her. "I very much need him dead. And then you can have him, right?"

"I will have him when he's dead, but to help you I need something valuable in return."

Simon fumbled inside his jacket, searching for something in the interior pocket. After a couple of seconds, he pulled out a small pouch made of what looked to be velvet. He struggled to open it in his enthusiasm, but finally pulled out a small vial.

"Hey!" I shouted, taking a step closer before I could catch myself. It was the fragment of my soul that Simon had stolen. "You said you didn't have it any longer."

The warlock looked at me, an evil grin spreading across his features. "I lied. Who could have more use for it than me? Except maybe this lovely woman."

"She's not a woman, Simon! She's a monster. You can't do this." Even as I spoke, I started summoning a spell. I threw one aimed to shatter the glass vial, but nothing happened. Desperate, heart hammering in my chest, I threw a second aimed to simply knock the vial out of Simon's hand, but even that failed. No spell touched them thanks to Lilith.

My breath lodged around the knot in my throat as I watched the vial slip from Simon's fingers into Lilith's glowing hand. The glass slipped through the nothingness, but as it fell to the ground, I saw that it was already empty. Focusing on her hand, I saw the small fragment of my soul wriggling around her fingers.

As she clenched her fist around my soul, I felt a tightening in my chest. She was strengthening her hold on me. I stumbled a couple of steps backward. I didn't know what powers she had topside, but I was willing to guess they were going to have an amplified effect now that she was in possession of my soul fragment. How did I defend myself against anything she threw at me?

Smiling, Lilith walked toward me. She gave her hand a little shake and my soul fragment disappeared. I could only guess that she had sent it somewhere for safekeeping so that I couldn't try to reclaim it.

"He can kill you," Lilith needlessly reminded me as she approached. As my gaze returned to Simon, who was watching with sickening glee, Lilith placed her arm across my shoulders. "You have to kill him first. Kill him with magic." Her soft, breathy voice wound its way through my brain, wrapping around my thoughts so that the world was in a type of fog. Everything slowed down but my heartbeat, which pounded in my ears like a tribal drum, urging me forward.

Simon's joy disintegrated before my eyes, replaced by anger. "What are you doing?" he snarled. "You said that you'd help me."

Lilith smiled at the warlock. "I lied. I need Gage alive to be useful to me. You, on the other hand, would be more useful to me dead." She then turned her attention back to me, looking serious for the first time since she had appeared before me. "I can't interfere anymore. You'll have to handle this on your own, and he can still kill you."

"She's right, Gage," Simon called. "I will kill you."

"So you can rule over your own genocide of the human race," I snapped, pushing through the lingering tendril of the mental fog as Lilith stepped away from me.

"Don't worry. I won't limit myself to just the human race. I think

I'll start with your friends before moving on to your family. I'll wipe away all memory of your existence."

"Kill him!" Lilith goaded, her tantalizing voice growing hoarse and more urgent. "Kill him in my name before he destroys your beloved Trixie!"

Fear clenched in the pit of my stomach and ripped through my mind, wiping away the last of Lilith's attempts at control. I bellowed at the warlock with all my rage, throwing out both my hands toward him, wand pointed at his chest as my fingers clenched and trembled. Magic pulled from deep in my soul surged and rushed out my extended arms toward him. Wild and barely controlled, the lightning white energy hammered against the glowing blue shield he had erected around himself. He rocked backward under the force of the blow, but his shield held.

Curling my left hand around to reach up from below, I created several sets of hands that rose from the asphalt below him, grasping his legs. The hands, made of black rock and gravel, grabbed his limbs and pulled on his clothes, tearing them as he fought to be free. The street beneath him grew soft and the warlock began to sink down into the earth, the hands pulling him lower and lower.

A strangled cry escaped Simon as he sank down to his chest in the street. His protective shield wavered as his panic at being buried alive overcame his ability to concentrate on the spell. I took advantage of the momentary distraction and sent another white bolt of energy at him. The spell shot straight through the shield like an arrow piercing an apple. Simon's head spun around with a sickening crack as his neck shattered, killing him instantly. The sound sliced through me, causing my heart to stumble for a couple of beats before resuming its pounding rhythm.

I took a step backward as I watched the asphalt hands continue to rise and pull his limp body into the ground. There were no thoughts in my brain. There was no room for them beyond the horror of what I had done. I hadn't thought about it, I'd simply reacted to his threat against the loved ones in my life. The power was just there burning inside my chest, needing to strike out at him. And I killed him. With magic.

Simon's body disappeared beneath the asphalt. The hands blended back in with the street and the surface became as smooth as the black waters of the Styx. He was gone. His soul was now in the hands of Charon for all of eternity.

I crumpled to my knees, my breathing fast and uneven, as I stared at the spot where I had last seen him. It was only when I felt a hand pat me on the shoulder that I looked up to find Lilith still standing over me. There was a thoughtful expression on her beautiful but frightening face as she stared down the empty street.

"Well, that's not exactly what I wanted," she murmured as if talking to herself. The mother of demon spawn then looked down at me and smiled, sending a chill down my spine. "But you did kill him with magic. That will put you into my hands for one year. Hmmm . . . maybe longer considering what I have in my possession now."

"No!" I gasped, terror rocking me to my core.

"Yes, I'm afraid so. I get to watch over those who die but are destined to return after a year. I'm sure we'll have great fun together." I watched as she took a step backward and disappeared like a puff of smoke dispersed on the air.

I lowered my head into my hands as I knelt on the ground. Not only had I killed a man, but I had also handed my soul over to the queen of the underworld. This was not how I had hoped the evening would go.

33

I TURNED THE folded sheaf of paper around, holding it with two fingers at the corner as the fire licked across the surface. The blackened ash curled and flaked off, dancing in the faint breeze that stirred the dense summer air. Sitting in the dark behind the tattoo parlor on the wooden steps leading up to the second-floor apartment, I watched the long letter I had written to my friends burn away to thin wisps of ash. Somehow, against the odds, I had survived. I had survived the planning and scheming of Simon as well as Gideon's group. I had even escaped the grasp of the grim reaper while prolonging Trixie's freedom from her own kind. Bronx was still stuck, but he was safe for now.

But sitting in the dark, crowded city, I felt alone and soul weary. I had killed a man. Simon and I had fought on several occasions, but I had never crossed the line I had drawn in the sand so many years ago. I had always sworn that I wouldn't take a life. I believed my powers could be used for positive, useful purposes. Warlocks weren't supposed to think like that. Or at least, that's what I had been taught to believe.

Gideon was different though. And maybe there were others out there like me who believed that our powers were something other than a god-given right to rule. Gideon had used his powers to strike fear in me, but he had done it to protect his own family. He loved. I could see when he looked at that picture of his wife and daughter that he loved them deeply. We weren't all monsters as it seemed.

And maybe I wasn't alone.

I dropped the last bit of unburned paper on the ground between my feet, allowing the fire to eat it without nipping at my fingertips. A bright light shined down the narrow alley along the side of the tattoo parlor, drawing my gaze up from the burning paper. My body tensed, but I didn't move. No one was supposed to come down the alley. They had no business back here.

A heavy sigh of relief hissed between my teeth as the front of Trixie's green Prius poked around the edge of the building. I didn't know what she was doing here, but at least I knew that I wasn't facing more trouble. I had already had my fill this evening.

Trixie parked her car next to mine in the empty lot behind the shop. A shocked smile quirked the corners of my mouth when I saw both Trixie and Bronx climb out of the little mint green vehicle. This was beginning to feel like an intervention. Bronx refused to ride in any car Trixie was driving, claiming the elf spent too much time multitasking while driving instead of just keeping her eyes on the road. As my friends approached where I was sitting on the second step of the staircase, I noticed that Trixie was walking around without her glamour spell. She looked beautiful. Her long blond hair was like a halo about her head, glowing in the nearby lamplight. Her green eyes were wide, scrutinizing my features as if trying to read my mood.

I loved her. I didn't know how long I had loved her, but it only mattered that the feeling was there in my chest, beating in time with my heart. I loved how she walked and smiled. I loved how she still loved her brother despite the fact that he was trying to destroy her life. I loved the tenderness she showed for Bronx when she drew on him each night. I loved listening to their arguments, ranging from sex to music to pizza toppings. But most of all, I loved her for standing before me with that worried look on her face when I needed her most.

"What are you guys doing here? You've got the night off," I said, forcing my stare away from Trixie's face and over to Bronx's ever stoic expression.

Trixie stepped around me and walked up the stairs. To my surprise, she sat down on the third step directly behind me while putting her long legs on either side of me. I twisted around to look up at her, raising one eyebrow in question at her sudden closeness, particularly in front of Bronx. While we had always maintained a harmlessly flirtatious relationship in the shop, this was a little closer than I had been expecting.

Leaning down, Trixie cupped my face in both of her hands and kissed me gently, stealing my breath away. Her soft lips were like feathers brushing against mine while her sweet scent danced around me. A sigh escaped me as her hands dropped down to rest on her legs and I turned back to find Bronx grinning at us like an idiot. Bronx was not the type to grin, but then Trixie and I had been dancing around each other for two years.

"Is this the new employee reward program?" Bronx taunted. He pushed off from where he had been leaning against the side of the shop. "If so, I'm ready for mine." As he approached, he puckered his fat lips and made some disgusting kissing noises as he drew near.

Raising both my hands and one foot to ward him off, I laughed as I fell back into Trixie's lap. He grabbed my wrists for a second and pretended to struggle with me before backing off again, making a disgusted sound in the back of his throat.

"It's about fucking time," he muttered as he returned to his spot at the side of the building. "The way you two have been flirting with each other the past couple of years has been disgusting. Hopefully, I can stop throwing customers out the window now."

My brow furrowed as I stared at my old friend. "What?"

"Every time one of Trixie's customers made a pass at her that crossed the line, I had to toss 'em out the window to keep you from getting your hands on them," Bronx answered with a snort. "Hell, the air crackled with magic when you were jealous and pissed. I was afraid you'd blow a hole in someone."

"I thought you were doing that to protect me," Trixie said, sounding as confused as I felt.

"Well . . . I was," he said, fumbling for a moment before his voice firmed again. "I was protecting you both. You can't run a respectable tattoo parlor with Gage blowing holes in anyone who takes a long look at you."

"Thanks," I said with a slight chuckle. Respectable was a stretch when it came to describing the Asylum, but then I liked to think of myself as an equal opportunity tattoo artist. A frown quickly tugged at my mouth as I continued to look at him. "Then you've known for a while?"

"That you were a warlock? Of course." Bronx sniffed, crossing his arms over his chest as if he were affronted by the idea that he wasn't smart enough to catch on to my secret. "Besides the antiglamour spell I noticed when I first walked in the door, the air tended to tingle any time you got seriously pissed."

I dropped my head, rubbing my face with my hands. "I'm sorry," I murmured. I thought I had had better control. Bronx made me sound like a ticking time bomb just waiting to go off at the slightest provocation.

Trixie's slender arms quickly wrapped around my shoulders and neck as she leaned against me. "No, Gage, he didn't mean it like that."

"I knew we were never in any danger no matter how badly you were pressed," Bronx said in a deep voice that rumbled through me. "You were thrown through a glass case and I had to come to your rescue because I knew you wouldn't do anything. You would never harm anyone."

I flinched at Bronx's words and I knew that Trixie had felt it because her arms tightened around me as if she could absorb the pain that cut through my body at the memory of Simon's head snapping around on his broken neck. For someone who would never harm another person, I'd proved to be quite good at it.

Trixie laid her cheek against the side of my head. "Tell us, Gage. What happened tonight?" she whispered, but I had no doubt that Bronx had heard her.

Wrapping one arm around her knee, I pulled her leg tighter against my body, just needing to feel her closer to me. Resting my cheek against her leg, I let my fingers trace over the soft, faded blue denim while my mind tried to put the events of the past few days in some semblance of order.

When I started talking, I didn't begin with Tera walking into the tattoo parlor. Instead, my first comments were about the day a guardian showed up on the doorstep of my parents' nice suburban home to tell them that their son was a warlock. Looking back with the eyes of an adult, I could see the tension around their mouths and the fearful look in their eyes as they spoke to the guardian who was demanding custody of their seven-year-old son. It was only after living in the confines of the Ivory Towers for several years that I came to understand my parents had had no choice in giving me up. If they had said no, I would have been killed on the spot. They had prettied up the separation with tales of going on an exciting adventure so I wouldn't be afraid.

I brushed over years of physical and mental abuse accompanied by squalid living conditions and rushed forward to my escape. I wove a tale of intense politics and fear that saw me living with a guardian constantly looking over my shoulder in hopes of bringing me back for slaughter. I left out Gideon's real intentions, as the warlock had a tough enough road ahead of him without anyone else knowing of his struggle.

My words slowed when I finally reached the present-day events that depicted Simon as an adept puppet master while he carefully maneuvered both Tera and Sparks into play with hopes of finally destroying me. The only detail I left out of the gruesome battle between Simon and me was the presence of Lilith. She represented my own private hell, waiting for me with my soul fragment in hand when my death year finally arrived. There was nothing anyone could do to help me escape the fate I had woven for myself.

When I stopped speaking, I noticed that my heavy breathing was the only sound in the night. There were no crickets, no swish of cars on the nearby streets. My heart pounded in my chest and my body ached from being slammed to the pavement. Most of all, I ached somewhere in my soul. Tera was dead and there had been nothing I could do to stop it. Simon was dead and I had everything to do with that.

"Did you have any choice?" Trixie asked after a long silence. I twisted around slightly so that I could look at her over my shoulder. Her sweet face was lined with worry and I wanted to take back all my words so she wouldn't feel that fear. But in the same thought, I knew it was better that both Bronx and Trixie knew the truth. There had been too many years of secrets and lies. A weight had been lifted from my chest when I told them my story, regardless of how ugly it was.

Reaching down, Trixie gently ran her fingers through my short hair, soothing some of the tension from my shoulders. "You said he was going to kill you and then come hunting for us. Did he give you any choice but to kill him?"

"No," I admitted with a sigh. I turned back around on the stair and looked over at Bronx, who was frowning at me.

"Then let it go," the troll said. "You did the right thing. You saved the lives of a lot of good people, and you tried to help one person. There's nothing wrong with that."

Squeezing Trixie's knee with one hand, I smiled at the troll staring grimly at me. "Thank you," I murmured before lowering my lips to press a kiss to Trixie's arm where it wrapped loosely around my neck.

I hadn't seen my parents or siblings in nearly ten years. During that time, I had forgotten what it was like to feel the love and concern of people who knew you. Sitting in the dark behind the tattoo parlor, I knew that Trixie and Bronx would rush to my side without a moment's hesitation if I needed them. I knew they would protect me, as I would do everything to protect them. I still loved my parents, brother, and sister, but I doubted I would ever see them again. It was for the best. I would miss them, but I knew they were safer without me around.

And it was okay. Bronx and Trixie were my family now. Even to a small extent were Gideon and Sofie. Since coming out to sit on the steps in the dark, I had felt a nagging weight in the air. Someone was watching over me. I had felt it for years and hadn't given it much thought. But now I knew that it was Gideon watching me, protecting me the only way he knew how.

"Well, I'm glad that's all over with," Bronx said, breaking the sudden silence.

I smiled at the troll as he shifted against the side of the shop, shoving his meaty hands into the back pockets of his brown cargo pants.

"Yes, I think it's time we turned our attention to more important matters," Trixie piped up.

I looked over my shoulder at her. "Like dealing with the Summer Court and your brother," I suggested.

Trixie flashed me a sour look as her voice become painfully tart. "I was thinking more like finding Bronx a girlfriend."

A wide smile slashed across my face as I looked back over at him. He frowned at the elf sitting behind me as she laughed lightly. Truthfully, I didn't know anything about matchmaking or dating, and even less about the love life of trolls, but I liked seeing Bronx squirm under Trixie's scrutiny.

"You know he's going to be even grumpier to work with now that we're dating," she teased, causing my heart to give a little flutter. It was wonderful that she was physically showing her attraction to me, but the words pinged against my heart, starting it pounding again.

"And here I was hoping that work would become a more tolerable place now that you're dating," Bronx snapped. "We can finally get over all the goo-goo eyes and the mooning when the other person goes on a date."

Trixie gasped, trying to pretend to be insulted by his comments, but I just blushed, knowing better than to deny it. I knew I was intolerable to work with whenever she announced that she was going out on a date. I liked the thought that she might have been too, when I stepped out on the rare occasion.

A soft meow captured everyone's attention before Trixie could argue with Bronx. I turned around to find Sofie sitting on the steps, just above Trixie, her wide yellow eyes taking in the cozy scene.

"Hey, Sofie!" I said.

"You have a cat?" Trixie demanded, her face turning from the large Russian blue to me. "Since when do you have a cat?"

"Recently," I replied with a bit of a sigh. I had left that part out of my story as well simply because in all the chaos I had temporarily forgotten about the exiled witch.

"She's beautiful," Trixie said, which earned a loud purr from Sofie. The elf leaned back and scratched Sofie behind the ear and under the chin. The witch-cat leaned into her hand, soaking up the attention as her purring grew louder.

"Do you like cats?"

Trixie continued to scratch the feline, rubbing along her cheek. "Oh, I've always loved cats."

My smile grew even wider as my gaze met Sofie's and a little chuckle escaped me. "You know, I'm really glad to hear that."

Hell was still waiting for me. I didn't doubt that. But as I sat on the rickety wooden stairs in the dark with my friends, I wasn't worried. With them, I would conquer hell too.